Rad Decision

A Novel of Nuclear Power

James Aach

Impressive Imprint

June 21st 2011

~ came across this
book when doing
research on
surviving a nuclear
disaster ~

hope you enjoy it

~ also the movie
"How to get ahead in
advertising" is
absolutely hilareous

love you both
Jay & Miriam
from mom xxooxx

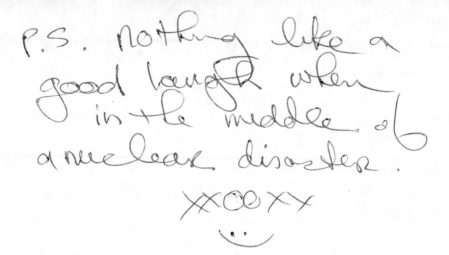

P.S. nothing like a good laugh when in the middle of a nuclear disaster.
XXOOXX

Rad Decision: A Novel of Nuclear Power
An Impressive Imprint / LAG Enterprises Book

Publishing History: First Edition. November, 2006

All Rights Reserved. Copyright © 2006 by James Aach

ISBN: 978-0-6151-3657-8

For information, address Impressive Imprint, 3073 S. 337 E., Kokomo, IN 46902, or see RadDecision.blogspot.com.

Rad Decision

List of Illustrations:

Figure A: Map of Potawatomie County, Indiana   Page iii
Figure B: Fairview Station Safety Systems   Pages iv - v
Figure C: Radiation Basics   Page vi
Figure D: Water Injection Summary   Page 54

Figure 1: Cutaway view of the reactor vessel   Page 31
Figure 2: Fig. 1 with electric power production equipment   Page 43
Figure 3: Fig. 2 with emergency water injection sources   Page 63
Figure 4: Fig. 3 with electric power for plant equipment   Page 84
Figure 5: The Event   Page 206

The Fairview Station Nuclear Power Plant, its employees, other characters, and certain key locations in this story are fictional.

i

DEDICATION:

For Nancy (of course)

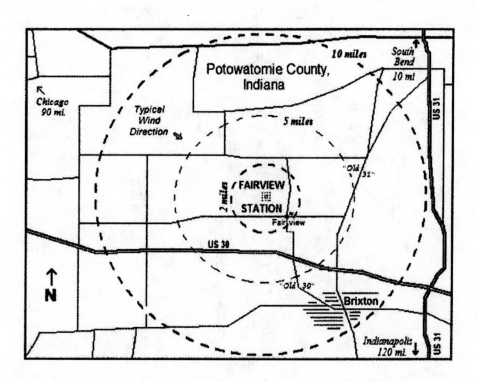

Figure A: Map of Potawatomie County, Indiana

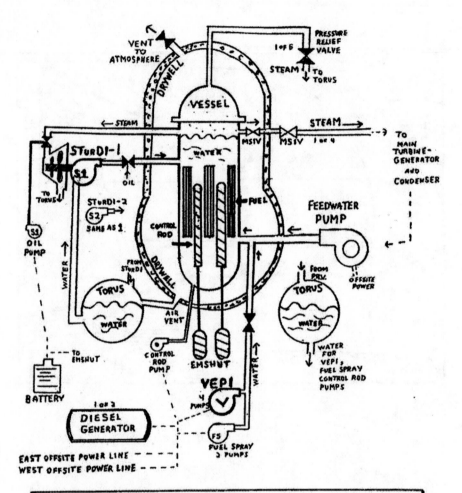

Figure B: Fairview Station Nuclear Power Plant - - Safety Systems

"So what <u>do</u> I remember?" Paul said.

Langford thought for a moment. "Oh, I would go with '**water is good**.' The rest will come to you in time."

Fairview Station Boiling Water Reactor

High Pressure Injection Sources

STurDI (Steam Turbine Driven Injection)

STurDI-1   3500 gpm   (powered by reactor steam and DC) . . . . *pg 49*

STurDI-2   400 gpm   (powered by reactor steam and DC) . . . . *pg 49*

Also Control Rod Pump at 65 gpm (AC powered) (*gpm* = gallons per min.) *pg 59*

Low Pressure Injection Sources (< 250 psig)

VEPI (Vessel Electric Pump Injection) . . . . *pg 51*

4 VEPI Pumps   7700 gpm *each*   (powered by AC)

Fuel Spray . . . . *pg 59*

2 Pumps at 3300 gpm *each*   (powered by AC)

ELECTRIC POWER SOURCES: . . . . *pg 82*

AC: 2 offsite power lines and 2 emergency diesel generators
DC: various battery banks located onsite

Normal Parameters at Full Power

- +200 inches of water over the top of the active fuel (TAF)
- 1000 psig reactor vessel pressure
- 500 F water/steam temperature in the reactor
- Drywell air = 120 F, 1.1 psig (*psig* = lbs. per sq inch > outside air)
- Torus air & water = 84 F, 0.8 psig
- 32,000 gpm supplied by 2 Feedwater Pumps at full power

Other Systems:

- 386 fuel bundles of finger-sized fuel rods . . . . *pgs 28, 34*
- 94 control rods of boron to absorb neutrons from the fuel . . . *pg 41*
- *EMSHUT* = Emergency Shutdown System. Shoves control rods in between the fuel bundles using compressed air. . . . . *pg 41*
- *M.S.I.V.* = Main Steam Isolation Valves (8 total, 2 per steam line.) . . *pg 56*
- *ARAFS* = Atmospheric Release Air Filtration System (removes some iodine / particulate from reactor bldg or drywell air before release) . *pg 96*
- *P.R.V.* = Pressure Relief Valve (sends extra steam to torus) . . . . *pg 61*
- *E.B.I.* = Emergency Boron Injection. (liquid control rods) . . . . . . *pg 46*

Figure C: Radiation Basics   *Fairview Nuclear Plant, 1984*

Radiation

Radiation is energy given off by a decaying atom in particles or waves.

Four types of radiation, alpha, beta, neutron and gamma.
                      Gamma penetrates much farther than the others.

Contamination – Abnormally radioactive material where we don't want it.
                      An object can receive radioactive energy but <u>not</u> become contaminated.

Radiation Dose is measured in Humans in REMs.
Other measurements include Curies (how radioactive something is) and Sieverts (1 S = 100 REM).

Radiation dose is often measured in "**milli-rem**" or 1/1000th of a REM.

1000 m.r. = 1 REM or 1 R. Often it is expressed in a rate, such as
                      "50 milli-rems per hour" (or 50 m.r. for workers, who often leave off the "h")

Acute radiation dose = all in a short time. High enough = immediate health effect.
Chronic dose is long-term, usually lower doses. Enough over time = health effect.

Acute Dose Health Effects (for adults, children's effects are greater)

   650 Rem = 650,000 milli-rem (m.r.) = death probable
   450 Rem = 450,000 milli-rem = 50/50 chance of survival
   100 Rem = 100,000 m.r. = nausea possible, likely not a lethal dose
   50 Rem = 50,000 m.r. = nausea possible, not lethal

Chronic, Long-Term, (lower) Doses

Health effects uncertain. Current estimate: a year with 1000 m.r. (0.1 R) dose
                      takes one day off your life (for an adult).

Background Radiation (South Bend Area)

        50 m.r. per year cosmic radiation (the sun, etc.)
        25 m.r. per year local rocks/soil
        25 m.r. per year food
        100 m.r. per year due to radon gas from soil

Man-made sources
          20 - 30 m.r. for a chest x-ray
          3 – 4 m.r. for a cross-country flight
          >1000 m.r. per year for smoking cigarettes
          1 – 2 m.r per year to public from a nuclear plant

5000 m.r. per year maximum allowed for nuclear workers per 1984 US regulations

FIGURE C: RADIATION BASICS

Prologue

South Bend, Indiana
May 11, 1986

Steve Borden could hear the woman's muffled fury as he reached for the door, and he was grateful for the distraction that allowed him to slip in unnoticed. She was standing at the front of the small, bare auditorium, a stout lady in a nylon jacket, unleashing a tirade at the Hoosier Electric spokesman on the podium. Lives had been ruined! Children would die!

Her anger spent, the woman quieted, leaving the rest of the crowd to clap and voice its approval. Ranging from teenagers to senior citizens, the onlookers filled half the room.

The spokesman, a sullen executive in a dark suit, waited until the clamor died down. When he continued, his comments were directed to the dozen reporters ringing the platform. "As I said, we do know a great deal of information about the radioactive- "

"All I know is, you're responsible!" the same woman interrupted. "You're gonna pay for this! Our farm is gone!"

Steve had settled in along a wall, shielded from the press by the other spectators, and watched as a security man stepped in. The woman began berating him as well, but then turned and stomped out the nearest exit, a few newsmen trailing behind. From the podium, the spokesman watched the doors slam shut, and then finished his response.

Steve tilted forward to hear the next question. Despite his lean frame, the back of the borrowed suit coat pulled tight across his weary shoulders. Though relieved that he was not involved in the press conference, he had felt compelled to look in -- and catch a glimpse of the future.

As the session dragged on, Steve's concentration began to give way to fatigue and fragments of tragedy: the urgent phone call, the worried looks, the core in trouble, and then the final, bitter results. The latest report still weighed on his mind. *How?* he kept asking himself. *How did it all happen?*

The briefing ended, and with a flurry of camera flashes the crowd began to break up. Steve shook loose from his thoughts -- from his doubts -- and headed toward a door that would take him backstage. He didn't want to linger.

"Steve Borden?" he heard a woman ask. He had almost reached the exit, but looked back. Approaching was a reporter, a slim blonde from local television. "Aren't you Steve Borden?"

"Yes," he said. "I'm Borden."

"Have you been to Fairview? What happened?"

Steve nodded. "I've been there." He ignored the second question. There was no easy answer.

"Have there been any injuries? Any deaths?"

The question shook him. How much did she know? Other reporters were now migrating towards him and he edged a little closer to the door. "We're giving regular briefings," he said. "We'll keep you informed."

"Whose fault was it?" It was a different voice this time, rough, male and demanding.

Steve had reached the exit, but he stopped and turned to the swelling group. It was <u>the</u> question, of course. And he would not dodge it. "I am the manager of Fairview Station," Steve Borden said. "It's my plant."

Part One: Beginnings

Richmond, Indiana
April, 1968

Steve reached down for his sister's hand before they crossed the street. It was a Saturday afternoon, the breeze carrying a hint of summer, and downtown Richmond was busy. Cars cruised along Main Street past the turn-of-the-century brick buildings while pedestrians came and went from the shops. Soon, Jenny began to yank him forward. She hadn't been in such a hurry earlier, while picking out a blue dress and searching for matching barrettes to place in her jet black hair, but now the State Theater was in sight. It was time for the children's matinee.

Steve bought the ticket and his sister went inside. Through the glass doors Steve saw her join some friends, all smiles and giggles as they picked out their candy. Closer still was his own reflection in the glass: a gangly six foot three inches, short chestnut hair above a pale face with sad brown eyes and a hawk nose. Turning away, Steve strolled down the sidewalk. He had finished helping his mother around the house and had the afternoon free. The following weekend he would also return for Easter, since any excuse to see Marie was enough to endure the long bus ride back to his hometown. But soon, his college days would be over. He would graduate, marry, and begin a career. Then his life would really start.

He was several blocks up the street now, across from the tan, limestone castle that served as the county courthouse. It would be a nice walk to Marie's . . .

THUMMM-WOOOM! The sound came first, and as Steve turned to look, the shock wave roared past. Down the street, from where he had come, a white cloud billowed into the sky.

Jenny! Steve began racing toward the theater as chunks of brick and glass started to plummet onto the sidewalk. A thick swirl of dust had descended over the street a few blocks ahead. Something hard bounced off Steve's leg before skittering across the pavement, but he kept running. He passed people fleeing from the cloud as cars also sped away, tires squealing.

WUUMMMP-SHHHH! A second explosion shook the ground and hurled Steve against a building. Ahead, a massive pillar of black smoke was roiling up hundreds of feet into the air. *My God!* Steve pushed himself from the wall and ran on. *Jenny!* The atmosphere grew thicker with debris -- shards of metal, brick, glass and plastic all tumbling from the sky. A woman staggered by, her white dress flecked with blood, and then a man, seemingly unhurt, rushed past in terror. Others in the street were yelling, screaming, crying.

Steve was now a block from the theater and could see its marquee: half the letters had been blown off. Beside him, a car screeched to a halt and a woman leapt out to join the others racing toward the movie house. Children from the matinee were spilling into the street: some terrified, others treating the event like a game. Beyond them, at the next intersection, there was a wall of dark smoke and flame.

"Jenny!" *God, please. Please!* Breathless, Steve searched the faces, and spotted his sister by the curb, holding onto her friends. He rushed up and grabbed her by the shoulders. "Are you okay?"

She nodded, her eyes wide and filled with tears.

Steve looked up, beyond the children. There was a break in the black cloud, and he could see that the next block of Main Street was a no-man's land of heaped, smoking rubble, like a scene from World War II. Then he spotted movement. <u>People</u>. There were people in there. He squeezed his sister's shoulders even tighter and peered down again at her worried face. Steve spoke slowly, yelling over the pandemonium. "Run straight home! Home! Tell Mom I'm okay! And have her call Marie! Now go! Go!" He gave her a nudge, and Jenny took off down the littered sidewalk, her friends close behind.

More cars were now arriving, with worried parents jumping out. "Be careful!" Steve said.

He moved closer to the conflagration. *The people. You can help.* A businessman stumbled out of the smoke, his suit coat shredded by flying glass. "Are you all right?" Steve asked, and there was a dazed nod as the victim moved past. Carefully, Steve began picking his way forward past mounds of waist-deep rubble and soon found himself in the middle of the street. There were fires on both sides, and above the roar he heard sharp pops -- like firecrackers -- along with frantic voices.

Keep moving. Waves of heat washed over the carnage, and Steve's eyes watered from the thick, acrid smoke. He reached out to shove aside a shattered door in his path, and a vicious sting jabbed at his right hand. *Damn!* He jerked back and shook his wrist to settle the pain, then held up his arm. The top of his thumb and half his forefinger looked as if they had been plunged into a meat grinder -- there was nothing but oozing, crimson flesh. Light-headed with shock, Steve willed himself to hang on. The wound had stopped hurting, and he pulled out a handkerchief and wrapped it as best he could. Then he remembered the leather gloves in his coat pocket, and forced one over his raw, torn fingers, and then onto his other hand as well.

Once more, Steve began to move forward, but then something smacked into the ground beside him with a sharp thud. It had come from the left. He peered past the sidewalk and into the flames. There was no building -- only a broiling pile of debris. What had been there? Steve tried to picture the street. Shoes. . . Drugstore. . . Sporting Goods. . . A distant POP! and another THUD nearby. Sporting Goods. . . Bullets! *God, it's bullets!*

He dropped to a crouch and scrambled ahead and toward the far sidewalk, negotiating piles of glass and shredded metal as he tried to put some distance between himself and the exploding ammunition. Steve stepped over a man's shoe and saw there was still a foot in it, severed at the ankle, the bone protruding past a blue sock. His stomach churned, but a cry for help carried through the heavy, shimmering air, and he kept moving until he had reached the flaming remnants of a small store. The plea was louder now, a woman's voice, and Steve called back: "Hang on! I'll get you!" The shattered storefront window crunched beneath his feet as he stepped up through the wide gap. Inside, the smoke and heat were more intense, but he could make out a figure, arms waving, that was struggling toward him. She called again for help, but Steve found his way blocked by an overturned cabinet heaped with broken dishes. The woman was just beyond.

Rearing back, Steve flung himself up onto the debris, a dozen jagged shards stabbing at his torso. The figure was now a step away. It was an older woman, a huge welt on her forehead beneath her tightly curled gray hair, her tan dress smudged and torn. "Here!" Steve said, beckoning with his hands. "You can! You can!" The woman stumbled ahead and fell into his arms, her face pressed against his chest. Steve then lurched in reverse, dragging the woman over the top of the pile, a mass of broken china trailing onto the floor.

"Oh, Jesus!" the woman said, as Steve shuffled back further until he had reached the sidewalk. Inside, he saw the ceiling come crashing down. "Jesus, Jesus," the woman kept saying. She could not stand on her own, and Steve lifted her in his arms and began working his way along the half-buried street. As the rubble field lessened, two teenage girls in bright summer dresses ran toward him.

"We'll take her," one of them said.

Steve set the woman shakily on her feet, and she began mumbling "Oh, bless you, bless you," as the girls led her away.

Steve turned back. There were sirens behind him now as he waded again toward the flaming ruins. The upper stories of the older buildings were beginning to give way, raining bricks and mortar onto the sidewalk, so he kept to the street, using heaps of wreckage as cover when clambering past the sporting goods store. The POP! POP! of its ammunition continued. Through the haze, Steve spied a small, wiry man in janitor's coveralls, clawing at bricks that had buried a parked red station wagon.

"It's my wife's car!" the man said, his tortured face covered in soot, and Steve joined him in his frantic effort to clear away the debris around the driver's side window, which had shattered into an opaque web.

"I got it!" Steve said when the majority of the window was in view, and he grabbed a broken corner with a gloved hand and pulled the crumpled pane aside.

The man shoved past him to peer in. "She's not there! She must be inside!"

Steve looked beyond the car at the battered storefront. Flames had not yet reached the building, but the showroom was a maze of toppled cabinets and fallen lights.

"I'll get there!" the man said as he charged into the structure. He heaved aside a filing cabinet that blocked his way and disappeared from view before Steve had a chance to react.

Peering back down the street, Steve saw two firemen struggling to guide a hose over a jagged pile of cement, bricks and steel. He headed in their direction.

Dusk was approaching as Steve helped two young black men keep the jerking fire hose pointed at the State Theater, which had now been overtaken by the flames. His injured right hand ached terribly, and he found it harder and harder to grip the slippery line. To his relief, another man came up and grabbed on, and Steve stepped aside. In the pulsing light of the fire he looked down at the leather glove, torn and soaked through with blood. As if sensing that his work was done, the pain began to rise into an agony that stretched the length of his arm, and he doubled over, cradling the hand. *God!*

An older fireman, his thick coat extended over an ample belly, stepped over to help direct the spray, but first he grabbed Steve's wrist and examined the throbbing wound. "Better get that looked at, son." He pointed. "First aid over there."

Steve nodded, and clutching his arm, he walked away. Before

entering the first aid station, he looked back at the still-flaming buildings, the police and volunteers, the piles of smoldering rubble, and the sheets covering those who had not survived. *What had the power to do THAT?*

****

Boussac, Louisiana
April, 1968

The humid factory air was filled with the hissing of gas and the rumble of machinery. Within a cluster of aluminum tubing and round brass dials, a lean, rangy technician in worn blue jeans was jotting readings on his clipboard. Glancing up, he caught sight of a co-worker lumbering by. Shorter in stature, the man wore a grease-smeared khaki shirt that was stretched tightly across his broad chest. "Hey, Charlie!" the technician called out. "I hear tomorrow's your last day."

"Yeah, one more," the mechanic said, flashing a single, stubby index finger. "Then it's back up north for me."

"Sure picked a good time. Hot enough already."

"Damn right." The mechanic peeled off his thick glasses and battered hardhat, then wiped the sweat from his round face and hairless scalp with a crumpled bandana. "I'll tell ya, Long Island is gonna be a hell of an improvement."

As the technician returned to his work, the mechanic continued on, descending a flight of stairs that took him deeper into the bowels of the chemical plant. For months he had carefully plotted out this day, step by step. His plan went against everything the Center had told him, but it was something he must do. He had served too long without striking back. And now time was running out.

Stepping off a metal ladder into the damp, dimly lit tunnel, the mechanic squeezed between rows of blackened piping and then knelt beside a valve. Only a few turns of the small handwheel would be needed. No one would ever notice. And then, in a few months, when they started the tank flush . . .

Moscow, USSR
October, 1968

Still growing accustomed to his new assignment, Dmitri had decided to relax with a stroll after work. It was a pleasant evening, and the well-lit sidewalks were bustling with young couples, families, and pensioners. The short, heavyset KGB officer halted to peer through his thick glasses at a copy of *Pravda* tacked to a display board. But the Soviet paper held nothing of interest, and he was soon on his way.

Today, like every other day for the past two months, Dmitri had scanned the American newspapers while at work, searching for a report on a factory disaster in Louisiana. But the notice had never appeared, and by now the time for the event was long past.

The future, he hoped, would bring other opportunities. If so, he would be ready.

****

Fairview, Indiana
September, 1971

The tour group of four men and three women, hardhats resting awkwardly atop their heads, stepped through a gap in the partially constructed wall and emerged into bright sunshine. Behind them came their guide, a large man in dusty jeans, well-used work boots and a denim jacket. He pointed and led the assembly past a bulldozer and cement mixer to a spot of relative calm amid the rumble of the construction site. The air smelled of burning metal, diesel fuel, and dust.

"So, that was the reactor building," the guide said. White sideburns framed his reddish cheeks. "In case you didn't hear me inside, that tall steel capsule is the reactor vessel. It's where the nuclear fission will take place." A piercing screech of metal upon metal from behind them caused several in the party to flinch. The guide only grinned. "Any questions so far?" he asked after the noise had faded. For a moment the small group offered no response, standing silent amid the hectic activity. To their left, welders were at work on a huge pipe which lay on the barren soil, and in the other direction a wall of concrete was rising to engulf a web of iron struts. Meanwhile, far overhead, a steel beam had just been lowered into place beside a half-finished dome.

"How big is this plant going to be?" an older man in a brown suit finally asked.

"Well, Mr. Mayor," the guide said, "at full power Fairview Station will generate about five hundred and seventy million watts. That should light up South Bend."

"And what will it cost?" a young woman said. The breeze ruffled her sweater and skirt.

"They're figuring around three hundred million. It's more than a fossil plant, but since our fuel's a lot cheaper than coal, we'll catch up once we're on line. Then Fairview Station will be the bargain producer for Hoosier Electric. That'll mean lower rates for everyone."

"Well, I'm all for that," the mayor said, his face lighting up in a politician's smile. "I like it already. Lots of jobs. Lots of visitors to the community. It's a real boost for Brixton."

"How many people will work here once it's finished?" the young woman asked. She was taking notes.

"They used to think about sixty full-time," the guide said, "but the estimate now is one hundred." He stopped and looked past the group toward a tall, slender worker in blue jeans and a flannel shirt who was making his way between buildings. "Now here's someone you might like to meet," the guide said. He waved. "Hey Steve! Come here a minute, will ya?" The man saw the gesture and approached.

"This is Steve Borden," the guide said. "He'll be one of the people running the plant." The young man smiled at the description. A few strands of gray tinted the chestnut hair that extended beneath his hard hat. "What ya doin' out here, Steve? They move the classes?"

"No, we're on self-study," Steve said in his soft, tenor voice. "I thought I'd see things firsthand."

"Steve's going to be a shift supervisor," the guide said. "They're the men responsible for operating Fairview Station day to day. He'll spend most of his time in the control room."

"How long have you been with Hoosier Electric?" the mayor asked.

"About three years," Steve said. "Since I graduated. I started the training program a few months ago."

"Well, learn your lessons well, young man," the mayor said. "Keep this place running right."

"Yes, sir. I intend to."

****

Moscow, USSR
October, 1973

Vitaly Kruchinkin had been in the reception area over an hour, and he had long since given up his study of the three aging chairs propped against the far wall. He shifted his taut, six-foot frame and flexed his knee. It was sore today. There would be rain. His eyes drifted along the faded wallpaper until they again fixed on the framed picture of a May Day parade. Grim soldiers marching past a podium of leaders. *Soldiers* . . .

When Vitaly Fedorovich Kruchinkin was ten years old, his father had asked what he wanted to be. The skinny boy, his tawny hair an uncombed jumble, had replied: "A soldier, just like you were, Papa!"

He could not remember a time when that hadn't been his dream. His father had spoken often of the Great Patriotic War and the fierce battles that drove out the Germans. To defend the *Rodina*, the Motherland, was the highest honor. The military academy had followed a strict regimen, and Vitaly had applied himself with vigor. In the evenings came his greatest pleasure, when he practiced gymnastics. The end had come so quickly. It was his last run-through on the high bar. He remembered letting go a little early on the dismount and instinctively twisting to compensate. But he went too far and one leg bore the brunt of an awkward landing. The rest was all pain.

There was a shuffling behind the door and then a prim matron in a gray dress appeared. "They will be ready for you in a few minutes, Comrade Kruchinkin," she said. The door shut again.

Vitaly smiled to himself, the expression only faintly visible on his sharp, intense face, with its aquiline nose, steel blue eyes, and cleft chin. In a few minutes . . . The woman had said the same thing when he had first arrived. But even the KGB could be inefficient at times, Vitaly had come to learn.

He had never given the Committee for State Security much thought until he was approached during his final year of trade school. The KGB wanted recruits with electronic skills, and they needed them badly enough to waive the Soviet Union's standard requirement for two years of post-graduation community service. If Vitaly joined up, he would avoid an unpleasant stay in one of the grime-smeared industrial centers of Siberia. He could remain in Moscow. "And my wife, Yelena?" he had asked.

"We would see that she stays in Moscow as well."

Since graduation, his few months in the KGB had been uneventful; his days spent testing miniature circuits. But on this morning, his supervisor had smiled and told him to report to an office across town. He was not to worry, his boss said. It would be a good thing.

There was movement again beyond the door, and then it was time. Ushered into a windowless room, Vitaly took the lone empty chair, a few feet away from three dour men seated behind a long table, each in a pale blue KGB officer's uniform. What was this about? Had he done something wrong? The somber questions began: on his education, his marriage, and then his background.

"You spent time overseas as a child, correct?" asked a small, intense man with greasy hair.

"Yes, in New York. My father was a Ministry of Trade official."

"And how long were you there?"

"My father was transferred to the U.S. in 1954. We left in 1966."

"How old were you then?" The question came from the officer in the middle, a bald man whose wide face was dominated by the bottle lenses perched across his pug nose.

"I was fourteen when I came home." Vitaly tried to maintain eye contact with the panel. He still did not understand what the meeting was all about, and the emotionless return gazes provided no clue.

"Did you have much contact with Americans?" The question again was from the bald officer.

"Some. I went to school at the Soviet Embassy, but I played in the park with American children, especially after my mother died."

"And you speak English?"

"Yes. I picked it up in New York, and I've taken courses in school."

After the interview had continued for some time, to his relief, Vitaly began to sense that it was not about some past transgression. The panel seemed interested in his daily life in America. Did he watch television? Listen to the radio? Did he go shopping? Then, finally, the purpose of the questioning was made clear. Vitaly was given the opportunity to think it over. But for him there could be only one decision. It was his duty.

"And after ten years they'd give you a good job here in Moscow?" Yelena asked that evening at home over dinner.

"That's what they said," Vitaly replied. "In the meantime, they'll triple my salary."

"But ten years . . ." Yelena looked down into her tea.

Vitaly gazed across the tiny, uneven kitchen table. His wife was beautiful -- a tall, willowy blonde with brown eyes -- and she was so much more. Yelena was his partner, and she had been there through the long hours of study, the death of his father, and his knee's rehabilitation. He wanted to ensure they had a happy life together, and the KGB's offer could be his path toward success. But she was right -- ten years!

"It's a long time, I know," Vitaly finally said. He had been assured that Yelena would be looked after. She could leave the cramped apartment they shared with another couple, with its peeling paint and cracked, moldy floor tile, and move with her parents into better accommodations. "I'll still be able to see you on occasion -- a week, maybe two weeks a year. Maybe more. And in ten years you'll only be thirty-two. We can have a family and live in comfort."

"It's important to you, isn't it?"

"Yes," Vitaly said. As his father had gone to war, so must he.

****

14

Cleveland, Ohio
November, 1976

John Donner climbed out of the car and crossed the damp driveway to the back entrance of his small, rented home. Once inside, Vitaly Fedorovich Kruchinkin set his bagged supper on the kitchen table and then checked the mailbox on the front porch. There was nothing for John Donner today.

"So you're going to train me to pass as an American?" Vitaly had asked his instructor.

"If we can," Dmitri had said. The bald, compact KGB officer had been at Vitaly's first interview. "The process will take two or three years. Once you're there, living as an American, you'll be what's known as an "illegal." After a time, headquarters -- we call it "the Center" -- will give you assignments to watch troop movements or gather other bits of data. Nothing too exotic. If we're very fortunate, perhaps your day job might lead to something." Dmitri had then tipped his thick glasses forward, and peering over them, had stared at the young recruit with cold, malevolent eyes. "Individuals like you, deep and unnoticed in enemy territory, are one of our nation's greatest assets."

Vitaly had nodded. Then, thinking of life overseas, he suddenly felt very lonely.

"How long until I see you again?" Yelena had asked, as they strolled through the Moscow Zoo a few days before Vitaly was to leave for America. "Will it be less often now?"

"Yes." Vitaly stared at the ground. He could tell his wife nothing of his mission, except its importance. "I'll be back at least once a year. You can keep writing, but you probably won't get letters from me very often."

"Oh . . ." Yelena stopped. Her brown eyes were fighting back tears. "I know it's something we agreed on," she said in a choked voice, "but sometimes it just hits me. I love you so much, and I see so little of you now. How can I stand to see less?" She looked away.

Vitaly stared at his wife's profile: the delicate face with its high cheekbones, the blonde hair streaming past. It was a beautiful image he wanted to carry with him, deep inside. "We'll make it, my love," he finally said, trying to sound hopeful. "Just think of what life will be like when it's over. I'll have so many benefits -- you've seen what they've given us already -- and we can live in comfort. It won't be a struggle for us, like it is for everyone else."

"I know," Yelena said. "It's just that all that doesn't help much right now."

Upon reaching the United States, Vitaly first spent time in New York, visiting his own childhood haunts, and then examining his alter-ego's neighborhood. The real John Evan Donner was an only child who had died with his parents in a train wreck while visiting France, just before his eighth birthday. In Vitaly's version, John Donner and his family had returned home, with his mother and father having later been killed in an accident in Mexico when their son was twenty years old. In order to explain the scars on Vitaly's knee, the teenage John Donner had been injured and operated on while taking another trip overseas. The records of his schooling, his short-lived jobs, and his time studying electronics were all in place or simply not available. After graduating from trade school, John Donner had traveled for a time, and then the quiet young man with the lithe body, strong jaw and youthful face had settled in Cleveland. Now Vitaly had only to be an industrious citizen. And await orders from the Center.

Finished with his fast-food meal, Vitaly settled into a worn easy chair with a magazine and began an article about life in America's inner cities. A car passed by outside, splashing through a puddle, and he found himself recalling the time years before when his father had taken him on a driving tour of New York. They had not visited the Empire State Building or Broadway, but rather the slums, the deteriorating South Bronx. His father had sat behind the wheel of the sedan, an older image of Vitaly, with graying hair and deepening lines on his face that bore witness to battles fought both in and out of war.

It was a slushy winter day, and Vitaly's father had pointed out the ragged figures trying to sleep on heating grates. "When we return home, you will not see this," the elder Kruchinkin had said to his lone child. "Our government cares for its citizens. It gives them food, shelter, and a job." Large drops of sleet hit the windows as they drove on. "Remember this, Vitaly Fedorovich. You may hear America called a land of opportunity. But theirs is an opportunity to starve. It may have had its moment in the sun, but the United States is crumbling now. And our Soviet Union will continue to grow stronger because the Party cares for all the people."

It was as true today as back then, Vitaly knew. Since his return he had seen enough to convince him of that. There was only one way -- Socialism -- and it must prevail. It must.

****

Fairview, Indiana
April, 1976

It was three in the morning, and Fairview Station was quiet. An operator on rounds out by the river water pumping station had reported a bad storm coming in from the west, but at his post in the heart of the power plant, Steve Borden was well isolated from the outside world. The paperwork was light this shift, and he took a moment to relax, absently buttoning and unbuttoning the collar of his white linen shirt. He thought of Marie. Perhaps she was finally getting a good night's sleep. Long before its arrival, their first child was making its presence felt.

Steve stretched his long legs beneath the desk as he looked through the glass of the shift supervisor's office into the central area of the control room. A row of curved countertops, covered with handles, buttons, knobs, and lights, jutted out from the far wall. Above these control panels were checkerboards of wallet-sized rectangles, each block labeled with a specific problem that could occur in the plant. At the moment, only a few of these "annunciators" were shining, backlit by amber lights. Over the central panel, splitting the banks of annunciators in two, was a circle, a yard in diameter, that was filled in by ninety-four glowing red tiles. The lights indicated that all of the control rods were withdrawn from the core. The nuclear reactor was at full power. Observing the plant's operation was the chief control room operator. A rotund figure, his permanently flushed face topped by curled blond hair, he was slowly moving back and forth from panel to panel. Reviewing a procedure at a nearby table was his assistant, a young Hispanic man in a blue and red baseball jersey. With a year now under its belt, Fairview Station was churning out over half a billion watts of electricity for Hoosier Electric and northern Indiana.

Steve returned to his work, but a buzzing alarm soon broke the quiet and an annunciator brightened and began blinking. The chief operator stepped over to the panel. He studied the flashing message, then pulled a hand from the pocket of his blue jeans and pushed a button. The buzzer and the blinking stopped. Steve had looked up, but only for a moment. There was no reason to be concerned. The previous shift had confirmed that the instrument that was setting off the alarm was malfunctioning, and maintenance had been asked to fix the device.

Alarms suddenly began blaring and most of the overhead lighting disappeared. Steve jumped up and rushed into the darkened control room just as the chief operator said: "Reactor scram!"

The core display on the wall was now changing colors: its solid circle of red lights switching over to green. The reactor was automatically shutting down.

"Main steam lines isolated!" the assistant operator reported. "Pressure relief valve lifted." He glanced at other readings. "We've lost offsite power. Primary dead, no transfer to backup!"

Steve hurried to a panel on the left. "Diesel generators running!" he called out. "Loading now." The room brightened as the absent lights overhead returned.

"Reactor level at 156," the chief operator said. He punched a button, and the alarm horns fell silent.

"Rods full in," the assistant operator said. "Reactor power at zero."

"Generator's tripped. Turbine's tripped," Steve said.

"Reactor pressure 10-50. Last pressure relief closed. Creeping on up."

With the situation under some control, Steve had a moment to piece together what had just happened. Normally, the safety systems at Fairview Station did not receive their electricity from the plant itself, but rather from transmission lines that passed near the site. But something had happened to that source -- maybe the storm had brought it down -- and then the backup supply lines had failed to automatically take over the job. The reactor had then shut down, as it was designed to do in such circumstances, and huge valves had also closed in order to seal off the radioactive core from the rest of the plant. Thanks to the diesel generators located on site, electric power for the safety systems was available again within a few seconds.

At the moment, Steve knew, no pump was running to supply the water that was always needed to prevent the reactor's fuel from melting, but there was plenty of time to get one started. With any luck, the shift supervisor told himself, repairs could be made and the plant restarted within a few hours. "Get STurDI-2 going and raise level back up to normal," Steve ordered the chief operator. "Then STurDI-1 in recirc mode, and the VEPI heat exchangers in torus cooling. Let's bring pressure down."

****

Paver, Illinois
May, 1981

Paul Hendricks waited for his burly classmate to squeeze beneath the thick pipe, then easily ducked under the obstacle with his smaller frame. Stepping out onto the polished concrete floor of the large industrial hall, his eyes were immediately drawn to the center of the open area, where three rumbling, bus-sized machines were lined up end to end, their smooth, pea-green casings reflecting sunbeams that streamed in through tall windows. "This, right here, is where electricity is born," the guide shouted above the din, as the small group gathered around him. "We have two turbines, then the generator."

A smile creased Paul's narrow face as he removed his hard hat and swept a stray lock of chestnut hair away from his brown eyes. Since high school he had been interested in how energy was produced, and he had learned the basics -- that household electricity was the vibrating of tiny electrons, that this invisible shuddering represented power and force just as surely as a locomotive racing down the tracks -- but it was here that the whole story came together.

The tall, angular tour guide, who was not far removed from Paul's age of twenty years, led the students up to the nearest huge machine at one end of the long row. "This is the generator," he said, patting the thundering device. "We're at 100% power right now. About four hundred megawatts -- four hundred million watts."

Paul gazed at the rounded green casing. Inside it was a huge magnet, a massive cylinder that was being spun round and round within a thick cage of wire. The moving magnetic field caused electrons in the wire to vibrate back and forth. This was electricity in the making: the power used to rotate the magnet was being transferred into the wire. One form of energy into another.

The guide gestured back toward the two turbines and pointed out the pipes, almost a yard in diameter, which plunged into the top of each enormous machine. "Those are the main steam lines, direct from the boiler."

"How much steam is going through?" one of the students asked.

"Over six thousand gallons a minute, at full power, to keep the turbines rolling."

Paul nodded. A lot of heat was going down that pipe. A lot of energy. Something had to keep the generator cranking round and round. The force could be a waterfall, or the wind, but if a great deal of electricity was desired, heat was usually the simplest way to extract the energy from nature and use it to maintain the magnet's rotation. Heat could produce a pressurized gas, such as steam, which could be used to spin the windmill blades of a turbine shaft that was bolted onto the end of the generator magnet. Some plants got their heat by burning coal -- a hundred railroad cars a day at a unit like this, Paul had seen -- while others used natural gas or even nuclear reactors. But it all came back to heat. Modern society hadn't really discarded the central hearth used for cooking and warmth. All those little fires, in little huts, had just been moved to one place. The power plant.

The tour stopped next in the control room, where the bemused utility crew stood off to one side while Paul and his classmates shuffled past the rows of dials, switches and colored lights. To Paul, it was like visiting the ultimate video game. The guide then led them down through a floor of metal grating and into the huge basement. The area was damp and smelled of grease, and there was a grimy coating of coal dust on every surface. In the distance, the rumbling of the turbines could be heard, and felt. The group quickly entered a maze of dull-colored piping that here and there curved aside to display a throbbing pump, or a hulking tank, or a complex assortment of valves. Paul found himself stepping around thin puddles of oily water. *Dad would get a kick out of all this -- he worked so hard just to fix that one leaky pipe.*

The last stop on the tour was the cooling towers: a pair of long, five-story-high structures, each with a row of funnels on top that from a distance had reminded Paul of ocean liners. Water poured out beneath each funnel and cascaded down the sides of the huge wooden frameworks, while clouds of steam billowed out overhead.

"Each cooling tower is longer than a football field," the guide said, his voice grown hoarse. "We use them to chill water from the river, which then goes into the plant to cool down the condenser. That's the big tank where the all the steam goes after it leaves the turbines. Cooling down the used steam helps suck the gas following along behind it past the turbine blades. It makes the plant more efficient." The guide cleared his throat. "Some units use a different type of tower. Huge funnels. Those big white things at Three Mile Island, for instance. They're just cooling towers. You need a really big facility for them to be effective, so you don't see many at coal plants. Mostly nukes."

As the tour broke up and Paul headed with the group towards the parking lot, he looked back over his shoulder at the collection of drab brick and glass buildings. It must be satisfying, he thought, to walk through such a place and understand what each piece of equipment was doing. Someday, he hoped, he could do that himself.

****

Leaving behind the roadside bar and its neon beer signs, Vitaly crossed the chilled gravel to his car. Few from the staff of Grissom Air Force Base had ventured out this evening, and he had heard little worth reporting to the Center. But not every attempt to gather intelligence was expected to be a success. His duty was to listen, or to strike up a conversation if that seemed a better way to glean information. Tonight, he had discussed baseball with a staff sergeant from New York. As a child, Vitaly had attended a Mets contest with a few of the other Russian children, and he had also tried playing the game in the park, where, because of his natural athleticism, the American kids had tolerated his ignorance. By the time of his return to the United States as an adult, his understanding of the sport was much improved.

Cold crept into Vitaly's fingers as he wiped the thin layer of condensation off the side windows of his aging brown, four-door sedan. Climbing in, he turned the key and flipped on the heater, then let the car bounce out through the rutted exit and into the street. Tomorrow, he would get some rest, and then it was back to his regular job. John Donner must keep putting in the time until he had earned another vacation. Then Vitaly could go home.

Yelena. He missed her: her soft brown eyes, her body in bed next to him, her laugh, her smile. His wife's letters were full of longing as well, but she was learning to cope, and her family had been settled into a comfortable new apartment because of his "contributions to the State." Vitaly was proud of that.

He pointed the car north along an empty highway. He was truly living the life of a soldier now. Cold, lonely, and in enemy territory.

Part Two: Fairview Station

<u>1983</u>

Paul worked his way around the stack of half-filled boxes and slipped into the bathroom of his new apartment. He looked in the mirror at the latest blemish to mar his dark complexion, brushed aside a few stray bangs of brown hair, then fiddled with the open collar on his white shirt. After buttoning the sleeves, he declared himself ready. *No more mowing lawns. No more sweeping up at the factory. This is the real thing.* Grabbing his padded blue coat, he headed out the door. It was a cold February morning in Brixton, Indiana.

He still found it hard to believe he had ended up at Fairview. There were power plants across the Midwest, but with several utilities close to bankruptcy after failed nuclear projects, the job opportunities after graduating had been few. The offer from Fairview Station was the best. He had little interest in nuclear power as a career -- *radiation* and *messy* were the first words that came to mind -- but an engineer had to start somewhere.

Paul had interviewed at Fairview Station in December. The recruiter, a chatty woman in a blue pantsuit, had first taken the carload of visiting students on a tour of South Bend, past the golden dome of Notre Dame and the Hoosier Electric corporate headquarters, and then had turned south for the thirty- minute drive to Brixton. "Fairview Station is located a few miles outside of town," she had explained. "There <u>is</u> a place called Fairview, just a mile from the site, but it's not much more than a crossroads. Maybe 300 people. Brixton is where most of the employees live. It's a typical small town, 15,000 or so."

Paul hadn't been that impressed with South Bend, but he'd seen things differently as they drove down Brixton's main street. It looked like Jameston, his hometown in the middle of Illinois. His father's insurance office might be just around the corner, and the realty company where his two older sisters worked could be a block further down.

Now, it was two months later, and in his well-worn car he was driving out of Brixton for his first day on the job. Paul went past the beauty parlor that reminded him of his mom's shop, and he thought of her smile, her hug, and let the ache surface for a moment. *You'd be proud of me. But you always were.* Ten years had gone by since heart problems had taken her away.

As he drove west through the plain of snow-covered cropland, Paul thought back to his first glimpses of the Fairview site. The misty plume had been visible even before leaving Brixton, and as the recruiter's car approached the facility, he had seen the cooling towers were the ocean liner variety. At the end of the dirt access road the vehicle had pulled into a gravel lot near a collection of gymnasium-sized, tan and white buildings that clustered around a bleached concrete dome. There had been something wrong with the power plant scene, but it had taken Paul a few moments to pin it down. No windows. Coal units always had big windows. And smokestacks. Here, there was only one tall chimney, and it jutted straight out of the ground some distance from the main buildings.

During his visit, Paul had never entered the plant itself. Instead, he had spent his day in interviews at a small office outside the twin chain-link fences that surrounded the main complex. He'd been pleasantly surprised that the supervisors with whom he'd chatted were young and informal, and they had seemed genuinely enthusiastic about Fairview Station. Now, as he was on his way to join them, he hoped his impressions had been right.

Paul parked near the same building where he'd interviewed, announced his presence to the woman inside the door, and then took a seat on a plastic chair. He tried without success to neatly fold his bulky coat, then gave up and piled it on his lap. Taking a deep breath, he tried to relax. *You've already been hired. So just go with it. Have fun.*

"Paul Hendricks?" It had been less than a minute.

"Yes." Paul stood, and found himself eye-to-eye with a smiling, chubby man in a gray sweater.

"Lou Tarelli. I'll be your supervisor in Tech Engineering." Tarelli extended his hand. He was probably in his late thirties, with a wide, rough face, a pug nose, and a thick neck. Dark hair lay sparsely across the crown of his head and was clipped close at the sides. "Hope I didn't keep you waiting."

"No, I just sat down." Paul said, in a voice he hoped would sound matter-of-fact. The back of his shirt had already grown damp with sweat.

"Good," Tarelli said. "Here's the plan. I'll be taking you inside as a visitor. That'll continue for a few days until you get some training." The supervisor placed a friendly hand on Paul's shoulder and directed him into a small office. "Just fill out these forms while I make some calls."

Tarelli returned a few minutes later, holding something inside his curled right hand. "On the other side of the fence, you'll always wear a couple of things to monitor your radiation dose," he said. "That's not a concern at your desk, but sometimes you'll go in the power block." Tarelli handed Paul a finger-sized metal tube. "This is a self-reading dosimeter. Hold it up to the light and look inside."

Paul did as directed, staring into the device as if it were a miniature telescope.

"You'll see a little scale in there, with the needle at zero. That shows how much radiation you've been exposed to."

"It's at zero," Paul said. *Cool -- and scary.*

"Just clip that onto your shirt pocket," Tarelli said, and he waited until Paul was done. "Also, we use one of these," he said, handing over a blue plastic rectangle the size of a matchbox, with a thumbnail's worth of photographic film peeking out from inside through a slot "That is a thermoluminescent dosimeter, or film badge for short. It's a little more accurate than the one you can read. It goes on your pocket as well."

It was a short, chilly walk across the gravel to the glass double-doors and the lobby that was the entryway to the main plant complex and the grounds inside the fence. Once there, Paul was frisked by a muscled, grim-faced security guard before following Tarelli through a metal detector and then a tall, rotating turnstile that his new boss unlocked by slipping his plant ID badge into a card reader. The two then moved down a long hallway, flanked by bulletin boards, framed photographs of men and women at work on machinery, and the entrances to several office areas.

Tarelli briefly quizzed Paul about his new apartment, then led him into a room full of gray-walled cubicles and down one of the rows. "This is your spot," Tarelli said, slapping an empty desk. He looked around. "Let see who's here." Tarelli glanced into the next spot down the aisle and Paul did the same, spying a man in a pale red turtleneck working at a computer. "Paul Hendricks, meet Mike Langford. He's our office Democrat, and another mechanical, like you."

"Welcome aboard." Langford stood to shake hands. A bit taller and sturdier than Paul, his rust-colored hair matched the tint of both his glasses and his well-groomed mustache. He was near Tarelli's age. "So what's Lou told you so far?" Langford asked, his voice a distinctive, mellow baritone.

"Not much," Paul said. "I get my own desk, I guess."

"Correct, and we shall bury it in paper soon enough." Langford peered over the top of the cubicles. "Meanwhile, Crutch approaches."

Paul turned to look as Tarelli introduced the massive blond, bearded man coming down the aisle, who was wearing a Chicago Bears sweatshirt and stood nearly a head taller than everyone else. "Crutch Pegariek, meet Paul Hendricks."

"Our newest sacrifice to the Nuclear Gods," Langford added, deadpan.

Crutch extended his hand, his blue eyes lit by a smile. "Lousy break, Paul. Ya go into the volcano at twelve."

In the quiet at his new desk, Paul yawned and turned back to the thick notebook:

> Fairview Nuclear Plant, Unit One, received its construction permit on January 11, 1970. The first criticality was achieved on September 21, 1973. The unit went on-line as a commercial plant on August 5, 1974. Designed by the NorthEastern Boiler Company (NEB), the 1750 thermal megawatt boiling water reactor . . .

When Lou Tarelli appeared, Paul was grateful.

"So, how much do you know about nuclear power?" Tarelli asked, cigarette smoke drifting up from the white stub between his fingers.

"Not a lot. I never had any courses in it." *Or much interest, either.*

"No problem." Tarelli grinned, displaying yellowed teeth. "Most people come in like that." He took a final drag and snuffed his cigarette out in an ashtray across the aisle, then pulled up a chair. As he reached across Paul's desk and grabbed an empty notepad, there was the faint scent of tobacco and aftershave. "So let me give you a quick rundown. You'll pick up most of this as you go along, but it's good to hear it in a nutshell."

"Sure."

"Well, basically, we're a power plant, and we use steam to spin a turbine-generator," Tarelli said, as he began sketching, "but instead of heating water in a boiler, we have this big pot called the reactor vessel. It's about seventy feet high, and fifteen feet across."

Paul studied the shape on the paper. It looked like a giant cold capsule.

"Inside this steel container," Tarelli continued, "we have lots of long, skinny tubes full of uranium. That's our fuel. We call it the reactor core." He drew several vertical lines inside the capsule. "Now, those uranium tubes can get real hot because of nuclear reactions and radioactivity. When that's occurring, we pump water into the bottom of the pot. The water goes up past the tubes to cool them off, and in the process it gets heated to steam." On the sketch, Tarelli drew arrows among the vertical lines that pointed upwards to indicate the water flowing past the uranium. "We keep the fuel completely covered with water at all times, and let the new steam bubble up and then flow out through the top of the vessel. From there, we send it on to spin the turbine."

Paul nodded. So far, so good.

"Now," Tarelli said, "if you remember one thing, it should be this: the safety of our plant is all about water." He pointed to the drawing. "Without water to cool them, those little uranium fuel tubes can get so hot they'll split apart. They even melt after a time. Then, basically, you have a puddle of uranium sloshing around the bottom of your pot. It might even burn right through. That's the famous 'meltdown.' Nasty stuff. Of course, a lot of things have to go wrong before a meltdown happens. A lot of things. So let's cover some of those. We'll start with the high pressure systems. Technically speaking, those are . . ."

Tarelli charged ahead, adding layer after layer to the drawing, gradually quickening his delivery. Paul tried to keep up, but thirty minutes later, the dazed look he feared was in his eyes had finally been noticed.

"Heh, heh." Tarelli chuckled and set his pen aside. "Anyway, Paul, we've got a lot of safety systems."

Paul nodded. "You seem to."

Tarelli stood. "How about I take care of a couple of things and then we head into the plant? See the real world."

"Sure." His new boss stepped away, leaving Paul to stare blankly at the wall of his cubicle. "So much…" he mumbled.

Mike Langford soon appeared from around the corner. He was wiping his glasses with a handkerchief. "Don't worry about remembering all that," he said. "Lou is an evangelist, and this is his religion."

"So what <u>do</u> I remember?" Paul said.

Langford thought for a moment, his tongue softly clicking against his teeth. "Oh, I would go with 'water is good.' The rest will come to you in time."

"Okay. Thanks." *That's better.* Paul leaned back in his chair. "So, anyway, what'd Lou mean when he introduced us, calling you the 'Office Democrat'?"

"Oh, that was just his sense of humor. I'm a rarity here, especially among the engineers and management. It's a conservative lot, and Lou is very much at home. Crutch, too, I'm afraid, though he's not as vocal about it. What persuasion would you be, by chance?"

"I never paid much attention. Politics to me always seemed like my sisters having a hissy fight."

"Oh, to the contrary, our political system is far worse than that."

Fairview Nuclear Reactor

Figure One: Cutaway view of the reactor vessel.

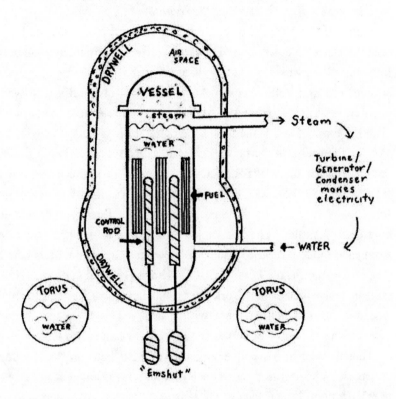

Additional Information: The vessel is surrounded by a concrete shell (the "drywell") and there is a large water tank nearby (the "torus") which together make up "containment".

Fuel is show inside, along with the "control rods" and their operating system "Emshut."

This drawing is not to scale. The vessel is 70 ft. tall and 16 ft. in diameter and has a 6 inch thick iron/steel wall. The top half of the drywell is 34 ft in diameter. Reactor fuel is 16 ft. long. The torus tank is 27 ft. in diameter.

Before leaving his desk to go with Tarelli, Paul had taken some time to adjust his new hard hat, but he'd never given any thought to the plastic safety glasses that were now perching at an angle on his thin nose as the two walked down the office corridor. At least they were on tight. Right now, he had other things on his mind. He was about to step inside the bowels of a nuclear power plant. *How will it look in there? And what about the radiation? . . .*

Paul followed Tarelli through a doorway and into a low-ceilinged area the size of a classroom. Its walls were a soft green, and the beige linoleum floor was split lengthwise down the middle by a swath of striped, red and yellow tape. Along the wall on Paul's side was a counter, behind which an older blonde woman was doing paperwork. Tarelli stopped, and leaned onto the countertop as he spoke with her. Across the room, in the far corner, Paul saw a wide steel door painted dark brown, with POWER BLOCK stenciled in white letters on its face. *That's it. The way in.* Beside the door was a long table holding four boxes of dull metal, each the size of a thick paperback and sporting a handle. The occasional sharp, chirping pulse that came from each made it clear to Paul that they were Geiger counters. As he waited for Tarelli, the POWER BLOCK door opened and three young men in worn blue jeans, work shirts and hard hats stepped through. The door closed behind them with a heavy THUD as the workers began using the Geiger counters to check their hands and feet.

Tarelli finished his conversation and patted Paul on the shoulder. "Okay, let's head into the reactor building." He pointed at the line on the floor, then the workers at the table. "Once we cross that tape, we don't step back until we've made sure we're clean."

Paul followed Tarelli to the metal door, taking an exaggerated step across the barrier. *Be careful. Just don't mess up.*

"First thing we do," Tarelli said, "is go through an airlock. As I explained, we keep the building isolated from the environment outside, just in case." He slipped his pass into a card reader by the POWER BLOCK door, then yanked open the thick metal slab. With the word "airlock," Paul had briefly pictured some type of metallic capsule on the other side, but instead there was only a short, narrow, cinderblock corridor with two exits. Tarelli let the first door slam shut and then opened the second.

For Paul, the next few minutes were less about gaining a foothold of knowledge and more a jumble of images and impressions. When the inner airlock door had opened, the first thing he noticed was the smell: a stuffy mixture of paint, insulation and grease. Next, as he and Tarelli began their tour, he was struck by the color. In a coal plant everything was dark and coated with grime, but here was only cleanliness and a multitude of paint shades. The floor was light gray and scarred with use, while the poured concrete walls were a sky blue as high as Paul's chin, then white up to the ceiling thirty feet above. Piping, from wrist size to two feet in diameter, was everywhere along the walls and floors. Painted red, orange and bright blue, here and there it sported valves of black or forest green, with pale yellow handwheels. Then there were the sounds. Apart from the occasional announcements on the plant page, it was easy enough to hear, provided no large equipment was in operation nearby. But always, in the background, there was a deep, vibrating growl that Paul could sometimes feel coming up through his shoes, and this rumble was overlaid by a high-pitched, fuzzy whine, like the sound of an leaking air hose in the distance. As the tour progressed, the two passed by pumps, compressors and other devices, ranging in size from that of a football to a railroad car, the equipment sometimes filling entire rooms or mounted off to one side in alcoves and cubbyholes that were accessible from the plant's wide main corridors.

Paul was surprised by how much he was able to see without donning special clothes or receiving advanced training. Always, he was acutely aware of the invisible danger of radiation. He took care not to touch anything unnecessarily, and twice he pointed the self-reading dosimeter up into the fluorescent lighting that dangled overhead next to long, metallic gutters full of cabling, but the instrument's needle did not budge from zero. As if to emphasize his concern, there were also doors they did not open, labeled "Locked -

High Radiation," and Paul saw other areas cordoned off by yellow and magenta rope, from which hung signs with the three-pronged symbol for radioactivity.

During the tour, Tarelli kept up a constant banter, pointing out safety systems for pumping water and stopping the nuclear reaction in the core, as well as answering the questions that Paul was working hard to devise. *Try to learn. Try to act like you're learning.* Here and there, they would stop alongside steel gray cabinets fronted with multi-hued, blinking lights, or long racks of round, black and white dials, or clusters of emerald green air tanks, like scuba gear, that were suspended just above the floor amidst a maze of aluminum tubing. Occasionally, workers would pass by, both men and women, some pushing carts full of instrumentation or carrying bright yellow garbage bags. Temperatures in the building varied from a few degrees colder than the office area to considerably hotter, and after some time spent in one of the warmer spots, Paul was glad to find himself in the pleasant outflow from an overhead duct as Tarelli gave another explanation.

"... and that run of pipe is part of VEPI," Tarelli said, pointing. He checked his watch. "Looks like I've got about twenty minutes, then a meeting." He thought for a moment. "Let's go up on the refuel floor. Top of the reactor building. A good place to finish."

Paul and his supervisor stepped off the elevator into a spacious hall topped by a rounded dome of off-white concrete. There was no one else about and it was quieter here than anywhere else they had been. At the far end of the room was a large pool of blue-green water surrounded by a bright yellow railing. Tarelli took off toward it, but then halfway there, he stopped atop a circular disc of cement thirty feet across, and turned to Paul, a twinkle in his eyes. "We're standing on top of the reactor now."

Shit! Paul instinctively looked down.

"Don't worry," Tarelli said, "you won't pick up any radiation here. There's a lot of concrete and steel and water between you and

34

the core. It's about ninety feet below, down inside the reactor vessel. Just a few hundred pounds of hot uranium. Everything else you've seen today is because of that."

Paul resisted the urge to look towards his feet again.

"Now over here," Tarelli said, heading on towards the pool, "we've got our old fuel stored underwater." He pointed over the railing. "Take a look, but keep a grip on your hard hat. If it goes in the water, you won't be getting it back."

Paul pushed down on his helmet and peered into the pit. The water was strikingly clear, and far below the surface, covering the bottom, was a shiny grid of metal -- rows and rows of squares perhaps ten inches on a side. Some were filled-in by a reddish-gray cap, while the remainder appeared black, deep, and empty.

"Many of those slots hold our used fuel," Tarelli said. "The uranium tubes in the core are kept in square bundles of twelve. Each of those is about the size of a telephone pole."

"And we're actually seeing them?"

"The very top, yes. The water shields us from the radiation."

"So the fuel gets used in the reactor," Paul said, "then you put it here." He looked back from the pool to the disk he had been standing on. "How do you move it?"

"Well, we do all the transferring underwater. We pull out that cement plug we walked over and then unbolt the lid of the reactor vessel. After that, we fill up all the empty space with water and then connect it with the storage pool. When everything's ready, it's basically just a matter of reaching down into the reactor hole, lifting out a fuel bundle, and then carrying it beneath the surface to the grid next door."

"That would be cool to see."

"It is," Tarelli said. "It's also the only chance we ever get to look at the reactor core itself. And the fuel does glow when you take it out. Or at least the water around it does. Bright blue, like a bug lamp. The tour groups love it."

"You have tour groups in here?"

"During refueling, sure. All that water is like liquid lead. Blocks the radiation, as its doing now with the spent fuel." Tarelli pointed down. "Without that water, we'd have been doomed from the time we walked in the door. That used stuff is dangerous."

"How long will it stay that way?"

Tarelli gave the question a moment's thought. "Oh, about a hundred thousand years. The government's supposed to put it deep underground, but they haven't picked a spot yet. They're looking at one in Nevada. I hope they get it sorted out soon -- having old fuel sitting around like this all over the country isn't such a great thing. The nuclear industry gives the Energy Department half a billion every year to keep working on it. To pay for that, we're allowed to add a fee to our customers' bills, and we also get to keep a little for a decommissioning fund, so we can clean up this place when we close after forty years." Tarelli stepped away from the railing. "But the end of Fairview Station is a long way off." He looked at his watch. "And I'm late for a meeting."

****

Paul reached into the box and pulled out three more science fiction novels, then crammed them onto the shelf. Most of his first day off had been spent settling into the apartment he'd rented in Brixton. A radio provided thumping background music, the components of his stereo still in boxes, stacked in the corner. A few paychecks, Paul kept telling himself, and he could afford a new setup, with more wattage, a woofer, the works.

Next from the box came a stack of *Playboys* and *National Lampoons*, then a plaque from his days in Little League, at a time when there was still a chance he'd turn out to be a decent athlete. He grabbed a few engineering texts, and between them found a magazine cover of Madonna that had been stuck on the wall of his dorm room.

The mindless task of unpacking was a welcome break after a long week of nuclear power. He had quickly learned that all the complexities of turbines and generators he had studied were taken for granted at Fairview Station -- but then so was nuclear fission itself. That process wasn't hard to manage. It was the safety systems that were the real focus, the special equipment built to ensure the fuel in the reactor vessel was always kept cool and covered by water. *Sturdy One*, *Sturdy Two*, *Veppy* and *Fuel Spray*, Paul repeated to himself. STurDI-1 and 2, VEPI and Fuel Spray. And there were other systems designed to shut down the nuclear reaction or keep radiation from escaping. EmShut, ARAFS. Langford had also mentioned that Kittleburg, Hoosier Electric's other nuclear plant over by Fort Wayne, was completely different. Paul had shuddered at the thought. He'd stick with Fairview Station. One reactor was enough.

The last item in the box was a book from a course he'd taken on the history of technology. Paul studied the cover. There was DaVinci, some Chinese guy, Thomas Edison. Edison, he'd learned, had been in at the beginning of the electric power industry. It was during his time that inventions, on a regular basis, began to exceed the understanding of the common man. A steam engine, or an improved clock, could be understood at some level by a simple craftsman, but electricity and the phonograph seemed like magic. Edison had tried to use this to his advantage when his power system, which used the one-way flow of electrons known as direct current, was challenged by the superior alternating current technology of George Westinghouse. This A.C. system featured electrons vibrating back and forth. While Edison's electricity couldn't be transmitted more than a few blocks without thick, costly wires, alternating current could travel for miles. To turn the public against his competitor, Edison had convinced the prison authorities in New York to build the world's first electric chair, using the more "dangerous" alternating current as the instrument of death. Ultimately, the ploy failed, as the prospect of needing an Edison power plant every few blocks pleased neither consumers nor investors.

In the end, Paul had learned, it was the public that decided what stayed and what went, balancing convenience and progress against the perceived difficulties that every new technology presented. It would be the same for nuclear power -- and for the time being, he had a ringside seat.

"So, how do you like work so far?" Crutch's wife asked as she passed Paul a bowl of steamed carrots. In contrast to her tall, Nordic husband, Maxie Pegariek was a petite brunette, with dark eyes and olive skin.

"It's okay," Paul said. "But the learning curve is pretty steep."

"You got that right," Crutch agreed. "Lou figures a year 'fore you're worth much. I've doubled that and still seem to run around like a chicken with its head cut off."

"It's a lot different than what I'd pictured," Paul said. "You get this image of scientists in lab coats."

"Nope." Crutch shook his head.

"Everybody seems real normal," Paul said. "They're just older versions of the guys I went to college with." He took a piece of roast pork from the center of the table. "How many people out there, anyway?"

"About three hundred."

"I can believe it." On a nearby wall, Paul had noticed a framed photo of a basketball player aggressively pulling in a rebound. "What's the picture from?" he asked.

"That's me at Valpo," Crutch said. "One of many glorious moments."

"Be sure and tell him what happened later in that game," Maxie said with a sly smile.

"I know that's the only reason ya let me put it up," Crutch said, "so you can mention that." He leaned back in his chair and looked at Paul. "Later on, I missed three straight lay-ups. We lost by two points. The campus paper had a headline the next day: 'Crutch Needs Guide Dog.' Saw a lot of bench time after that."

"So why do they call you Crutch, anyway?"

"Everybody has since junior high. I broke my left ankle, then my right foot. Hell, I lived on the things for a year."

"I thought he was cute," Maxie said.

"So you two have known each other a long time."

"Oh, yeah. I was just a simple farm boy an' she was a city gal from Logansport."

Maxie rolled her eyes. "He lived two miles outside of town."

"I think I drove through there on my way up," Paul said.

"Probably," Crutch agreed. "It's two counties south.

"So, do you still play basketball?"

"Hey, this is Indiana, boy. It's the state religion. I play up'n South Bend."

"And come home bruised and battered," Maxie said.

They ate for a while until Crutch spoke up again. "You 'dressed out' yet?"

"I don't even know what that means," Paul said.

"Is that when you have to undress in front of everybody?" Maxie asked her husband.

"Yep," Crutch said. "Out in the middle of the plant, gals strolling by, whatever. Ya strip down to your shorts, climb in a suit–"

"For real?" Paul said.

"Don't worry, you'll get trained on it soon. If ya go in a contaminated area, ya wear a yellow jumpsuit instead a your street clothes. Anti-contamination clothing. 'Anti-c's'."

"That keeps the radiation out?"

"Nope, you'll still get exposed," Crutch said. "To stop rads ya need somethin' thick and dense. Lead or steel or water. It's like tryin' ta block radio waves."

"So the suit's just to keep you from getting dirty?" Maxie asked.

"That's the idea. It stops ya from carryin' radioactive dust and grime back into the clean areas. When ya come out, ya toss it all in a barrel."

"And that keeps the radiation in the plant?" Paul said.

"Sorta. It keeps radioactive <u>particles</u> inside. You know the difference 'tween exposure and contamination?"

"No."

"Well, the best explanation I've heard is that exposure ta radiation is like exposure ta sunlight. On the other hand, contamination would be if ya actually had a piece a sun stuck to you. They call it being 'crapped up.' That's what the suit prevents."

"The whole thing sounds bad to me." Maxie said. "It's the part of Crutch's job I don't like."

"They take a lotta precautions," Crutch said. He speared a bit of salad. "Anyway, in our job ya don't hafta do it much."

Paul watched as Mike Langford pulled hard on the airlock door, and then the two stepped inside the narrow hallway. He had completed the required training and now had his own security pass. In three days of class work he had learned a lot -- particularly about radiation. A nuclear reactor produced four types: alpha, beta, gamma and neutrons. All four could affect humans by changing the chemical structure of their body tissue -- just how much depended on the amount of radiation present and the exposure time. Most of the radiation at Fairview was in the form of gamma rays, which were invisible waves of energy that could be stopped only by dense materials like lead. As a safety measure, the federal government had set limits on the total amount of radiation each plant worker could be exposed to. These were in units called "milli-rems," or "m.r." for short.

Langford yanked open the second airlock door and the two entered the reactor building. The older engineer led the way as they walked alongside a thick orange pipe, and then past a bank of gray metal cubes, each with its own handle, that resembled lockers at an airport. These were large circuit breakers. Finally, they turned a corner and Langford pointed toward a rack of bright green, high pressure tanks the size of scuba gear. "The emergency brakes."

"You mean EmShut?"

The older engineer nodded. "Correct. This is EmShut."

Paul had read a little about the Emergency Shutdown System. "So this is what they use to turn off the reactor."

"True, but only when they need to shut down the whole core at once. EmShut pushes all the control rods up between the fuel bundles at the same instant. That halts the nuclear reaction. Have you had a chance to study the details of nuclear fission yet?"

"No, and I get the feeling I'm not going to enjoy it. It looks like a lot of chemistry. I hate chemistry."

A smile appeared beneath Langford's mustache. If Tarelli was the office evangelist, Paul had come to understand, then Langford was the quiet professor.

"Oh, it's not too difficult. The nuclear reaction goes like this: a few of the uranium atoms in the fuel are always falling apart. U-235. Radioactive decay. When that happens to an atom, it shoots out little neutrons. These end up smashing into other uranium atoms, which then shoot out even more neutrons. Soon enough, you have neutrons flying all about the place. That's nuclear fission, and it creates a lot of heat."

"That's the chain reaction?"

"Correct. Of course, to keep a handle on things, you need the ability to catch some of those neutrons that are flying around. That's where the control rods come in. Each one is a neutron sponge. If you shove enough rods up into the core between the fuel bundles, the chain reaction will stop." Langford paused to allow some workers to go by. The three men each carried a plastic bucket full of tools. "When EmShut is activated, it's like slamming on the brakes. That happens automatically if something goes wrong." The engineer pointed to the row of green cylinders. "Every control rod has a tank beneath it filled with high pressure gas. All that's needed is a signal from EmShut and that gas is released. Then VOOM! -- the rods are in the core and the reactor is shut down. It's known as a 'scram.'"

"That sounds like we're supposed to run away?, Paul said.

"No, that would be too easy. 'Scram' is just an acronym. When they built the first reactor during World War Two, they had only one large control rod, and they would use a rope to winch it out of the core from above. When they were trying to get the reaction started, they would pull the rod up and tie it off. But someone always stood by with an axe, ready to chop the rope. Standby Control Rod Ax Man. Scram. Shut down fast. My father worked with one of those fellows later on."

"At a nuke plant?"

"No, he was a physics professor at Iowa State. Retired now. My mother taught psychology."

Paul stared at the long row of EmShut cylinders. "How many control rods we got, anyway?"

Langford furrowed his brow. "386 fuel bundles and 94 control rods," he finally said.

"Somehow, I didn't picture that many."

"Oh, they build nuke plants big. It's not worth it otherwise."

Fairview Nuclear Reactor

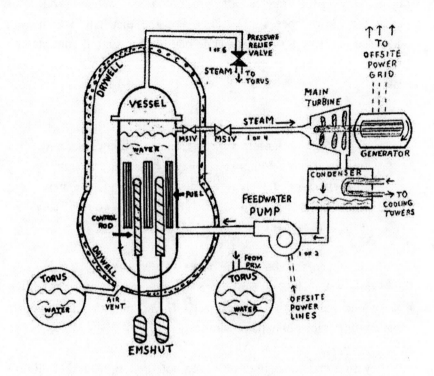

Figure Two: Previous Figure One, with the addition of Fairview's electric power production equipment. Water is heated to steam in the reactor and the steam is used to turn a turbine-generator which produces electricity. The "used" steam falls into the condenser, is cooled back to water, and goes through the cycle again via the Feedwater System. At full power, Fairview will be boiling over 16,000 gallons of water a minute.

Also included in the drawing is the Pressure Relief Valve (P.R.V.) for removing excess steam from the reactor vessel.

****

Vitaly sat at the old desk in his basement, the ground-level curtains drawn, copying the broadcast of dots and dashes. When it ended, he began the slow process of deciphering the dispatch, which was addressed to "Blue Raven," his code name. As usual, it consisted of little more than encouragement -- until, at the end, his hopes were realized:

> Vitaly, My Beloved Husband,
>
> Things are going well here. I am feeling fine, and my parents are doing well. They were so surprised with the gift I gave them for their anniversary! -- a new refrigerator I bought with some coupons your office sent. We're all so very proud of you . . .

Vitaly longed for the chance to see Yelena again. It would be some time before he had any more vacation, and by then almost a year would have passed since the KGB had provided they young couple with a dacha outside of Moscow.

They'd sat one morning drinking tea, looking out from their hilltop perch toward the capital, the spires of an old church glinting amidst the gray concrete of the modern city. Vitaly had gazed across the table at his wife. She wore only a robe, loosely tied in the middle so that the pale skin between her breasts was exposed to the light. Her new earrings dangled behind a thin haze of shimmering blonde hair. "So, you like your new job?" Vitaly had asked, in Russian.

"Oh yes, the work is much nicer. Shorter hours, and I get more management duties."

"It was great to hear about the apartment," Vitaly said. "I can't wait to see it next time I'm home." Soon, his wife and her parents would move into one of the best housing complexes in Moscow.

Dmitri had kept his word. Yelena was being well provided for.

"Like I said, Mama and Papa just couldn't believe it. They thought it was some kind of mistake for a while. The area director had to come down and show them the letter. I still wake up and think it's a dream sometimes!"

"I felt that way this morning," Vitaly said softly. Their brief times together were passionate and precious. Neither asked about the months spent apart, how each coped with the loneliness. Neither wanted to know. It did not matter.

His weary evening of decoding at an end, Vitaly re-read Yelena's letter a final time, and then gathered up the papers for burning. *A few more years of John Donner. Just a few more years.*

The senior shift supervisor looked up from behind the glass separating his office and the main Fairview control room. An annunciator alarm had sounded, and he scanned the board. After nine years, the tall, broad-shouldered man knew each rectangle on the wall by heart. As he stepped through the door, the chief operator pushed a button to silence the buzzer. "E.B.I.?" the supervisor asked.

"Yeah," the operator said, arms crossed in front of his T-shirt, his bony face in need of a shave. "Temperature problem."

"John still out on rounds?"

"He called in a minute ago and said he was heading back."

"Turn him around."

The operator picked up the page microphone. "John Donner, call the control room."

As the elevator carried him up to the Emergency Boron Injection pumps, Vitaly took off his hard hat, DONNER stamped across it, and wiped the sweat from his brow. Now that spring was turning into summer, the plant was beginning to heat up. He checked his watch.

The shift was only half over, and already he was tired. The most recent decoding session had interrupted his sleep.

John Donner had been working for Delco Electronics in Kokomo when he'd seen the ad for jobs at Fairview Station. The idea had intrigued Vitaly. Moscow told him to proceed cautiously, as U.S. atomic plants were required to perform background checks on their employees. Vitaly hired on at Fairview and now had advanced to reactor building operator, assigned to monitor the equipment spread throughout the five-story structure. He enjoyed the work, and his quiet intensity was a good fit with his coworkers, many of whom were happy to tell stories of their Navy days to a willing listener.

The elevator door opened, and Vitaly headed for the E.B.I. tank. It contained a liquid version of the control rods that could be pumped into the reactor vessel. The fluid needed to be kept warm, and there was a problem with the tank's heater. Vitaly soon found a circuit breaker had tripped. He reset it and then headed back for lunch. John Donner was hungry.

****

Steve Borden laid the report on his desk. FAIRVIEW STATION, YEAR NINE OUTAGE SCHEDULE. A bemused smile crossed his face. *Nine years!* He had started out as an engineer fresh from reactor training. Stacey and Martin hadn't even been born yet.

The old days -- the good old days. When you could walk right into the plant without all the security hassles, when the NRC dropped by only a few times a year, and when the thought of having 350 full-time workers -- let alone hiring more -- would have seemed absurd. But that was a past now long gone. Nuclear power had grown up, and Steve had too, right along with it. His rise up the ladder had been swift: supervisor in the control room, head of plant maintenance, then running Fairview day to day as the operations supervisor; he'd left each department better for his having been there. He'd worked hard at it too, both in the technical area and in learning people skills such as cultivating the voice and attitude that would signal authority without stifling dissent. And now he directed the whole show.

Plant manager. It was more than a full time job. He rarely dealt with the immediate decisions anymore -- when to fix a valve, how to deal with a bad pump. His concerns were on a broader scale, orchestrating a delicate balance between what was necessary for plant safety, and what Hoosier Electric could afford to spend. His time was spent approving projects, setting priorities, and discussing Fairview's performance with company executives or the Nuclear Regulatory Commission. Dealing with the NRC was difficult, but it was the corporation's money men he found the most trying. They were not unreasonable, but neither were they schooled in the science or politics of nuclear energy, and expenses he thought were easy to justify often proved baffling to those who watched over the purse strings.

Steve looked out the second floor window. It was a beautiful late summer day, a blue sky supporting puffy clouds, the nearby farms a sea of green and gold with their long rows of corn and beans. The next refueling outage would start in a matter of days, and the schedule called for it to be completed in fourteen weeks, which meant they'd finish up just before Christmas. Every day they were down was money lost, around a quarter of a million, but the work had to be done. The reactor needed new fuel bundles of uranium, and other plant equipment had to be inspected or repaired. They would also be installing a number of improvements -- a new pipe here, an extra valve there. Provided there weren't too many unexpected problems, and no new government regulations or safety concerns added to the workload, Fairview just finish on time and on budget.

His eyes still fixed on the bucolic scene outside, Steve began squeezing and pulling on his right hand, starting with the thumb that ended at the knuckle, then moving on to the index finger, which had a callused stub just below where the final joint had been. The hand had ached more than usual the past few days. Perhaps the arthritis was finally taking hold.

The injury was the one tangible souvenir of that terrible day in Richmond. He still had dreams on occasion, but he wouldn't call them nightmares -- those were reserved for the survivors, and the families of the forty-one who had died when a gas main ruptured beside a store that sold wholesale gunpowder. His wound had not been from a bullet after all, as these were harmless when exposed to flame unless they were also being squeezed within a gun barrel. Rather, the impact had come from shrapnel -- a stray piece of metal, or concrete, or plastic driven outward by one of the many detonations.

He had brought away another important memento from the catastrophe and its aftermath as well -- the confidence that came from knowing he had been tested under the worst of circumstances and had responded with his best. At the time, he had been mentioned as a hero, but he had never thought of it that way. It was the right thing to do, and he had done it. That was enough.

Steve watched a crow circle and land on a fence post. A few years ago he might have been playing golf in the fading sunshine, shooting the breeze with a few cohorts from church. But the days went by too quickly for that now — there were so many decisions to be made. This had its own rewards, the time he spent with other professionals, sifting through solutions and working toward common goals. And over the weekend, he did plan to spend some time with the kids and remind himself that Fairview Station was only a fraction of his world. They could watch cartoons together, or perhaps play in the yard. He might take a long walk with Marie. Then, later, if all were quiet, he would sit in the den and spend a few hours catching up with paperwork.

****

Gary Halvorsen had known this would happen. Things always broke down late on Friday afternoon. One of the last free weekends before the outage could well be shot for both he and his partner. Now, together, they headed down the reactor building hallway. Physically, the two mechanics were opposites: Halvorsen was a burly six footer, his rugged face bearing a few acne scars and a five o'clock shadow, his coal black hair sprinkled with gray. Doug Tama was four inches shorter, blond and pale, with thin features and a wiry build.

"Why did they test STurDI-1 today?" Doug Tama asked.

"Gotta test the safety systems every month," Gary sighed. "It was time for STurDI-1, I suppose." The Steam Turbine Driven Injection System could be important during an emergency. Normally, the reactor core was kept under sixteen feet of water. Steam boiled off the top and went on to the turbine, while replacement fluid was sent into the reactor vessel by the two huge feedwater pumps. But if those pumps failed, the water covering the fuel would gradually boil away with nothing to replace it, even if the nuclear reaction was turned off. That was the time to use STurDI. It could keep the core covered with water and safe from a meltdown.

Outside the STurDI-1 area, Gary grabbed a stack of anti-contamination clothing off plywood shelves. The skull cap was white, but the thick cotton jumpsuit, the hood that wrapped around at the neck, the rubber gloves, and the plastic booties were all a bright yellow. Rubber overshoes of black and a roll of tan masking tape to seal all the loose openings completed the outfit. Because there was no radioactive dust floating free in the STurDI-1 room, Gary would not have to wear a respirator to filter the air. The clothing requirements were no different than in his Navy days.

"So they couldn't get steam to the STurDI-1 turbine?" Tama asked, as he pulled off his jeans. The STurDI system used the vapor boiling up out of the reactor vessel as the power source for two turbine-driven pumps. It was like using the energy of a fire to fill the fire hoses. The pressure inside the reactor vessel was often very high, and against that force, only the electric feedwater pumps or the steam-driven STurDI units were powerful enough to shove large amounts of water into the huge container.

"Steam valve didn't move," Gary said, "so no power for the turbine. The rules say we've got a week to fix it or we shut down." Gary slid his stocking feet into his anti-c jumpsuit. "Hell, at least STurDI-2 tested okay," he said, referring to the smaller of the two pumps, "or we'd be coming down right now."

A few minutes later, two baggy yellow figures opened the heavy door to the STurDI-1 room and headed down the three flights of metal grillwork stairs. The area was like a dungeon, with its bare cement block walls and odd noises. At the bottom of the stairs sat the van-sized STurDI-1 turbine, a lumpy collection of metal parts painted green and black, with protruding tubes, pipes and cables.

"You guys ready to go?" the health physics technician waiting beside the turbine asked. He was a small man with a thick torso, his round face framed by a yellow hood. The boxy Geiger counter in his gloved hand was clicking slowly.

"Yah," Gary said, with a touch of a Scandinavian accent. "Give us the rundown."

"Well, it's not very 'hot' down here, about seven milli-rems an hour in the general area," the HP said, referring to the radiation level. "The valve's twenty m.r. on contact, and it smears clean. But if you tear into it you'll need masks."

Gary looked at the broken valve. Encased in a shell of burnished sheet metal packed with insulation, the device was a silvery knob the size of an easy chair. It sat atop a large and equally well-insulated pipe that extended from the wall to the valve and then on to the turbine. "Let's give it a try," Gary said.

The problem was soon narrowed down to the electric motor that moved the valve. The six hundred pound device would have to be unbolted and hoisted back to the shop. If parts were available, Gary calculated, they could have STurDI-1 back in working order by Monday. Then, perhaps, he could take a day off – and rest up before the refueling outage.

****

"Aw, hell." Gary's crew had just finished removing the pale green casing that surrounded a large pump when he spotted a jagged crevice in the polished metal shaft. VEPI pump #2 was cracked, and Gary knew he was looking at a serious problem. The VEPI system -- Vessel Electric Pump Injection -- provided a backup to the feedwater and STurDI pumps for injecting water into the core. There were four VEPI pumps, any two of which were enough to keep the fuel bundles from melting even with water pouring out of a gaping two-foot hole in the side of the reactor vessel. These pumps were much bigger than the STurDI units, but with that size also came a price -- unlike STurDI, the VEPI system could only push water along at half the pressure normally found in the reactor. To use VEPI, the vessel first had to be bled down. Precious fluid was lost in this process, but it was quickly replaced by the flow from VEPI.

"Get Karl's ass down here," Gary said over his shoulder to Doug Tama. "He'll wanna see this crack."

The standing joke around the plant was that Karl Leeman had been trained by Henry Ford, and though an exaggeration, the raw-boned maintenance supervisor would occasionally remark that when he had started with Hoosier Electric, the only nuclear power plant in the world was cruising the oceans aboard the *Nautilus*. Leeman's graying, bushy eyebrows furrowed as Gary shone a flashlight on the crevice, and he put his weathered face within an inch of the shaft, careful not to touch the contaminated surface. Lifting his stubbled chin, he peered through the bottom of the bifocals that perched in silver frames on his thin, crooked nose. "Yessir," Leeman said, his eyes fixed on the thin line, "that there sucker won't do."

"So only one is cracked?" Steve asked as the two men found seats in his office.

"Jest VEPI 2," Leeman said in his Southern twang. With one thin hand he massaged his narrow lower back. "X-rayed'em all. That crack ain't so bad. Not deep."

"Did we see any evidence this was happening?" Steve asked. "Vibration when we did our tests-"

"No," Ted Cervantes said. In charge of operations and responsible for running the plant day-to-day, Cervantes had a wide, Hispanic face, an unkempt mustache, and a receding hairline. He had perched his short, broad body on a table alongside the wall. "That pump's always worked. Ran it when we first shut down." Even with the nuclear reaction turned off, the fuel would still produce some heat, so VEPI was used to circulate cool water through the core.

Steve's hand was aching, and he was flexing it: open, closed, open. "Any idea what caused the shaft to crack?" he asked.

"Castin' error, maybe," Leeman said. "Can't know yet fer sure. Vendor's sendin' a guy."

"How much will a replacement cost?"

"Ninety thousand fer nuclear grade. We git it in twelve weeks."

"After New Year's," Cervantes said in his clipped voice. His dark eyes narrowed. "That blows the startup schedule."

"Vendor can speed up the fix," Leeman said. "Fer a price."

Steve sighed. The new fuel was now in the vessel, but without all four VEPI pumps in working order Fairview Station would not start the reactor. He saw no choice. "Find out how much they want for a new shaft by Christmas."

There was a knock on the door frame, and Steve saw it was Mike Langford, accompanied by Fairview's resident NRC inspector, Phil Guthrie. A tall, pudgy man with brown hair and deep-set eyes hidden behind thick, tortoise shell glasses, Guthrie maintained the site office of the Nuclear Regulatory Commission. Steve smiled. "I suspect you'd like to discuss the VEPI pumps."

"If you're ready," Guthrie said.

Steve motioned to some empty chairs. Over the next week, he knew there would be several such meetings, as Fairview finalized its repair plans. If Guthrie approved, and his superiors at the regional office in Chicago had no concerns, the work could go ahead. Or, there might be questions: some simple, some difficult and expensive to answer. When it came to a subject as complicated as nuclear power, no two engineers ever thought exactly alike. Steve knew Phil Guthrie, knew him as a man who was fair and knowledgeable and decent. But always, there would be a barrier between them, a line between acquaintance and friendship that could not be crossed.

"So, start from the beginning," Guthrie said.

FAIRVIEW ATOMIC PLANT

Emergency Water Injection Sources

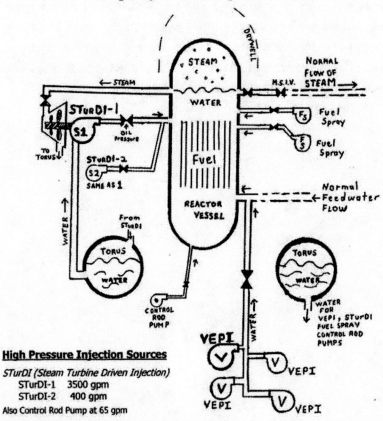

High Pressure Injection Sources

STurDI (Steam Turbine Driven Injection)
    STurDI-1   3500 gpm
    STurDI-2   400 gpm
Also Control Rod Pump at 65 gpm

Low Pressure Injection Sources (< 250 psia)

VEPI (Vessel Electric Pump Injection)
    4 Pumps   7700 gpm each
Fuel Spray
    2 Pumps at 3300 gpm each

NOT TO SCALE: Actual injection pathway not shown.

Figure D: Water Injection Summary

****

"Well, Paul, you've been here a few months now," Tarelli said, opening the airlock door into the reactor building. "You like it?"

"It's interesting," Paul said. It was. His department investigated problems and also worked closely with the NRC. "There's new stuff thrown at me every day."

"Me, too, and I've been in this business fifteen years."

"Did you start out here?"

Tarelli smiled. "Heh, heh. No, this is plant number four. Granger Ridge, Bayford and T.M.I. after the accident -- a lot of people went through there."

Paul followed his supervisor, counting on him to find a path through the clusters of helmeted workers and portable equipment that filled much of the main passage. The two were tracing a wide circle around a curving central wall. In the middle of the reactor building, Paul now understood, the steel reactor vessel sat within a larger container known as the drywell, like a yolk within an egg. The massive concrete and steel shell shielded the rest of the plant from the core's radiation. It was also watertight.

"How thick is the drywell wall?" Paul asked, gesturing at the cement barrier.

"Six feet of concrete, with some steel mixed in. Then there's thirty feet of space full of equipment, then the vessel."

The two picked their way through the busy crowd, while around them dials, meters, pumps and valves were being examined or repaired. Some workers were behind colored ropes in full anti-c's, while others remained in their normal work clothes. "Hang on a second," Tarelli said, putting a hand on Paul's shoulder. He stepped over to a petite young woman with curled blonde hair who was leaning against the wall, reading through a procedure. Tarelli thwacked his finger against the back of the paper. "You got safety glasses?"

She looked up. "Yeah."

"Then put'em on!" Tarelli stared at the woman until she complied, then turned back to Paul and continued walking. "Watch those people," he said.

They passed into a wider space, where workers were climbing into their anti-c's. One, fully decked out with only her face visible through the gap in the yellow hood, was helping another adjust the straps on his gas mask. Paul could hear the man's muffled voice forcing its way through the air filter, his features hidden behind smooth, fly-like eyes.

"They're getting ready to go in the drywell," Tarelli said. "Probably for M.S.I.V. work."

Main Steam Isolation Valves. The four thick pipes that delivered steam from the core to the turbine jutted out from the reactor vessel into the air space inside the drywell. At that location each line had an M.S.I.V., and all of the huge valves would automatically slam shut if there were a break in any of the pipes. That would keep the radioactive steam within the "primary containment," as the drywell was sometimes called. An additional set of M.S.I.V.s was also in place just outside the containment.

Paul stepped aside to let a group of technicians scurry past. "Man, it's busy." Usually, he saw only one or two other workers.

"Outages are like this," Tarelli said. "If refueling were all we needed to do, we'd finish up in a month. It's checking all the other stuff that keeps people busy. And nothing ever goes as smoothly as we'd like." He paused. "Ever work on a car engine?"

"Sure, a little, with my Dad."

"Ever have a simple fix turn into a real bitch?"

"Of course."

"Well, multiply those problems by something like a million, and you've got a good idea what a refueling outage is like. Technically speaking, it's one long, expensive pain in the butt."

****

Gary was tired. And hot. Some of the air coolers in the cramped, cavern-like drywell were not working and the temperature inside the cement shell stood above ninety degrees. He sat down on a pipe and leaned against a ventilation duct. At least some chilled air had passed through this one recently, and the coolness of the metal surface seeped into his thick, cottony anti-c's and mingled with the sweat on his back. It felt good.

He'd worked under far worse conditions in the drywell when the reactor had first been shut down a month before. Wearing a respirator that had filled his nose with the smell of polyurethane, he had climbed around in a darkness illuminated only by his flashlight, the valve on the mask slapping open and closed with each breath. The assignment was to search out any small leaks that might go unnoticed once steam was bled off from the piping within the drywell as part of the outage. Carefully, Gary had probed ahead, always listening for a hiss, and trying to spot a small, billowing cloud of white. Such a plume could appear out of thin air with no discernable source, since steam itself was perfectly clear. It was only cooling, liquid drops of water that gave it color. Somewhere below the cloud would be the leak. If he wasn't careful, Gary might suddenly encounter the leak itself, and find the lenses on his mask melting from the heat. But during this year's search, he had found nothing.

Gary stretched his sore limbs and then shuffled in his black rubber overshoes across the metal grating to the desk-sized Pressure Control Valve that he would soon unbolt from its base. The steam lines to the turbine were not the only exits from the reactor vessel. Opening a Pressure Control Valve allowed steam to blow from the reactor straight down into a huge tank known as the torus. The P.C.V.s would automatically open if pressure in the reactor vessel became too high, and they could also be used to reduce pressure so that the VEPI pumps could inject water back in to cool off the core.

What was it . . . Tuesday? It was easy to lose track of time, working fourteen-hour days, six days a week. To Gary, it was like a long cruise in the Pacific. And since the health physics technicians were required to monitor all jobs, his wife Carol had been putting in horrendous hours as well.

When he had enlisted in the Navy after high school, Gary's knowledge of other cultures was limited to several choice words of Norwegian his grandfather had used while he shuffled about the family home. A few of these had lodged in Gary's vocabulary from a young age, including "yah" and "dritt," and it was only later that his grandfather had explained the latter was the Norwegian equivalent of saying "shit." Leaving the service after four years spent babying the power train of a nuclear sub, he had thought about running a tool shop or garage, and even took a few business courses, but it was soon clear to him that he was not cut out for the crap that owners had to deal with. All he really wanted to do was salt away some money and then plunk it down on a boat for his own charter service on Lake Michigan. He'd grown up around the harbor, watching the pilots return at the end of the day, and he'd gone out a few times as a kid, serving as a free deckhand. Once, he and some Navy buddies had rented a boat in the Philippines. He had dreamed of showing the neophytes how to really fish, but the experience hadn't proven nearly so grand. It had rained, continuously, and the jarhead Marine one of his shipmates brought along had spent most of the day heaving over the side. Still, there were few better places than on the water and behind the wheel.

And he wouldn't have to do it alone. Before coming to Fairview he'd found a wonderful local girl who would never be confused with the port trollers that had sent him scurrying to the infirmary after shore leave. His friends had always said he seemed like a moose on ice when dealing with women, but with Carol he had felt comfortable from the start. Somehow, she was able to overlook his fumbling ways and acne scars and return his affection. With enough savings, they could move back home to Michigan . . .

CLANG! The sound came up the ladder from below, and Gary knelt to grab the bucket full of tools being handed up. *Keep going. Hell, some day we'll start this place up again. Then you can get some fishing in.*

****

Paul had spent the morning watching repairs on a fuel spray pump. There were two of these which could shower the core with a cooling mist if the feedwater, STurDI and VEPI systems were all broken. He'd also had a chance to watch the mechanics tear apart the small control rod pump that pushed water up past the rods and on into the reactor vessel. The flow kept the moving parts of the rods from overheating, and it could also be used to make small adjustments to the vessel's water level.

Now, for the first time, Paul joined a procession of sweaty workers in underwear, socks and shoes, as they inched toward three young women at a table. At least he didn't look any more ridiculous than anyone else. A few spots ahead of him he could see Langford squinting into his finger-sized dosimeter. Paul had already checked his. It read just above zero -- he had been exposed to little radiation during his trip into the restricted area. After peeling off his anti-c's, he had also run a Geiger counter probe across his body. The intermittent "click . . . click" of background radiation had not changed to the roaring static that meant radioactive dust was clinging to his skin. He was not 'crapped up.' It was an odd feeling, dealing with a source of danger he could neither see nor feel. Nuclear workers obviously became somewhat callous towards radiation after a lot of time spent in the plant, but Paul was not sure he would ever feel that laid back. There was just something about it, something ominous.

He'd seen too many old science fiction movies, too many monsters, he thought sometimes. He needed to remember that this was real life. But, still, he would be careful.

"So what's Lou up to?" Paul asked Langford, as the two left the power block and headed towards the break room. He had seen little of Tarelli for several days.

"Oh, he's attempting to answer some questions INPO had about the crack in the VEPI pump."

"What the hell is 'In-poe' anyway?"

"The Institute of Nuclear Power Operations," Langford said. "The utilities formed it after T.M.I. to help exchange information among themselves."

"So it's a self-help group? People don't seem to talk about it like that."

"Oh, it's supposed to be helpful, and it is sometimes, but now we have to keep INPO happy, just like the NRC. Their opinion of us has an effect on our bond ratings and insurance."

The lunch area was awash in cigarette smoke as Paul and Langford entered, the room resonating with the mumbling of a hundred voices. Paul quickly chose a sandwich, and while Langford studied the vending machines, he glanced around at the rugged men from the outage construction crews: seated at long tables, they played cards or ate from their lunch boxes, their hardhats taking up much of the table space. A heavy-set man, with close-cropped hair, bloodshot eyes, and several tattoos, finished off an apple and tossed the core down at his feet.

"Where do they get those guys?" Paul asked, once he and Langford had left.

"Some are out of the local union hall. The rest are Nuclear Cowboys."

"Huh?"

"Oh, they travel from plant to plant, outage to outage, doing specialized jobs. They will work seventy hours a week, perhaps do some drinking in their time off, then head down the road to the next site. There can be good money in it, but the work itself may be unpleasant." Langford bit into a candy bar. "I did contract work for a time. Nothing too bad, but it was a definite change from teaching" -- Langford had briefly been a high school science instructor -- "and it paid far better. Cindy didn't care for it, though, and once Trisha was on the way, she suggested a change. That made good sense to me." He took another bite of candy. "I once ran a job in Taiwan. They built their scaffolding out of bamboo. It was very odd."

"I've only been here a few months," Paul said. "Believe me, it's all very odd."

Paul finished off the last of his sandwich just as Langford peered around the cubicle. "Ready to view the torus?"

"Sure." Paul had read of the doughnut-shaped tank that surrounded the base of the reactor vessel and served as the final stop for any steam removed by the pressure relief valves. Soon, he and Langford were climbing down through a hatch into the huge cylindrical container, fifteen feet across, its walls painted a light gray. They stepped out on a brightly lit, bare metal catwalk, hung from the ceiling above clear water that curved away in both directions. The torus was usually kept half-full. "I never could picture how big it was," Paul said.

"Well, in an emergency they need some place to dump all of the energy coming from the reactor," Langford said, pointing to a huge pipe extending from the tank's ceiling to below the pool's surface. "To do that, they blow the steam from the P.R.V.'s directly into the water. This chills the steam down. Dissipates the energy."

Paul saw some smaller lines nearby. "What are those?"

"Torus cooling. The water in here can heat up rather fast when the steam arrives, and that's not a good thing. You want it cool for the next batch. So a VEPI pump can be used to run cold water through those pipes. This will pick up the excess heat and carry it away."

"And if they can't cool the torus down?"

"Oh, it's a rather long chain of events," Langford said, looking at the clear surface, "but if all the water in here is heated into steam, this tank will burst."

Fairview Nuclear Reactor

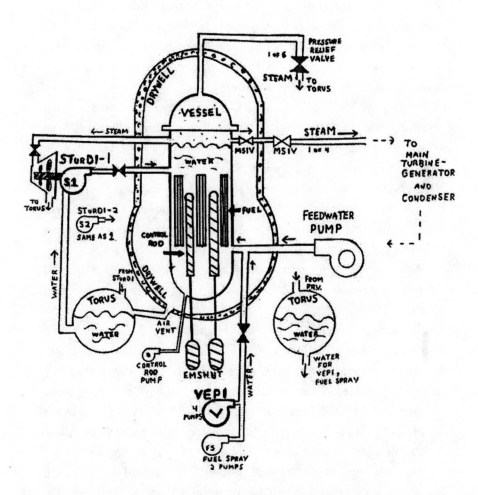

Figure Three: Previous Figure Two, with addition of the emergency water
injection sources for the reactor vessel: STurDI-1, STurDI-2,
VEPI (1 of 4 pumps shown), Fuel Spray (1 of 2 pumps shown)

1984

Steve swallowed the last of the lukewarm coffee, unbuttoned the collar on his shirt and loosened his tie. Both had been selected by Marie, who fortunately felt the same responsibility toward his wardrobe that he felt toward maintaining their cars. Periodically, she would spend a Saturday in South Bend shopping for business outfits that would look proper in her own job as a school administrator, and selecting items for her husband as well.

Turning the page of the budget report, Steve continued reading about the just-completed outage. Forty-four million dollars had been spent inside the plant, and an additional twenty million had been required to purchase replacement electricity from other utilities. The VEPI pump crack had been only one of several issues that had prolonged the shutdown. No flaws were found in the other three VEPI pumps, but their shafts would still be replaced during the next refueling outage, and they would be monitored closely until then.

Steve glanced at his watch and saw it was time to go. He peeled the gold watchband from his wrist and rewound the spring as he tried to study a final set of figures, but soon found himself staring at the small inscription on the back of the timepiece. "S.B. Sr. to S.B. Jr." His father had presented the watch to him for high school graduation, less than a month before fatally slamming his car into a highway median. As clearly as the day he had received the gift, Steve remembered the week previous to it, when he had twice driven to the county jail to bring his drunken father home. The senior Borden had fought for years to control his alcoholism, but after discovering his partner had squandered all the money, he seemed to give up. Somehow, his mother had held the family together, and Steve and his sister had turned out well. But he had never taken a drink – nor taken any success for granted. Steve Borden, Jr. would always be responsible for his actions. And he would not allow himself to fail.

"You moving in?" Steve looked up to find Lou Tarelli filling the doorframe, a grin plastered across his wide face.

"That might be more efficient," Steve sighed. He tried to remind himself not to be a workaholic, but Tarelli, on the other hand, seemed interested in becoming a case study. In college, Steve had taken some psych courses, and found he enjoyed trying to understand why people moved in the ways they did. With Tarelli it wasn't hard to figure out. Mozart had his music and Rembrandt had his art. Lou Tarelli had nuclear power. He loved the work.

Steve stood up and began packing his briefcase. "Better get home. Parent-teacher thing tonight. Marie will kill me if I'm late, and it'd be hard to blame her. I was a no-show at everything the whole outage." Steve thought briefly of school plays and band concerts, but it was the church activities he'd missed the most. It wasn't the religion itself — to him that was more a background hum of guidance and ethics than a wellspring of deep, spiritual feeling. What he regretted giving up was the time spent chatting with friends and fellow businessmen about things other than pumps and valves and regulatory concerns. For Tarelli, of course, that technical world was heaven itself.

Tarelli pulled out a cigarette. "Ann wasn't happy about the things I missed either."

"She lives over in Fort Wayne now, right?"

"A little east of there. Not too bad of a drive."

"You get to see Timmy much?"

"On weekends, or maybe some event." Tarelli lit his cigarette and took a long drag. He smiled. "He'll be playing Little League this summer. That'll be fun."

"Martin started last year. Good hit, no field. He loves it."

"Fun to be that age. I go talk to the bigger kids tomorrow."

"High school?"

"College." Tarelli took another puff. "I just hope I don't get another know-it-all activist like last time. She was a bitch."

"As I recall, you said the professor kept breaking up your little debate."

"Like a referee. She had nice legs, though." Another puff. "If I remember right, it was fun to be that age, too"

"There were moments," Steve said as he flipped out the lights.

"So, basically, that's how the plant works," Tarelli said. "Any questions on the process?" He turned off the overhead projector. The fifteen students slouching in the small desks of the classroom remained silent.

"All right," Tarelli said, "a quick word about the advantages of nuclear power. A big one is no fossil fuels. Fairview Station doesn't use oil, so we're not dependent on the Middle East, and we don't burn coal so we don't have to deal with all that smoke. Even if you filter away the sulfur, you're still pumping out a lot of carbon dioxide, and there's some concern now that all that CO2 might cause the blanket of air around the earth to start holding in more of the sun's heat. The 'Greenhouse Effect.' Sort of like leaving your car sealed up in the parking lot on a sunny day. Nuclear doesn't produce CO2, so no problem there." He shrugged his thick shoulders. "That's my pitch. Any questions?"

"What about radiation?" a clean-cut male in a blue T-shirt asked.

A smile lit up Tarelli's face. "Heh, heh. Well, you don't come to speak on nuclear power without being ready to talk about radiation. So let's cover it. Anybody want to give me a definition of what radiation is?"

"Killer energy," a tall young man with reddish hair said from his seat in the front row. The rest of class laughed quietly.

"Killer energy," Tarelli said, scratching his chin. "Not a bad try. It is energy, and, as our military has shown us, it can certainly kill people." He glanced around the room. "Anyone else?"

There were no takers.

"Okay," Tarelli said. "So, what is this thing called 'radiation'?" Well, for our purposes, it's energy given off by an atom as it falls apart. Subatomic waves, or particles such as electrons, protons, neutrons, and helium and hydrogen nuclei. These are all ionizing in nature, do not require matter for their propagation, have differing penetration properties-" Tarelli stopped himself. "Anyway, you can't see it, smell it, or taste it." He looked toward the student in the front row. "Invisible killer energy, if you like."

Tarelli went on. "So, the first thing I should do is explain how we measure radiation. We do it in 'Rems.' That stands for 'Roentgen Equivalent Man'." He stepped back to the overhead projector. "We were talking about how radiation can kill you. So how many Rems does it take?" Tarelli put a slide on the projector, but left the machine off. "The guaranteed answer is six hundred and fifty. If you are exposed to 650 Rems of radiation all at once, you've likely taken a lethal dose. Without the best medical attention and some luck, you'll be dead within a few days." The overhead projector came on now, displaying a slide entitled 'Radiation.' "As you can see," Tarelli continued, "at 450 Rems, you've got an even chance of surviving, while an adult who is exposed to less than 100 Rems all at once should live." The Fairview supervisor paused to take a breath. "And I say 'adult' because the levels are a lot lower for children. The younger someone is, the less they can take."

The tall student raised his hand. "What about cancer?"

Tarelli nodded. "That's the other big risk, of course. When radiation hits, your body absorbs that energy, and it can cause damage that increases your risk of cancer. Anything more than a few Rems at once may be enough, and the bigger the dose, the greater the chances. On the other hand, if you get enough little doses over time, that might cause problems too. They call that 'chronic exposure'."

The class remained quiet, and Tarelli continued. "So now that we've talked about death and cancer and all that, let me ask you something else. How many of you realize you're being exposed to radiation right now?" Tarelli gazed at the ceiling, as if expecting something to fall, while a few students reluctantly raised their hands.

"Well, you are being exposed -- and not because the guy from the nuclear power plant is here. Don't forget, radiation isn't something that man invented. It's always been around. The sun and other stars emit radiation, and so do rocks and soil."

"How much radiation we talking about?" someone asked.

"Compared to the numbers I just gave you, not very much," Tarelli said. "We were speaking of Rems before. Now I'd like to switch to a smaller unit called the milli-rem. It takes 1000 milli-rems to equal one Rem. Sort of like pennies to a ten dollar bill." He rubbed imaginary money between his fingers. "So, remember I said 100 Rem might just kill you? That's 100 thousand milli-rems, or 'm.r.' as we call them."

Tarelli turned off the projector. "Now, as I said, we are being exposed to small amounts of radiation all the time. 'Background radiation' we call it. But how much? How close are we to that possible death sentence of a 100,000 m.r.?"

A few students shrugged.

"Well, not very close. Around here you're exposed to about 50 m.r. a year from cosmic radiation, thanks to our sun and other stars. Another 25 m.r. comes from the rocks and soils, which have a little bit of uranium in them. Then there's the food we eat. Add another 25 m.r. for that. Potassium isotopes, mostly. That makes us radioactive, too. So if you sleep with someone every night," Tarelli said, flashing a smile, "put one more m.r. on the list. It all adds up to about 100 m.r. a year. And I should mention that the background value varies from place to place. You move to Denver and you'll get more cosmic radiation because the atmosphere is thinner there. At one site in Brazil you pick up twenty times more radiation from the ground than you do around here." He pointed down. "And there's also another natural source we're just starting to get a handle on. It's a gas called radon that naturally seeps up out of the soil and accumulates inside houses. It's a little bit radioactive. You may be getting an extra 100 milli-rems a year from that."

Some of the students nodded with interest, others glanced at the clock.

"So basically, that's natural radiation," Tarelli said. "Then we dump some more on ourselves, thanks to civilization. Your average chest X-ray is about twenty or thirty milli-rems, for instance. Fly across the country and back and you'll pick up an extra three or four m.r. because of the altitude. And, of course, there's smoking." Tarelli patted the pack of cigarettes in his shirt pocket. "A regular smoker will deliver a few <u>thousand</u> milli-rems to his lungs every year. Luckily, for me anyway, individual organs can absorb a lot more radiation by themselves than the whole body can take." Tarelli looked around. "Can anyone name another example of man-made radiation?"

"Nuclear power plants," someone said.

"Heh, heh." Tarelli flashed a smile once again. "Right. So just how much radiation <u>is</u> Fairview Station giving off? How many hundreds of milli-rems every year? Anyone want to hazard a guess?"

There were no volunteers.

"Well, if you lived on the farm next to the plant, you'd pick up an extra dose of a milli-rem or two every year. Almost nothing."

A few students traded looks.

"It's a small number, I know," Tarelli said, "especially given the reputation of nuclear power. But, I swear, honest-to-God, it's the truth. It's my job to know."

"How about other plants?" asked a thin young woman seated in the corner.

Tarelli gave the question a moment's thought. "I'd say, overall, we're about average for a plant in the U.S. Go much higher and the government steps in."

"Isn't your kind of radiation different than the stuff from rocks or stars?"

Tarelli gave a knowing nod. "The radiation from rocks, stars, radon, potassium and sources like nuclear power are each a little different. But as far as your body is concerned, a Rem is the same, no matter where it comes from."

"So how do you know exactly what the plant is giving off?" the tall student asked.

"Well, basically, we monitor our ventilation and water releases, and we've got a lot of instruments set up around the area. We also check milk from the farmers nearby, and we're required to take tissue samples from plants and animals to see if they've absorbed anything unusual. Road kills come in handy for that." Tarelli pretended to hold a smelly object at arm's length. "Our tests are pretty sensitive, too. Back in the mid-seventies, when the Chinese were setting off H-bombs, we detected the residue on grass near the site."

"What about Three Mile Island?" someone asked.

Tarelli nodded, and ran a hand across the top of his nearly bare scalp. "They released more than normal, for sure," he said. "But in the end, that accident wasn't too bad, at least as far as dose to the public goes. The official estimate is that no one living around the plant got more than one hundred milli-rems." Tarelli shrugged. "A few chest x-rays worth. Most people got a lot less. Of course, some people don't buy those numbers. But even if you figure in a few hundred percent worth of error, it still doesn't amount to much. Plant workers see that kind of dose from time to time with no problems." Tarelli briefly raised his palm to halt any response. "Not that T.M.I. wasn't a serious event. It was a partial meltdown. But it wasn't the killer it's been made out to be."

Some of the students began filling their backpacks, and Tarelli looked up at the clock. "Okay, I'll wrap it up. Basically, let me leave you with my outlook. You won't remember all these numbers, but you might take this away: Radiation is kind of like booze. If you have a drink once in a while -- no big deal. It's not gonna hurt you. Drink a lot, day in, day out, and you'll have problems later on. And if you really pound it down all at once, you can kill yourself. Same goes for radiation."

The bell rang and the class got up to leave. Tarelli was packing his materials when a short, plump coed in a green sweatshirt approached. "So how much radiation do your workers get out there?" she asked.

"Well, the government sets our limits. Right now, it's no more than 5000 milli-rems for a worker in a year -- and you have to spread that out. And there are lifetime limits, too."

"How do they know what limits to set? What's a safe amount?"

Tarelli fiddled with his cigarette pack. "That's a tough one. They've studied animals, and the Hiroshima victims, trying to figure it out. But the time span for problems like cancer is so long. It's still being studied. They may change the limits in a few years, as they know more. I'm betting they'll lower them a bit."

"Are most of your folks hitting the maximum every year?"

The supervisor shook his head. "No. We get a few edging up near it, but if you work in an office like I do, you don't see much more than background. I think the best answer on health I can give is that there are a lot of folks who've been working in nuclear power for years, since the sixties even, and some of them have picked up a fair amount of dose. And they're not dropping like flies. I did some jobs myself, maybe ten years ago, where I took in about a Rem at a time." Tarelli patted his round stomach. "And so far, so good."

****

"We'll go over it one more time." The man's voice was soft and patient. He spoke in Russian. "And then we'll go over it again. And again. And again -- until you tell us the truth."

The cellar was musty and dim. Strapped in a hard wooden chair, and seated in center of the room, a light in his eyes, Vitaly could see only the outline of the speaker.

"You know," the voice said, "the truth is a funny thing. For it is singular. You can lie, and lie, and then lie to cover up your lies. But the truth just sits there, waiting. It is the only thing that is real." The voice took on a great weariness. "And when you're tired of lying, it is all you have left."

Vitaly said nothing. How long had he been here? Six hours?

Twelve? A day? Two? He was between flights . . .

It was a routine trip back to Moscow. He was passing through Rome this time. His identity would change there, once he reached the locker at the far end of the airport. There was a jab in the back of his leg . . .

"Again!" The voice was harsh, and spoke in a flat, unaccented English. "What is your name?"

"John Donner. John Evan Donner. What are you doing? Call my Embassy." When he had come to, his bare feet on the cool, cobbled floor, his arms and legs immobilized, Vitaly had remained silent for some time, feigning sleep even as the interrogators tried to gain his attention in Russian and English. *Who am I now?* he had tried to remember. *Rome. Still John Donner. Those were the documents.* And what to do? *Stay with that. Be consistent.* But who was he being consistent for? As a spy, he had always lived on the edge, knowing some day it could crumble beneath him. Was it all over now?

"Where do you live?" The question was gentle, like a teacher guiding a student towards the right answer.

"South Bend, Indiana. United States." Vitaly focused on a stone at his feet. Looking up was a waste of time -- all he could see were the shadows of three men, gathered around him in a semi-circle beyond the reach of the light. He sensed there was another behind his chair.

"What is your name?"

"John Donner. I told you."

"*Erunda!*" the voice said. "Bullshit!"

Vitaly heard the scraping of metal on rock behind him. Then came a startling chill as cold water was dumped on his head. He shivered.

"That should clear your mind. You might try this, too." A hooded figure appeared from the shadows, jerked up on Vitaly's hair, and shoved smelling salts beneath his nose.

Vitaly struggled against the caustic smell, twisting his neck left and right, but there was little he could do. He coughed violently as the salts were pulled away.

"All right. . ." the voice said, in English, with a sigh, "your name?"

"John Evan Donner. Call the Embassy." Vitaly mumbled this time, wanting to give the impression he was beaten down.

"Your home is?"

"Indiana. South Bend. United States."

"You are a very smart man, comrade." There was a pause. "What is your occupation?" The question was in Russian.

"I don't understand. I speak English." *Stick with Donner. Careful . . .*

"No, no, no, " the voice gently scolded him in Russian. "We know you speak your native tongue. You are a spy. You only pose as an American."

"I don't understand what you're saying!" Vitaly said. "Who are you? What do you want?" *Keep acting the victim.*

The voice answered, in English. "Oh, my friend, you must know. We've found you out. The game's finished. It's time for you to come over to our side now. We can make you very comfortable."

Our side. Western Intelligence. That's it. "You've made a mistake. I'm an American."

"No, we have not made an error." And now in Russian: "You are a spy. You have been caught."

"I don't understand when you talk like that! Let me go! Let me call the Embassy!"

"No!" the voice shot back in English. "Now, what is your name?"

Vitaly straightened. His damp shirt gave him another chill. "John Donner. John Evan Donner of South Bend, Indiana."

"Ahhh," the voice said. "You're not as tired as I thought, comrade. No mumbling that time. Good, good! Are you hungry? Of course not! You've done nothing but sit in a chair all day. Still, my colleagues and I have been working hard, and I think we'll get something to eat. Perhaps it would be better for you if you stayed here and thought about things for a while. Don't contemplate a rescue -- there's no chance of that. Think about how you can help us. Think about how you can save yourself -- how you can make life easy. Just cooperate. You could really become an American if you wanted too. You wouldn't have to pretend. Think about it." A figure came out of the shadows in a blur, and grunted as he swung something downward. One of the back legs of the chair gave way at the impact, and Vitaly tipped over, his shoulder battering against the floor. Then there were shuffling footsteps, the sounds of creaking stairs, and a door being locked shut.

Vitaly tried to make sense of it all. His interrogators knew something wasn't right with his story, but could that be all? Could he ride it out long enough to escape? Yelena was waiting in Moscow. And he was a soldier. *Never surrender.*

There was only the low hum of the city beyond the boarded-up window. Vitaly knew if he yelled he would not be heard. And who would he yell to? He was in enemy territory. Left alone for a time, he had nodded off, still on his side with his face pressed against hard stones. He tightened his leg, and felt the bruised muscle contract. It would heal in time. But did that matter?

Yelena. He knew he would never see her again. But the pain would not be his to endure. Given the chance, he would end it now, quickly. But she would have to go on. What would they tell her of her husband?

The figures plodded down into the room, and from the shadows, one hooded figure ambled behind Vitaly. He could hear the scratching of the man's shoes against the rocks. CRACK! Vitaly's arm was suddenly on fire, bolts of white heat shooting into his clenched hand. Something had struck him on the elbow.

The hood appeared just inches from his face, lips protruding through a hole. "YOU ARE A KGB SPY! ADMIT IT! YOU ARE A KGB SPY!"

There were other whispers throughout the room. "Spy . . . spy . ."

"WHAT IS YOUR NAME?" the voice screamed into his ear in Russian.

Vitaly twisted his head away. "I don't understand!"

His tormenter stood. "What is your name?" he asked, softly now, in English.

"John Donner. For godsakes, stop this! Call the American Embassy!"

PAIN! His feet. A strap across the bottom of his feet. Vitaly's face contorted as he let out an involuntary scream.

"You are a spy, are you not?"

"I . . . don't know . . . what you're talking about." Vitaly wanted to vomit. He struggled to sound innocent. Dmitri had once told him: "You can be a victim who knows nothing -- just believe in that person, be that person."

The hooded figure shuffled around, and then Vitaly felt something pushing on his stomach. "Look!" the man said.

Vitaly focused. He could see the arm, the hand, the pistol pointed at his gut.

"Talk," the figure said, in Russian.

"I don't know what you want," Vitaly said. "Who are you? What have I done?" *That's right. Get frustrated. Kill me. Pull the trigger.*

The barrel pressed harder, and slid down into his crotch. "I fire now, and you'll live, but not as a man." The voice was in Russian. "Is it worth that?"

I'm a dead man already, you bastard. I'm a soldier. "What do you want? Just tell me!" *Please, let them take care of Yelena.*

There was a click, as the hammer of the revolver was cocked into place.

"I don't know what you want! If I did, don't you think I would say it? Who are you?"

Vitaly saw the finger squeeze, and his body tensed, awaiting the pain. But there was only another click. Then silence. No motion. *Fooled me. Now I break down. No!*

A few more seconds, and then the man in the hood spoke, in Russian. "We are KGB, like you, comrade." The pressure of the barrel disappeared as the tormentor rose to his feet.

Vitaly had anticipated the trick. He would not fall for it. "I don't understand. Let me go!"

More silence.

"Comrade Kruchinkin, I commend you on behalf of the Soviet people."

Vitaly instantly recognized Dmitri's voice. More lights came on and the man with the gun moved back as another figure approached. Vitaly looked up into the round, familiar face.

"You have done well, " Dmitri said. "The test is over now."

Vitaly could not think of a response. He felt only a numbness, tinged with relief.

"Doctor, see to him," Dmitri said, and a figure moved in with a black bag, as two other men began to release Vitaly's hands and feet. "Right now, Vitaly Fedorovich, you're in shock," Dmitri said. "An hour from now you'll be calling me a son of a bitch. But in time you will understand the reason for this. We had to test you. Now you may be of more service than ever."

Vitaly winced as firm hands slowly straightened his legs. Out of the corner of his eye he saw the doctor preparing an injection, holding the needle up to the light. "Yelena?" he asked.

"She's not expecting you for a few more days," Dmitri said. "And she'll have quite a few new luxuries to show you. She'll also be hearing about a pay increase. First, though, you'll need to rest and recover. Then we'll go home."

****

"Yeah, fire in a nuke plant is a big concern," Tarelli said to Paul as the two walked toward Fairview's river water pumping station, a half-mile from the main complex. In the bright spring sunshine they were strolling down a dirt road that passed between a patch of woods and a plowed field. "The Browns Ferry incident back in '74 really brought the fire issue home-"

"That the one the guy started with a candle?"

"Right, he was using the flame to check for drafts beside a sealed-up hole in the wall. Then some of the sealant caught fire and burned a lot of wires going to the control room. Nobody knew it was happening and they ended up losing control of a bunch of their safety systems. It was probably the most discussed event until T.M.I."

"You were at Three Mile Island after the accident, right?" Paul shook his head. "I tried reading the reports one day, but I couldn't quite make sense of it."

"Well, basically, T.M.I. is a pressurized water reactor, not a boiling water like we've got."

"Like Kittleburg," Paul said, referring to Hoosier Electric's other nuclear plant.

"Right. More than half the plants in the country are P.W.R.s. Anyway, T.M.I. started out with a scram, which wasn't a big deal by itself. But they didn't realize that a pressure relief valve had gotten stuck open, so steam and water were slowly leaking out of the vessel. The panel lights in the control room indicated the valve was closed, and the instruments monitoring the water level weren't designed to handle the conditions the open valve was creating, so those meters were acting screwy. The operators thought they had more than enough water in the vessel, and one of them even shut off an emergency pump that had started up. Basically, it was a confused mess. When they finally did refill the reactor a couple of hours later, it actually made things worse. The fuel had been uncovered by then, and the top of the core was starting to melt. Some of the tubes in the fuel bundles were so hot that they shattered when the cold water hit them. Then bits of fuel started leaving the vessel through the stuck valve and getting outside of containment." Tarelli pointed up and out.

"And things went on for a few days. I remember that."

"They kept having problems. And the info getting out was so mixed-up that nobody in the real world could tell what was going on." Tarelli shrugged. "Hell, I don't think most of the folks on the inside knew either."

"Didn't they have a gas bubble inside the reactor?"

"Hydrogen. Basically, melting fuel reacted with the water, and a lot of hydrogen was formed. Some of it got in the drywell too, and they actually had an explosion a few hours after the accident, but fortunately it wasn't big. You know, technically speaking, their containment -- their version of the drywell -- did a reasonable job, once they got the right valves closed. They had a mini-meltdown, but 99% of the core stayed put."

Tarelli suddenly stopped and looked up the road. "Deer," he said, pointing.

It took Paul a few moments to see the three motionless animals staring back at him from the edge of the plowed field, barely a stone's throw away. Then they took off, gliding silently across the road and into the woods, the last one presenting a flash of white as it leapt through a gap in the trees.

"Nice to see that," Tarelli said. He started walking again. "Anyway, the thing about T.M.I. that hurt the most was that the same valve had stuck open at other plants before, but everything was handled right and there wasn't a big problem. So the word didn't get passed around. If the guys at T.M.I. had been trained on those other events, the accident wouldn't have happened."

"So now we review reports from other sites."

"You got it." Tarelli smiled. "We're one big, happy nuclear family."

****

Weary from carrying boxes into Mike Langford's new house, Paul sank onto the front steps. The evening was cool for June, and the breeze felt good.

"So, Paul," Crutch asked as he sat down beside him, "are you still dating that friend of Maxie's? Vickie whatever?"

"Yeah," Paul mumbled. "She's okay."

"She must be. It's been a few months."

"No complaints." She was a gift, Paul thought, this pretty girl who took him seriously. High school had given him a one semester romance, but after that there had been nothing more than a few brief dates until his junior year in college, when he had made the mistake of falling for a close friend of his roommate's fiancée. She was very kind, but it was clear the interest was not mutual. Such things were supposed to fade away, but venturing out with companions meant her constant presence, and Paul often drank too much trying to kill any feelings. At other times he would escape into the video arcade, spending what little money he had playing Defender and Pac-Man. But all that was over now. He had finally moved on, and Vickie was for real. It was a good thing.

Langford stepped out his front door, clutching a diapered young girl against his chest with one arm. "Here you go," he said, handing out cans of beer.

"Good deal, Boss," Crutch replied. Tarelli had recently moved a notch up the corporate ladder and Langford had taken his place.

"Cindy decide you were in the way?" Paul said.

Langford stepped out onto the freshly sodded lawn. "At the moment, yes. Between her, Trisha and Maxie, it is a very efficient operation inside." He set the little girl on her feet, and she took two wobbly steps, toppled over on the grass, and then began playing quietly with the toys clutched in her hand.

Langford sat down, and the three savored their drinks, looking out at the field on the edge of the subdivision, the cooling tower plume of Fairview Station visible a few miles to the northwest.

"You see that NRC report on the guy gettin' zapped in Brazil?"

Crutch asked between gulps. "I peeked at it just before hittin' the door."

"It was Argentina," Langford said. He took off his glasses and began wiping away the sweat. "A small reactor was in operation, testing new fuel designs. It was shut down, and a worker was over the top of the core looking into the water and moving some bundles around. Then the reactor came to life. Apparently, they didn't follow all the safety rules. He got 2000 Rem, whole-body."

"Jeez, that's two <u>million</u> milli-rem." Crutch grimaced.

"How much to kill you?" Paul said. "Six hundred Rem?"

"Anything over 650, it's guaranteed." Langford said. He slid his glasses back on. "The worker had no chance. In half-an-hour a headache came, then the vomiting. I believe he survived two days."

"I guess this blows the claim that no one's ever died from the radiation at a reactor," Paul said.

"Not quite," Langford said. "That's just for commercial reactors in the U.S. It doesn't include the units overseas, or the government plants here. This Argentina event sounds a bit like SL-1."

"What?"

"SL-1 was a Navy test reactor in Idaho. They lost some people there in 1961."

"Didn't a guy get pinned to the roof by a control rod?" Crutch asked as he set his empty can on the cement.

"Correct. There was just one rod, and it was pulled out from above by hand. The operator was standing over it, and apparently he yanked up too fast. That was a problem. The water around the fuel boiled instantly and the steam pressure shot the rod right through him and into the ceiling."

"Holy shit!" Paul said. "How many people were at this place?"

"Three, I believe," Langford continued. "Two others were nearby. They all died before they had a chance to explain, so it took some time to figure out." Langford leaned forward and handed his daughter a toy she had tossed out of reach. "I met a fellow once who was on the initial response team. He was sent through the building holding a Geiger counter, trying to find the missing men. He ran by the top of the reactor and his counter got very noisy. It went upscale."

"Did he see the guy stuck in the ceiling?" Crutch asked.

"No. He told me that he never thought to look up. After they were finally located, the bodies had to be buried in pieces because of their radioactivity. Their heads and hands were sent to a special landfill. Then the reactor site was bulldozed away."

"God," Paul murmured, looking down.

"It sounds awful," Langford said. "But a few factory workers are killed on the job every year."

"Still sounds bad," Crutch said.

An aging brown station wagon pulled up in front of the house, and a tall young man in a colorful shirt jumped out, leaving the car in idle.

"I believe it's time for pizza," Langford said.

****

Beneath his hardhat, Wendell Auterman's copper-colored hair was dark with sweat from the mid-day heat, and he stepped into a patch of shade beside the transformer. His knit shirt clung to his five foot, nine inch torso of medium build, and perspiration was dripping down past his blue eyes and onto his sharp, freckled cheekbones and his thin nose. Uncomfortable as he was, there was still much to learn before he could go home. Then dinner and more studying. But at least this time he knew what he was getting into. When he had first brought his new wife from Philadelphia, he hadn't been entirely sure. The job market was tight for graduates, but Hoosier Electric had offered him the chance to become a shift technical advisor. The STA program was a result of Three Mile Island, where the control room personnel, taught to operate the plant on a minute-by-minute basis, had been unable to step back and figure out the cause of their problems. Wendell had undergone training and then stood a watch in the Fairview control room. Now, with the additional senior reactor operator's license he hoped to earn at summer's end, he would qualify as a shift supervisor. Ted Cervantes had felt it was worth the $100,000 it would cost to train him prior to his taking the NRC exam.

Come on, back to work. Wendell studied a sketch of the plant's power sources in his sweaty hand, then looked up at the massive, humming transformer that sat on the baking gravel. Fed by lines a few miles to the west, the Offsite Power Transformer supplied the plant's electric safety systems, such as the VEPI pumps. A backup unit also sat nearby, powered from a different set of high voltage lines that passed east of the plant.

Finished with his review, Wendell gladly turned his back on the shimmering heat and headed inside. *So what happens if both transformers go dead?* he asked himself. *We'd lose all the normal electric supplies for our safety systems, of course. But what else?* First, he knew, the reactor would automatically scram and the main steam isolation valves would close. *No feedwater for the vessel either.* There would be no offsite power available to the huge pumps. *That's not so good.*

Wendell added it up. If all the offsite power sources were lost, he would have to deal with a nuclear reactor that was shut down, with no water going in and no steam coming out. The vessel would be "bottled up." It wasn't a stable condition, but it wasn't that bad either. Some safety systems <u>would</u> still be available. The emergency diesel generators and the plant's battery banks would provide their power.

The smell of diesel oil hit Wendell well before the door slammed shut behind him. In the small, cramped room, he began making his way along the head high, orange and green, painted mass of metal that was an emergency diesel generator. The locomotive-sized machine, with pistons the size of a large man's fist, stretched thirty feet. It could provide enough electricity to run half the VEPI and Fuel Spray pumps, and there was a twin unit in the next room. Just down the hall, Wendell knew, were several battery banks that were kept fully charged and ready. These batteries were used to signal the STurDI turbines and also to power the instruments in the control room.

Wendell examined the controls for the diesel in detail. Finally, he headed out the door. A few more hours of review, and then home -- to Karen.

Fairview Nuclear Reactor

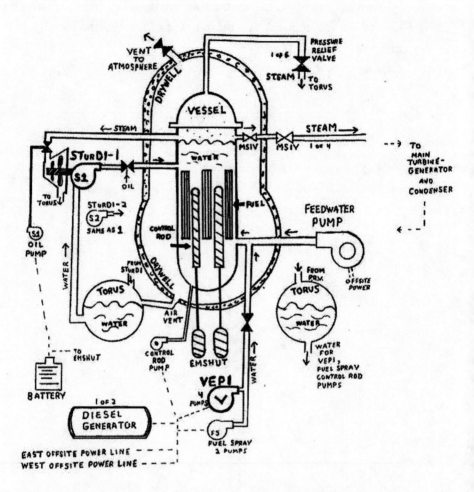

Figure Four: Previous Figure Three, with the addition of the electric power
sources for plant equipment. These are the two offsite power
lines coming from the grid, the two Emergency Diesel
Generators, and the plant's battery banks. The STurDI
Startup Oil Pump is also shown.

****

A young Japanese technician in white overalls and a blue helmet stood at a panel beside the emergency diesel generator, waiting for the start signal. The machine served Minoto Units 1 and 2, and had since the NorthEastern Boiler Company completed work on the plant in 1976. The nuclear industry in Japan was now the fourth largest in the world behind the United States, France, and the Soviet Union, and new plants were still coming on line.

CLANG! The huge diesel engine began turning over, and within ten seconds the roar had become deafening and the machine ready to provide electricity. Foam earplugs made the noise tolerable while the technician took some readings. He was turning to leave when an odd scraping noise caught his attention. The sound grew louder and more distinct and then the locomotive-sized engine began to vibrate. Suddenly, there was a loud CLICK! and the machine gradually slowed to a stop, the strange noise fading away.

****

"Misha, you are indeed the optimist," Morozov said. "Of course, in your position, you <u>can</u> make a difference. Perhaps it's not just optimism after all."

"You're right on both counts, my friend," Mikhail Gorbachev said. "I do have a streak of optimism -- and there are things I can do."

"But will it be enough?" Morozov said. He had known Gorbachev since their college days in the crowded student barracks. Now they were strolling along a wooded path at a plush dacha near Moscow. Morozov had flown in for a technical conference. "I'm just not sure the seeds are there for change," the scientist said to his classmate.

"Yes, I know," Gorbachev said, his accent betraying his southern origins in the Caucasus. "But change can happen, and when it does, our people will respond. Don't think that because I'm a Politburo member I don't notice of what life is like for the workers. I see the lines, I know about the black market. We must find a better way."

"But is the Party ready for this?"

"It will have to be."

****

"Yeah, Dan, I wouldn't buy it either," John Donner said as he got up to leave the control room. "If you think he's screwed with the engine, that'd be enough for me." The door slammed behind him, and Vitaly headed on toward the power block and his normal rounds. When on night shift, he was often alone in the reactor building except for the walkie-talkie that kept him in touch with the control room. Such walks gave him time to think. He had quickly recovered from the mock kidnapping and accepted Dmitri's assurances that he had passed his last test. Vitaly Kruchinkin had performed honorably, as a soldier should. As to why the exercise was necessary, this was a mystery to him at first. Then he had returned to Moscow. The time with Yelena had been wonderful, but it was his debriefing with Dmitri that was on his mind:

"The Center is very pleased with your work, Vitaly Fedorovich," the stout instructor had said. "I imagine the information you're getting from those air base trips seems trivial to you, but it's very useful."

"Thank you, comrade." Vitaly had been off the plane barely an hour, and responding in Russian still felt awkward.

"So tell me more about this promotion," Dmitri said, leaning forward with interest. "It sounds encouraging."

"Well, I'll be in training over a year. To get a reactor operator's

86

license. It's a difficult course. When I finish, I can work in the control room if there's an open spot. It may take a while for that to happen."

They talked for another two hours about his job, his lifestyle, America in general. The conversation had begun to wind down.

"One more item," Dmitri said, looking intently at Vitaly. "As I mentioned last time, you are getting a promotion of sorts. From time to time an agent will advance such that we feel it's appropriate to plan ahead for more active measures. Just in case. And you, Vitaly Fedorovich, are now in that group. After all, if we wanted to wreak havoc in the enemy's rear, you might give us an ideal way to do it."

"Take out a nuke plant." *That's why they tested my loyalty.* Vitaly felt little surprise, but still, it was an idea he did not wish to hear.

"Yes. Give it some thought. How you'd go about it."

Vitaly nodded, his firm jaw now tensed. It was one thing to spy, to gather information in the abstract. But to take action -- to hurt people he knew -- that was a big step. The American system was corrupt, he could see that, but its people were no better or worse than any other. Still, such an act would be his duty if the Motherland required it. But how far must he go? "In my planning, am I supposed to consider this a suicide mission?" he asked.

"Both ways," Dmitri replied. "High-risk to you, and undetectable sabotage." The senior KGB man then paused for emphasis. "And remember -- do not take any action or even mention this in any communication unless you are given the go-ahead by me. Never."

****

When the annunciator sounded, Wendell Auterman looked up from his desk in the office. The new junior shift supervisor saw it was a routine alarm, given the plant's shut down condition. Fairview Station had come off line to investigate a leaking pipe inside the drywell. Special tanks within the hollow structure collected the trickles of water that seeped from the equipment inside. Some leakage was acceptable, but that limit had been passed. At least the problem had come at a good time: with the arrival of fall, the demand for electricity had dropped.

Wendell returned to the paperwork that his partner, Darrel Fleck, had once again asked him to handle. He was pleased to be paired with the long-time Fairview employee. The two made an interesting contrast: the wiry new supervisor, always in pressed slacks and a fashionable knit shirt, while the burly, affable Fleck's apparel often looked old and slept in. Towering over Wendell as the two stood at the panels, his wavy blond hair a tousled mess, the older Fleck had a perpetually blank expression that hid a keen mind, and was the calm voice of experience. Wendell knew he could do the job, but he wanted to be the best. Fleck would help him get there.

And he would work for it, as he always had. Wendell was the eighth of ten children. His father was a draftsman at the Naval Yard in Philadelphia, his mother at home whenever they could possibly afford it. Higher education was never a given, but like most of his siblings he had scraped together enough money to cover his college bills. When he started classes at Temple, he was living at home and was almost engaged. But then he moved out, and two semesters with little contact broke the bond with his girl. Actually, Wendell was almost relieved. She now seemed too simple, too stuck in his old neighborhood. A few months later he met Karen.

The document before him called for replacing an instrument in ARAFS, and Wendell whistled at the cost, which included a huge markup for the quality checks and legal requirements a nuclear plant required. It was no wonder Fairview was running out of companies to deal with. There just weren't enough nuke plants around to make such things worth the hassle.

The rear door opened and Ted Cervantes strolled in and perched on the other desk. Wendell's supervisor rarely chose to sit in an actual chair.

"So, got the routine?" Cervantes asked in his dour manner, as he picked up a pen and absently twirled it between his fingers. A gold chain hung around his neck, a cross peeking out above his open collar.

Wendell lifted the pile of forms. "With as much paperwork as it takes to run one of these," he replied in his light Philly brogue, "I doubt if anyone will ever want to build one again."

"And the bullshit keeps gettin' worse," Cervantes said. His head tilted back and his eyes narrowed as he spoke. "Darrel probably tells you that all the time."

"He does mention it." Wendell's partner had also told him a little about Cervantes. The intense operations supervisor was the son of migrant workers who had settled in the area. Like Fleck, Cervantes had joined the Navy out of high school, spent time on a nuclear submarine, and then signed on at Fairview a few months before the plant first started up. Something else Darrel had related popped into Wendell's mind. "Did you really come on shift one night dressed as Superman?" he asked his boss.

A brief smile appeared under Cervantes' mustache. "It <u>was</u> Halloween," he said. "But that was years ago. Different world now."

****

Steve considered the point, his eyes fixed on his desk, then looked up at the visiting NRC inspector. "So you feel we should check these pressure monitors more closely?"

"Yes," the inspector said. He was in his mid-twenties, with a long, slender face. "I've seen these instruments fail at other sites."

Steve turned to Crutch Pegariek, who'd been showing the inspector around. "How many are we talking about?"

"Twelve total," Crutch said. "All just for information. They don't control a safety system."

"If I recall, we read them daily, don't we?" Steve said.

Crutch nodded. "Operators check'em on rounds. We'd quickly see a problem."

"That's all correct," the inspector said, "but at another plant I visited, several of these monitors failed. I believe that can be prevented if you check them out internally from time to time."

"I see," Steve said. He had encountered the inspector's type before: young, confident, eager to assert his power and make a mark. But also, perhaps, lacking in wisdom. "How hard is it to open these instruments up?" Steve asked.

"It's not easy," Crutch said, his features betraying tension. "They're not built for it. It takes a lotta time and you might just break something."

"Well, anyway," the inspector said casually, "I just thought I'd put that forward as a suggestion. I'll mention it in my report."

"The bastard wants to tear'em apart!"

Paul sipped at his beer and listened to Crutch complain. Along with Tarelli and Langford, they were seated in the old bar that comprised most of Fairview's business district. Outside, a cold rain was pulling down the last of the fall leaves.

"Internal inspections -- what a joke," Crutch said. "Crack up one monitor, and you're lookin' at a thousand bucks down the hole."

Langford nodded. "That is a problem. But if he writes it into his report, we'll have to do it."

"I still don't get it," Paul said. "Why don't we talk to his boss?"

"Heh, heh." Tarelli chuckled and gave a thumbs down. "Bad politics. Basically, if you complain too much, NRC management thinks you're not taking them seriously -- so you're not paying enough attention to safety. That kind of perception can sway big decisions."

"This is true. The little things count," Langford said. "When I was at Craymont, they were visited by a commissioner. The plant spent a least a hundred thousand dollars preparing for the big day. Much of it was cosmetic. The entire plant was repainted, and a number of shiny new doorknobs were installed."

"You'd think being an old nuclear plant guy, he wouldn't just go on appearances," Paul said.

Langford shook his head. "Many in the NRC have never worked at a power plant. This is particularly true of top management."

"The commissioners aren't from power plants?" Paul said, referring to the five executives who controlled the federal agency.

Tarelli put down his beer. "Not one, unless you count a nuclear sub. They're usually admirals, lawyers or academics."

"How can they know what's going on?" Paul said. "It doesn't make sense."

"Basically," Tarelli said, "the NRC is supposed to be independent and watch over us, not be our pals. So Congress doesn't want a bunch of old utility guys running the show. But they've overdone it. Now there's hardly anybody in Washington who's actually tried to run one of these things. The liberals seem to think you've sold your soul if you've worked in the industry."

"A bit over-stated, but you do have a point," Langford said. "Still, you must give the NRC credit for being correct a good deal of the time."

"Yeah, sometimes," Crutch said. His eyes were focused on twisting a napkin into a tight spiral. "The guy today was a loser, but the one here last month was sharp. Forced us to keep better track a spare parts."

"A bad inspector can cost you, with dumb ideas and useless paperwork," Tarelli said, "and a good inspector will cost you too -- but it's money well spent. He'll help you keep the plant out of trouble." A waitress walked by and he pointed at the empty pitcher.

"Phil Guthrie is helpful," Langford said, referring to the plant's resident NRC employee. "He seems to focus on the things that are genuinely important."

Tarelli lit a cigarette. "It's not an easy job -- especially if you're a resident, like Phil. It's a hell of a life. You move every few years, and you can't make friends-"

"Ya know," Crutch said, "when my Dad first took me out to the barn to castrate hogs, he held up a knife and said, 'Before ya get too cocky, make sure you're on the right end a this.'" Everyone laughed. "I know which end we're on here. An' squealin' don't do no good. We can't even complain if the NRC screws up."

"We can do a little behind closed doors," Tarelli said, "but they've got the upper hand, right or not. We go public and bitch about something and it ends up sounding like the evil utility is trying to get out of making their plant safe." He took a sip of beer. "No way you can look good with that. You're better off just doing what the government wants and billing the customers."

"Seems like on the news, people say the NRC is not tough enough," Paul said.

"Just say 'radiation' and people are spooked," Crutch said, twisting his napkin even tighter. "It's a boogey-man."

"True," Langford said, "But you cannot see it, or smell it, or taste it. And in the right amounts, it can cause you great harm. I'm afraid many in the population would rather not live with something like that lurking nearby, however well-managed it is."

"Like your fellow Democrats," Tarelli said, smiling.

Langford nodded. "Yes. Most. Their hearts are in the right place, but their science is not." He gave a sly grin. "I will refrain from discussing the hearts of Republicans."

"Good." Tarelli rolled his eyes. He slapped his palm on the table. "I got an idea. Let's go back to the good old days. Put in a coal-fired unit and let the flyash float out the stack, like they did in the fifties. That's a bigger rad release than anything Fairview puts out. Coal's got uranium in it." The waitress returned with a fresh pitcher, and Tarelli reached for his wallet.

"The media's no help," Crutch said. "You saw that thing in the paper last month. The reporter's here one day, then calls her article 'AN ACCIDENT ABOUT TO HAPPEN?' Jeez, that sucked."

"It's too complicated a subject," Langford said. He took off his glasses and began cleaning the lenses. "Unfortunately, most of the literature available that the general public can understand is propaganda from one side or the other."

"At least she didn't say we could blow up like a bomb," Paul said. "Vickie's friends seem to think that."

"Heh, heh. Can't happen," Tarelli said. "Not enough U-235. You need a special reactor, and the government runs those. About all we could do is make heavy water."

"That may be true in this country," Langford said, sliding his glasses back on. "But in some nations, what begins as an atomic plant to generate power soon becomes a factory for bomb material."

"Hey, not us though," Crutch said. "We just make electricity."

"Hard enough doing that," Tarelli said.

1985: January – August

"Halvorsen," the burly man said, reciting the name on the hard hat of the petite young health physics technician at the entrance to the power block. A few locks of curled auburn hair framed her delicate face, with green eyes and a small mouth that seemed set in a permanent frown. "You related to Gary Halvorsen, the mechanic?" he asked.

"Just married to him," Carol said. The laborer must be new. He certainly needed a shave. She passed a Geiger counter once more over the knee of the man's blue jeans, and again the slow click. . . click. . . click increased to a static-filled roar. Shoot. "Still got some hot stuff on you. Where were you, anyway?"

"Down by the VEPI pumps. Can ya get it off? I'd like to get outta here."

"We'll try again." Carol reached for the duct tape. There were several possible explanations for the worker being contaminated. He might have followed all the rules and still gotten crapped up. It happened sometimes. An area that should be "clean" could have a bad spot. Or perhaps he had ignored one of the safety ropes, maybe just for a second, in order to get a job finished. That happened as well. People got in a hurry or just didn't care. Even Gary did it from time to time, Carol knew. She wished he would be more careful. Fortunately, everyone coming out of the power block had to pass through sensitive monitors. Her current client was a good example of why.

With a thin, gloved hand, Carol slapped gummy tape on the denim fabric and peeled it back, then checked again. The steady click. . . click. . . click did not increase. Whatever had been on the blue jeans had stuck to the tape. The worker was now decontaminated.

"I can go?" the man asked.

"Fine. Go home," Carol said. *And then I will.* It looked to be a nice summer night, and she and Gary could sit out on their deck. When they had first started dating, she would often meet him after classes at the junior college for a walk along the eastern shore of Lake Michigan. Together they would watch the sun drop down into the cool, blue water. They had grown up in nearby towns, but had never met until that day in the commons when the young veteran had struck up a conversation. Carol had never really fallen in love before -- apart from a few dates and the occasional beer party, her bookish social life had revolved around her family and a few friends. She had fretted often in high school about her small figure and the green eyes she felt were too close-set, but she proved to be a late bloomer, with subtle changes to her hips and a filling out of her face after she started college.

She might have been studying music at another school -- and never met Gary -- had she not decided against music as a career. She'd been a state finalist in clarinet and piano, but hated being onstage, and the other choice of giving piano lessons and teaching classrooms of giggling students didn't seem worth the large debt and small salary. Watching her Mom had taught her that. Eventually, she had brought Gary home to meet her mother and sisters, and then introduced him to her father down at his garage. Gary had even helped out there in the months before he had gotten the job at Fairview. Soon after, they were traveling to work together, her radiology credits making her a good recruit for health physics.

Carol cleared off the countertop. She thought again of the quiet evening ahead. Perhaps they might listen to some music. When they had first met, Gary's taste had run to the kind of country and western she couldn't stand, but it turned out he also had an affinity for classical, provided it sounded more like a cavalry charge than a springtime morning. His mother had often played symphony records when he was growing up. Or, perhaps tonight the two would just sit back on the deck at the rear of the trailer, hand in hand. Either way, it would be nice.

****

John Donner massaged the back of his neck. The class had been given the afternoon to tour the plant, and Vitaly was tracing the reactor building's ventilation system, staring up at the main air shafts leaving the building. Sensors monitored the air for radiation, and if it was detected, dampers would shut and the building's exhaust would be diverted through the Atmospheric Release Air Filtration System. ARAFS would clean the air of radioactive particles and some gasses before sending it up the tall smokestack outside. At the same time, huge fans would also be sucking air into the reactor building to keep the structure at a lower pressure than the outside world, ensuring nothing leaked out without first being filtered. A similar system protected the crew in the control room.

How could I break ARAFS? The question was in the back of Vitaly's mind with every system he studied. Dmitri wanted a sabotage plan, and searching for weak spots in the plant's design also helped him with his class work.

Vitaly did not want to believe the plant's destruction would ever become necessary. His co-workers were his friends: he had been to their homes, played with their children. Growing up in New York, he remembered watching *Father Knows Best* and *Leave It to Beaver*. To the youthful Russian, that was America away from the city. Small towns and pleasant lives. He knew now there was more to it than that -- and rural poverty -- but spending time in the backyards of Indiana, cooking hamburgers with kids racing underfoot, was a life not so far removed from what he had first pictured.

Still, Vitaly knew where his duty lay. He remembered his father telling him of a time during the war when he was guarding German prisoners. One of the captured soldiers spoke Russian, and Private Kruchinkin had talked with the man of families and home. "Few people are evil, Vitaly," his father had explained. "But one doesn't fight against people. It is ideologies that do battle. Soldiers are just tools, after all." The prisoner had later escaped, the elder Kruchinkin also recalled. "And if I had met him again, on the battlefield, I would have killed him. Or he would have killed me. That is war."

****

The debrief was nearly over, and Vitaly was anxious to start his vacation. Five precious spring days with Yelena.

"One more item and we're done," Dmitri said, folding his hands atop the table. "How are you doing on the sabotage plans?"

"Well, I've given it some thought, but I haven't worked out the details. No time. The training class is a real challenge."

"I'm sure it is," Dmitri nodded. "Still, we'd like to get your thoughts. You'll be back in a few months, after your course is over. Perhaps you can forward an outline to the Center before you return. Then our experts can go over it."

Vitaly sighed. *Tough job.* "I'll try to work it in."

"You'll do fine," Dmitri smiled. "You're one of the best."

Yelena unwrapped her arms from Vitaly's waist and reached up to his forehead, gently playing with a tawny lock. She examined it closely, then looked away.

"Something wrong, my love?" Vitaly asked. Around them, a birch grove trembled in the breeze.

Yelena smiled. "You have gray hairs, my husband. It just reminded me of how much time has passed."

"I know, I know," Vitaly whispered as he again took his wife in his arms. "And I can't say it's gone quickly." He meant every word. For all the satisfaction of doing his duty, and the short moments of pleasure he occasionally found with American women, it was Yelena that he needed.

"Nine years. . ." Yelena gazed toward the treetops above the path, her ear resting against Vitaly's chest. "Sometimes I feel I'm growing old."

"You're only thirty-two, my precious one," Vitaly said, stroking his wife's blond hair. "And a young and sexy thirty-two at that."

"Thank you." Together, the couple swayed back and forth. "How much longer?"

Vitaly felt the warm breeze drift across his face, carrying with it the scent of Yelena's perfume. He hated to think of the time they had yet to spend apart. He took a deep breath. "I don't know. They told me at the start it'd be ten to twelve years. I think they'll keep their word. . ."

"But?"

"But it will probably be closer to twelve. I'm doing valuable work, and it's becoming more important all the time."

Yelena sighed, and pressed tighter. Together, they stood in the forest, not speaking.

****

The office lights cast a harsh pallor as Anton worked on the dispatch, his white uniform shirt stretched across thin shoulders. His writing hand grew tired, and he paused to stroke his narrow black mustache and peer out with his sunken gray eyes at the dense forest that surrounded the KGB complex. Days in the S Directorate could grow tedious. Anton's role in helping to manage the elite corps of Soviet illegals abroad often consisted of composing inspirational messages or editing chatty letters from family members. Occasionally there would be more -- making travel arrangements for a spy's trip home; or arranging a 'dead drop,' where the agent would pick up or deliver a package without ever seeing his contact. But there was never any continuity, never any clue as to where the undercover operatives were located or what they were doing. Anton might not even know if he was writing to the same agent as he had the time before, since each illegal had both a code number, such as C393-111, and a code name, like "Six Tiger." Messages were addressed to either designation to prevent subordinates from learning too much about a particular operation. Only Anton's section chief, the pug-nosed, near-sighted Colonel Dmitri Ivanovich Bykov, knew both the number and code name for the agents his office was handling.

Anton hated Dmitri Bykov, as he hated all those who did the KGB's dirty work. He knew firsthand how they could tear one's soul apart but leave the body behind, untouched. Only seventeen at the time, he was still growing, still learning about himself, when he had met the love of his life. Everything had clicked from the very first, and he was walking on air -- but also looking over his shoulder. They were to meet one night at the club, and Anton had been running late. He only saw the end of it -- the unmarked trucks, the nightsticks beating his friends as they were dragged out of the dingy basement. And then he saw Viktor, head bloodied, as the van doors slammed shut. Why hadn't he rushed in? Anton had asked himself that question a thousand times. Why hadn't he burst past the thugs to hold on to the only thing in the world that meant anything to him? Why? Was it cowardice? Shame? The will to survive? It did not matter once the truck had pulled away. Viktor was gone forever.

Someone was walking up the aisle, and Anton went back to work. In a few weeks, he would have enough for another "dead drop" himself, taking vengeance on the system he loathed. Six Tiger had been to White Sands, Blue Raven to the naval yards in Chicago, and Steel Deer had picked up a package near Barstow. All were little things, but perhaps the Americans could piece the puzzle together. And if they could, Anton consoled himself, then Viktor would not have died in vain.

****

Wendell grimaced as he reached for the report, and he squeezed his swollen wrist. "I never knew owning a dog could be so dangerous."

"He bite the hand that feeds him?" Darrel Fleck asked from his desk.

"No, I tripped over him."

"I thought you said Karen wanted a cat."

"She did. We settled on a dog and a new refrigerator."

Fleck chewed thoughtfully on his gum. "I'm glad Marcia doesn't drive those kind of bargains."

"I got off easy. I promised her a trip down the shore last summer an' we never made it."

"Where?"

"The beach. The ocean." Wendell grinned. "That's how we say it back home."

Fleck shrugged. "To each his own, I guess. So how'd you sweet talk this girl into marrying you, anyway?"

Wendell began studying the document in his hand. "You don't wanna know."

He had always wanted a dog, but there was no room for one while growing up in a crowded urban townhouse. But now, he and Karen had a place of their own, just east of Brixton. There, it was an easy drive for Karen up to the Hoosier Electric offices in South Bend, and her job as a corporate attorney. Her sister was also barely an hour away in Fort Wayne.

Wendell had sensed her drive and ambition from the first time they had met, around a table with mutual college friends at McGillan's. Soon, they were spending long nights together, studying side by side for a few grueling hours before falling into each other's arms. Two years ahead of Wendell, slight, blonde, and an inch taller, Karen had passed her bar exam a few weeks before he had received his diploma. A brief honeymoon cruise and then they had headed west to Indiana. Apart from the lack of cheesesteaks and his beloved Tastykakes, Wendell found he liked the small town atmosphere in Brixton, and he now busied himself with all the repairs that an old home needed. He also enjoyed having friends over after Mass, and they'd even had a Knights of Columbus picnic. Karen, too, was spending her free time on the house, browsing through stores looking for furniture or carpeting. Wendell had laid out a plot for a garden, but she'd been so busy that nothing had yet been planted. Still, they were settling in.

Finished with his reading, Wendell put the report down and stared through the glass into the control room. The control rod display was a circle of red lights, and the chief and assistant operators were casually monitoring the wide array of instruments, while the STA sat nearby at his desk. The reactor was at full power, with the feedwater pumps maintaining the boiling water inside the vessel at its usual 190 inches above the fuel. Steam, pressurized to 1000 pounds per square inch, was flowing into the main turbine.

With the plant coasting along, the young supervisor had been catching up on the latest industry news. "Yo, Darrel, did you read this?" he asked his partner. "Davis-Besse really took a run at it. They were losing water fast, and had to race 'round the plant opening valves by hand."

"Saw it. A bad deal," Fleck said. He blew a bubble with his gum.

"Looks like if they hadn't gotten things back under control, the core would have been uncovered in an hour or so."

"Maybe." Fleck blew another bubble. "But that's why they keep us on shift. Nothin' beats the human touch."

The laborer was striding through the reactor building with a yellow trash bag. Once the package was delivered to the radwaste department, he could head home at last. He cut a corner, and the heavy bag tapped the edge of a rack full of instruments. Loud noises came from the EmShut tanks further down the corridor, but the worker ignored them. The plant was always full of sounds he couldn't explain.

When the bank of annunciators sounded, Wendell and his partner jumped from their chairs.

"M.S.I.V. closure! Reactor scram!" the chief operator called out.

Christ! Wendell halted in front of the control rod display. The rods were automatically being shoved into the core by EmShut, and the last of the ninety-four lights was turning from red to green.

"All rods in!" the chief operator said.

A glance at the annunciators told Wendell the main steam isolation valves had slammed closed because high radiation had been sensed nearby. That might indicate a pipe leak -- but if so, it was now sealed off. The pressurized reactor vessel was "bottled up." Still, the hot fuel in the shutdown reactor would continue to boil water for some time, and that new steam needed a place to go . . .

"P.R.V. lifted," the assistant operator said. A pressure relief valve had automatically opened, allowing the new steam to flow down to the torus. This would keep reactor pressure within safe limits.

"Level down to 160 . . ." the chief operator reported. When the control rods had inserted, causing the tremendous heat output of the core to change to a warm glow, the bubbling foam over the fuel had collapsed. Water level in the vessel was now three feet below normal.

Come on, feedwater. Back up.

". . . 155 . . ." the operator went on, ". . . 150 . . . there . . . feedwater 's on it . . . level going up." The feedwater pumps were automatically responding to the problem by sending more water to the vessel.

"Good."

The STA had begun scanning the radiation meters for the plant. "All rads normal," he said. "Even by the steam lines."

"P.R.V. has auto-closed," the assistant operator said. "Vessel pressure 925. Rising."

"Good. What about the weld temps?"

The operator next peered at a recorder. "Temp change okay."

Reducing pressure with a P.R.V. also cooled off the water in the reactor vessel, but too rapid a temperature change would create stress in the huge container at the welds where pipes were attached. Hairline cracks could form and then expand over the years until there was a leak. If there was any chance of that long-term problem, months of testing and repairs would have to be undertaken. But the pressure relief valve was operating according to plan, and automatically closing on time to prevent any concerns.

Thirty seconds into the event, Wendell had seen no complications after the initial, unexpected closing of the M.S.I.V.s. EmShut had scrammed the reactor, a P.R.V. had lifted for a time to divert excess steam, and feedwater had adjusted to return level to normal. There had been no need for any of the other emergency systems: STurDI-1, STurDI-2, VEPI, Fuel Spray, ARAFS -- all remained unused. And if radiation near the M.S.I.V.s was normal, as the STA had reported, there might not even be a real pipe leak.

Fleck stood nearby, a few steps back from the main panel. Arms crossed, chewing his gum, he watched impassively. "Larry, get torus coolin' started," he said. "Both trains." The steam blown into the torus through the P.R.V. had warmed the water-filled tank, and that energy must be removed. There would soon be more steam arriving -- the core would remain hot for several hours.

"Torus cooling," the chief operator repeated, as he shifted over to another panel.

"Pressure control mode in auto," the assistant operator reported. "Valve open. Going 1000 to 900." Periodically, a P.R.V. would now open to vent off steam into the torus.

Wendell moved up beside the assistant operator to check some of the key readings. "Level back to normal," he said. "190."

"Pressure control-" the assistant operator began, before catching himself in mid-sentence, "-wait . . . 875 . . . P.R.V. still open . . . 850 . . . still open. Not right."

Oh, shit. Jesus! Wendell's mind raced ahead. The P.R.V. should close automatically. If it allowed pressure to fall much farther, the rapid temperature change could still do long-term damage to welds on the reactor vessel.

"Still dropping . . . 800 . . ."

Either the valve was stuck, or the auto controls had failed. If the valve had jammed open, nothing could be done. The plant would be shut down for months, at least, checking the welds.

". . . 750 . . ."

But if the automatic controls were the problem, they could be turned off. *Maybe that's it.* Wendell opened his mouth, but the order came from Fleck:

"Disable auto pressure control. Go to manual."

"Auto control . . . off," the assistant operator said. "Manual. P.R.V. to close."

Wendell watched the pressure meter. It wavered. And again. *Come on...*

A light on the panel changed color. "P.R.V. closed," the operator said. His shoulders sagged with relief. "I've got manual control."

At the same instant, Wendell saw the pressure meter halt its downward slide, and he let out a deep breath. *Now the weld temperature...* The young supervisor checked the recorder himself, tracing the thin red line across the marked paper. "Temp change still okay," he reported. Wendell felt a weight being lifted from him. Still, it would be a long, long evening. An operator would now have to carefully watch pressure and manually open and close a P.R.V. while the reactor slowly cooled off. But it was far better than the alternative.

In his baggy anti-c's, Gary walked down the main plant hallway, a bucket of tools dangling below one hand. The unexpected shutdown was giving maintenance an opportunity to work on one of the VEPI pumps.

"So, an oil leak?" Carol said. Also in a yellow jumpsuit, she had been assigned to monitor her husband's work to ensure his radiation dose was kept as low as possible.

"Yah. But leak may not be the right word," Gary said. "More like weep. Maybe just a nut or two to tighten."

"Fine. You think we might get home at a reasonable hour?" Both had been working overtime for several days.

"I suppose. Gonna fix me a big dinner?" Gary said, smiling.

"No, husband, but I will buy you one. Any place with a nice salad."

"Aw, and you're gonna make me eat some of it, too."

"Yes. Then you can have your huge slab of meat. We wouldn't want that gut of yours to get any smaller."

"Aw, Miss Car-o-l-l-l." Gary looked at his wife with a mischievous grin.

"You're welcome." The two came to metal stairs and began clattering down to a lower level. "Think we'll be online by Saturday?"

"So we can catch the concert? Probably. And this gal is good?"

"Very."

"Will she do some Russian stuff? Prokofiev or somethin'?"

"Possibly."

"Then I'll work extra hard to get everything fixed," Gary said, as they stopped in front of the VEPI room door.

"A little piece of metal?" Paul said, as he followed Langford through the reactor building.

"Correct. It was lodged inside the pressure sensor, so the P.R.V. never got the signal to close. They believe it's scrap remaining from the factory. It must have been within a crevice and then was jarred free during the last calibration. Typically, there would also be a backup sensor, but given that the operators can work the valve themselves, a second unit was not installed."

Langford came to a stop in front of an instrument rack and pointed at two black cubes.

"And these started the whole thing?" Paul said. "Bumped?"

"Yes. M.S.I.V. high radiation detectors. They receive signals from sensors on the other side of the wall. There are four of them in total, but only two are needed to scram the reactor. Such as this pair."

"And the guy didn't realize what he'd done?"

"No. But nothing else was found to be wrong, and this fellow was the only one in the area. He recalls nudging into something, and it appears he heard the activation of EmShut. That was a problem."

Paul shook his head in disbelief, repeating the language of the official report: "The reactor scram was due to the impact of a bag of refuse upon plant instrumentation."

"Oh, nuke plants are very sensitive," Langford said wearily. "They are quite easy to shut down. It's keeping them up and running that's difficult."

****

Anton strolled among the summer crowd, reading the cardboard signs held up for inspection, as all around him his fellow Muscovites bartered for apartments. He had already passed the permanent billboards, and out of the corner of his eye Anton had spotted the slip of blue paper. He soon returned, making a show of reading the numerous ads. The blue card was for a one-room apartment at a suburban address. Anton smiled. *Message received.*

The drop had gone without incident. As usual, he hadn't provided much information, but he was doing the best he could: "C393-275 requested to revisit military storage site in Utah. . . . . . Blue Raven will soon complete a long training course. . ."

****

Vitaly closed the binder and rubbed his eyes. The NRC exam for the reactor operator's license was fast approaching, and he would soon have to prove himself in the simulator, pass a written exam, and answer questions during a walk through the plant with an NRC inspector. As if preparing for that wasn't enough, there were the sabotage plans for Dmitri. But for now, his concentration was at a low ebb. *Time for a walk.*

Vitaly slipped on his running shoes and stepped out on the tiny front porch. The neighborhood was alive: down the hill, near the entrance to the cul-de-sac, little children were playing kickball, while closer by, older kids stood astride their bikes beneath an unlit street lamp. He noticed one was Ken Prager's son, whom he'd played volleyball with a few weeks before at a backyard party. Vitaly gave the boy a nod as he strolled past, trying to relax. He thought back to summer evenings in New York, playing in front of the apartment. There was Alexi, and Yuri, and the two American kids from across the street. Where had they all gone? He knew Yuri was in the Army, and Alexi had gone north to drill for oil. But Tommy and Matt? -- he couldn't even recall their last names. It did not matter. Such playmates were best left as a pleasant memory from a time before he understood the huge gulf that separated their world from his.

At the bottom of the hill, Vitaly moved onto the shoulder of the old country lane that skirted the southern edge of South Bend. His knee was stiff. That's what he got for not exercising more. As he strolled past the cornfield that climbed the incline behind his house, his thoughts returned to work and the day's lesson: Public Relations.

If a nuclear plant was in trouble, how could it be explained in simple terms to the public? This was the challenge the industry faced, and the solution was Emergency Action Levels. There were four of these. The first was the "Unusual Event," which meant only that the plant needed to take extra precautions to avoid any trouble. Fairview itself had experienced several over the years when safety equipment had failed routine tests. An "Alert" was the second step up the ladder. It meant there was a serious problem, but it could be resolved without any effect on the public. Next came the "Site Area Emergency." That was bad news. People living within a few miles of the plant might be asked to take shelter or evacuate, since a release of excess radiation was considered a possibility. Finally, there was the "General Emergency." That was the worst. Evacuations might be extended to ten miles downwind.

Vitaly stopped. *Take a break, John Donner. Relax!* The piercing staccato of crickets filled the air as he thought of the long nights of study in college. When he'd been tired or frustrated, Yelena had always been there. But not here, now. He must do it alone. And survive.

****

Steve stared out the small window and tugged on his aching hand as the corporate jet began its final descent into South Bend. The day's meeting had been a disappointment, and all he could do now was look past his anger and make the best of the NRC's decision. Checking his schedule book, he grimaced at the reminder that he was having dinner with Brixton's mayor. This was one night he would rather stay home. But Marie already had a babysitter arranged, and it was too late to cancel.

Paul put his beer down and flexed his ankle where the grounder had bounced off. *Vickie's gonna laugh, but those linemen really beat the hell out of the ball. Best in the company league.* Now he, Langford, and Crutch were drowning their sorrows.

"Jeez, guess we gotta do it, huh?" Crutch said, referring to the day's big news.

"At least we were permitted a few days for planning," Langford said.

"Why now?" Paul asked. The plant was shutting down to replace the wiring on valve motors located near the steam pipes.

"Oh, we believed the wiring was 'environmentally qualified'," Langford said, "but one of our fellow utilities performed a retest and found a large steam leak would ruin it." He shrugged. "Therefore, we fix it."

"Third time down since spring," Paul said. "Couldn't we wait a few months to the refuel outage-"

"That argument was put forward," Langford said wearily. "The odds of having an accident that would destroy the wiring are remote. It didn't seem appropriate to upgrade the wires immediately, since that would mean changing the state of the reactor, and also subjecting our workers to a large dose."

"And the NRC didn't agree?" Paul took a sip of beer.

"No. They were under pressure from activist groups, and Congress also expressed an interest."

"Ya know," Crutch said, a frown appearing within his beard, "the papers'll say the NRC shut us down to take care of 'n emergency. Like we're inches away from disaster. But it's an extreme precaution."

"Kind of ironic," Paul said. "Some people think we're out of control, and we feel over-regulated."

"Oh, the NRC must be having some success, if everyone is mad at them," Langford said. "Of course, in 1979 the task force that looked into T.M.I. said there were too many regulations. Workers were getting distracted from the most important items. Since then, to our infinite regret, the situation has only gotten worse."

"Jeez, ya wonder if other countries have ta deal with this shit,"

Crutch said. With one long finger, he traced circles on the table. "Hard ta picture protesters at a Russian plant. Or them shuttin' down for something like this."

"They don't even have a drywell, do they?" Paul asked. "I know they're different."

"They have little in the way of containment," Langford said. He took off his glasses and cleaned them. "But you don't have to leave the country to find plants that operate without a great many controls. The D.O.E. units aren't monitored by the NRC."

Department of Energy. "They make the bomb stuff, don't they?" Paul said.

"Correct. I've spoken with workers from there. It seems a bit more haphazard. They contaminate a great deal of ground."

"Didn't Karen Silkwood work at one a those?" Crutch said.

"No, she was at a factory where they processed uranium for fuel," Langford said. "A private company was in charge."

Paul took another sip of beer and rubbed his shin again. "Speaking of screwups, did you see the report on the African who picked up the x-ray source?" The other engineers shook their heads, so Paul continued: "They were x-raying some welds at a coal plant in Morocco and the rad source fell out of the machine. A pellet. Some worker picked up this cute little chunk and took it home. The thing was so radioactive his whole family died, and nobody figured out why until the last one was gone."

"Don't go tellin' that to Maxie," Crutch said. "Let the Africans worry by themselves."

"Cindy would just remind me to come home with clean pockets," Langford said. He slid his glasses back on. "Of course, there was a natural reactor in Africa at one time."

"Huh?" Paul said.

"Over a billion years ago there was a great deal of high grade uranium ore in one location, as well as a lot of water. The pile went critical-"

"How'd they find that out?" Paul said. "Was it still hot?"

"Prospectors in Gabon located a uranium deposit, but when it was tested, it contained abnormally low amounts of U-235. It had been burned up by the reactor."

"How big was this thing?"

"Very small. We would call it a baby reactor. It just bubbled slowly away for a few hundred thousand years."

"Not to change the subject," Crutch said, smiling broadly, "but speakin' of babies, Maxie had another ultra-sound. Looked fine."

"What could you see?" Paul asked.

"Not much -- only the head. Kid's the spittin' image of me."

"Your child has a beard?" Langford said.

"Kind of a bad time for you folks to be shutting down, isn't it?" the mayor said, just as the dinner party of three had finished passing around the food. "A lot of air conditioners running right now."

"Certainly summer is when you need the power," Steve said. After apologizing for his wife's remaining home with their sick boy, he had explained the current issue. "But we'll have things fixed up in a few days."

"Can your company produce enough electricity with Fairview shut down?" the mayor's wife asked.

"Well, we always keep a little in reserve, since you've got to take down plants for maintenance once in a while. But we'll also have to get power from other utilities. Everyone feeds into the same grid, so we'll ask someone else to pump in a little more to make up for Fairview."

"Have you thought about building more plants?"

"Someday we'll have to," Steve said. "Our older units are starting to wear out, and the need for power keeps increasing." He took a sip of iced tea, grateful the subject was drifting away from his own responsibilities. "You know, back in the early 50's, Eisenhower first talked about using atomic power to generate electricity. To give you an idea how much demand has grown, U.S. nuclear plants will soon be producing more electricity, by themselves, than the whole country was using back then."

"What would happen if those anti-nuclear folks got their way, and all the plants shut down tomorrow?" the mayor asked.

"There would be brownouts, and maybe some blackouts. Nuclear is more than fifteen percent of the country's production. We'd probably end up buying hydropower from the Canadians for a few years, and perhaps have some rationing. The country could get through it, but it wouldn't be pleasant. And I'm not sure how we'd replace it over the long haul. Nobody wants a power plant of any kind built in their backyard."

"How much does Fairview generate?" the mayor's wife asked.

"About 580 megawatts," Steve said. "580 million watts."

"You're a big employer, I know that much," the mayor said. "How many people you got out there now?"

"Nearly five hundred. And we'll be adding more next year. These days, it takes a larger staff to comply with all the rules."

"Has Hoosier Electric ever looked into solar power?" the mayor's wife asked, dipping a fork into her salad.

"A little, yes," Steve said. The question invariably came up when he talked to civic groups. "But solar cells aren't very practical in this area. It's too cloudy and we're too far north. If we wanted to replace Fairview with photovoltaics, we'd need about four square miles of collectors and batteries. A bit less if we added windmills."

"That's a big chunk of farmland," the mayor said.

Steve nodded. "Solar is nice, inexpensive energy, but it's spread awfully thin. Even in Arizona, you need a square yard of the best collectors to light up a seventy-five watt bulb."

"So do you think solar will ever work?" the mayor's wife said.

"It will keep growing," Steve said. "They're generating a few megawatts in California right now, with both cells and windmills. But to produce the amount of power the country actually uses --

300,000 megawatts at any given time -- would take up a great deal of room and cost a fortune."

"People complain about their utility bills as it is," the mayor said.

****

"Comrade," Dmitri said, "I'd like you to meet Doctor Gregori Ivanovich Berdyayev."

Vitaly extended his hand. "It is a pleasure to meet you."

"Thank you, comrade," the doctor said. His trim black goatee fit perfectly with his angular face and high forehead.

The three men took their seats at the table. "Did you enjoy your tour, Vitaly Fedorovich?" the doctor asked. "We thought you might like to see one of your own country's plants for a change."

"Yes, it was interesting. A little different from Fairview. Not as many contaminated areas, but I understand that's one of the advantages of a P.W.R. Is that what we have, mostly?"

"Yes," the doctor said as he opened his briefcase. "We also have a few graphite-based B.W.R.'s and some Fast Breeders. Those are quite different from U.S. commercial plants." The Doctor retrieved a folder. "Now, perhaps we should get started. I understand the colonel," he nodded in Dmitri's direction, "has filled you in on my background."

"Yes, comrade." Vitaly knew Berdyayev had been involved in Soviet reactor design for many years. "Now he works part-time for us," Dmitri had said on their chartered plane flight to Kalinin. "He's reviewed your sabotage plans quite thoroughly."

For the next hour Vitaly's roughed-out ideas were discussed. With the little time he could spare, he had devised three approaches: obvious sabotage that would allow him to escape, sabotage that would lead to his capture or death, and damage to the plant that would not have a clear cause.

"I can anticipate one question my superiors will ask," Dmitri said. "Why risk discovery of an agent during wartime when we could just send in a commando team? Vitaly has given me some input on that, but I'd value your opinion as well, Doctor."

"As I understand it, U.S. plants must all meet certain security standards," the scientist said. "Armed guards, a monitored fence, constant patrols, and so on-"

Vitaly nodded agreement.

"-and *Spetsnaz* troops shooting their way in would be unlikely to accomplish much beyond scramming the reactor and sealing things off. These plants are built to shut down, not keep running. But I wouldn't consider destruction to be the real objective here. The goal should be to cause massive fear among the public. You only need a radiation release to do that."

"So a big rad release is the target, you think?" Vitaly asked. *A little different than my approach.*

"A release <u>must</u> happen," the doctor said. "If the plant is damaged but nothing gets out, the public will only care for a little while. You've got to impact the common man directly, or national concern won't continue. You need interviews on American television with people who've been exposed to radiation, who've been evacuated. That is the lesson of Three Mile Island."

"So, a big rad release."

"It does not have to be large," the doctor said. "With the Americans, five or ten milli-rems per hour will suffice. Of course, that's not much at all- "

"But the public won't understand that," Vitaly said, completing the thought. *Of course. I was too close to see it.* "So I just need a little puff. Enough to get a Site Emergency declared."

"Exactly." The doctor looked through his notes. "And it's the undetectable sabotage that's the real challenge for you, correct?"

"That's the tough one. How can I make them think it's an accident? So many things have to go wrong."

"I understand. Somehow, you've got to stop water reaching the core, so there will be fuel damage and a release."

"And there's a lot of ways to get water in there," Vitaly said.

"A real challenge," the doctor agreed. He smiled. "But perhaps I have a solution. Some American utilities are experiencing this problem." He slid a sheet of paper across the table.

Vitaly scanned the short newspaper article. *Obvious again. And I can pull it off from outside.* "It would work," he said.

"You might consider this as well." The doctor pushed another photocopy across the table.

Vitaly looked at the report from the NRC detailing a recent event. "It might work, I suppose." He shrugged. "STurDI-1 is dead without the oil pump."

"Good," the doctor nodded. "And we may be able to help in other ways. For example, we have a method of producing a short circuit that has a built-in time delay -- and it will also be undetectable later on."

"Now that's something I'd like to see."

1985: September - December

In his small, unfinished basement, Vitaly was spending the night decoding a message from the Center. His superiors asked for an update to his sabotage plans. At least he had the time for it now. John Donner had passed his exams, and the proposed attack upon Fairview Station was finally foremost in Vitaly's mind. The plan for a radiation release, versus catastrophic destruction, was easier to develop, and the lesser goal also helped assuage any guilt. His co-workers -- his American friends -- might lose their jobs, but there would not be a massive sacrifice of lives. A good soldier only killed when it was necessary. And, of course, his plan was destined only to sit on a shelf, gathering dust.

Vitaly reached the Center's salutary farewell, and, as he had hoped, there was more text. He began decoding another of Yelena's chatty notes, reading as he went -- but then until a word stopped him in his tracks, and he hovered motionless over the paper, the pencil tip still pressing down. His heart beginning to race, Vitaly blinked and refocused. *Calm down. Finish the message first.*

> My Dearest Love,
>   I have missed you so very much these past few
> months, and I so look forward to your return. Mama and
> Papa are fine. Papa's emphysema is much better now
> that he is getting that new medication you arranged.
> Now for the big news -- by the time you come home
> next spring, my dear one, you will probably notice that I
> have changed a bit since your last visit. I'm pregnant!
> I'm so excited, and so are Mama and Papa. I know we
> had planned on waiting, my love, so that you could share
> in our little one's early years, but perhaps it is better this
> way. We can have more children -- an even larger
> family--after you return! I am feeling fairly well,
> although I have some morning sickness. I have not

begun to show yet. The due date, as you would expect, is at the end of May. I love you, my darling, and miss you very much. BOTH of us miss you.

Yelena

Filled with happiness and anticipation, Vitaly read the message over and over. He was going to be a father -- Yelena was carrying his child. She had made that clear. The due date was nine months from his last visit.

The pregnancy was due to a combination of circumstances. Yelena had always had trouble with the Soviet birth control pills, and even the superior East German ones had bothered her. The last two years they'd gone back to using western European condoms he would pick up at airports on the way home. But on the last visit his connection was tight, and there hadn't been time. Yelena was not at the right point in her cycle, so they'd foregone any precautions. Vitaly couldn't stand the Russian condoms -- they were commonly known as "galoshes."

So, my love and I have made a child. Dmitri had asked many times if his young protégé was thinking of starting a family, and Yelena's parents, too, had dropped many hints. Now, when spring came, he and his wife would celebrate in Moscow. But, at this moment, in his small house in South Bend, Vitaly was finding it hard to control his excitement. *I'm going to be a father, and I can't tell a soul!* There was still one traditional way available to mark the occasion, and he headed upstairs. The bottle of vodka was waiting.

****

"As you can see," the instructor said, "there are two principal ways to detect an illegal. Either observation of suspicious behavior or intelligence information." Clean-cut, with a white shirt and black tie, the lecturer appeared every inch the FBI agent. "Overall, we believe the apprehension rate is still very low. That means, of course, there are lots of trophies still out there."

Liz Rezhnitsky smiled and brushed aside a stray lock of her short, cinnamon hair. It looked doubtful the seminar would break any new ground, but then, little had changed when it came to catching spies. Nine years before, she had first learned of illegals in this classroom at the Quantico training facility. She could also remember the time spent sweating and aching in the gym, and practicing at the target range. *Nine years!*

When it was first announced the FBI was dropping its height requirement of five foot seven inches to allow for more women recruits, the investigator for the Pittsburgh D.A. had been curious. Two inches shorter, until then she had given little thought to the Agency, which had only recently accepted females at all. Soon the stocky young woman with the soulful blue eyes had submitted her application.

It was time for lunch, and a chance for Special Agent Elizabeth Rezhnitsky to pick up a few tidbits about the FBI's activities.

"REZ--NIT--SKI." The agent in line behind Liz slowly read her name tag aloud. "Sure you're working for the right side?" he said with a laugh.

"Third generation." Liz sized up her new acquaintance. He was about her age -- thirty-five -- and tall with close-cut blond hair. He seemed pleasant enough. "It's the ones who stayed behind in the old country you should worry about," she said.

"I suppose you're right," the man responded, as each slid their tray along the food aisle. "Your family get out to escape the Communists?"

Liz took an apple. "No, the Czar was bad enough."

"He must have been, for Lenin to get a chance," the other agent said. "So you're the C.I. coordinator for Indianapolis?"

"That's me."

"I thought Bud Ferguson was at Indy."

"He was." Liz moved further down the line. "He took a preferential to Bowling Green back in March. Stayed around just long enough to turn it over."

"You been a C.I. chief before?"

"Coordinator? No," Liz said. She fought the temptation to have a dessert. "I was on the squad up in Boston, and I did a little work in Silicon Valley."

"Well, you should be up to speed then. I've been handling Raleigh for a couple of years now. Routine stuff most of the time. But you've got to keep your line in the water."

"And hope you're in the right spot," Liz added. She understood the fishing analogy: her father had often taken his only child to a nearby pond.

"Well, keep at it," the agent said, heading for a table.

"I plan to," Liz replied. "I want to hook a big one."

****

Anton was always nervous in the days before a drop. Much of his new message would be the usual, low-grade material: "Blue Raven recently visited Grissom AFB" and so on, but he had recently been involved in bigger projects as well. One was the return of C393-492, who had visited from the United States in August. Anton had chartered a plane to take Colonel Bykov and the agent to a meeting in Kalinin. As instructed, he had also forwarded a copy of the travel plans to Directorate T, the KGB science department.

Tonight, the classical concert had been providing Anton with a welcome diversion -- until he noticed the woman. Twice during the evening he had caught her discreetly staring in his direction. Dark hair, brown eyes, black skirt, ankle-high boots. The concert over, she had followed him out of the auditorium and then, waiting for the subway, he had seen her again, thirty feet down the platform. She had abruptly looked away. *Am I imagining things?* He took his seat on the train next to a tired housewife, and reaching back to adjust his collar, he spotted his pursuer six rows behind. *Is this a routine check?* The KGB did such things from time to time. *Or have they caught on? Did I slip up somewhere?* Sweat trickled down Anton's spine. *It can't end this way!*

The train was approaching Park Kultry Station, and Anton decided he would get off and head for Gorki Park, a short walk across the Krymsky Bridge. It would appear a natural thing to do: a stroll on a mild evening. A few twisting pathways and he would have a much better idea of what was going on and perhaps how many were watching him. As Anton shuffled onto the platform, he faked a sneeze and glanced to the right. The woman had gotten off at the other end of the car. Anton followed the crowd up to the street, where he spied one of the newspaper bulletin boards. It was under a light and a Babushka was intently surveying the day's events. Quickly, Anton moved behind the display and watched the subway exit. There she was, at the top of the stairs. His pursuer was looking around, and then she spotted him. She headed in his direction.

Anton tensed. *There will be a black Volga pulling up. Two or three men will step out. Someone will ask me to go quietly.* The American operative clenched his fists. *I won't. They can shoot me here, in the street!* The enemy was a step away.

"So, Mother, did you have a nice time in the park?" Anton's pursuer asked the old woman reading the other side of the display.

"Oh, hello dear," the Babushka said. "Yes. I walked around a bit, fed a few birds. It's good to get outside. How was the play?"

"It was a string quartet, Mother. Fine. About average. Are you ready to head back?"

Anton strolled about Gorki Park, relieved, and a little humiliated. *Oh, Viktor! If only you knew!*

120

****

Wendell tucked in his shirt for the third time. *Come on. Let's have a disaster.*

Two operators paced in front of the panels. The drill had started thirty minutes before, and they had begun by making a minor adjustment to vessel water level using the control rod pump, but since then only a few nuisance alarms had broken the tedium. The control room simulator was housed in a non-descript building within a South Bend industrial park. Wendell had spent many hours training in the computerized mock-up. Often, he'd join Karen afterwards for dinner with some of her fellow lawyers. He enjoyed spending time with these educated, ambitious men and women, listening to the kind of insights on the business world that could not be gained from the management books he liked to read.

An annunciator broke the quiet. "High Flow, Main Steam Lines, Reactor Building," the chief operator reported, silencing the alarm. The buzzing horn immediately returned, and then the wall was awash in blinking lights. The core display began to change from red to green.

"Reactor scram!" the chief operator announced. "Main steam isolation! High flow!"

A pipe break. Here we go.

Thirty minutes later, Wendell stepped to the center panel to check the pressure in the reactor vessel and watched as the needle crept up past the red line and then took a nosedive. It was as he expected. All control rods were inserted, but the core was still boiling off some water. Because the M.S.I.V.'s had closed, the simulated reactor vessel was 'bottled-up' and in pressure control mode. Newly created steam was being periodically bled off to the torus, and the fluid then replaced using a feedwater pump. Unlike the real event he had gone through a few months before, this time the P.R.V.'s were working correctly. But the drill would not end this way. Drills never did.

In the busy staging area, Gary Halvorsen had finished climbing into his anti-c's and was attaching his film badge and dosimeter, along with a second tube that could record higher rad levels. Doug Tama was doing the same.

"Carol on the offsite team today?" Tama asked.

"Yah. She'll be out there," Gary said in his rough voice. He and his wife had each performed in many drills, and they hadn't bothered to discuss their assignments during the drive to the plant that morning. Gary had just stared straight ahead and said little rather than glance over into Carol's green eyes. His wife was a born worrier, and over breakfast their finances had become the topic of the day. The cost of his fishing boat, paying off the truck, their plans for a house. It was not a conversation he wished to continue.

In the control room simulator, little had happened in the hour since the scram, as Wendell and the rest of the crew monitored the shutdown reactor.

The room went dark. Then alarms began, and dim emergency lighting flickered on.

Oh, Christ. Not so good . . .

"Loss of primary offsite power!" the assistant operator said. "Auto transfer to backup supply has not occurred! . . . Both diesels have started . . . loading!" The room grew brighter as more lighting returned.

So much for offsite power. Wendell grimaced. Electricity was no longer being directed into the plant from either of the transmission lines passing nearby. Now, only the emergency diesel generators, the battery banks, and steam from the reactor would be available to power Fairview's equipment. That meant the feedwater pumps could no longer be run to replace the vented steam. It was up to the emergency systems to take over the job.

The first two hours of the drill had been tedious for Carol Halvorsen. She had helped load the white, company SUV and then rode to the site boundary with her driver, Marty. Also along in the back seat was a young engineer from Kittleburg. Blonde and balding, wearing a blue nylon jacket and clutching a clipboard, he would serve as the drill controller.

In the nearby woods there were splashes of red, yellow and orange as maple trees began to show their autumn colors. Carol soon reported over the radio that they were in position. And that had been it so far. She wished more would happen. *At least the company isn't bad.* Marty was much easier to get along with than her past drivers. The short, pudgy laborer, with unruly charcoal hair, a bulbous nose, and a chuckling sense of humor, was good at his job as well. And now, finally, the drill seemed to be picking up. Drill controllers had just informed the health physics personnel patrolling the yard that they had detected an invisible cloud of gas, giving off at least 1000 milli-rems -- one Rem. It was moving away from the turbine building, a few hundred yards upwind from the sport utility vehicle, where Carol sat in the passenger seat holding the detachable probe of a Geiger counter out the window. The meter box rested on her small lap, clicking at random from background radiation.

The controller looked at his schedule, then his watch. "Your meter will show that rads are starting to creep up."

"Fine." Carol picked up the radio mike. "Offsite Leader, this is Drill Team One. Beginning to see the plume." She quickly exchanged the counter on her lap for another at her feet. The first device was useful for detecting an approaching source of radioactivity, but it would be too sensitive once the cloud had arrived. Carol stuck the new probe out the window. "Mr. Controller, what am I reading now?"

"5 m.r." the controller replied. "Now 10, now 50." He paused. "150. . .300. . .400."

"I'm putting my hand over the probe," Carol said, as she covered the sensing area with her small palm.

"Your reading dropped to 200," the controller replied.

"Ground-based release," Carol announced. "We're in the plume." A cloud of radioactive gas could produce several forms of radiation, but one type could only be sensed from within the cloud itself -- a subatomic particle with so little energy it was able to travel just a few feet in open air, and could not pass through a human hand.

Carol removed her palm from the probe face. "Now reading . . . ?" she asked.

The drill controller glanced at his notebook. "Back up to 500. . ..700. . .900. . ."

"Marty," Carol ordered her driver, "start moving slowly, and cut across the wind. Let's see how wide this thing is." She reached over and grabbed the radio handset as the vehicle lurched into motion. *Finally, some action.*

Steve sat behind his desk at one end of the emergency center. The long, low-ceilinged space was near the staging area in the basement of the site's administration building. Before him, staff members were studying blueprints, or the floor plans of Fairview Station posted along one wall. Also on display was a map showing the surrounding countryside. An arrow indicated the direction of the wind.

The crew at the simulator finished their update, and Steve set the phone back on its cradle. A damaged vent had already allowed a release of radiation into the environment despite the use of ARAFS, and now with STurDI-1 and STurDI-2 having just broken down, the situation was even worse.

At least I won't have to deal with the public. That duty belonged to Bill Chambers, the Offsite Emergency Coordinator. A self-described "big galoot in a business suit," the tall, bald and heavy-set Chambers operated out of the corporate offices in South Bend, working with the Civil Defense to coordinate shelter warnings and evacuations. While Steve's interactions with the NRC on a daily basis could be difficult -- trying to balance technical arguments, arcane regulations, and the needs and interests of the government's personnel -- he knew this would be nothing compared to confronting an angry, fearful, distrusting citizenry.

Lou Tarelli came out of a nearby room where radio contact was maintained with personnel both inside and outside of the plant. "Steve," he said, "our repairs aren't going well."

In the simulator, the water covering the fuel had boiled off, and the procedures now called for Wendell and the crew to replace it once and for all. *We'll have to blow down.* The VEPI or Fuel Spray pumps could be used to force water back into the reactor vessel -- if the pressure inside the steel capsule was first reduced by a considerable amount. To do that, all of the pressure relief valves would have to be opened at once. It was a drastic step. If the crew could think of another option, the procedures allowed them to pursue it -- but there were no alternatives. It was time to blow down.

From his office window, Steve watched the sunset as a Beach Boys song quietly played in the background. Marie had given him the radio as a birthday present after noticing he tuned in to the oldies station while working in his den. She had been right, of course -- at the end of a long day the music helped him relax. Memories of simpler times.

The drill had been challenging, but it had gone well. Steve's biggest concerns had come early in the simulation, as his staff battled a few simple problems, for he knew such things could actually happen. But as the test moved along, he always had trouble playing the game, for he believed -- he knew in his gut -- that no event at Fairview would ever be allowed to progress to the big accident. The plant had been built well and it had many backup systems. There were also good people in all his departments. They were focused on safety, and he was confident they could handle any concern while it was still minor. And, if he ever had an inkling that something was amiss, he would see that it was corrected. His people would -- he didn't shoot messengers. The plant would remain safe. <u>His</u> plant would remain safe.

Steve got up and prepared to go home, then spotted the thick document in his in-basket. *I should review the outage schedule.* Refueling was just a month away. He smiled and turned toward the door. Not tonight. Stacey had a tennis match – and her backhand was getting better.

****

"Hey, Liz," a special agent asked from a nearby desk, "what's Russian for beer belly?"

"*Bpiukhop,*" Liz Rezhnitsky said, not looking up from her paperwork. "Why do you want to know?"

"No reason, really. I saw a picture last night of one of those big Russian weightlifters. He had a massive 'Bff-you-hop' or however you say it."

Liz turned to her co-worker. "*Bpiukhop,*" she said again, slowly. "You thinking with a little work, you might match him?"

"If I lift enough doughnuts." The agent laughed and leaned back in his chair. The squad room was quiet and nearly vacant. "How hard was it to pick up Russian at school, anyway? I've always wanted to give Spanish a shot sometime. It'd be nice to work down south."

"I never took it in school," Liz said, "except for refresher courses. I learned at home."

"Your family spoke Russian?"

"At dinner we did," she said. "My Dad grew up speaking it in New York. He wanted me to learn too."

"That was back in the fifties, right?" her fellow agent said. "Kind of a tough time to be speaking Russian, wasn't it? You'd figure the neighbors would call the cops."

"My Dad <u>was</u> the cops." Pride crept into Liz' voice. "Police chief, Darwin, Pennsylvania."

It had been another routine day for the Counter-Intelligence Coordinator of the FBI's Regional Field Office in Indianapolis. Perhaps someday she would move up to the premier squads in Washington or New York, but for now she kept an eye on visitors to Indiana from Communist countries and ran down leads from other offices. It was an unglamorous job, but her Dad had always said police work was a tedious business. "The gun's just for decoration," he'd remark, patting the bulky handgrip jutting from his holster. Liz could see the truth in that. In the line of duty, her own gun had never left her purse.

****

The operator hung up the phone and reinserted his earplug. The control room of the Vorney, Nevada, power station had said it was time, and with a hiss and a growl, the diesel generator's huge engine soon began turning over. The operator prepared to log a reading, but then stopped and looked again at the rumbling machine. The vibrations in the floor had changed, and through the dull filter of his earplugs, he could hear a peculiar noise -- a sort of scraping sound. Then, with a screech, the generator shifted gears and began to shut down.

****

Paul rolled over and hit the alarm, then slid out of bed. Mondays always sucked, but with the outage dragging on, today would be worse than usual. He showered, dressed, and with his brown hair still damp, leaned down and kissed Vicki on the cheek. His girlfriend barely stirred. Christmas break must be nice for a teacher. He gazed at her for a long time. From his vantage point as a child, he could remember how happy his parents had seemed together. Perhaps this was his own chance. Or was he getting ahead of himself? He slipped out the door.

"Talked to Mike yesterday," Crutch said, as he and Paul entered their office area. "He's feeling a lot better. They're gonna let him out soon."

"An ulcer." Paul shook his head. "Why am I not surprised?"

"Yeah, he was really gettin' stressed out," Crutch said. "Ya had management, then the NRC -- jeez."

"That boot thing must have been the last straw." A temporary worker had contaminated a new pair and then had tried to sneak the radioactive shoes offsite by tossing them over the security fence.

"Yeah, the boots did it. If the guy'd just let the H.P.'s wash'em instead of stealin' 'em back, he'd probably have walked out fine. But noooo, Mike had that mess on top a everythin' else. Too much."

"So I imagine you're really looking forward to filling in for him." Paul grinned.

"Hey, you bet," Crutch said. "I got a month-old baby boy who only sleeps when Dad's at work. An ulcer's just what I need."

1986: January - April

Sergei watched with only mild interest as the jetliner banked and the lights of New York were replaced by the darkness of the ocean. After eight months abroad, he was returning home to Moscow and the Ministry of Energy. He had made the most of his time in America, the young Russian thought, as he scratched the short, blond hair on his neck. He had studied reactor physics and plant design, and visited a number of sites, including Three Mile Island. The Americans, Sergei had decided, were a fearful people. The event at T.M.I. had been minor, yet the nuclear industry in the U.S. was being strangled by endless hearings, inspections, and upgrades. In his own country, Sergei knew, such delays were not tolerated. There had been problems, of course -- a few cases of damaged reactors and melted fuel -- but no one had panicked.

Overhead, the NO SMOKING light blinked out. Sergei pulled the pack of cigarettes from his shirt pocket, lit up, and thought ahead to his upcoming training at plants in Russia and the Ukraine. The young engineer smiled. Some time off, then a chance to see his own country. Things couldn't be better.

****

"They never knew what hit 'em," Karl Leeman said.

Steve nodded. "That's something at least." His maintenance supervisor was referring to the space shuttle Challenger, which had exploded that morning.

"Tough break," Tarelli added.

Ted Cervantes walked into the office and slid onto the table along the wall. "Challenger?"

"Yep," Leeman said.

Cervantes looked down and made the sign of the cross.

"I think that puts our problem in perspective, anyway," Steve said. *Like Richmond always does for me.* He held up a thin document. "Have you all seen the NRC Bulletin?"

"No," Cervantes said. Borden handed it over, and the operations supervisor scanned the contents. "So an NEB diesel failed in, and then Nevada," he said. His eyes narrowed. "Our diesel's the same, right?"

"Yessir," Leeman drawled. "Model n' vintage."

Cervantes continued to read. He pulled a pen from his pocket and slowly twirled it in his free hand. "Improper screws. Vibration kicks 'em loose, huh?"

"Over a long period," Steve said. "You just can't build a perfect machine."

"The kicker's on the last page," Tarelli said, pointing.

"We got 'til end a May to replace them screws," Leeman said, "and we'll be taring them machines down ta do it. Five days."

Cervantes' hard gaze shifted to Steve. "Damn overkill. But we can run seven days with one diesel out."

"Karl, how long before the new screws arrive on site?" Steve asked. He began squeezing his aching hand.

"Mid-April. Every NEB plant wants 'em. They're not easy to get. Odd little fuckers."

"Understood," Steve said. "Let's get the work scheduled."

****

"Sticking around for the main event, huh?" the operator said to Gary as they stood near the STurDI-1 turbine.

"Yah. Gotta stay on site anyway, just in case." Gary turned to the health physics technician. "Thing don't get very hot when it runs, right?"

"Fifty, maybe sixty milli-rems an hour," the HP responded. "Not much."

Gary nodded. He was confident of the repairs he had made. From before his days in the Navy he knew he could fix anything that had bolts and grease. Now, he faced the STurDI-1 turbine, a chest-high lump of metal hidden beneath thick, gray blankets of insulation. A large pipe penetrated the machine from above, bringing steam from the reactor vessel to spin the turbine shaft and power the pump. Jutting out from the turbine's rear was the pump itself, and at the front of the machine sat its brains -- the hydraulic oil control system, with its low tank and maze of finger-sized pipes.

The operator picked up a nearby phone and checked in with the control room. "Any time now," he reported back.

At the base of the oil tank, a small black object no larger than a loaf of bread began whirring. *Startup oil pump's going,* Gary noted. *STurDI-1's coming up.* The small, battery-powered pump was providing a surge of high pressure fluid to force open the valve separating the turbine from the reactor vessel. A low, straining groan cut through the air, and after a hiss and puff of steam, the STurDI-1 turbine rumbled to life, filling the room with an ear-splitting roar. The operator read some gauges and then gave Gary the thumbs up.

****

Carol spotted the metal cabinet bolted to an electric pole alongside the country road, and she pulled over. Humming a Mozart concerto, she climbed out of the truck, and was greeted by a cold, February wind. *Shoot.* Checking the sample units within the ten mile emergency zone was usually a choice assignment for a health physics technician, but not this day. Dry leaves crunched as Carol stepped to the box. There were forty such stations, containing film badges and air samplers. The government required that Hoosier Electric monitor the environment around the plant. Fortunately, in comparison with industrial chemicals like dioxin, keeping an eye on radiation required little technology.

Carol replaced the film badges. *Maybe I'll be doing more of this next year.* She and Gary had decided they would soon start a family – or she had, at least, and Gary wasn't against it. It was a decision their parents would surely greet with approval. Her mother-in-law had been mentioning grandchildren for years -- her other son and his wife having made it clear that Gary was the only hope. There were many things to consider, of course -- their careers, their savings, their thoughts about returning home -- and Carol knew it was she who would do the heavy thinking. Gary was more of a dreamer, and said she worried too much, but she couldn't help it. Even as a child -- a tomboy, no less -- she had always felt the need to watch out for others. There were four girls in her family -- the twins, who were six years older, herself, and Natalie, the youngest by eighteen months. Carol had reveled in the role of older sister, and she had spent hours playing with her favorite companion. The maple tree in the back yard was a popular spot -- they could climb higher than the roof of the garage, and look out over the neighborhood. Carol was ten when Natalie slipped on a branch, and the vision of her sister screaming as she lay helpless on the ground was still with her. If she'd reached out quicker, Carol often thought, she might have pulled her in. Instead, she had helped with the long years of physical therapy. Natalie did walk again, and over time the cruel limp became less noticeable. Now she was married with two rambunctious daughters of her own. And Aunt Carol was the one afraid of heights, battling herself each time she had to scale a ladder in the plant.

Carol slid back into the truck. Perhaps, next winter, Natalie would be the one helping her, as she carried her first child. If that happened, she would be given temporary assignments away from rad areas, since the risk from radiation was greatest for an unborn child. Slow and boring jobs. But to Carol, it would be a wish come true.

****

Midnight was approaching when Vitaly heard the page from the control room. The shift supervisor reported that condenser vacuum was rapidly falling, which meant the huge metal box would soon be unable to suck steam through the main turbine. John Donner needed to check things out -- fast -- before the reactor was shut down to prevent any damage to the turbine and generator.

Vitaly raced through the plant, his key ring jingling, and at the condenser control panel he confirmed that pressure in the huge box was inching its way up towards the red line on the dial. A minute to go before reactor shutdown. Scanning the panel, Vitaly spotted the problem. Two small pumps in another room had to continuously remove air from the condenser to keep pressure low, but neither was now running. *The breaker must have tripped.* Vitaly quickly found the large circuit breaker bolted to a nearby wall and saw he'd been right. He grabbed the handle and twisted it to ON, but it snapped back to OFF when he let go. His mind raced through the possibilities: *What's causing the breaker to trip? Did one of the pumps burn up?*

He considered his choices. *If I force the breaker closed, one of the pumps might still work. That would be enough.* But his plan was against the rules, and Vitaly wouldn't do it without permission. His training, in both Moscow and America, had emphasized that. He grabbed his radio and explained the situation to the shift supervisor.

Procedures called for a great deal of paperwork before taking such an action. But there was no time, and the supervisor knew it. "Try it," he said.

Slamming the breaker to ON, Vitaly braced himself for the recoil. The handle pushed back, but he kept it in place and twisted to look at the control panel. A pump was now running. The condenser pressure needle was perilously close to the red line, but it didn't seem to be moving up. After watching the gauge for what seemed an eternity, Vitaly saw the needle begin to creep back down.

"You're John Donner?" a younger man asked when Vitaly entered the control room a few hours later.

"That's me." The shift supervisor had already warned him he'd be interviewed.

"I'm Paul Hendricks," the engineer said to the lean man with the strong jaw and intense expression, "and I'll be writing the report on the condenser event. You got a minute?"

The beginning of the sunrise was evident as Vitaly headed east along Highway 30 towards Brixton. John Donner had stayed late to finish his interview and then accept the congratulations of the day shift personnel. But now, speeding past the snow-covered landscape, he realized he couldn't share his glory with his wife. Dmitri yes. Maybe Dr. Berdyayev. But not Yelena.

Yelena. His wonderful partner, and soon-to-be mother of his child. A few more weeks and he'd be home again, he reminded himself, as he turned and headed north to his small house on the outskirts of South Bend.

****

Anton stepped across a rivulet of icy water and ducked into the cramped second-hand bookstore, where an edition of the works of General Secretary Gorbachev was prominently displayed in the window. Browsing the shop's musty interior, Anton selected a copy of *SOVIET AGRICULTURAL PROGRESS: 1960 to 1970* as his purchase, then worked his way back into a narrow aisle that was out of sight of the store manager dozing at the register. From his coat pocket, Anton extracted a small, sticky package and secured it to the underside of a shelf.

The drop now complete, the KGB officer left for the subway. Just before heading underground, he passed a polished young man in a knee length coat, striding with purpose in the opposite direction. Briefly, Anton thought of another young Soviet who would soon be in Moscow. That visitor would also try to make every minute count. Somewhere next month, probably in an obscure safe house, C393-492 was to attend a meeting.

As with the illegal's last trip, Anton had set up a conference between the foreign-based agent and members of the KGB's technical branch. This time he had stumbled upon an interesting, though likely trivial, item: one of the meeting participants would be a Dr. Berdyayev. Anton had no idea who the doctor was, but perhaps the CIA would -- after one of their own had returned from a little book shopping.

****

"Well, Vitaly," Doctor Berdyayev said as the meeting finished, "I think you have some excellent plans here."

"Thank you. Your advice was very helpful," Vitaly replied, closing his copy. The instructions would be stored at the Center for safe-keeping.

"Yes, Comrade Doctor," Dmitri chimed in, "you've given this project a great boost."

The doctor stroked his dark goatee. "To be frank, as an academic exercise, I found it quite intriguing. Of course, it's unlikely it will ever be put to the test."

"Of course," Dmitri said.

Vitaly and Yelena were spending the day shopping in Moscow. They had first visited one of the *Beriozka* stores, off-limits to ordinary citizens, and used special coupons to purchase a crystal vase for her mother. Then it was on to GUM, the huge department store, where they roamed the glass-roofed arcade, drifting in and out of the small shops.

As Yelena looked over some merchandise, her long blonde hair flowing to her waist, Vitaly gazed at his wife. She was seven months pregnant now. Her face had grown larger, and softer, as well. He watched as she examined some china, and then stepped up and hugged her from behind. Yelena smiled and arched her head back, one tender cheek brushing against Vitaly's as his chin rested on her shoulder. "I love you," Vitaly whispered. He was as happy as he could ever remember. The woman he loved was carrying his child, and through his service to the State they were able to afford some of the better things in Soviet life.

"I love you, too," Yelena sighed. "I feel so good when we're together."

"All three of us." Vitaly smiled. He patted his wife on the tummy and then released her from his embrace.

She turned to face him. "I'm so glad you feel that way. After all, it wasn't in our plans."

"I think it's wonderful." Vitaly stroked his wife's shoulders. "It's just like you said when you wrote to me. Maybe it's better this way. When I'm home for good in a year or two, I'll have a child to play with."

"And more to look forward to," Yelena said.

"Oh, yes, my love. More children, and more time with you."

****

Crutch briskly entered the office area. "Got the O-ring report." He held up a document. "Came in over the fax."

"The one from the paper?" Paul said.

"Yep. Challenger blew up due to O-rings, and the anti-nukes say we've got 'em too an' they're a big problem." Crutch rolled his eyes. "Hey, of course we got O-rings. Washing machines got O-rings. Car engines got O-rings. They ain't that special."

Tarelli and Langford looked up when Paul knocked on the open door.

"The O-ring report came in," Paul said, as he and Crutch stepped inside. "In the back there's a list of events. We're in there twice."

"I'd heard your liberal friends were at it again," Tarelli said to Langford as he took the report.

"And I specifically told them to call me first," Langford replied.

The two read the marked sections, Langford peering over his boss' shoulder.

"Did our events occur because of O-rings?" Langford finally asked, looking up. "It isn't clear."

"Nope," Crutch said. "We checked. One was an instrument outta cal made by O-Ring America Corporation. Nothin' says O-rings were the problem -- and hell, it was hardly a problem to begin with. The other's even more cock-eyed. A valve kept gettin' stuck, an' when it got worked on it, they went ahead n' replaced the O-rings. Routine shit. But it made the list."

"It looks like they went through all the reports sent to the NRC, and if 'O-ring' showed up, that was good enough," Paul said. "That bugs me. I'd be tossed out the door for work like that."

"They're just playing mind games with the public," Tarelli said with a wave of his hand. "Don't let it bother you."

"It's a fuckin' cheap shot." Crutch said.

"True, but there appears to be a little more to it than that," Langford said. He had continued to read the report. "They have some good points about rubber not holding up under high rad conditions. The industry has just begun to deal with that issue."

"There's usually some thought to these things," Tarelli agreed. "Most of the folks who write them aren't idiots. A few even worked in the industry. But they're absolutely convinced nuclear power is unsafe, and that seems to justify a lot of distortion."

"Of course, our own public relations staff can also turn information to their advantage," Langford said.

Crutch took the report off the desk. "These guys are just playin' on the fear of radiation."

"It's more than that," Tarelli said. "It's risks, and choice. People don't mind taking some risks, as long as they aren't forced into it." He tapped the cigarette pack in his shirt pocket. "But basically, a lot of people feel nuclear got rammed down their throats. Some kind of evil conspiracy is putting them in jeopardy."

"Just who are 'Hoosiers for a Safe Tomorrow'?" Paul asked. "Their director was quoted in the paper as saying Fairview is a real threat-"

"Heh, heh." Tarelli smiled. "That's Evelyn Davis. Technically speaking, she's on the fringe." He tapped his skull.

"So how come the paper talks to her?"

"They need a local opinion," Tarelli said. "The paper gets the pro-nuke side by quoting our press release."

"As I recall, wasn't there another group in this area?" Langford said.

"Some farmers," Tarelli replied. "After T.M.I.. But they were willing to learn and took a long look at the stuff we put in the public document room."

"Brixton library, right?" Paul said.

Tarelli nodded. "Most of the reports you guys write to the NRC are down there. In the end, the farmers decided we weren't all that bad. It's a complex subject if you're an outsider."

"But it's a black 'n white world," Crutch sighed.

"And we seem to be with the Forces of Darkness," Langford said.

****

Liz entered the squad room. The April morning had been routine: two interviews with the former employers of a California man suspected of selling computer secrets to Bulgaria. Back at her desk, Liz found a note saying a dispatch had arrived over the teletype, and at the communications window she signed for the sealed folder. Pulling out the single page, Liz scanned the decoded message. Then with growing interest she read it a second time.

"An illegal, huh?" the Special Agent in Charge remarked from behind his desk.

"Yes, sir," Liz said. "We don't see many of those popping up."

"You're right about that." He nodded. The FBI veteran scratched his chin with a leathery hand. "Washington must know something, huh?"

"It sure looks that way. They've got a source somewhere they really believe in."

"Well, whoever that guy is, he's not giving away the whole story."

"He may not know everything," Liz said. "The Soviets compartmentalize pretty well."

"Of course," the S.A.C. agreed, glancing again at the report. "This isn't too bad really. It certainly narrows the field. We've gone from the whole population to a nuclear power plant worker."

"And one who was out of the country last August, and again this March," Liz said. "That shortens the list even more. Maybe just enough."

"How many nuke plants we talking about, anyway?"

Liz was glad she'd done her homework. "About a hundred in the U.S. We've got two in Indiana. They're both up north. Fairview and Kittleburg."

"Whatever happened to Marble Hill?" The S.A.C. was referring to a unit that had been under construction beside the Ohio River. "They gave up, didn't they?"

"Over a year ago. I think I can forget about that one. So I'll just need to make a trip to South Bend. That's Hoosier Electric's headquarters."

"Sounds reasonable. Have you met the S.R.A. up there?" the supervisor asked, referring to the city's Senior Resident Agent. "His name's Walt Kreveski."

"No sir, I haven't. I think he's been in here a couple of times when I was on assignment."

"Well, you'll like Walt." A smile crossed the S.A.C.'s lined face. "Nice guy. Been around a long time. He was stationed in South Bend about twenty years ago, and enjoyed it so much he listed it as his office of preference. He's gonna retire there. Lot of Polish in town, and Mr. Kreveski likes that. Be sure and talk with him awhile -- he's been a lot of places. Wounded Knee for one."

"Interesting," Liz said. "I'll ask him about it if I get the chance." The occupation of Wounded Knee by the American Indian Movement in 1973 had produced heroes on both sides.

The S.A.C. handed back the dispatch. "At least H.Q. gave you a good cover story so you won't create too much of a stir."

"Not until I find him."

****

Paul pulled out of the Fairview lot. Tarelli had explained the situation to him: the FBI was doing a routine check of the station's personnel records and someone from the plant was needed in case there were any technical questions. None were expected. Even so, it would be interesting, and he'd have a good story to tell Vickie when he picked her up. He smiled to himself. A cool job and a wonderful girl. *You can't beat that.*

The FBI Field Office in Indianapolis was 150 miles behind her as Liz cruised up the wide street that led into downtown South Bend.

She had little trouble locating the Hoosier Electric building, and the company's personnel manager met her in the lobby. They grabbed an elevator.

"We weren't sure, but we thought you might want some nuclear expertise handy," the manager said, "so Fairview sent us an engineer to sit in on the meeting. As you requested, I've also got the personnel files for the folks at both sites who know about your visit."

"Would it be all right if I looked at those first?" Liz said.

"Sure, we can swing by my office. To tell you the truth," the manager said, "I'm very curious about all this."

"So you haven't been filled in?" *Good.* Liz had provided her cover story to a vice president at Hoosier Electric, but requested it be kept confidential.

"They just told me that you were coming, and to pull the files. The VP said he'd leave it for you to explain."

The door opened in the conference room and Paul rose from his seat as a stocky woman with short, reddish-blond hair entered, followed by the personnel manager.

"Paul, I've already explained to Agent Rezhnitsky that you're here to answer any technical questions," the manager said after the introductions.

"Sure. And if I don't know, I can probably find out pretty fast."

"That'll be fine," Liz said. The engineer fit the description in his file: five-ten, rather thin, brown hair, brown eyes, mid-twenties. The three seated themselves. *Time for the cover story.* "As I've explained to your vice-president," Liz began, "the Agency is looking for some fugitives from a major narcotics operation several years ago. There was an FBI agent killed. I'm afraid I can't give you any more details than that. But we have some indication that one or more of these individuals have recently been working in a nuclear power plant. So what I'd like to do is review your company's records for the present employees at your two plants."

The personnel manager frowned. "We have over a thousand

people in nuclear right now. That's a lot of records."

"I understand. There's one thing that should narrow down the search. All the suspects were out of the country in August of last year, and again this past March. Can you check for that sort of thing? Vacation records?"

"We can do it." The manager jotted down a note. "But it'll take some time."

"I understand," Liz replied, hiding her disappointment. Too bad.

The manager stood. "I'll go see what we can do. Be right back."

"Thanks." After a brief silence, Liz looked across the table at Paul. "So what do you do at Fairview?"

"I investigate problems," Paul said. "Then write reports to the NRC."

"I've seen films from nuclear plants where the workers were dressed up in special suits and gas masks," Liz said. "You do a lot of that?"

"Not really. Most of the plant you can walk through in street clothes. I usually work in an office, so I don't even wear my hard hat that often."

The door soon opened, and the personnel manager reappeared. "Well, Agent Rezhnitsky, I checked, and it'll take about a week for us to sort out what you need. I'm sorry for the inconvenience."

"That will be fine," Liz said. By now she had resigned herself to a wait. "I'll come back when you're done."

"So, have you ever been to Fairview or Kittleburg?" Liz asked, after she and Walt Kreveski were seated in the restaurant. They had already discussed her mission.

"I was at Fairview once," Kreveski said in his hoarse voice. He was six feet tall and heavy-set. His large, reddish nose supported horn-rimmed glasses. "A few years ago I took a tour. It's an impressive place. I see the vapor cloud when I'm driving west of Brixton."

"I was thinking I might go by there when I head back." Liz picked up the menu.

"It's not too far out of your way. When we go back to my car I'll show you a shortcut." A waitress appeared and took their order, then Kreveski went on: "I still find it hard to believe there might be an illegal out there. They do background searches. How'd our man beat that?"

"Our friends are careful," Liz said. "They make sure there's a good story in place. And, of course, he's probably not at Fairview anyway. There's a hundred other plants out there."

"I've never gone in much for this spy stuff," Kreveski said. "I'm more of a cops-and-robbers guy. Just an old 'Brick Agent'."

"I heard you were at Wounded Knee."

"Yeah, I was working out of St. Paul then. That was a mess. Why the Indians picked early spring, I'll never know. It was cold and muddy."

"Were you in any of the fire-fights?"

"No." Kreveski shook his head. "It depended on where you were. The only time I've ever fired my gun is on the pistol range. I'm a good shot there, aiming at paper. Of course, I also do some hunting, but that doesn't count."

Liz continued to listen to Kreveski's tales for the next thirty minutes. The elder agent took a last sip of coffee. "So tell me about you," he asked. "All I really know is that you've got a lot of patience to listen to my old war stories. How long have you been with the Bureau?"

"Since '76."

"You married?"

"No." Liz shrugged. "It's kind of tough when you're moving around."

"That must mean you've got boyfriends all over the country, huh?" A grin crossed Kreveski's face.

"Well, one anyway, in Indianapolis," Liz said. "He's a state police instructor." It was the kind of question her older relatives might ask. But, of course, Walt Kreveski was about that age. Liz saw the waitress was returning. "Here's the check."

Guided by the misty plume, Liz followed the back roads northwest of Brixton until she reached Fairview Station. She cruised by the plant, gazing at the fenced-in collection of buildings. One of them featured a dome, and she also could see the source of the vapor cloud: two cooling towers a few hundred yards away. She stopped to get a better look. *What if he's really in there?*

****

Vitaly pulled out his radio, and the dispatch soon came in:

"... The Center has developed criteria under which the various versions of your plan, designated A6,B2,V3: Alpha-Six, Bridge-Two, Vector-Three, will be enacted. At such time as these criteria are met and the decision is made, you will be given instructions involving the location of the written plan and the items required for its completion. Until that time, you are not to attempt any enactment of the plan, nor maintain a copy..."

So it's sitting in a file somewhere. And I'm sitting here. How much longer? It's been nearly ten years. Vitaly stared at the wall. *I wish they'd tell me. It's just like what Father said about the War -- they never knew when they'd go home...* He refocused his attention. *Finish the message. There might be a letter from Yelena.* He was right:

". . . I miss you dearly, my love, and wish you could be here to share this time with me. But I know you're doing a great service for our country, and you're probably sleeping better than you would here too, what with me tossing and turning, and getting up all the time! Mama and Papa pass along their best wishes for your success. Thanks to your work, I've been given a bonus week of vacation, and near the end of April we're going down to Kiev to visit some of my aunts and uncles, while I can still travel. I'm not looking forward to the train ride, but it will be nice to see them again. I hope you know how much I love you and await your safe return. When you come home you can hold our child in your arms. I hope he or she looks just like you!"

I Love You,
Yelena

After burning the message, Vitaly sat for a long time, rocking back and forth in the old chair that took up a corner of his living room. It all hurt more that it used to. The first years had been difficult, but they were also filled with the excitement of a grand adventure. Then he had become somewhat hardened, and had allowed his job to fill the void. But now, with his family about to grow, there was sadness and regret at not being there.

Like the men in the muddy trenches, longing for home.

1986: Late April

Sergei smoothed out his shirt on the bed of the small guest apartment. The dinner was with plant officials welcoming his group of observers, and he wanted to look his best. Satisfied, he stepped out onto the balcony to have a smoke and look over Pripyat. A Ukrainian city of forty-five thousand, it was dotted with cement block apartment buildings, though twenty years before there had only been a few wooden huts in the forest beside the Pripyat River. Just three miles to the east was the reason for the new town -- the V.I. Lenin Nuclear Power Station. There were four reactors in operation there and a fifth under construction. Sergei could see the massive gray buildings and the tall, red and white ventilation stacks. When the facility was begun, the nearest town of any size was an ancient hamlet eighteen miles away. It was from that village that the atomic plant drew its more commonly used name -- Chernobyl.

During the eighty mile drive up from Kiev, Sergei had reviewed the design of the Chernobyl reactors. Most nuclear plants in the world were either pressurized or boiling water reactors, and his own country had over twenty P.W.R.s in operation. But the four units at Chernobyl were different. All were RMBKs, a type of reactor exclusive to the Soviet Union. While most plants kept their uranium immersed in water, the fuel in RMBK reactors remained dry. These tubes of uranium were surrounded by black graphite, which helped regulate the nuclear fission. Water was still used to keep the reactor cool and to generate steam, and it was pumped past the hot fuel through more than a thousand small pipes imbedded in the graphite. Control rods were also moved in and out of the solid mass. The RMBK was a design with a number of unique advantages, which Sergei would soon have the chance to see firsthand.

Finished in the control room, Sergei stepped into the long hallway that ran through Units Three and Four. A group of workers approached, each wearing the same white pants, shirt, smock and cap that Sergei had been issued. He gave them a nod, then climbed the steep stairs to the catwalk overlooking the refueling area. The floor of the cavernous room below was a checkerboard of gray and black metal squares. This was the top of the reactor. Each square was the end of a long column, at the bottom of which was either uranium fuel or a control rod. The column passed down through the lid of the reactor -- nearly thirty feet of concrete and steel -- before entering the graphite core. To Sergei's right was the enormous refueling machine, all 350 tons of it, that ran along rails built into the walls. It could remove and replace a fuel bundle while the reactor remained in operation.

Sergei found the RMBK design intriguing. Because the water flowing past the fuel was contained within small pipes, there was no need for a huge steel reactor vessel. Plants in the United States, Sergei recalled, had both a vessel and a drywell shell. The architects of the RMBK had also sought to safely enclose the atomic core, using thick walls and water tanks to block the radiation, but they had not gone overboard like the Americans. Western plants also featured a more complex array of safety systems than the RMBK, and some nations even felt the need to provide all their workers with devices to read their radiation exposure.

Sergei's next stop was the turbine building, but first, he thought, a little spring air and a smoke. Of course, the RMBK wasn't perfect, he reflected as he strolled outside. In American plants, if water flow to the reactor were interrupted, the atomic reaction would slow down, while in the RMBK, less water meant more energy. The Soviet reactor was also harder to control, and power would shoot up when the control rods first began dropping into the core because their tips were made of graphite. But these were minor concerns. Sergei took a drag on his cigarette. Up ahead lay the huge pond that took the place of a cooling tower. The finger-shaped lake was a big hit with local fisherman.

His break over, Sergei stepped into the turbine hall, where a row of rumbling machines shared by Units Three and Four stretched in a line of more than a thousand feet. Sergei saw some workers nearby, including a friend of his; a fellow observer who was a specialist in turbines. Moving on, he considered his upcoming schedule. Toward the end of the week, Unit Four would begin shutting down for maintenance, and a special test was scheduled to see if the generators could provide emergency power as they were coasting to a halt. Sergei looked forward to watching the experiment.

****

The personnel manager laid an armful of folders on the table between Liz and Paul. "Here's the thirteen we came up with. Seven from Fairview, and six from Kittleburg."

"Thanks." Liz reached for the first file.

"If you need anything more, just ask," the manager said. "I'll be around the corner."

"Is there anything you'd like me to do?" Paul said.

"Well . . . perhaps you could skim through the files and get a feel for what these people do. That might help if I have any questions."

Paul retrieved a folder. Inside was the complete employment record of a radwaste technician at Kittleburg.

Liz combed each of the files, picking out a few facts she could verify. She also asked Paul about the individual and their job.

"I think one more and then let's take a lunch break. I'm supposed to meet with the local agents here in town." Liz picked up another folder. "You know a John Donner?"

"I've talked to him a couple of times. He sort of saved the plant a few months back from having to shut down. That can cost a lot of money. I interviewed him and wrote a report."

"He's a 'Licensed Reactor Operator.' What's that?"

"They're the guys in the control room who run the plant day to day. Some of them also go out on rounds, checking up on equipment. They're sort of the pilots of the ship."

Liz studied John Donner's record further. Born in New York, two year electronics degree. In 1981, he'd hired on with Hoosier Electric. Excellent work record. For closest living relative, Donner had listed an uncle in New Zealand. Liz jotted down a few details, then closed the file. "Lunch time."

Liz was looking forward to another talk with Walt Kreveski, and walking into the local FBI office, she spied him behind a glass door. He waved her through. "Hi, Walt. Ready for lunch?" She could see now that he was talking to a tall, much younger black man.

"Sure thing, Liz," Kreveski smiled. "Let me introduce you to the other resident here. Liz Rezhnitsky, Taylor Winn."

"*Privet kak della. Dobralsya bes problem*," the younger agent said, his thin lips parting in a smile.

"*Vsyo horosho. Spasibo*," Liz replied, surprised. "So how'd you know I speak Russian?"

"Walt told me," Winn said. "Not much call for it here in South Bend, though."

"Yeah, and all I speak is bad Polish," Kreveski said.

"I don't get much chance to use mine either," Liz said. " I use tapes to keep myself fresh."

"Same thing here," Winn said. He looked at his partner: "Where we going for lunch? I'm starved."

"Well, today," Kreveski said, with a mischievous look, "I thought I'd treat Miss Rezhnitsky to a little genuine Polish cuisine."

Winn looked toward the ceiling. "God have mercy."

Paul cruised down the highway towards Brixton. As far as he knew, his role in the investigation was over. If something did turn up on the drug dealers, he'd probably read about it in the newspaper. And until he got the all-clear, he couldn't even discuss the search. *What if one of our people really is a fugitive?* Paul found the idea hard to believe. *Guess I'll find out.*

****

From the rear of the Unit Four control room, Sergei watched as the Chernobyl operators prepared for the test on the generator. On the curving front wall, he could see the circular control rod display, with two operators seated below it, wearing the standard white uniform. It was two o'clock on the afternoon of Friday, April 25, 1986, and Sergei had been joined by the turbine specialist from his team "How much longer?" his acquaintance asked.

"A while yet. They have to reduce power slowly. This reactor gets touchy." The experiment would simulate the sudden loss of offsite power, with its accompanying scram. The massive rotor of the generator would also coast to a halt, but it would continue to produce some electricity as it slowed, and the test was to demonstrate that this power could be used to keep pumping water through the core. In the past, during similar experiments, there had been problems. But the plant was ready to try again. While still above twenty percent power, the experiment would be run. Below that level, the reactor was too hard to control.

The time for the test was approaching, and the shift supervisor paced back and forth, glancing down at the papers in his hand. He gave some orders.

"What now?" Sergei's companion asked.

"They're turning off the emergency cooling system for the reactor," Sergei said. "During the test it could screw things up. They won't need it anyway. They have some feedwater pumps, just in case."

The shift supervisor took a call, frowned, and spoke to the management representative standing nearby. Then an announcement was made: the test was on hold. The load dispatcher had asked that Unit Four keep producing power for a few more hours due to a shortage of electricity in the Ukraine.

Sergei turned to his friend. "Let's take a break."

Sergei yawned. He was determined to wait it out, as was his companion. It was after midnight now and the test still had not been run, but there was light at the end of the tunnel. The plant was reducing power again. A tall, broad-shouldered shift supervisor, who had come on duty a few hours before, was monitoring the reactor's progress, while the same management representative, a trim man with graying hair, stood nearby.

Suddenly, one of the operators announced that reactor power was dropping fast. Too fast. The automated system being used to insert the control rods had not been adjusted properly. The shift supervisor cursed as he moved to the control panel, where he was joined by the reactor engineer, a chubby young man with a thin mustache. There was a flurry of orders and adjustments, but it was no use. Reactor power had plunged to a mere one percent, far below the minimum required for the test.

Sergei glared at the ceiling. He had wasted the entire evening waiting for a test that could not be run.

"It shouldn't take them long to get power back up, right?" Sergei's friend said.

Sergei shook his head. "No, it's not that simple. It'll take a long time. Many hours. The core's 'poisoned' now. There's a chemical reaction that takes place in the fuel if you don't run things right. Sort of like flooding a car engine." Sergei was going to explain further, but the management representative had begun berating the control room crew. Core output must be raised, the manager said, and the test completed. The shift supervisor and reactor engineer began arguing against such an attempt.

"Let's take a walk," Sergei said to his friend. "No use listening to this."

Once outside, Sergei lit a cigarette, and the two strolled towards the cooling pond and the distant lights of fishermen. "That manager is wasting his time. Poisoning makes it very hard to get the nuclear reaction going again right away. The only thing you can do is pull out control rods like crazy. But with this type of reactor you've got to keep a certain number of them in the core at all times just to keep things stable. They won't get enough power back for hours." Sergei tossed his cigarette. "I don't know about you, but I'm tired. Let's find out when they'll try again, and then get some sleep."

When the two returned to the control room, Sergei was surprised to see that preparations for the experiment were continuing.

"It looks like they're going on," Sergei's friend whispered.

"Yeah," Sergei nodded. "I guess I was wrong." He could see the operators were pulling more control rods out of the core. But could they get back up to twenty percent power for the test and still keep the reactor under control? Additional pumps were now turned on to ensure that enough cooling liquid would continue to flow past the fuel after the test was started. But as the new pumps moved water faster through the core, the reactor engineer reported that power level was dropping off again. Sergei quickly realized why. In the RMBK design, too much unboiled water in the core acted like a brake on the reactor. To compensate, the operators began pulling out even more control rods. By now, Sergei thought, they must be close to the maximum number that could be removed while still maintaining control of the nuclear reaction.

One of the operators now reported that signals from the reactor might cause an automatic scram before the test was started. The shift supervisor conferred with the manager, and then the worrisome signals were turned off. More control rods were withdrawn. *How many will they pull?* Sergei leaned back against the wall with fatigue. *They've got to be at the limit.*

The clock passed 1:20 a.m. A nearby printer came to life, and the reactor engineer studied the fresh output from the plant computer. Sergei saw the engineer's look of concern as he reported that too many control rods had been withdrawn from the core to ensure proper control. There was more discussion, and then the test continued. It was important, and it would soon be over.

Sergei was shifting from curiosity to concern. Operating the reactor under the present conditions was like driving a car with both bad brakes and a sticky, unpredictable accelerator. But, then again, he reassured himself, this car was just slowly cruising along.

"Getting close," Sergei's friend said.

"Yes," came Sergei's flat reply. He had just heard an order to turn off the scram signal that was to occur at the start of the test. This would allow the crew to repeat the experiment if things didn't go right the first time. Sergei knew the test wasn't designed that way. Was this how they always did things? On the fly?

With preparations complete, the shift supervisor announced the start of the experiment. Valves were closed in the plant, and the steam supply to the turbine-generator was suddenly cut off, simulating the effect of losing offsite power. Still producing some electricity, the massive rotor of the generator began coasting to a halt, and several of the pumps supplying water to the reactor drifted to a stop along with it. Meanwhile, other pumps continued to cool the reactor core.

The test was only a few seconds old when an operator reported that power in the reactor was gradually increasing. Sergei nodded. With less water traveling up through the core, that was expected. But then another reading came, and another. Core power continued to rise, and there was a hint of fear on the reactor engineer's face. The test was only thirty seconds old, and the reactor of Unit Four was not responding properly.

"We may have to scram," Sergei whispered. "Things aren't right."

He pointed at a control panel. "You'll see a blip upwards in power just as the rods start in." Even before Sergei finished, the reactor engineer, beads of sweat glistening on his forehead, asked that the test be stopped. Like a car coasting down a slight incline, the Unit Four reactor was slowly picking up speed.

The shift supervisor thought hard for a moment, the manager looming behind him, and then firmly pushed the scram button, ordering all control rods into the core. Sergei squinted at the power meter, expecting it to jerk up as the graphite tips of the control rods entered the reactor, and then to plunge as the boron in the rods began bringing the atomic fission to a halt. It was one final push on the car's sticky accelerator before slamming on the brakes. . .

Sergei flinched as the lights on the control panels flared. One of the operators yelled that the control rods were not going all the way in. Another voice announced that reactor power had gone right off the scale.

That's not right. Not right!

A deep rumble swept into the control room from the direction of the reactor hall as the shift supervisor punched at switches, trying to get the control rods to move further into the core. But the accelerator of the nuclear reactor had been pressed too many times. It was stuck. The core was now speeding up fast -- and the brakes weren't working.

Sergei watched in disbelief as alarms sounded and lights flashed. Banging and cracking could be heard in the distance. The shift supervisor didn't know what was happening, nor did the reactor engineer. The manager's face was pale. Water flow into the reactor was at zero, someone announced. More buttons were pushed.

"What's going on?" Sergei's friend asked in an anxious voice, as the floor vibrated beneath them.

Sergei didn't answer. *They've lost it.* If the power surge didn't stop, the reactor could damage itself. There could be steam leaks. Some radiation might be released . . .

The thunder and clanging grew worse. It had been half a minute since the scram button had been pushed. The shift supervisor barked out more orders.

Kablaaack-WUMPFF! Sergei was thrown back against the wall by a huge shock wave. The floor beneath him crumpled, and debris crashed down from above. The room went dark.

Hunching over, his back pressing against the trembling rear wall, Sergei covered his head as he was showered by bits of plaster and metal. The thunderous deluge soon ended, and gripped by shock and fear, he opened his eyes. A few emergency lights now illuminated the dusty scene as the operating crew, coughing and cursing, began to extricate themselves from the debris. Around them battered control panels hummed and sparked, while torn cables dangled from the ceiling, crackling with energy. In the distance, beyond the leaning walls and shattered glass, there was the hiss of steam and the gurgle of water running free. There were now loud questions: What happened? What was it? And orders, sounding more like demands, were given by the shift supervisor. Cooling water! The reactor must have water! Buttons were pushed, again and again, as the crew tried frantically to comply.

Sergei glanced at his friend, who was crawling to his knees. "You okay?"

"Yeah." The man wiped at his chin, where a small cut was oozing blood, and the two pulled themselves upright, avoiding the cracks in the floor. "What the hell happened?"

"I don't know," Sergei replied.

The door to the control room flung open and a worker rushed in. Sergei heard him report that he had seen the top of the reactor in motion: the checkerboard of fuel channels had been jumping up and down a few moments before the blast. It was hard to believe. The steel columns above the core weighed several hundred pounds apiece. Soon, there also came reports of flames in the turbine hall, and the town fire brigade was called out.

More minutes passed, but it was still not known what had happened. Had there actually been an explosion in the reactor? The crew did not want to acknowledge such an idea. The reactor must be intact. It had to be. Clearly, the control rods must be pushed the rest of the way into the core, and the shift supervisor sent two young men, training for control room jobs, up to the refueling area to operate the rod mechanisms by hand. No one knew if radiation levels had changed anywhere in the plant. The instruments that might tell them were no longer working.

The trainees soon returned, and Sergei leaned forward, trying to hear their report. Even in the dim light, it was easy to see that both men were distraught. Their white suits were covered with a moist film of dirt and grease. They had climbed through rubble, they said, to get to the refueling floor, and . . . it was torn apart. The ten thousand ton lid of the reactor lay askew -- blown off. They could see fire belching up from below. The men in the control room immediately began to second-guess the report, telling the trainees they couldn't possibly be correct. The reactor must be intact!

Sergei did not have that faith. *An open reactor. And on fire. If it's true . . .* It wasn't hard to picture what it meant. Thousands of Rems per hour. Millions of milli-rems. He studied the two young workers as they answered more questions. They were soaked in sweat, their hands shaking, their faces flushed. If indeed they had edged up near the exposed core, they were dead men. And what of himself? His legs grew weak. *Go!* his mind began to scream. *Go!* Sergei grabbed his friend's arm. "Let's get out of here," he whispered, trying to sound calm.

His acquaintance glanced back. There was determination in his eyes. "They might need me," the man said. "For the turbine."

"You don't know how bad it is!" Sergei said, squeezing his friend's shoulder. "High rads! Way too much."

"There's a job to do," his friend replied. He took a step away and with a look that mixed compassion with disdain, he motioned towards the door. "Go on," he said softly. "You can help later."

Sergei nodded. He wanted so badly to leave. To survive.

The way out of the plant proved difficult. Few lights remained, and the hallways were filled with debris and drenched by an acrid, metallic smell. Sergei passed by the entrance to the turbine hall and a blast of hot air greeted him when he peered inside. There was a hole in the roof, a jagged cut, and chunks of the ceiling had fallen onto a turbine. There were fires as well, and workers scrambling about the catastrophe. For a few moments Sergei stood transfixed in the doorway, but then regained his senses. *Get out!*

The sky overhead was crimson and shimmering when he finally burst outside onto the asphalt tarmac that surrounded much of the complex. He could see fire trucks parked near the cooling pond and started in that direction. Something crunched under his feet and then his toe struck a fist-sized rock. He kicked the black, angular object aside and continued on, stepping around other pieces of debris. Anxious to get further away, he broke into a run. The fire trucks represented safety. From there he could move on to Pripyat, just three miles distant. Out of breath, he reached the vehicles and then turned back to look.

Oh . . . A huge column of bluish flame was belching up into the sky behind the Turbine building, with thick puffs of black smoke climbing even higher. Closer, atop the Turbine building roof, firemen were at work, while their comrades on the ground hurriedly unrolled more hoses and struggled to get them up the wall. One firefighter came down off the ladder, clutching at his stomach through his thick coat. Staggering toward the trucks, he kicked at the dark rubble littering the ground, and in a brief, horrible moment, Sergei realized what the rocky objects were. Graphite! Chunks from the reactor's core, intensely radioactive, had somehow been blown up through the roof and landed here. *Here.* Terror again coursed through Sergei's body. This place was not safe. Not safe at all. He turned and ran.

Sergei awoke, sticky and uncomfortable, atop the bed in his apartment. On the way into town he had peeled off much of his plant uniform before plopping down, exhausted. He had lain there, shaking, trying to decide what to do. Now it was 8:00 a.m. He must have drifted off. Sunlight was streaming through the thin curtains as he relived the night and its terror. It hadn't been a dream, Sergei knew. It had been very, very real.

His joints uncharacteristically stiff, he stepped onto the balcony, squinting in the light. Five kilometers away he could see the Chernobyl plant. Beside one of the tall ventilation stacks, the reactor building of Unit Four was now a blackened hulk, from which a dark column of smoke was rising.

That's it then. It was really gone. He had witnessed the impossible: the destruction of a nuclear reactor. And he had panicked. But the fear had now subsided, to be replaced by shame. He ran, like a coward. You ran. Laughter drifted up from the street and Sergei peered over the railing. A group of children seemed to be on their way to school. Those kids should be indoors. Surely someone told them!

Just how bad was it? Sergei suddenly realized he could find out. As a gift before leaving the United States, he had been given a self-reading dosimeter like those used in American plants. He located the finger-sized metal tube in his bags, checked that the needle inside was close to zero, and then laid it on the balcony railing.

After a shower, Sergei stepped back into the springtime breeze on the balcony to pick up the dosimeter. It had been thirty minutes. The needle would probably still be hovering around zero, he thought, as he held the small tube up to the light. But the thin black line was near the high end of the scale. 500 milli-rems.

500! That can't be right. Can't be! Sergei checked again, and then looked beyond the apartments of Pripyat to the burning reactor. *At this distance? Is it possible?* For the first time, he noticed a faint smell in the air, an acrid, almost metallic odor. *Maybe . . . maybe it's true.* He began to feel sick to his stomach and stepped back inside.

Weakly, Sergei sat on the bed. Had he underestimated the true impact of what had happened? Had he been trying to fool himself? The dosimeter indicated a radiation level of nearly one Rem per hour. That was tens of thousands of times higher than normal. It meant one shouldn't stay in Pripyat for very long. A few days at most. Nausea was building up within him as he tried to reassure himself. He was jumping to conclusions. The dosimeter could be broken. And there were children in the street. Surely that was a good sign. A funny taste filled Sergei's mouth, and he got up to get a drink of water. He had barely taken a step when his stomach began convulsing, and he flung himself toward the sink.

Sergei perched on the edge of the thin cot, dining on crackers and water, his striped hospital gown hanging about his shoulders. It was midnight now, and he felt much better than when he had slowly climbed the steps of the clinic that afternoon. He had barely managed to keep down the potassium iodide tablet given to him upon his arrival. Sharing his room this night were two others who told similar stories of nausea a few hours after the explosion: a laborer working the night shift at a construction site near the plant, and a fisherman who had been at the cooling pond.

And they were not the worst, Sergei knew. Anxious for a cigarette, he taken a short stroll that led him past other wards where the firemen and operators lay, their skin blistered and burnished to a reddish black. Among them lay his friend and companion from the night before. A team of physicians had already arrived from Moscow and were evacuating the sickest patients. Sergei could only feel lucky. As near as the doctors could tell, he had not absorbed a lethal dose.

They explained that he would feel much better for a few weeks, and then the symptoms of his exposure would return. He would use that time well, Sergei thought. He would volunteer for whatever was needed. He would redeem himself.

****

The clock flipped to 9:30 a.m. and the radio came on. Vitaly sat up and ran a hand through his disheveled hair. His knee ached as he shuffled across the room. *Rain.* Slipping into a pair of jeans, he considered his plans for the day. John Donner needed to pick up groceries before his three to eleven shift. The radio had begun a news report, and when the Soviet Union was mentioned, Vitaly focused in:

". . . up to forty times normal levels. The Russian authorities have not yet accepted responsibility for the radioactive cloud detected by the Scandinavians, but evidence is beginning to mount of a nuclear disaster somewhere in the Soviet Union. Based on prevailing weather patterns over the past few days, experts are speculating the source may be a nuclear power plant in the Ukraine. One unconfirmed report has stated U.S. Government satellite photos indicate an explosion may have occurred among a group of reactors at a site approximately one hundred miles north of Kiev.

In other news, . . ."

Vitaly continued getting dressed. *So maybe it's happened. After all, my homeland isn't as safety conscious as the Americans. But our economy must move forward, and there will be sacrifices.* He pulled on a sweatshirt. *They did it here, too, with their factories and pollution.*

There was something else about the report, something that gnawed at the back of his mind as he began threading his belt. What was it? Something familiar. The Soviet agent stopped one loop short. *Yelena! She was going to Kiev. When?* Vitaly concentrated, trying to recall. *You got the message two weeks ago, and it said end of the month . . . the last week. What is it today, the 27th? 28th?* The pieces all came together. *She's in Kiev. Damn it, she's in Kiev!* His training back in Moscow had taught him how to avoid panic, and this, combined with his calm personality, had stood Vitaly well through the years. But now a wave of cold tension enveloped him. He could accept whatever his own fate might be. He was a soldier. He could accept a nuclear accident in his own country, if it were just a bump in the road to progress. But Yelena -- and the baby!

Calm down, calm down! Kiev is a hundred miles from the spot, that's what they said. That's a long way. But, shit, it's showing up in Sweden! Vitaly raced through his memory. *Where do her relatives live exactly? It's outside of Kiev somewhere.* He couldn't pull up the name. *I'll have to look at the map. I've got to get more information!* Vitaly pounded on the bed, and recalled what Dmitri had once told him: "Panic comes from not knowing."

He spent the day switching between the TV and the radio, but only the most general news was reported. What exactly had the Swedes and Finns picked up? Milli-rems? Less? Vitaly had looked at a map, and felt sure Yelena was in Irpen, twenty miles northeast of Kiev. There were rumors the accident had taken place at a reactor in Chernobyl. Irpen was seventy miles from that site. His wife was in no danger, Vitaly reassured himself, as he climbed in the car and headed for work. *She's okay. And the baby is too. Seventy miles. They have to be.*

****

Sergei dipped his spade into the sand and then dumped the load in a bag held open by another volunteer. With a grunt, the man swung the bulging sack over his shoulder and trudged off toward one of the waiting trucks. Content to take a break, Sergei leaned on his shovel and wiped his brow. Even in the cool spring air it was easy to work up a sweat.

There was much idle talk about the cause of the event. Sabotage had even been mentioned, but Sergei knew the truth. The reactor had simply been pushed too far and it had suddenly slipped into overdrive. That rapid, vast production of extra heat had caused the cooling pipes running through the core to burst, which had damaged the reactor fuel. Chemical reactions had then generated enormous amounts of hydrogen and oxygen. Eventually, the explosive mixture had detonated, blowing fuel and graphite into the sky.

To both douse the ongoing fire and cover the horribly radioactive debris, sand was being dumped into the gaping reactor cavity by helicopter. Sergei had spoken briefly to one of the pilots. The man had felt the heat rising up from the core, and as the dumped sand sent dust and ash billowing upward, radiation levels around the helicopter had reached a million milli-rems per hour. The pilot had gotten sick even before pulling away.

Several kilometers distant, in Pripyat, conditions were not quite so intolerable, but the entire area was covered by an invisible layer of radioactive dust. Finally recognizing the danger, the authorities had evacuated the town more than a day after the accident. An enormous fleet of buses had converged on the city, and its 45,000 inhabitants, calm for the most part and clutching what few possessions they could carry, had climbed aboard. Sergei had remained behind. He would never run away again.

****

When Paul returned to his desk he saw Crutch and Langford looking over a document. "More on Chernobyl? I caught the end of the news at lunch. They said it was still burning."

"INPO reports that as well," Langford said. He handed the paper to Crutch.

"I guess they're worried about other reactors at the site," Paul said. "Apparently, we've got satellite photos."

"Says here the fire is probably the graphite in their core," Crutch noted, studying the report. "They asked Sweden and West Germany for help. Sweden told 'em to talk to England. Some kinda graphite fire there back in the fifties. 'Windscale'."

"I've heard of that event," Langford said. "It occurred at a reactor up near Scotland. They contaminated some of the countryside."

"Does it say how the thing works?" Paul asked, looking over Crutch's shoulder. "The Russian reactor?"

"They provide an outline," Langford said. "It is a much different machine than ours, you can determine that much."

"Whatever they got," Crutch said, "it's really fucked up."

****

Reactor building operator John Donner checked the charger for the emergency battery cells and logged the reading. He glanced at his watch and saw he was running behind on his rounds. Vitaly wasn't surprised. It had been hard for him to concentrate all week.

Was Yelena safe? He could not know for sure. He had sought out every bit of news about Chernobyl, but little was known thus far. The death toll was anywhere from two to two thousand, and some in Kiev were leaving due to fears about the water supply. If Yelena had indeed made the trip to Irpen, Vitaly kept telling himself, she would have little exposure to any fallout. But he also knew his unborn child was especially at risk. What was happening to his family? It was a heavy load to bear, but there was no choice. In an extreme emergency there were ways to get in touch with the Center, but that could jeopardize his whole mission, and his fellow countrymen probably couldn't tell him anything more about the confused situation. His best hope was that something would be reported in the next regular message. That would be in four days.

Vitaly kept reminding himself what his father, and so many others, had gone through during the war. Far away from their homes, they could never be sure that their families weren't being bombed, or starved, or marched off into slavery. But as soldiers, they had done their duty. They had kept on fighting. And Vitaly would do the same. But right now, the battle wasn't with the enemy, it was within himself.

****

Liz returned to her desk with a mug of coffee. This first day of May she had a busy schedule, with three interviews, leaving only a few hours to finish some important paperwork. She also hoped to put in more time on the search for the illegal working at a nuclear plant. She had continued to collect data, both for her own investigation and for agents in other states, and responses to her own requests were now beginning to filter in. Methodically, she was comparing her findings with the backgrounds provided by the Hoosier Electric files, hoping to spot some clue that would put her on the right trail. It was a long shot, but there was no other way to go about it.

****

During the KGB's long years of service to the Soviet Union, the intelligence apparatus had developed an imposing bureaucracy to ensure secrecy. Information was carefully guarded so that few of the half-million employees of the Komitet Gosudarstvennoy Bezopasnosti could form a clear picture of any given activity. But within the massive organization there was also intrigue. Alliances were formed, and risks taken, by those with ambition and a yearning for power. A venture that was successful could provide many benefits for its supporters.

Anton picked up the folder, strolled past two of his fellow KGB officers and into Colonel Bykov's unoccupied office. Tossing the report in the overflowing IN basket, he glanced at the cluttered desktop. A single sheet of paper, lying face down, caught his attention. On its back was a neat, hand-printed note: "File C393-492." Anton recognized the number, and on this slow-paced morning he found the impulse to look too great to resist. After checking over his shoulder, he retrieved the report he had just delivered, then snatched up the overturned memo as well and slipped it inside. Then he quickly scanned it:

> To: -------Bykov
> From: -----------Sveshnikov
>
> . . . recommendation reviewed. . . . . .in light of present circumstances. . . . . . .Pursuant to the plan drafted at meetings K3v... . . in August, 1985 and T3v ..000. . . . subsequent plan approval via 1CKxxx..x. , Blue Raven, plan . . . 3 . . . . . . ordered for implementation during the period between 10 May and 1 June, 1986. . . . . utmost caution . . . . cessation of the plan . . . if at any time detection . . . . dead drop. . . . ."

Plan . . . ordered for implementation? Blue Raven? Anton was just beginning to grasp the content when a phone rang outside the door. He quickly returned the memo and exited the office. *You shouldn't have looked, stupid!* With relief, he saw no one could have seen his folly.

Back in his cubicle, Anton thought more about the document. He remembered arranging a meeting a few months before for C393-492. And Blue Raven -- something about the American Midwest. Then there were the instructions: "utmost caution," "cessation if detected." Anton had never seen anything like it. The dispatch was important -- something big was about to happen. He must pass it on to the Americans as soon as possible. If he was right, it would be more than just a token jab at the State. And that was what Anton wanted, most of all. For Viktor.

****

Vitaly stared at the brief message that had begun the transmission. It was unusual for the Center to begin with personal news, but this time they had made an exception -- a wonderful exception:

> "Your wife has returned from her vacation in Kiev. She
> is in good health, and sends you her best."

He wanted to hear more, of course, but for the moment it was enough. Vitaly let Yelena fill his thoughts. Everything was all right, after all.

A drop of sweat fell onto the paper as Vitaly gazed at his decoding handiwork. The remainder of the message had contained none of the usual exhortations for him to continue his great service to the State. There was no discussion of America as a land of capitalist evil, no reminders of the superiority of the communist doctrine. Vitaly tried to remain calm as he re-read the instructions:

> "You are hereby advised to proceed with Operation Blue
> Raven Five, Plan Vector-Three, repeat, Operation Blue
> Raven Five, Plan Vector-Three, between the dates of 10
> May and 1 June, 1986. All pre-requisites as stated in
> this plan must exist. Performance of the plan's
> requirements must be undertaken with the utmost
> caution, using all means to avoid suspicion, and
> cessation of the plan is to occur if at any time detection
> appears possible. The plan and associated equipment
> will be provided by dead drop, instructions to follow. . ."

Vitaly's heart continued to pound. The message was clear.
It was time for John Donner to attack the enemy.

****

Paul set his cooler on the desk and headed back up the aisle to
Mike Langford's office. "Did you see the Chernobyl pictures they
released yesterday?"

Langford looked up. " It appears that they blew the top right off
the building. That is a problem."

"They're evacuating out to eighteen miles." Paul took a seat.

"And there is quite a plume in the atmosphere," Langford said.
"The West Coast is even reporting a miniscule amount. Just micro-
rems, so it means nothing with respect to health. But apparently
there's been a run on potassium iodide in California. I imagine they
believe the tablets will protect them from radiation."

"It would be a wonder drug if it did," Paul said. He knew taking
KI only ensured the thyroid gland was full of 'normal' iodine, which
in theory would keep the user from absorbing iodine-131, a

radioactive isotope released by a reactor in trouble. Settling on grass eaten by dairy cows, the substance could become dangerously concentrated in milk. But I-131 was just one potential source of radioactivity during an accident.

"It appears the farmers downwind in Europe are going to feel the economic effects for some time," Langford said. "Iodine, at least, decays away in a few weeks. But if Chernobyl's core is truly on fire, the plant is releasing other isotopes that will remain rather toxic and radioactive for a long time to come."

****

Vitaly carried the heavy trash bag through the kitchen and down into the basement, where he already had spread newspapers across the floor. Crouching, he emptied out the sticky, odorous contents of the sack. After an assortment of filthy cans and soiled paper plates, he found the metal box, sealed in green plastic.

Since receiving his orders two days before, Vitaly had given a lot of thought to the reason for the mission. The Center had directed him to sabotage Fairview Station in a manner that could not be detected. *Why?* Chernobyl must be a big part of the equation. The Soviet government was being buffeted by a storm of international protests, both for the accident itself, and for its unwillingness to pass along details. Vitaly had concluded his task was to create a diversion so his country could recover. The United States would now have to contend with an accident on its own shores. Such an event would bring the American nuclear industry to a standstill. That would deal a painful blow to the economy.

It would also be a blow to his companions at work. When the idea of sabotage was just a theory, Vitaly could make allowances for his potential actions. But now it was for real. He was going to destroy the livelihood of his coworkers and perhaps endanger their lives.

That it was his duty was a good justification, but not a comfort. For that, he was thankful the plan Moscow picked was the least brutal of the choices. And he was confident of the strength and resilience within the men and women of Fairview Station. *They'll get by. There will still be jobs, or other places to go.* His own countrymen had survived far worse during the war.

The sealed aluminum container was the size of a briefcase. Inside, Vitaly found a copy of his plan and the special materials needed for the job. He held the small, clear vial up to the light, and peered at the thin strand within. It was a sublimation wire. Once exposed to air, it would carry current for a brief period and then disappear, the electric energy changing it directly from a solid to a gas.

Vitaly jerked, as a gust of wind rattled one of the ground-level windows of the basement. There was thunder in the distance. He tried to relax, thinking about the momentous achievement in which he could take pride the rest of his days. He understood the danger, but within him there was little fear. Vitaly Fedorovich Kruchinkin was fighting the war he wanted to fight. He looked down at the gadgetry spread out before him. *And I have my choice of weapons.*

****

Anton lifted his coat from the basket by the door and stuffed the sticky, tightly folded message into his pocket. The streets of the Moscow suburb were still damp from a spring rain as he strolled to the bus stop. After a walk in a nearby park to ensure he wasn't being followed, Anton headed into the movie theater. Twenty minutes later he exited. His package remained behind.

****

"Well, we've made some headway," Doug Tama sighed as he finished winding the extension cord.

"Smoother than I expected," Gary agreed. He stacked the last of the copper tubing in a corner, and took a final look. The #2 emergency diesel generator had been torn apart, the pieces lying on the floor around him. All to replace a few screws. But, with any luck, a few more days and the machine would be back together. Then it would be time to move on to the generator's twin, in the next room.

"You goin' bowling tonight?" Tama asked.

"No, more house hunting."

"Well, if you ever need a butler, let me know."

Gary climbed into the truck as Carol started the engine. Together, they watched the realtor back out of the driveway of the older, two story house and cruise off down the tree-lined street. The strip of sky overhead was fading from blue to black.

"What'd ya think?" Gary asked.

Carol sighed. "I don't know. It had some good points." She snapped on her seat belt, and left her hands in her lap.

"New kitchen.

"That was nice."

"And the dining room was a good size. You could have one of those tea parties in there, like you're always spendin' time at."

"You mean the Lutheran women's group? It would be nice. I can't volunteer our trailer. And we'd be close too. Maybe I could drag you down there once in a while.

"Let's not get into that again," Gary said. "What else did you like?"

"Oh, the bathrooms didn't look too bad."

"But…"

"Well, neither of the bedrooms were very big, and three would be better…"

170

"For your folks"

"And yours. You know they'll be coming."

"Yah, but I figured a tent in the back yard."

Carol flashed a sarcastic look, then turned away and stared out at the newly green grass in the front yard. "Your turn. Plusses and minuses."

"Well, location's good. Price is good. House is in okay shape. But I think the garage is too small. Backyard too. Not much room for your garden."

"I noticed."

"And no place for my fishin' boat." Gary rolled down his window. "But I liked the basement. Roomy. You could put your piano in the corner."

"And still fit in a pool table."

Gary grinned. "That's the idea, Miss Carol-l-l."

"At least you'd have something to do in the winter."

"I got pretty good in the service. It's fun. Relaxing."

"As long as it's not too expensive."

"Second-hand." Gary reached down and buckled his seat belt. "But we need a house first. And I don't think it's this one."

Carol put the truck in gear. "I know. So we try again tomorrow."

****

There it is. Vitaly spotted the round white barn up ahead as he drove along the country lane a mile east of Fairview Station. Beyond it came a small patch of woods and an intersection, and then he was in the open again, a field of freshly planted crops on one side of his brown Chevy, an empty pasture on the other. There were no buildings in sight. Slowing his car to a crawl, Vitaly stared up through the windshield. The power lines passed overhead, three of them, stacked one above the other. He glanced over into the meadow at the nearby tower, then tapped on the accelerator and coasted on to a grove of trees. *There.* A track extended into the woods.

Satisfied, Vitaly headed for the plant to begin his three to eleven shift. His work schedule was ideal, and the ground was drying out, with no rain in the forecast. May 10 was just two days away. It was a Saturday. Conditions would be perfect.

> "My Dearest Love,
>
> I hope you have not been worried about me because of the trip I took with Mama and Papa to Irpen. Everything is fine. I assume you know about the accident at the atomic power plant in Pripyat. We were not very close to it at all, and we left for home on the 29th, a few days after it happened. Since I have come back I have been to the doctor, and she says everything is just right. We are going to have a healthy baby! So do not be concerned.
>
> Mama and Papa really enjoyed their visit. Do you remember Aunt Ivana? She wanted me to tell you . . . "

Vitaly read the letter twice more. It was wonderful to hear from Yelena herself -- to be told that all was well. Before destroying the night's work, he re-examined the rest of the message. Expecting his mission would be discussed, he had found there was only one sentence on the topic: "Instructions of May 3 still apply." The brevity was a little odd, but his orders were clear. The plan would go through. And then someday, soon, he would return home to his wife and child.

****

The squad room of the FBI Field Office was bustling with activity as Friday wound down. Liz checked the clock on the far wall and began gathering up the files from Fairview and Kittleburg. Thus far, she had pieced together enough information to eliminate five of the thirteen suspects.

One of the other female agents walked by on her way out. "What you up to this weekend, Liz?"

"Oh, Stan and I are going out tonight and tomorrow. He's got the weekend off."

"Tonight __and__ tomorrow? Sounds serious," her colleague said, smiling.

"It's fun," Liz answered. Certainly it was the best relationship she'd had since Boston.

"I remember how it was before Josh and I got married," the other agent said. "It gets better, too," she added mischievously, before turning away.

Liz smiled to herself, thinking of the weekend ahead. She looked at the pile of records on her desk. *Gde bi ti he bil ya nayou tebya*, she said to herself. *If you're in there, I'm going to find you.* She picked up the files. *Ne seychas. But not today.*

The printer in the corner had ceased its chattering, and the night clerk tore off the printout and scanned the top. The dispatch was from the New York Field Office, and was addressed to Special Agent Elizabeth Rezhnitsky, CI Coordinator, Indianapolis. The priority code indicated it was a routine response to an inquiry she had made. The clerk placed the printout in an envelope and stuck it in the incoming mail slot. He then left to see if Agent Rezhnitsky was on duty this evening. If she wasn't, he would leave a note at her desk.

Part Three: The Event

Vitaly pushed up the glove and checked his watch in the harsh light of his unfinished basement. 12:35 a.m. It was now Saturday, May 10, 1986. He had been home from work about an hour, and used the small tank from the Center to fill seven balloons. There were just a few left, lying flat atop the old desk against the wall.

More and more in the proceeding days, Vitaly had come to understand the wisdom of his superiors. The accident at Chernobyl had truly been catastrophic, and there was even concern the molten mass of the core would melt its way down to the water table. *Thank goodness Yelena left.* From his distant vantage point, Vitaly had watched as his country was vilified as never before, even by its allies. Anything that might ease the pressure would be of tremendous benefit. The Soviet economy had been hurt by Chernobyl, but his country would not be deterred from its industrial expansion. In America, though, the story would soon be different.

Finished with another balloon, Vitaly added it to the shiny cluster pressed against the ceiling. In the corner, a rustling sound inside a pet carrier was followed by a cat's howl. He connected another balloon to the tank. If there was no message from the Center in the morning, he would take the next step in the plan. Then it would all really begin.

****

Saturday, May 10
Time: 4:30 p.m.

Moving through the reactor building, Vitaly felt only a calm determination. There had been no order to halt the preparations. His superiors had one last opportunity this evening. Otherwise, by tomorrow it would all be over -- and Vitaly Fedorovich Kruchinkin would have served his country well.

Heading down the stairs toward the STurDI-2 room, Vitaly paused and listened, peering above and below through the metal grating. He did not expect to see another worker on a Saturday afternoon, but he must be sure. Confident he was alone, he reached into a pocket of his jeans and withdrew two plastic vials.

****

Time: 8:07 p.m.

In his cubbyhole within the Langley complex, the young analyst looked at the clock. Only two hours until his shift was up and the rest of the warm Saturday evening was his. He would catch up with some of his fellow CIA employees across the river in Washington.

But first there was work to do. The researcher opened the packet from the Moscow Embassy. Usually these were examined on the day shift by senior personnel, so tonight's late arrival represented a rare opportunity -- but likely a tedious one as well. The analyst knew most embassy dispatches from behind the Iron Curtain were filled only with low-level gossip to be catalogued. He read through the message. Apparently a memo from the KGB's First Directorate had been intercepted, discussing a plan to be implemented in May or June by a "Blue Raven." A dead drop might be involved. It was probably nothing, the analyst thought, but there were some things he could check, so he turned to his terminal and activated the search program, beginning with "Blue Raven." A list of files appeared and he examined each in turn. Blue Raven was the KGB code name for a Soviet illegal operating in the United States. The researcher began taking notes.

Other words and phrases turned up no hits. Perhaps, the analyst thought, he'd been right to assume the dispatch was of limited value. It would serve only to provide a few more bits of information on Blue Raven. But the message also referenced "C393-492" as another possible code name, and the researcher punched it in, tapping his pen until the screen came back to life. C393-492 was also an illegal, he found, and the Agency had taken action recently based on this spy's possible activities.

Intrigued, the analyst read the full dispatch again, then made a list:

If Blue Raven = C393-492:
Illegal.
Midwest.
Plan.
A Drop.
May/June.
Nuke Power.
Experts - meeting.
Cessation if detected.

Setting his pen aside, the researcher studied the items.
"Oh, my God," he whispered.

The analyst perched on the chair while his boss studied the paperwork. "So Blue Raven seems to be operating in the Midwest, huh?" the older man finally said.

"Yes, sir, it looks that way. We know Illinois and Indiana for sure."

"And he's up to something, maybe starting tomorrow?"

"Yes, sir, according to a source."

"What's the source's rating?"

"The Blue Raven and C393 sources are rated as excellent. They're top classified."

The man behind the desk returned to the report, his eyes betraying nothing. "Something to do with nuclear power, huh?"

"Yes." The analyst shifted in his seat. "Directorate T -- that's the high technology group, of course. And the Doctor Berdyayev could be a nuclear physicist in the Soviet power program." He tossed a newspaper photograph onto the desk -- an image of a distinguished-looking man with black hair and a goatee -- and watched his supervisor for a reaction. There was none, as the senior man gave the snapshot a glance and then continued studying the report. "One of C393's Directorate T meetings was in Kalinin, too," the researcher went on. "I checked, and there's a nuke plant there. We also sent out an advisory to the FBI on the nuclear connection last month."

The supervisor turned his gaze back to the young subordinate. "Did anything turn up?"

"Not so far. There was no location fix, and the U.S. has over a hundred plants to choose from, plus fuel factories and storage sites."

"But now we're told C393-492 may be Blue Raven."

"Yes, sir. That gives us an illegal at a nuclear facility in the Midwest."

"Who may be thinking sabotage." The older man grimaced.

"There's a real chance. And Chernobyl is another factor."

"So," the supervisor mused, "the Soviets are taking a lot of shit for their mess, and they decide to take the heat off."

"It's certainly possible."

"Possible yes, but goddamn risky. What if they got caught?"

"They must be confident they won't."

The room grew quiet as the supervisor again studied the report. Finally, he looked to the analyst. "Let's take this upstairs."

****

Time: 8:15 p.m.

There. Vitaly slithered from beneath emergency diesel generator #1. He was relieved to be done. It was one of the more dangerous elements of his plan. John Donner went many places on rounds, but he was not responsible for checking the diesels. Fortunately, curiosity about the repairs at unit #2 gave him an excuse to be in the area -- and having to disable only one of the generators also made his plan much simpler.

It was now time to head back into the reactor building to continue his rounds. Among other duties, he still needed to go into the torus area and inspect the outside of the huge tank. And while John Donner was there, Vitaly Kruchinkin would make a few temporary adjustments.

****

Time: 9:11 p.m.

Liz Rezhnitsky flopped on her boyfriend's couch as the bathroom door swung closed. She stretched her arms above her head, the sleeves of her sky-blue sweatshirt sliding down. It had been a full Saturday, and a pleasant one. She glanced at the clock. She should check her machine. It had been awhile. Even when off-duty, the Bureau expected its agents to stay in touch. Liz pulled the phone off the end table and punched in her home number. There were no messages. She smiled. Nothing to ruin a nice day.

****

Time: 9:45 p.m.

Vitaly wiped the wrench clean of fingerprints and hung it back on the wall, then took a final look at the STurDI-1 turbine. *Perfect.*

A few minutes later, sweat began rolling down Vitaly's back as he again raced up the reactor building stairs. He legs ached from the effort. When John Donner reported back to the control room before going home, he would talk about coming down with the flu, and grumble that he had planned to spend his two off days working on his car. But though John Donner might be sick, in a few hours Vitaly Kruchinkin expected to be feeling just fine.

****

Sunday, May 11
Time: 12:16 am.

Liz spotted the red dot blinking in the darkness when she opened the door to her apartment. Maybe it was Stan. Did she leave anything? She pressed the button.

"Special Agent Rezhnitsky," the voice began.

"Yes," Liz mumbled. Work.

"...This is the night clerk at the Field Office. It's 12:10 a.m. Sunday, May 11. You have a priority C.I. communication from Washington. Please call in to acknowledge. Thank you."

What could that be? Liz picked up the phone as her curiosity began to take hold. She'd probably have to drive downtown and find out.

Liz began examining the printout even as she wove her way back to her desk. A second, routine message was also tucked under her arm. Halfway across the nearly deserted squad room, she stopped. *Oh, God. Active measures. For real.* She scanned further. *And maybe one of mine!* She hurried to her desk and then read the dispatch again. The message out of the Bureau's Washington headquarters began by discussing secrecy requirements and noting the previous reports regarding an illegal at a nuclear plant. Then came the real news:

> "Intelligence information now indicates a reasonable possibility that the illegal noted above will attempt some form of action, which may include sabotage, at the aforementioned nuclear facility. This is likely to occur between May 10 and June 1 of this year...."

Liz' hands gripped the dispatch. What was today? The tenth? Eleventh? She checked the calendar. May Eleventh. Already in the window. But the window for what? Something simple, maybe harmless, or would the Soviets actually try to destroy an American nuke plant? She resumed reading:

> "...The individual in question appears to have completed a long training course, probably employment-related, in the June/July, 1985 time frame..."

That should cut out most of the suspects. She had those records.

> "...There is also evidence to suggest the individual is operating in the Midwest, particularly the Illinois/Indiana area..."

That's it then. The burden was on her. Liz continued:

> "... Any suspects who meet all criteria ... should be placed under surveillance immediately and detained as soon as practicable for questioning. If on duty at said facility, take whatever steps are necessary to detain the suspect without alarming this individual. The Nuclear Regulatory Commission is being contacted. Further instructions in this regard will follow shortly..."

A few moments of shuffling through the first technician's file and Liz had found the training records. June or July of '85 ... *Nope.* The list of suspects was thinning out fast. The next file was labeled DONNER, and the training forms were tucked in the back. She rubbed at her eyes and began scanning the list of courses: turbine building operator training, December, 1982 . . . Completes reactor building operator training. . . . Requalification testing. . . . . control room reactor operator training completed, July, 1985. . .

July '85. A hit? Liz retraced her steps. *Began in the summer of '84. Finished in summer of '85. . . . So a full year. A long course!* Her excitement grew as she rechecked the records against the dates given in the Washington dispatch. *It fits. It all fits. Vacations at the right time, training at the right time. It could be. It just could be.* At the very least, it was enough to take the next step. John Donner, of South Bend, Indiana, would have to be put under surveillance as soon as possible.

Smiling broadly, Liz checked her data once more to be sure, and then examined the rest of the file, searching for any clues she had missed. She saw she had asked for Donner's birth certificate, his high school records, and a check on his first job. Since the suspect had grown up in New York, the field office there was to gather the information. *New York.* Abruptly, Liz remembered the other letter that had come in. Grabbing the envelope, she spotted the New York Field Office designation and tore the package open. Scanning the top of the message, she saw that background work had been completed on two individuals. The first was an employee at Kittleburg. The second was -- John Donner.

Fueled by nervous energy, Liz read on. A long search had turned up Donner's birth certificate. Of his high school records nothing remained, the building having burnt down in the mid-seventies. There was no information on the suspect's first job either. That factory had closed long ago.

Her heart skipped a beat as Liz recognized the pattern she had long dreamed of seeing, and she slapped the table in triumph. *Got him!* There were too many gaps in Donner's past to be a coincidence -- especially given the other clues. She checked the background search Hoosier Electric had conducted and saw that, other than an obscure relative in New Zealand, none of Donner's references had known him longer than nine years. She knew why.

What does he do at Fairview? Liz looked at her notes. "Control room," the handwriting read. "Runs plant minute-to-minute." A chill crept down her spine. If sabotage at a nuclear plant really were the mission, John Donner would be the perfect man to carry it out.

****

Time: 1:05 a.m.

In the bedroom of his small house, tucked away near the top of a hill on a dead end street, Vitaly sat beside his short-wave radio. There had been nothing but static. The Center had sent no message. He scanned the nearby frequencies, just in case, but found no signal. It was going to happen. After all this time.

****

Time: 1:06 am.

"Yes, sir," Liz said into the phone. "I double-checked. It all fits, and then some." She paused as the Special Agent in Charge asked another question. He had been asleep when the phone rang, but the S.A.C. showed no signs of weariness now. "Yes, sir, I think right away," Liz answered. "The dispatch from H.Q. pegged yesterday as the start date. It calls for immediate surveillance. . . . . Right. I thought I would call Kreveski in South Bend."

The S.A.C. asked Liz if she planned to travel to South Bend herself.

"I'd like to," she said. "I thought I might accompany you." Liz bit down on her lip. Tradition held that the S.A.C. be given the opportunity to make the big arrests.

"It's yours, Liz," came the reply, "unless we get into a manhunt."

"Thank you, sir." *Yes!*

"Can you find out if Donner is at the plant right now?" the S.A.C. asked.

"I'm not sure." Liz had already considered the idea. There was no easy way to do it. She could go through official channels, but that would take time and give the appearance that something was up -- but perhaps she could try another approach. "I don't think calling Hoosier Electric's VP would work too well," she said, "and nothing's come in over the wire yet on how the NRC wants to handle it. But I do have a contact who works at Fairview. He might be able to help."

"Use your best judgment," the S.A.C. said. "I don't want to tip anything, but since we're in the window, we've got to move quick."

"Yes sir. I'll give it a try."

"All right. And call Walt. Then let me know."

Liz placed the receiver back on the hook. *It's gonna happen. It's really gonna happen.* She leafed through her notes and retrieved Walt Kreveski's home phone number. "You better be there, Walter," she mumbled, punching in the digits.

The phone rang once. Twice. Three. *Come on, Walt!* Four times now.

"Hello?"

The voice on the other end of the line was sleepy, but Liz thought it sounded familiar. "Is this FBI Special Agent Walter Kreveski?" she asked.

"Yes. This is Agent Kreveski." The voice grew more alert.

"Walt, this is Liz Rezhnitsky down in Indianapolis. I've got something here and I need your help."

"Now?" the older agent said. "Is this about your spy?"

"Yes. Some new stuff came in, and I've got a suspect who matches the profile. It's got to be him."

"Well, I'll be."

"It looks like he's up to something, too. Maybe out at Fairview. Sabotage. It could be right now."

"Oh, shit," Kreveski said. "Then let's find the bastard."

Liz passed on the story, and promised to telecopy enough details to get a warrant. Walt would get hold of Taylor Winn, and send the younger agent out to watch the suspect's house.

Liz hung up and dialed again. *Now, let's see if I can find out if Mr. Donner's at work.*

Settled into his easy chair, Paul was well into a science fiction novel. It had been some time since he'd spent a Saturday evening alone, but with Vickie's sisters in town it was the lesser of two evils. When the phone rang, he glanced up at the clock. This late, it could be Langford calling to tell him the plant had scrammed, and he needed to come in "Paul Hendricks."

"Paul, this is Agent Liz Rezhnitsky of the FBI. We worked together a couple of weeks ago."

"Um ... yeah, sure, I remember."

"I apologize for calling you this late. I hope I didn't wake you."

"No, I was reading."

"Fine. Let me explain the situation. We have strong reason to believe that one of the fugitives we're looking for does work out at Fairview. And we think he may try to leave the country, so we want to pick him up as quickly as we can. I'm hoping you can help me find him."

"Anything I can do," Paul said. *Oh, man!*

"Great. Now here's the problem. We need to know if the suspect is at work. I was hoping you'd have a way to get that information without arousing suspicion. He can't know we're asking. If I started making calls, it might leak out."

"Yeah, okay," Paul said, trying to put his surprised mind to work. "You know most folks are off until Monday," he said. "It's just the shift crews out there right now."

"Yes, I understand. The suspect is a shift worker." There was a pause. "His name is John Donner. He's a control room operator."

Whoa! "I know him." Paul tried to think of a way to see if

Donner was on shift. *Concentrate. How?* "I could phone the control room," he said, "but then he would know someone is asking for him."

"You're right, that wouldn't be any good. It's got to be more subtle."

Paul kept thinking. *Why would I want to call the control room at one o'clock Sunday morning and ask who's there? What would make me do that? Because. . .* an idea began to form. "I think I might know how to do it," Paul said. "I've got an excuse to get them to read me the work schedules for the next few days. I'll listen for Donner's name."

"You can do that now?"

"Sure, right now. I'll sound like an idiot to the guys in the control room, but it won't be the first time."

At his desk in the shift supervisor's office, Wendell fiddled with his shirt collar as he scanned a new procedure. Darrel Fleck was in the main control room speaking with the operators. The phone rang.

"Control. Auterman."

"Yeah, Wendell, this is Paul Hendricks from Tech Engineering. I know this is a really strange time and everything, but I need some information from you. Have you got a minute?"

At one-thirty in the morning? Is he drunk? "Yo, what do you need?"

"Well, I was gonna wait till tomorrow to call, but this is driving me nuts," Paul said. "I just remembered I've got a report due on Monday, and I'm not close to being done. I really need to interview some operators to get it finished up. I was hoping you could tell me who's on shift and who'll be in tomorrow. Maybe I can get lucky."

Wendell had fought enough deadlines to understand the engineer's problem. And Hendricks sounded fairly normal. "Anyone in particular you're looking for?" he asked.

"Oh, there's about eight guys I could talk to in various combinations. It'd probably be quicker if you just read me the list."

"All right." Wendell retrieved the scheduling book. "Let's see..."

****

Time: 1:27 am.

The objects floating in the basement varied in shape: some were round pillows, others fluffy hearts; but all were metallic. A cartoon face grinned above his head as Vitaly gathered together seven of the balloons into a lumpy sphere. Now for the tail. He attached more balloons in a column, and then tied a crowbar wrapped with string to the lower end. Carefully, he guided the silvery object up the stairs, out the kitchen door, and into the garage. Shoving the floating mass into the back seat of his car, he covered it with a blanket.

Vitaly gave the contents of the trunk a final check. The fiberglass fishing pole was there, along with the canteen and the lifeless body of the cat in its harness. He leaned in and disconnected the trunk light.

Satisfied that all was ready, Vitaly tried to relax, strolling out onto his deck. His back yard was not large, a fact accentuated by the tall wooden fences on each side. The grass sloped down to barbed wire at the rear, beyond which lay a thin strip of field and then a patch of woods. The weather this early Sunday morning was pleasant, and he would need nothing more than the black leather jacket he was already wearing. He looked up at the solitary maple tree a few yards beyond the deck. Its leaves barely fluttered. *Perfect.*

****

Time: 1:35 am.

At her desk in the squad room, Liz tried to form a mental picture of John Donner. It was hard to do. The records could only tell a small part of the story, and there was no photograph or even a good physical description. The phone rang. "FBI. Rezhnitsky."

"Yes, this is Paul Hendricks. I've got what you wanted. John Donner is not on shift right now, and he won't be for a couple of days."

Liz sighed with relief. "That's tremendous, Paul. Thanks."

"Nobody should have any idea who I was looking for," Paul went on, "and I got something else for you too. John Donner was on the three-to-eleven shift tonight. I didn't ask about it, but the guy I talked to said he was pretty sick when he left."

"So he went home?"

"That would make sense."

"Yes, it would," Liz said, her mind already racing ahead to the arrest. "Thanks, Paul. You've helped a lot. That's what I needed." *Now we just pick him up.* Liz set the scene in her mind, but Donner's face wasn't clear. *Bad description, no picture . . .*

"If there's anything else I can do," Paul said.

He knows Donner. It would help. "Yes, Paul, there is something else. It's a big favor, but it would simplify things."

"Sure. What?"

"Well, I've never seen John Donner," Liz said, "and I don't have a picture. If we pick him up, it would make things easier if we had someone there to make a positive ID. Can you do that in a few hours? I think you said you knew him."

Liz had just finished speaking with Walt Kreveski again when the overnight clerk handed her another message. She read the teletype:

"... The Nuclear Regulatory Commission will provide assistance as necessary if apprehension at a nuclear facility is to occur or if information is required regarding a suspect's whereabouts at the facility. Immediate assistance can be obtained from the NRC Operations Support center listed below. A liaison office between the Agency and NRC security personnel is being established at this time ... "

Liz put the message aside. *I don't think we'll need their help for the moment.* She would let the S.A.C. figure out how to deal with the NRC. In the meantime, she had an illegal to catch.

****

Time: 1:47 am.

Taylor Winn rubbed his blurry eyes as he pulled up to the deserted intersection. The FBI special agent had been asleep when his partner's call had come. Winn had quickly dressed and kissed his wife goodbye, and then shoved two cans of soda and a bag of cookies into the deep pockets of his overcoat before heading out the door. Now he was well on his way across town to John Donner's house. Overhead, the light changed to green.

Dressed in his leather jacket, blue jeans, and dark cap, Vitaly reviewed the checklist one last time, then held the paper over the sink and set it aflame. He stepped into the garage, shut off the overhead lights, and climbed inside his car. The garage door slid open and Vitaly nudged the vehicle into the driveway and then let it coast to the bottom of the street before he turned on his headlights and sped away.

A mixture of suburban homes and farm fields bordered the road where Winn drove along the southern edge of South Bend. There had been no traffic to speak of -- just one oncoming car a few moments before -- and with the turnoff to the suspect's address up ahead, Winn flipped his headlights over to bright to read the street signs. Spotting the road, the FBI special agent turned and cruised up the slight incline. Near the top of the hill, he spotted Donner's home off to the left. Illuminated in the glow of a street lamp, it was a small, single-story white house, with an attached garage. Two steps led up to the landing outside the front door. There were no lights on inside. Winn cut the ignition and let the car drift back down the hill a short distance before he pulled alongside the curb across the street.

****

Time: 2:07 am.

Liz felt a sense of relief that she was finally headed north on the two hour drive to South Bend. Still in her sweatshirt and jeans, her gun in the handbag on the seat of the Bureau car, she ran through her preparations one more time. She had set up a rendezvous with Walt Kreveski and Paul Hendricks, telecopied the appropriate papers to South Bend, informed the S.A.C. of her plans, and sent a brief message to Washington. Everything was ready. All that was left to do was to capture the suspect.

John Donner. An illegal. Her background search suggested Donner had been in the U.S. for at least nine years. *Nine years.* Such a very long time. Did he have a family back there? Someone who misses him? He was a highly trained individual: a licensed operator in a nuclear power plant. His records indicated he was conscientious

190

about his work and well thought of by his superiors. Yet all that was only a masquerade, a disposable part of his life that he would someday shrug off. Who was he, really? And what had he been up to all these years? Special Agent Liz Rezhnitsky pressed a little harder on the accelerator. *With a little luck, I can ask him myself.*

****

Time: 2:28 a.m.

Vitaly made a right turn and drove on through the farm fields a few miles east of Fairview. He tuned his car radio to a strong AM station. Country music filled the speakers.

The round white barn came into view and Vitaly let his car drift by the darkened farmhouse. Soon, as trees on either side gave way to open fields, static began to fill the speakers. Vitaly took note of the landmarks: a bent fence post, an asphalt repair along the road's edge, a slip of paper stuck in the high grass. The static crescendoed, then faded back to music. He turned off the radio. There were trees beside the road again. *There.* Vitaly spotted the small gap. He stopped, then backed up into the undergrowth.

With the car idling in the darkness, Vitaly stepped well beyond the vehicle and listened. Except for a dog barking in the distance, the night was silent. Returning, he worked quickly, using his flashlight only for brief glimpses. Inserting an earphone, he clipped a small radio to his belt, put on a black motorcycle helmet and flipped up the visor, then grabbed a pair of thick, electrically insulated gloves and pushed his hands inside. The balloons were next. Vitaly took hold of the attached crowbar and carefully maneuvered the light, bulky mass out of the back seat. He let it rise in the air just above him as he gauged the direction of the breeze. *Now do it.* He crept to the road, the balloons in tow. Vitaly listened for oncoming traffic, but there was nothing. He waited a few seconds more to be sure, and then, in a low, crouching run, he moved off into the nearby field.

****

Time: 2:34 am.

Wendell stretched in his chair. It was another slow night on backshift. And sleep had been harder to come by the last few weeks. He and Karen seemed to be arguing more now. She had dreamed of a lawyer's life in the big city, handling tough cases in the financial and corporate worlds -- or at least by this point watching how it was done. The work for Hoosier Electric wasn't as exciting as she would like, and while Wendell worked his way up the ladder, she was growing more and more restless. Wendell had never thought they could grow apart, but perhaps that was happening. Or maybe it was just another rough patch. His odd hours didn't help, but the experience on shift could allow him to move into a higher management slot. And it was interesting. They would work something out. The love was still there -- he was sure of it.

Seeking a break from his thoughts, Wendell opened the glass door, crossed to the front of the control room, and slowly paced the length of the curving panels. Behind him, the two control room operators were seated at a table, casually monitoring the panels as they discussed a fishing trip. The only thing out of the ordinary this evening had been the call from Hendricks about the weekend shift schedule.

Wendell stopped for a moment at the center panel with the full core display above -- the circle of lights entirely red, showing the control rods were fully withdrawn. A check of the meters below found reactor vessel level and pressure were normal, and power sat at

100%. Fairview Station was currently supplying 580 million watts of electric energy to the grid.

"Wendell, they're gonna have the #2 diesel back on Tuesday, right?" The question was asked by Larry, the chief operator, an angular bald man with a bushy mustache.

Wendell turned. "That's what they tell us. Monday night or Tuesday. No problems so far."

"Control!" The operator's table held the plant radio, and a voice had just crackled over the loudspeaker.

The man seated beside the radio, the assistant operator, picked up the microphone. "Control."

"Yeah, DeMira here. Just letting you know I'm heading over to the air compressor building." The turbine building operator was checking in with his walkie-talkie.

Wendell turned back to the main panels. On the wall to the right of the core display, crimson lights showed that all the valves carrying feedwater and steam to and from the reactor vessel were wide open. Every minute, 14,000 gallons of water were pouring into the bottom of the huge steel capsule, passing up through the hot fuel bundles and being heated to a gas, and then sent on to the main turbine and generator. At the far end of the controls, Wendell finished his tour beside the shift technical advisor's desk. "Yo, Tom," he said to the young engineer, who was reading. "Anything interesting?"

"For once," the STA said. "Chernobyl. Man, they really screwed up."

"Sounds like it," Wendell said. "Drop that on my desk when you're done, okay?"

At the back of the room, a thick door closed with a thud, and Wendell saw through the glass that Zabowski, the reactor building operator, had returned from rounds. Fleck got up from his desk and began reviewing the results, the heavyset supervisor nodding as his man in the field explained an item. Wendell walked back to the office door and stepped inside. "Something up?"

"Well, there's a drywell cooling valve drippin' a little," Fleck answered without concern. The air in the drywell was heated by the hot reactor vessel and required constant chilling. "We'll have Leeman's boys look at it Monday. Soon enough."

"You want me to write up the work request?" Wendell asked.

"Yeah, sure," Darrel said. "I hate paperwork."

"I know," Wendell said, a freckled smile forming beneath his copper hair. *I know.*

****

Time: 2:38 am.

Vitaly moved at an even pace across the darkened pasture, the cluster of balloons trailing in the sky behind him. After thirty paces, he stopped and peered into the night. He could just make out the transmission tower that lay ahead. Ninety feet up from its base was the lowest of the three electric lines. A few more steps and the metal framework of the tower was clearly in view. Vitaly knelt and pulled in the silvery balloons. He watched the floating mass sway. *Light breeze.*

When Dr. Berdyayev had first suggested the balloon idea, Vitaly had recognized its advantages. The metal-coated decorations had proven troublesome to utilities, frequently drifting into power lines with damaging results. Now, above him, high tension wires stretched across the field on their way to Fairview Station, where they served as a backup source of three-phase power for the plant. If any of the lines gave out, the rest would be useless. Vitaly studied the tower against the backdrop of stars. The three wires were suspended, one above the other, along the side of the structure. *There. Right there.* In the gloom he had spotted his target: a column of dish-shaped, porcelain insulators that hung down from a crossbeam and held the center line aloft. If that connection were broken, the line would drop and ground itself on the tower or the wire just below.

There was a puff of wind, and Vitaly felt a tug from the balloons overhead. The shiny formation stretched nearly eight feet in height from the top of its rounded cluster to the tip of its tail, each balloon filled with an explosive mix of gasses. If the metallic mass touched both the metal crossbeam and the center power line below, there would be a short circuit. The brief surge of power and detonation of the balloons would then allow the center line to drop free of the insulator column and fall onto the lower line.

Still kneeling, Vitaly fed out the string, letting the balloon-kite rise until its tail was two stories above him. He gauged the breeze, then stood, and keeping his eyes on the column of insulators, he stepped back upwind a few paces, away from the tower. He had practiced this maneuver only once before, in Moscow. It hadn't been difficult.

Vitaly took a deep breath and tried to ignore the adrenaline surging through his system. *Careful now.* Slowly, he uncoiled more string and the balloons rose higher in the darkened sky. He came to a knot in the string and, peering back at the tower, decided he was far enough from it to make the final adjustments. He kept unwinding, twisting off the string with his thick glove. A second knot appeared. Then a third. On a perfectly calm day, the middle of the balloon formation would now be even with the center power line, and the top of the metallic sphere would be the same height as the crossbeam holding the insulators. Vitaly unwound a little more string to compensate for the angle of the floating mass in the wind, then glanced back and forth between the tower and the balloons. *Looks even.*

Reaching down, Vitaly fumbled with the radio on his belt, and static began to roar in his ear. He edged closer to the tower, the balloons overhead. When they were a few feet from the lines, he stopped again. The height was correct. It would work. He slid down the clear visor of his helmet.

Ready . . . Go! Vitaly took two steps forward, his eyes fixed upward. The balloons drifted closer to the center power line and the insulator column that held it in place. Closer still. From his angle of sight, it seemed to Vitaly the balloons were already touching the wire. *That's it . . .*

CRACKKKKK! A searing blue flash lit up the night, followed instantly by a fireball, twenty feet in diameter, extending out from the tower.

Yes! In the first fraction of a second after the explosion Vitaly thought he saw the center line fall free. Shards of porcelain showered down around him as music began flooding into his ear. He turned and ran towards his car.

Only after he had reached the woods, fighting for breath, did Vitaly peer back. In the darkness, a few small spots of burning material lay near the tower. *Got it!* Jumping into his idling car, he jerked the vehicle into gear. *Move!* Vitaly pulled onto the road in the direction he had come and flipped on the headlights and the radio. Music filled the speakers. He tapped once on the accelerator, then slowed when a landmark appeared beside the road. *About here.* The music from the speakers remained clear. Leaning forward, Vitaly gazed up to the sky through the windshield. It was too dark to see, but he knew that somewhere overhead a group of deadened power lines were no longer supplying energy to Fairview Station. *One down, one to go.*

****

Time: 2:42 am.

Wendell finished up some paperwork and gazed into the control room. The assistant operator, a chunky figure with tousled brown hair and silver-rimmed glasses, was checking a panel, while at the table a few feet away, the chief operator chatted with Fleck. In the corner, the STA was still reading.

An annunciator alarm cut the quiet and everyone looked up to the blinking, lighted rectangles on the wall. *Two at once. Something's up.* Wendell stepped inside just as the assistant operator read off the alarms:

"Loss of Backup Offsite Power. Backup Transformer Low Voltage."

"Well, well," Fleck murmured, as he and the chief operator rose. "Anything else from the transformer?"

The assistant operator scanned the dials. "Nothing I can see. We'll get DeMira to check the local readings," he said, referring to the operator on rounds in the turbine building.

"I'll call Load Dispatch," Wendell said. The backup supply for offsite power came from lines running east of the plant. If they had gone down, the dispatcher in South Bend would be able to tell. Otherwise, it was a problem at the plant. Although it needed to be dealt with promptly, the loss of the backup supply wasn't a critical concern. Fairview Station still had its primary offsite power source for the plant's safety systems -- a set of lines from the huge towers three miles west of the site. And there was one emergency diesel generator in reserve, as well as the batteries for STurDI-1, STurDI-2, and the control room instruments.

"L.D. said the lines went down a few miles from here," Wendell soon reported to Fleck.

Fleck chewed his gum for a moment, then looked to the chief operator, now in radio contact with the man in the turbine building.

"Larry, just in case, have DeMira go and check everything out. Never hurts."

****

Time: 2:44 a.m.

The radio provided a steel guitar background as Vitaly sped through the countryside. To the east was the well-lit exterior of Fairview Station. The next intersection appeared. Two hundred yards and he would go under the lines. Another fifty and he would park. He touched the brakes, and as the music disappeared in a haze, he caught sight of his final target. Sixty yards back from the road was a substation; a light illuminating its fenced-in area. Letting the car drift on, Vitaly searched for the tractor path. A song reappeared from the static, and then two ruts came into view at the edge of a woods. *There.*

His helmet back on, the insulated gloves in his pocket, Vitaly laid his beaming flashlight in the trunk. He opened the canteen resting inside the spare tire, drenched the lifeless body of the cat, then lifted the carcass, along with the collapsible fiberglass fishing pole beside it. The rod was joined to the dead animal by a few feet of cord; one end wrapped around the cat's neck and shoulders in a makeshift harness. Clutching the objects, Vitaly stole out across the field.

Gravel crunched under his feet as he crept along the chain-link fence of the humming substation until he reached the cement-block shed in the far corner. A service light glowed above the door. Behind the building, shielded from the road, Vitaly knelt on the sharp stones. His heart pounding, he laid down the soggy cat and then extended the fishing rod to its full length. Now, wearing his thick gloves, he grabbed the pole and rose, jerking the cat into the air.

Vitaly slid one hand up the rod to counterbalance the cat, then stepped around the building. Just over the fence was a large transformer; columns of stacked, porcelain insulators jutting from its top like spines. That was the feed. Primary Offsite Power. Thanks to the energy flowing through the device before him, Fairview Station was still supplied with an independent power source for its safety systems.

Vitaly peered toward the road. There was no traffic. *Perfect.* He flipped the helmet visor down and shifted his feet for balance, then slowly swung the carcass of the cat over the fence and maneuvered the wet object toward the top of the transformer. Drawing close to the target, Vitally stepped sideways to shield himself with the edge of the block building, awkwardly extending his arms around the corner. *A little more . . . good . . . good . . .*

The lifeless cat now hovered a foot above the insulator columns on the transformer. In the shadowy light, Vitaly eyed the animal's position and shifted the carcass to the left. Then he braced himself, and carefully lowered the cat still further.

Right there . . .   Right there. . .

NOW! Vitaly let the carcass plunge onto the transformer as he tucked his head behind the wall.

SNAP--CRACK! !

An explosion shattered the night as the short circuit burst the insulators into fragments. Vitaly felt shrapnel smack into his gloves as the area went dark, the service light broken by porcelain debris. He yanked the fishing pole back, the cord holding the cat having burned away, and let the rod collapse into itself as he began sprinting for the car. He looked back once, but there was nothing to see in the darkness, and soon he was driving away from the scene. A flood of relief, of completion, washed over him. *That's all. It's over now.*

But, he knew, for Fairview Station a nightmare had just begun.

May 11, 1986
Time: 2:51:12 am.

Reactor Water Level (above Fuel): *192 inches* (normal)
Reactor Pressure: *1000 pounds per square inch* (normal)
Drywell Pressure: *1.1 pounds per square inch* (normal)
Drywell Temperature (Air): *120 degrees Fahrenheit* (normal)
Torus Pressure: *0.8 pounds per square inch* (normal)
Torus Temperature: *84 degrees Fahrenheit* (normal)

Electric Power Systems:

Offsite Power Line (normal source)*:*   *Operable*
Backup Offsite Power Line: *Down*
Emergency Diesel Generator #1:   *Operable*
Emergency Diesel Generator #2:   *Under Repair*
Batteries: *Operable*

Water and Safety Systems:

Electric-Powered:

   Feedwater : *Operable*
   VEPI: *Operable*
   Fuel Spray: *Operable*

Steam / Battery-Powered:

   STURDI-1: *Operable*
   STURDI 1: *Operable*

Compressed Air and Battery Powered:

   EmShut: *Operable*

Wendell finished up the log entry regarding the loss of the backup offsite power supply, while through the glass he could hear Fleck describing his new car to the two men at the operator's table.

Darkness.

The control room exploded with alarms, the walls lit with blinking rectangles as horns began to blare. Wendell jumped up. *What.....?*

"Reactor scram!" the chief operator announced.

"No offsite power! I'm covering diesels!" the assistant operator said.

"Main steam valves have closed," Fleck said. He remained beside the table. "The vessel is isolated. We've lifted a relief."

Wendell ran into the control room and headed for the center panel. *Loss of offsite power: steam lines fail shut -- feedwater pump dies -- you get a diesel start.*

"All rods full in!" the chief operator announced as Wendell came up alongside. On the wall above, the circular control rod display had changed from red to green.

"No diesel start!" the assistant operator shouted from a panel on the left. "No diesel start! Trying manual!"

Shit! Wendell began scanning the center panel. *Where we at? What's level?* It was difficult to see in the faint emergency lighting. Alarms continued to blare.

"No manual start!" the assistant operator said. "No diesel start on manual! Damn!"

There. "Level at 1-5-6 inches!" Wendell said.

Fleck pointed at the chief operator. "Larry, get STurDI-1 running."

"STurDI-1!" the operator replied, as he began manipulating controls.

"Reactor pressure 920, falling," Wendell reported. "Torus temp nearing 90 .... rising." Excess steam was being diverted into the huge torus tank by a pressure relief valve.

"Tried manual again, no diesel start!" the assistant operator said. "No bad readings, but no R.P.M.!"

Come on, we gotta have that diesel.

Fleck grabbed the radio mike off the table. "DeMira! Get to the #1 diesel on the double!" he said to the turbine building operator on rounds. "Start it locally! Acknowledge!"

"Roger, on my way!" the speaker crackled.

"Zabowski!" Fleck said next, addressing the reactor building operator in the plant. "Diesel! Go help DeMira!"

"Roger!"

"Level at 152!" Wendell said. "Creeping down!"

"Starting STurDI-1!" the chief operator shouted over the alarms.

"Drywell air at 175 degrees, mid-level," Wendell reported. *Not so good.* He turned off an alarm.

The assistant operator cut the annunciator horn at his station as well, and, abruptly, the control room was quiet.

Wendell's rapid breathing punctuated the stillness. He watched the water level indicator for the reactor vessel. *STurDI-1 should be kicking in...*

A new alarm began blaring.

"STurDI failed to start!" the chief operator said. "Startup oil pump shut off early!"

"STurDI-2," Fleck ordered.

"Trying STurDI-2!" the chief operator repeated. "Lining up."

"P.R.V. has closed, pressure rising again," Wendell announced. "Level's down to ... 147." *STurDI-2 better work, or we're screwed.* The small turbine-pump was now the only way to put water into the reactor vessel.

"Starting STurDI-2!"

Come on, come on...

"STurDI-2 no start!" the chief operator yelled frantically. "Trying again! ... No start! Nothing!" He smacked his leg. "Fuck!"

Wendell grimaced. *Jesus, this can't be for real. Can't.*

At the operator's table, Fleck spoke into the radio: "Zabowski!" he ordered the reactor building operator, "skip the diesel and get down to STurDI-1! ... then 2!"

Wendell continued to watch the vital indications. "Level at 145, slow decline," he said. "P.R.V.'s are in pressure control mode. Auto circuit on."

Behind him, Fleck put aside the mike. "God damn, this is screwed up."

Wendell could only agree. Fairview Station was in deep trouble. They had lost all offsite electric power, and the one available diesel generator, designed to operate VEPI or Fuel Spray, was not working. Neither were the STurDI-1 and STurDI-2 systems. Slowly, the water covering the core was boiling away due to the heat remaining in the shutdown reactor -- and there was no way to replace it.

"I'm trying STurDI-1 again," the chief operator said. "Then STurDI-2."

"Good," Fleck said. Behind him the STA was now feverishly reviewing the emergency procedures.

An alarm horn sounded and was promptly quelled. "Control!" a voice now crackled on the radio.

Fleck grabbed the microphone. "Control."

"This is Zabowski." It was the operator sent to the STurDI area. "Reactor building is locked!" he reported. "Access cards don't work. I'm going over to Security to get a key."

Fleck signed off. "Damn. All the doors with card readers will be like that."

"He should have most of the keys with him," Wendell said.

"Yeah, but it's gonna fuck up a lot of other people," Fleck replied. He pushed the mike button. "Control to operators! If you unlock a door, prop it open. Repeat -- prop all locked doors open!" The supervisor laid the mike aside. "Wendell, where we at on level?"

"142."

"How fast we losing it?"

Wendell did a quick mental calculation. "Maybe … six inches a minute." As expected, the level had instantly dropped three feet from the scram when the water inside the vessel had ceased its intense bubbling. But since then, the height of the water above the core had continued to lessen due to the boiling away of steam being created by the heat still remaining in the fuel bundles.

"Starting STurDI-1!" the chief operator announced.

Wendell looked toward the controls. *Come on...*

"No go!" the chief operator reported. "Startup pump didn't even come on!"

Shit. We've gotta get some water in! The reactor vessel was sealed off from the rest of the plant, the valves on the steam lines having slammed shut when offsite power had vanished. To remove the steam still slowly building up inside the huge steel container, pressure relief valves were now periodically venting the hot gas into the torus. That automatic system was working as designed to keep pressure in the vessel at a safe level. But the crew at Fairview Station had no way to replace the steam removed by the P.R.V.s with fresh water.

"Control!" the speaker crackled. "This is DeMira." It was the turbine building operator. "I'm at the #1 diesel. Had to unlock the door. Ready to try a local start."

Fleck glanced at the assistant operator manning the diesel generator panel. "Go!" the operator said.

The senior shift supervisor stared at the floor, thinking. "Any alarms on the local panels?" Fleck asked into the mike.

"Negative on alarms," the man in the diesel room responded. "Black board. Over."

"Try local start," Fleck ordered.

"Trying local start."

A few seconds passed. Wendell bit into his lip. *Jesus, please.*

"I'm not seeing anything!" the assistant operator reported from the diesel panel. "No R.P.M.s! Nothing!"

Wendell frowned. *How?...*

"Control," the radio confirmed, "no diesel start. It didn't turn over."

"Damn," Fleck murmured. "Not that easy." He spoke into the mike. "We copy. Go to full manual override. Over."

"Roger. It's dark in here. Hang on."

Fleck released the mike. "Damn it, I should have kept Zabowski headed there to help." He looked at Wendell. "How long before the next venting?"

"Maybe a minute." The torus would soon receive more excess steam when a P.R.V. again opened.

"What's torus temp?"

"About 105. Not too bad."

"Drywell?"

"230 and still rising. Getting hot in there." *Too hot. Christ.* The drywell cooling system was without power, and heat from the reactor vessel was now raising the air temperature inside the cavity. The concrete and steel shell could withstand up to 300 degrees. Above that, it would begin to weaken.

"Control! DeMira!" the man at the diesel generator called over the radio.

Wendell looked hopefully toward the assistant operator at the diesel panel, but his face had only soured further.

"No go!" reported the voice on the speaker. "I tried three times. Air's okay, but it won't keep rolling."

"God damn," Fleck muttered. "All right, take a look around. We need that diesel." He put the microphone aside and shook his head. "We better get something working soon."

Fairview Nuclear Reactor

May 11, 1986   2:52 a.m.

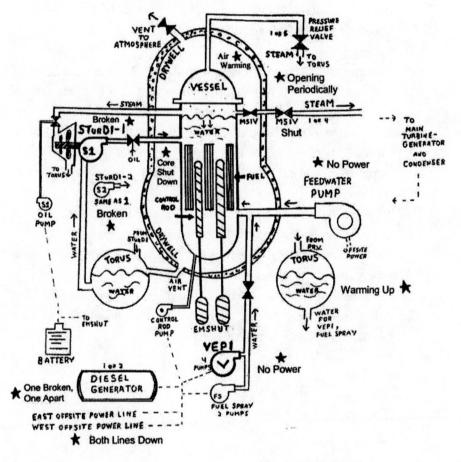

Figure 5: The Event

"Why won't it start!" the chief operator cursed beside the STurDI-2 controls. "I ran the test last week. It worked perfect!"

Wendell looked up through the glass at the outburst as he continued on the phone. They were six minutes into the event, and the load dispatcher <u>had</u> to be made to understand. "We need it bad here. Bad. Do anything you have too. Temporary fix. Re-route shit. Anything! But we need power back. Otherwise, we're gonna have a fucking mess on our hands! What?... Good. Whatever it takes. Just soon!"

Back in the control room, Wendell found the two operators still at work on the broken safety systems, while the STA stood between them at the center panel, monitoring the conditions in the vessel. An alarm went off and was quieted within seconds. In the rear of the room, Fleck was using a pocket flashlight to scan an emergency procedure. "The L.D. says our primary supply is down a few miles from here," Wendell told him, "just like the backup. They're trying to get crews on it, but it's gonna be awhile. He thought ninety minutes."

Fleck looked up, his normally placid features now hardened. "We haven't got ninety minutes."

"I told them. They got the picture." *Christ, I sounded desperate enough.*

"Darrel!" the chief operator said. "I'm gonna start checking fuses."

"Right."

The operator dropped to his knees and removed the lower door of the STurDI-1 panel. An alarm went off, and he checked the flashing annunciator, then slapped at a nearby button. The horn ceased.

"Control! DeMira!" It was the man in the diesel room.

The assistant operator stepped away from the diesel panel and picked up the radio mike. With his counterpart he began discussing what to try next to get the huge engine started.

Wendell moved to the center panel. "Tom, where we at on level?"

"122," the STA said. There was ten feet of water over the core --

six feet less than normal.

"Drywell air temp?"

"255. It's on a slow rise."

Jesus. If that keeps going up, we'll need to act. What else to check? What else could go wrong? ... A radiation leak? Could we detect it? "Rad meters?" Wendell asked

"The working ones show normal," the STA said.

"Which ones? How much coverage we got?" Only battery-powered instruments were still in operation.

"Could be worse," the STA said. "We've got drywell, torus, a few in the reactor building. We'd catch anything big, I think."

"Good."

Wendell heard the assistant operator at the radio looking for an answer. "All the racks okay?"

"Yeah," the speaker crackled. "All normal."

"Shit. There's gotta be a reason. What the hell's happening?"

Wendell frowned. *Good question.*

Wendell paced near the panels. *How do we get some power back? How do we get water in the vessel?* Neither STurDI-1 or STurDI-2 were working, and they needed the diesel generator to run VEPI or fuel spray.

"Okay, try the bypass line," the assistant operator ordered the man in the diesel room.

"Control!" A different voice came from the radio speaker.

"Control. Go ahead."

"This is Zabowski," the breathless voice said. "I just got out of STurDI-1. It's a mess! The startup oil pump broke away and spewed oil. Nothing I can do. Phone down there don't work either. And the radio won't carry till I get up the stairs."

The chief operator crawled out from working beneath the STurDI panel. "Let me talk to him."

Wendell stopped his pacing and listened. At the center panel, the STA turned, and Fleck left the procedure books on the back table and came closer. The attention of all five men in the control room was centered on the radio as the chief operator took the mike. "Zabowski, this is Larry. Broken oil line on SturDI-1?"

"Roger, right by the pump."

"Okay. Get down to STurDI-2 . It's not responding at all. Check the control box. The fuses, switches, wiring, whatever. The start signal's not getting there."

"Roger. Out."

The chief operator turned to Fleck, his face drawn tight. "Unless he finds something, we're screwed. You heard what he said about STurDI-1."

"Yeah, oil everywhere," Fleck said. He looked to the assistant operator. "The diesel? You tried all the bypasses?"

"Yep. Nothing."

"Damn," Fleck sighed. Well, keep trying. Tom," he asked the STA, "what's our level?"

"113 inches."

Wendell cringed at the number. *I've heard figures like that a hundred times in the simulator -- but this is for real.*

"Drywell temp?" Fleck said.

"260."

Wendell turned to Fleck. "Sounds like it's leveling off. It was near that a couple of minutes ago."

"It's not screaming up like it was," the STA agreed.

"Control!" the radio speaker blared yet again. The assistant operator took the call, which came from the diesel room.

Wendell and Fleck conferred. "I'll hit the Emergency Procedures and figure out the Action Level," Wendell said.

"Yeah," Fleck nodded. "Probably a Site Emergency. Call out the troops. And I'll talk to Borden."

Wendell headed for the office as Fleck addressed the STA: "Tom, get Leeman on the phone. Tell him I want some people out here right now. Mechanics, electricians, I & C, the works. Then get Cervantes."

At his desk, Wendell flipped through the thick binder to the Emergency Action Levels. *Loss of power...* In the faint glow he could barely read, and he opened a drawer and pulled out a flashlight.

Fleck came in and grabbed a phone as he sat down. He began dialing a number taped to the wall.

Loss of power...there. Wendell began reviewing the criteria.

"Steve?" Fleck said into the phone.

Wendell kept reading while trying to listen as his partner explained the situation to the plant manager.

"Steve, this is Darrel Fleck. We have a major problem here. We've got a station blackout with no makeup to the vessel." Fleck listened a moment. "Yes, that's right, a loss of offsite power. Lines down, I guess. We scrammed okay on that, but then the #1 diesel failed to start, and we couldn't get STurDI-1 or STurDI-2 to pump. Nothing's going in the vessel." Another pause. "Below 110 by now. Our steam isolation valves closed when we lost offsite, so we're bottled up. Residual heat's just boiling down the vessel level bit by bit. We got P.R.V.'s lifting to keep us near normal pressure. The drywell air is heating up good too. It's around 260 ..... No, we've got a few rad instruments left -- nothing abnormal."

That's it. The paragraph illuminated by Wendell's flashlight left no doubt. He turned to Fleck. "Site Emergency. No choice."

"About ten minutes ago," Darrel said, in answer to another question. "Yeah ..... We just finished reviewing the Action Levels. It's a Site Emergency ...... Yeah, that's what I thought too. What? ...... We're calling Leeman right now......."

Wendell read through the list of actions the public could take for its own safety, then laid the book on Fleck's desk, shining his flashlight beam over his partner's shoulder.

"Yeah ... that's correct." Fleck ran his finger along the chart. "Okay, I've got the Protective Action matrix. Where we're at ... well, we've got no release yet ... nothing wrong with our vessel and drywell so far... we've got a little time ..." Fleck's finger stopped, and he tapped at the chart.

Wendell nodded. *Looks right.*

"I think we fit the minimum, Steve," Fleck said into the phone. "Yeah -- shelter two mile radius around the plant and five miles downwind. Animals on stored feed.....Yeah...Okay. We'll notify the authorities and have Security start calling our people in. Hopefully, Leeman's ahead of us on that... Yeah.... Oh, right.... Okay. Bye."

Fleck stood and reached for the door to the control room.

"I'll make the calls," Wendell said. He began dialing. It was time to let the authorities know what was happening at Fairview Station.

****

The radio played softly as Liz sped through northern Indiana, still an hour from South Bend. *Why now?* she kept asking herself. Why would the Soviets risk it? Something to do with Chernobyl? To take the heat off? Or was there more? The start of a war? What if Donner wasn't the only spy who would be taking active measures?

Questions you can't answer, Liz reminded herself. Tonight, the big issues were not her concern. Quietly, efficiently, she must arrest John Donner.

****

The first ring of the phone wrenched Gary from the fog of sleep, and after the second ring he fumbled for the lamp. Carol groaned and rolled away. "Hello?" Gary answered, his eyes locked in a squint.

"Gary Halvorsen?" asked a firm, familiar voice.

"Yah." Gary glanced at the clock. *3:07.*

"This is Leeman. You awake?"

"Yah, Karl." *Something broke. Crap.*

"All right," Leeman drawled. "Now lissen closely. This ain't no drill. They're having problems at the plant. Offsite power dropped away an' the diesel didn't pick up. No power. There's other shit went bad too. I need ya in thar right now. Ya understand?"

"I'll be there."

"Good. Fast as ya can. Call Tama first and tell 'im the same thing. You hurry!"

Gary pulled himself upright. He was wide awake now. *Shit, no power!* Gary punched in Doug Tama's number. The phone rang once... *Be there...* twice ... *Wake up!*

"Hello?"

Good! "Doug, this is Gary."

"Now?"

"Listen, Leeman just called. Plant's all fucked up. Diesel's out, for one. They want us now. This is no drill. Okay?"

There was a brief moan on the other end of the line. "Boy, I had a few beers ... but I'm okay. See you there."

Blue jeans and a flannel shirt from his Saturday work on the diesel lay across a chair, and Gary was ramming his legs into his pants when Carol rolled over.

"What are you doing?"

"Trouble at the plant. Power problems, I guess." Gary latched his belt. "I gotta go in."

Carol propped herself on one elbow. "Shoot. They down?"

"Karl didn't say," Gary buttoned the shirt across his wide chest. "Probably. He just told me to call Doug and get the hell out there."

Carol sighed. "Fine. I wish they wouldn't always call you, but go fix it, I guess." She fell back amid the blankets. "Let me know when you think you'll be home."

"Yes, Miss Carol-l-l," Gary said.

****

"Yes, thank you." Wendell hung up, his first call completed. He had awakened the Civil Defense director for Potowatomie County, explained the situation, and provided the plant's recommendations for actions the public could take. The director would make the final decision. After an initial curse, he had been all business: "How much radiation could you release? How much time before it really goes to hell?" To the first question, Wendell had no answer. To the second he could only hazard a guess -- within the next ninety minutes if nothing was fixed. It had already been twenty minutes since offsite power was lost.

Before his next call, the junior shift supervisor stared through the glass into the darkened control room. The STA was still at the center panel, the chief operator was working at the STurDI controls, and Fleck was busy on the radio. Wendell assumed his partner was talking to the two men now at the diesel. Fleck had dispatched the assistant operator from the control room to help.

Wendell punched in the next number. He would tell Fairview's town policeman to expect a call from the C.D. director. The 300 people in the nearby community would probably be advised to take shelter and stay indoors. Since it was only three a.m., that shouldn't prove much of a problem. *Even the farmers aren't up yet.*

****

Vitaly continued home via the back roads, his sense of accomplishment growing with each mile. He had done his duty. He had struck back. After all these years in enemy territory, he had struck back! Only briefly was his elation tempered when he thought of the men in the control room. It was Fleck's crew tonight. *They're good*. He would not want to be in their shoes, but he had no regrets. This was a battle his country must win.

"Roger. 41 out."

The voice on the scanner was distant and full of static. Vitaly had yet to hear anything from the County Police about the plant.

". . . units!   All units.   We have a report of a Site Emergency at Fairview. Repeat: Site Emergency at the Fairview Nuclear Plant.   You are to head towards Fairview and await instructions. 10-25 to Fairview and standby. 10-12. Dispatch out."

Yes! Vitaly slapped the steering wheel. *YES!* The plant was definitely in trouble. The only question now was how bad it would get. Letting his car coast through a lonely intersection, Vitaly already knew the answer. *Bad enough.*

Time: 3:19 am.
Time from Start of Event: 28 minutes
Reactor Water Level (above Fuel): 53 inches

As the light turned to red, Joel Wermager brought his police car to a halt at Brixton's busiest intersection. There was no traffic at the mini-mart, so Joel drove ahead through the four blocks of the business district. It was early on a Sunday morning, and the town of 18,000 was quiet.

At another light, the policeman stretched his tall, spare frame. In three hours he could head home, have some breakfast, and then crawl into bed beside his wife for a little sleep.

"All cars," the radio blurted out. "10-12. Standby."

Probably a fight.

> "All cars. Be advised there is a 10-33 at Fairview Station. A Site Area Emergency has been declared. Civil Defense is requesting public shelter to five miles downwind. No recommendation yet for Brixton. Return to station for your emergency packets. All cars. Acknowledge."

Joel stared at the radio. *Fairview Station. The nuke plant.* Was there an accident? Another Three Mile Island? He hadn't been back long from his army tour when that had happened. *And then there's Chernobyl...*

"Dispatch, Unit 9," the radio broke in as another car responded. "Is this one of their drills?"

Good question. Say yes.

"Negative, Unit 9. This is not a drill. Repeat: not a drill. Report to station. Out."

****

Wendell perched on his desk. The event was thirty minutes old now, and his initial rush of adrenaline had been replaced by a steady flow of nervous energy. He watched through the glass as Fleck paced in front of the long, curving panels, while the chief operator wiped the sweat from his bare scalp with a handkerchief as he manned the radio. Off to one side, the STA was punching numbers into a calculator. Nothing new had occurred, but that in itself made the situation worse. There was still water covering the reactor core, but it was slowly boiling away. Once the fuel was uncovered, it would be less than an hour before the uranium-filled rods began breaking apart.

"Fairview, are you still there?"

"Yes," Wendell replied into the red phone balanced on his shoulder. He was speaking with the NRC crisis center in Bethesda.

"Very good. Any change?"

"No. Same as before." Wendell had already provided the story. Now the NRC wanted to stay in continuous contact.

"Very good. We'll have supervision on the line shortly."

"Right." Wendell waited impatiently, scanning procedures with his flashlight. *If we keep heading downhill we might have to go to a General Emergency.* He shuddered. *But we've still got some time...* Apart from the level of water over the core, air temperature in the drywell was the other concern. The steel reactor vessel was holding a mixture of fluid and steam percolating at 550 degrees Fahrenheit, and nestled within the drywell shell, the huge tank was slowly heating up the air around it. The drywell's cooling system would be out of service until power was restored, and the air temperature inside had now reached 270 degrees. If it got above 300 for very long, the intense heat could cause the hollow structure of concrete and steel to weaken and then crack open or collapse. Such a failure would be catastrophic. There was an alternative: some of the hot gas could be vented off into the atmosphere, but that was not a step to be taken lightly. The air might be radioactive.

Wendell heard a click in the phone. "Fairview, what is your reactor vessel level?" a different voice asked.

"We were just under 60 inches a few minutes ago," Wendell said. "Dropping slowly."

"Any values more current? How fast is level dropping?"

"I'm not close enough to see," Wendell said. "If you'll hold, I'll find out."

"We'd prefer you to stay in continuous contact."

"My sitting here, not knowing the answer, isn't going to do much good!" Wendell snapped. *Jesus!* He sighed. "Look, until we get more people, I can't hang on every second. Do you want the current readings?"

"Yes."

"Very well. Just a minute." Wendell let the receiver fall hard against the desktop as he headed into the control room.

Fleck and the STA were now talking by the center panel. The STA swallowed hard. "I've averaged out the level drop," he said, "and we're losing three inches a minute."

"Where does that put us for uncovering the core?"

"It'll slow down some, but I'd say 3:35, maybe 3:40."

Fleck looked at the clock. "Under twenty minutes."

Christ! That fast? Wendell came up alongside. "How about drywell temperature?"

"Best guess is we'll hit 300 degrees a little before 4:30." the STA said.

"Too soon," Fleck said. His arms folded across his chest, he stared at the center panel. His jaw worked hard on his gum, and the dim light revealed a line of sweat down his back. "Okay, Tom," he finally said to the STA. "Next job. Get a walkie-talkie, and go to the front door. Catch people as they come in and brief them. Until Leeman gets here, here's what I want ..." The shift supervisor paused: "...First thing: I need an I & C tech down in STurDI-2."

The STA nodded. "STurDI-2 first."

"Yeah. Somewhere there's an open circuit, and we've gotta get that turbine rolling. Then I need an I & C or electrician down at the diesel. Once Leeman gets here, give him your radio and then come

217

on back."

"Got it." The STA turned to leave.

"Hey," Fleck added, "and prop the God damn door open as you leave. Get us some air. It's too damn hot."

Wendell glanced at the nearby level indicator. *Forty-seven inches.* Just four feet of water now lay above the fuel. Without a solution at hand, they might have to raise the warning level to the public. He looked back at Fleck. "I checked the criteria again. We're sneaking up on a General Emergency."

"Yeah, maybe. Kind of stupid, though. Everything's intact. No releases. For a General, you start evacuating around the plant." With all the barriers still in place, both men knew that even the melting of some fuel would not lead to a large radiation release.

"Jesus," Wendell said. His job was to keep any fuel damage from happening. "If we don't get this under control soon-"

"We're screwed, I know."

****

Get there! The lines on the highway sped by as Steve's mind raced ahead to Fairview. A station blackout left no electric power except the batteries, and with the STurDI pumps gone, there was no way to put water back in the vessel. Then there was the public. Emergency Action Levels. *If we don't get this under control, they'll start evacuating...*

At last, he turned off the highway and pulled his car onto the Fairview access road. He spotted Karl Leeman's rusted truck up ahead. *Good.* The two came to a jarring stop beside the darkened front entrance.

"Karl! What do you know?" Steve asked as he jumped out.

The maintenance supervisor recounted his phone call as the two hurried towards the entrance. Another car sped into the lot behind them.

At the door, a figure waited in the darkness. "Who is it?"

"Borden and Leeman," Steve said.

"Great," the STA said. "Shift sup's got me down here directing traffic."

"Where we at?" Steve asked.

"No offsite power, the diesel and STurDI-2 didn't move, and STurDI-1 blew an oil line. So far, I've sent an electrician to the diesel, and an insty tech to STurDI-2. Sharpley and Crayvick. Nobody down at STurDI-1 yet."

"Jeez," a voice said from behind. Steve glanced around. It was Crutch Pegariek, from Tech Engineering. The plant manager turned back to the STA. "What's the status of the reactor?"

"Shutdown and bottled up. Losing about three inches a minute to boil off, then blowing that to the torus. Level must be down to plus-forty by now."

"Understood." The story was not getting any better. *What first? Power? STurDI-2? Got somebody at each. STurDI-1 sounds messed up...* Steve glanced over at Leeman. *He knows the diesels. If we can get power back....* "Karl, start with the diesel. Anything it takes."

"Yessir," Karl nodded. Behind him, another vehicle pulled into the lot.

Good, more help. So what now? Get the control room some help too. Steve turned to the STA. "Tom, you brief Crutch and then head back to control." He looked over his shoulder. "Crutch, run things out here until we get set up in the emergency center."

Crutch nodded. "Right."

"Diesel didn't roll. Give me I & C an' electricians," Leeman said. "And run a mechanic by STurDI-1. If he can't fix it, send 'em my way too."

****

Taylor Winn used his flashlight to check his watch. 3:26 a.m. He had been on stakeout duty across from Donner's house for ninety minutes. The suspect was either asleep or not at home. Restless, the FBI agent turned off the radio, pulled a cookie from his coat pocket, and nibbled as he flipped on the police scanner. There was silence, and then a South Bend unit reported they were coming back to the station.

More silence.

"Dispatch," the scanner broke in, "Unit 249. Any more on Fairview?"

****

The last of his equipment now in the muck below the isolated country bridge, Vitaly headed on towards South Bend. The scanner was busier now with Fairview activities, and the public living downwind was being asked to take shelter. And the plant itself? *Water level will be getting low -- unless something's fixed.* Vitaly dismissed the thought. He had thought of every contingency -- and how Fairview Station was coping didn't matter so much anymore. People in the area had been warned that a nuclear disaster was on their doorstep. If things got worse, if there was an actual release of radiation, so much the better. But the die was already cast. Fear was now hard at work among the good citizens of Potowatomie County, Indiana.

****

220

Gary put his truck into a tight turn and headed into the parking lot. Fairview Station was dark. He had never seen that before. *Crap.* He cut the engine. A flashlight was playing across the sidewalk near the plant entrance, and he popped open the glove compartment and grabbed his own light, then jogged towards the door. The bright beam soon caught his unshaven face.

"Who we got now?"

"Gary Halvorsen."

"Mechanic, right?"

"Yah." Gary came to a stop. It was fifty degrees outside, but he was damp with sweat.

"Crutch Pegariek, Tech Engineering," the greeter said. "I'm handing out work for Leeman."

"Karl's here?"

"He's headed for the diesel already. Listen, the plant's a mess. Leeman wants a mechanic down at STurDI-1 to check out an oil leak. You're the first one here. No rules, no paperwork -- just get the damn thing running! Fast! Level's dropping. And if you can't get it fixed quick, get over to the diesel."

"Right." Gary headed inside.

****

The radio station began fading away, and Liz flipped the dial until a strong new signal appeared. A jingle promptly identified the source as South Bend, and an announcement began:

> "To repeat, there appears to be a problem at the Fairview nuclear plant, eight miles northwest of Brixton."

What? Liz leaned closer.

"As of 3:25 this morning, the Potowatomie County Civil Defense began advising those persons within a two mile radius of the Fairview plant to take shelter. As soon as we hear anything more on this, we'll let you know. . . ."

A sinking feeling washed over the FBI special agent. *Too late. It's got to be him. Got to be. . .* She grimaced. *Just a few hours!*

As she drove on and the sharp edges of her anger began to wear away, Liz thought of what lay ahead. There was nothing she could do until she reached South Bend. Then she would bring the suspect in. John Donner must not escape. She switched the radio to the State Police band. *Let's see what the Troopers know.*

****

Steve entered the dim, stuffy control room through the propped-open door. *We look dead in the water.* In the supervisor's office, he spied Auterman on the phone and then spotted Fleck by the main panels.

"Goddamn it, just try it and see!" Fleck said into the microphone. "It worked for me a few years ago. Or try something better. Just keep trying!" He saw Borden and handed the mike back to the chief operator.

Steve looked closely at the shift supervisor. He appeared hot, tense, and irritated, but still in control. Darrel Fleck was not panicking. "I heard some of it from the STA," Steve said. "Where's level?" *Start off with the worst.*

"We're around plus 27 inches."

God... "How long have we got?"

"Right now, we figure on hitting top of fuel a little before 3:40."

222

Fleck glanced at his watch. "Ten minutes."

"Have you made the calls?"

"Yeah, got 'em done. Site Emergency."

"Good. So what happened?" Steve's initial shock was gone, replaced, in part, with anger. This was *his* plant. *His* plant was falling apart.

Fleck ran his hands through his sweaty blond hair. "Well, we lost backup offsite about 2:40. Around 2:50 we lost the primary. We scrammed, and the main steam lines bottled us up. But the #1 diesel didn't start, and #2's still in pieces."

"What's the load dispatcher say?"

"Another hour, maybe."

"Batteries okay?"

"As far as we know," Fleck replied. "It looks like the reactor building isolated fine too. All the vents slammed closed when we lost power."

An alarm went off and the chief operator moved to deal with it.

Fleck continued, raising his voice until the buzzer was silenced. "We tried a manual diesel start, and a local, but it won't turn over. No real clues." The tall, stocky supervisor shrugged his shoulders in frustration. "The scram took level down to 155. We tried to fire up STurDI-1 but the startup oil pump is torn loose. We tried STurDI-2. Nothing moved."

Steve listened carefully -- there wouldn't be time to go over it again. He tried not to think about what it all meant.

Fleck continued. "As far as the reactor goes, we're losing around three inches a minute to boil-off. And drywell temps at 280 and still creeping up. No cooling in there."

"Understood," Steve said. "Where we at on repairs? The STA said we have maintenance at STurDI-2 and the diesel."

"They're headed there, yeah. And we'll have operators at both."

"Control!" the radio speaker crackled. The chief operator picked it up as Fleck and Borden moved a few feet away.

"One more HP has come in so far," Fleck continued, "and we got another operator and shift sup. on their way. Leeman just got on site, too."

"I talked to him outside," Steve said. "What do we need first?"

Fleck crossed his thick arms. "Well, I'd go after STurDI-2 and the diesel. Both look electrical." He worked his gum. "And we're gonna have to start thinking about venting the drywell. It's getting hot in there."

God, we don't need that -- opening up primary containment. "How long before we hit three hundred degrees?"

"Forty-five minutes, maybe an hour," Fleck said.

At least there's a little time there. "What are rad levels in the drywell?"

"Near normal. A little something from the steam going in the torus." The huge tank was connected to the drywell in a few locations. "I wouldn't expect high rads anyway," Fleck said. "No reason to think we've had fuel damage."

Steve nodded. As long as the reactor fuel held together, the air in the drywell and torus would remain relatively clean -- a good thing if some had to be released to the environment. *The public*, Steve reminded himself. "Where do you think we are on Action Levels?"

"Just finished checking." Fleck pointed his flashlight at an open manual nearby, and Steve leaned over to look. "You could argue we're near a General. But that usually means you're gonna dump out a hell of a cloud, and we've got no release path at all."

Steve nodded as he studied the criteria. *A General Emergency – Civil Defense would call for evacuations.*

"I don't know, Steve," Fleck said. "Everything's bottled-up. I can't see it's worth clearing out a bunch of people. More harm than good."

Steve's gaze remained on the procedure. *Unnecessary evacuation ... Uncovering the core ... Not much chance of a large escape of radioactivity at this point ... But if the fuel starts to crack and we also have to vent ... At T.M.I they were slow ... still paying for it ... Better safe than sorry.*

He decided. "Let's call it a General and get folks moving. If we get out of this with no release, I'll be happy to take the abuse for the evacuation." He looked back down at the procedure. "What's our minimum action?"

"Evacuate a two mile radius and recommend shelter to five miles downwind," Fleck said, pointing.

Steve's mind flashed ahead. *If we're evacuating ...."* Anyone on site we should get out?" he asked.

"There's nobody extra here," Fleck said. "Maybe the janitor, but he should've been sent home by now."

"Understood. Anything else I should know?"

"Well, most of the in-plant phones are down, the page is out, and none of the card readers work. We've been unlocking the doors and propping them open."

Steve nodded. "All right, Darrel. Keep at it."

"Sure." Fleck hesitated a moment, his eyes downcast. He looked back up. "Damn it, Steve," the supervisor murmured, "I never thought...."

"Neither did I."

****

The emergency lights in the reactor building lit a shadowy path for Gary as he ran toward STurDI-1. Since grabbing his film badge and dosimeter at the plant entrance he had encountered no one else. Reaching the metal-grating stairs, he hurtled down into the darkness, his flashlight pointing the way. At the bottom, the STurDI-1 door was jammed open by a pipe wrench.

Inside, one small light backlit the turbine: a hulking shape the size of a garden shed. The area stank of oil. Gary stopped at the entrance and played his flashlight across the floor, finding the surface coated with syrupy fluid. *Crap.* The oil was used to hydraulically open the valve that brought steam to the turbine from the reactor vessel.

Gary swung his light atop the low, square oil tank in front of the machine, and the beam hovered amidst the finger-sized piping above the container. *There!* Near the tank's leading edge, a line had separated at a coupling, leaving gaping ends of pipe hanging a few inches apart. With the light, Gary traced back from one of the loose ends. The pipe dropped over the front edge of the tank, and after a right angle turn and a short run above the floor, it attached to a small motor. STARTUP OIL PUMP was stenciled in white on the black device.

So, the busted line is the outlet from the startup pump. Something about the unit didn't look right either, and, careful not to slip on the greasy floor, Gary stepped closer, knelt and put his hand on the pump. He could easily rock it. The small machine, the size of a loaf of bread, was supposed to be bolted down. *Damn thing shook itself loose. Then it whipped the outlet pipe free.* And that was why the STurDI-1 turbine hadn't worked. Without the high pressure oil from the battery-powered pump, the steam inlet valve could not open. No hot gas could enter the STurDI-1 turbine to spin its shaft and provide the power needed to shove water into the reactor vessel. Gary looked at the dirty brown puddles spread out across the floor. *Lost a lot of oil.* He ran his hand along the pump's outlet pipe, and found it had bent slightly before tearing itself loose at the coupling. He played his flashlight over the rest of the thin piping. *No other leaks. Maybe this is it. How? The pump? A loose coupling? -- it doesn't matter.* The question, Gary knew, was could he fix it? Fast?

He stood. *To get the turbine running, what?....* He stared at the pump. *It blew a lot of oil. Might be out of alignment a little, but I'll bet it's still working ... New piping, some oil, bolt the pump down... No!! No! No! -- Think quick fix! Cheat a little...Maybe some tubing from the warehouse....welding.... or just tape... Need something to hold the pump down....Wait. WAIT!*

Gary's mind braked to a halt. The answer had come. But would it work? *The #2 diesel...Thing's torn apart. There's tubing ... tape...and oil too.* In his mind he heard Crutch Pegariek's words. "...get the damn thing running! Fast!" He turned toward the phone on the wall, sliding on the greased floor. Control room. *Get help.* But there was no dial tone. *Crap!* Gary slammed down the receiver and headed out the door.

****

Led by a security guard with a flashlight, Lou Tarelli entered the pitch-black emergency center in the basement of the administration building. "There's lights in the cabinet," he said, pointing, and soon a pair of battery-operated fluorescent tubes had been set up on a table.

"What happened?" a deep voice said from the doorway as Mike Langford entered the room.

****

The stereo grew quiet as the album ended, and Paul saw it was finally time to go. He had done a lot of thinking since Agent Rezhnitsky had called over two hours before. *John Donner, a drug dealer?* It was hard to believe. How had Donner made it through the background checks? And, with all the security around, why would he want to work in a nuke plant in the first place -- in operations no less, a job that took a lot of training and commitment? Paul thought back to the few times he had dealt with the man. Had there been anything odd there? Not really. John Donner was on the quiet side, but he seemed like a normal guy. Still, if the FBI said Donner was it....

Paul sorted through the cassettes atop the stereo. Loud music would keep him alert on the trip up to South Bend. Once there, he would have no trouble staying awake. Not for this.

****

"I'll get the latest," Wendell said, pulling open the glass door.

The STA gave a distracted nod. The red phone pressed to his ear, he was listening to the next question from the NRC officials in Bethesda.

Wendell headed for the center panel, detouring around two men crouched over a drawing spread out on the floor. The assistant operator had returned from the diesel and was working with another shift supervisor who had just arrived. At the operator's table, Fleck was on the radio, while the chief operator and another reinforcement were beside the STurDI panel.

The reactor level indicator now showed twelve inches of water remaining above the top of the core. *Twelve inches.* Wendell could hardly bring himself to believe it. *Jesus, we're almost uncovered.* He thought of Karen. She had been going to bed when he'd left for work. *She probably doesn't even know. The sirens would only be to five miles.* Their small house on the east edge of Brixton was nearly twice that distance from the plant. *If we could just get this under control, by the time she wakes up it'll be over.*

"Got to be a way to get water in there," Wendell heard the chief operator say, as he and his companion racked their brains.

"Hey, wait a minute," the newer man said. "Remember when they cleaned out that old oil tank last month?"

"Yeah?"

"They used a high pressure pump. Diesel, wasn't it? I'll bet we still got it. We could get some water in the vessel with that thing."

The chief operator's face brightened. "Maybe..." Then his features sagged. "No. That pump had an electric motor. I hooked the damn thing up."

There was pained silence. Then, without warning, the chief operator swung around and kicked a metal wastebasket, the sound of the impact echoing across the room. "How the FUCK could this much go wrong?" he yelled, his face growing red. "Didn't fucking maintenance do their job!" As abruptly as he had snapped, the tall, gangly man regained his composure. He took a deep breath, then pulled out a handkerchief and mopped the sweat off his scalp.

Turning back to the panel, Wendell watched the level indicator jiggle and then slide down another fraction of an inch. The water in the reactor vessel was boiling away at a high pressure and 550 degrees Fahrenheit. Even if they pumped water in right now, they couldn't prevent level from dropping below the top of the core. Compared with the hot fluid in the reactor, any new water would be ice cold. The sudden chill would collapse the steam bubbles holding vessel level as high as it was, and the fuel would briefly be uncovered. But, Wendell reminded himself, those tubes of enriched uranium were built to take that punishment -- up to a point. After a few minutes with their tips exposed, the finger-sized tubes would begin leaking -- first a radioactive gas, and then bits of melted uranium itself.

"What we at?" a terse, familiar voice said.

Wendell looked over his shoulder as Ted Cervantes came up alongside, his brown eyes narrowed with intensity. "We're plus twelve inches. Maybe four or five minutes 'til we start to uncover. Have you been briefed?"

"Just a little. Do it quick."

****

"Ya got continuity?" Karl Leeman asked the man kneeling behind the panel in the darkened #1 diesel room.

"Yeah, it's there." The electrician's flashlight framed his face in shadows.

Leeman's bushy, graying eyebrows turning up at the corners as he frowned. "So where's the fool problem?"

Time: 3:37 am.
Time from Start of Event: 46 minutes
Reactor Water Level (above Fuel): +7 inches

Steve raced down the murky hallway and into the emergency center. The low-ceilinged room was filled with an antiseptic glow from the fluorescent lights on each table. The plant manager was glad to see Tarelli on the phone at his desk. Nearby, Langford stood beside the in-plant maps conversing on a walkie-talkie, while two other staff members were retrieving drawings from a cabinet.

Tarelli looked up as Steve approached. His face was smudged by an unshaven beard. "I got Cervantes in control."

Good. He's here. Steve picked up the phone on his desk and punched in. "Ted, this is Steve. I just missed you up there."

"I know," was Cervantes' sullen response. "We're in deep shit. Get as many people on STurDI-2 and the diesel as you can."

"We're on it."

"Level's gonna hit top of fuel in a minute," Cervantes said. "Not many options 'til something gets fixed. What do you think about drywell temp?"

"We have some time on that, don't we?"

"Some. 280 now. Slow rise."

"I don't want to do anything just yet," Steve said. *No quick decision when I can avoid it.* "If we have to vent later, we will, but let's hold off. We could get ourselves in worse trouble."

"I agree, but don't cut it too close. Takes a while to set up. No power at the vent valves."

"Understood. We'll get someone on it."

Steve hung up. Vent the drywell. *God, what a lousy option.* There hadn't been any release of radiation thus far, and if they vented now it wouldn't be too bad -- the air in the drywell was still fairly clean. But some radioactive gas would escape. A plant releasing any radiation in an emergency was an ugly scenario. T.M.I. had brought that lesson home. Yet, if they waited and things kept deteriorating, they would have gas from damaged fuel to contend with. That would make any release much worse. What were the alternatives? If the drywell kept heating up, Steve knew, there wouldn't be any. They had to keep the concrete shell surrounding the reactor vessel from falling apart. Steve turned to Tarelli. "Lou, give me status. Plant condition and repairs."

"There's an HP in the reactor building now, getting some quick readings," Tarelli said, nodding towards Langford on the walkie-talkie. "Nothing out of the ordinary yet." He pointed to the back of the room. "I've got two guys looking at the diesel logic, and there's a mechanic headed out to help Leeman and his electrician. Another I&C is going to STurDI-2. People are starting to come in."

"You aware we went to a General?"

"Cervantes told me. Two mile evacuation, five mile shelter downwind. By the way, winds are out of the northeast," Tarelli said. "Light. We should have a team at the site boundary in a few minutes."

"Good," Steve said. "You're way ahead of me."

Tarelli shrugged. "I'm afraid this thing is way ahead of both of us."

****

Using his flashlight to guide him, Gary hurtled up the four flights of stairs outside the STurDI-1 room, catching himself on the hand-railing when the oil on his boots caused him to slip. He ran on into the turbine building and toward the diesel generator area. Almost at his destination, a figure approached. Lifting his flashlight, Gary caught a glimpse of Doug Tama's face.

"Gary?"

"Yah." Relieved to see his fellow mechanic, Gary began to explain between heavy breaths: "Listen, I can get STurDI-1 back. Where you going?"

"Diesel. I just got here."

"Help me first." Together they hurried on.

"Plant sure is fucked up, as dark as it is," Tama said. "What's wrong with STurDI-1?"

"Oil line's busted. We got the stuff to fix it in here." Gary put his access card in the reader beside the door to the #2 diesel. Nothing happened. He tried the door, but it wouldn't budge. "Card readers don't work. We need Ops to unlock it." *Crap.*

"I think there's somebody at the other diesel," Tama said. "Maybe they got keys."

The two rushed to a nearby door and found it propped open. Inside, emergency diesel generator #1 was a huge, hulking shadow. There was light behind the control panel and Gary found two men examining circuits, with Leeman crouching over them.

"Good, another body," Leeman said, glancing up.

"I got Tama with me too," Gary said. "I think we can fix STurDI-1."

Leeman cast a stern look at the mechanic. "Then do it!"

"I've gotta get in the other diesel room for parts. It's locked."

"I got a key," the operator in front of Leeman said. He stood.

"I'll tell Control," Leeman said. "Git that turbine ready."

"God, yes, get it working," the operator added, as he came out from behind the panel. "Things are going to hell."

Gary caught a glint of fear in the man's eyes. He began to feel it too, but pushed back the ugly mood. *I can fix it.*

"What do we need?" Tama asked as they stepped around the parts strewn about the floor of the #2 diesel room. There was a single light overhead.

"Tubing and tape," Gary said as he gathered up a few short pieces of copper piping and two rolls of duct tape. "Need oil, too. There's a couple of five gallon buckets in here someplace." Gary peered over at his fellow mechanic. "I'm going back. Find that oil and get it down there."

****

"What we at, Wendell?" Cervantes said. He had perched on the table beside the radio. An alarm began blaring and was cut off.

"Just under an inch," Wendell's attention was focused on the wavering level indicator. No boiling water reactor had ever been this far. *Christ, we're really gonna do it. Uncover the fuel.* All his training, all those nights of study, and it had come to this. He remembered how Karen would bring him snacks and kiss him as he reviewed for his exams. And now? Was her husband part of another T.M.I.? Or worse?

Fleck came up alongside and studied the panel. "God damn it," he said. "Where's STurDI-2? Where the fuck is the diesel? We're running dry here."

"There's a chance at STurDI-1," Wendell offered. Leeman had called in moments before to report that some mechanics thought they could fix the turbine-pump.

"Better be damn quick," Fleck said. "Cold water's gonna be tough on the core." Even before the fuel became hot enough to crack apart on its own, the sudden introduction of a cool fluid might cause damage. It would be like dumping ice water in a hot glass. Fleck leaned forward to get a closer look at the reactor level. "Zero," he announced in a loud, steady voice. "Level is at zero."

****

Phyllis Broeder scrawled some notes as she listened to the sheriff on her headset. He was at the civil defense office a few miles east of Brixton, and they were preparing to evacuate the area within two miles of Fairview Station.

"That's it," the sheriff said. "Get the word out. What's our patrol status?"

"Four cars near the plant. Fifth on the way."

"They got their radiation monitors?"

Phyllis fingered the dosimeter and film badge clipped to her blouse. "The car en route is delivering. Barry and Don have also called in. They're taking their own cars out there."

"Good. Sheriff out."

Phyllis sat quietly, gathering herself. The youthful grandmother had been with the county police for fifteen years, and she had taken many bad calls, but never anything like this. For the first time, she herself was afraid. The outside line rang and Phyllis looked across the squad room to be sure the detective on duty answered. The calls hadn't stopped since the sirens had begun.

It must be <u>very</u> bad if they're evacuating, Phyllis reflected, trying not to shudder. She thought of her husband, and her daughter and grandson. They would all be headed out of town. She had seen to that. The evacuation didn't extend as far east as Brixton, but Phyllis wasn't taking any chances. Now all she could do was pray for her family's safety. And her own. She was in the center of town, eight miles from the plant, in a windowless basement. During the drills, the Hoosier Electric trainer had said it was a good place to be in an emergency. Phyllis could only hope he was right.

****

Liz had been listening to the state police direct it's officers towards Fairview Station, and when passing the exit for Brixton, she instinctively looked to the west, but all that was visible was a hazy glow from the lights of the town. The plant was miles beyond that, she knew. What had John Donner done? Was it a plan out of *Mission: Impossible*, or more like a terrorist bombing? And what were the results? Injuries? Deaths? The dispatcher on the radio was saying little except that no radiation had been released.

South Bend was thirty miles further north. She pressed harder on the gas.

****

Karl Leeman grimaced and dug a thin hand into his back as he pulled himself from his crouch behind the electrician. "Hey!" Leeman yelled to the operator working nearby, "gimme that radio!"

The operator pulled the walkie-talkie from his belt and Leeman took it. "Control!" he said. "Leeman at the diesel. Gettin' close. Thar's a trip signal, but I can bypass it."

"How long?" the control room asked.

"Figure ten minutes. Then we do a local start an' give ya some power."

****

Beneath an emergency light, Carol Halvorsen began going through the crates pulled from the locker. Unable to sleep after Gary had left, she had put on some gentle music and started to pick up in the kitchen. Briefly, she'd thought about arranging things to pack, or working on a list of the items they needed to get done, but there was too much thinking involved. They might have found their house, in a nice neighborhood in Brixton, and they were hoping to close the deal next week. But what was happening this night? She had never seen Gary in such a hurry. The next call had answered none of her questions. There was only a recorded message, ordering her to report.

Arriving at the staging area, Carol had tried asking about her husband, but the few workers present had not seen him. *Shoot.* Information about the plant was lacking as well. It was dark everywhere, which she knew was a terrible sign, but beyond that she could only hazard a guess. Then she had run into Marty, her driver, and they had each thrown on a set of anti-c's over their clothes before he left to get the truck while she checked the supplies. It's real this time, Carol kept telling herself, wishing it wasn't true and trying to concentrate on her work. *This is no drill.*

****

The phone at Steve's desk buzzed twice. "Steve Borden."

"Good, you're there." Steve recognized the voice of Bill Chambers, the offsite emergency manager, at corporate headquarters in South Bend.

"I just got in," Chambers said. "How bad is it?"

"It's serious," Steve said, his stomach curled tight. "We lost offsite power and our good diesel, then STurDI-1 and STurDI-2. The water over the core is boiling off and we can't replace it."

"Oh, Lord. That explains the General Emergency. Any rad releases?"

"No. The vessel sealed off when we lost power."

"Good."

"For the moment. But the fuel is going to split open in a few minutes from the heat, or before that if we put water back in. The gas from those cracked tubes will get blown down to the torus, and a tank that big always has a few air leaks around the seams. So hot stuff could bleed on into the reactor building.

"How about it getting outside?"

"The building is closed off," Steve said. "No ventilation. But it's not airtight, and there's no power for the ARAFS filters. So no guarantees."

"Got it. Anything else?"

"Drywell temperature," Steve said. "It's getting too hot in there. That'll make the whole structure unstable. Either we restore power to the cooling system, or we vent in about thirty minutes. That might include fuel gas from the torus."

There was a pause, and Chambers sighed. "Steve, you know if this keeps going much longer, we may have to upgrade on protective action. If you really do release some high rads, clearing out two miles may not be enough."

Steve finished with Chambers and hung up. *Something's got to give. Something.* He glanced around as he composed himself, spying Tarelli just outside the small radio room, working with Langford to dispatch the new personnel who were just arriving.

The phone rang again. It was Cervantes. "Leeman thinks he'll have the diesel soon."

"Great!" *Karl, you old bastard, turn this thing around.*

"We need to talk strategy," Cervantes went on. "We don't know how much the diesel can handle. But I can't see an option except blowdown and flood up with VEPI."

"Understood." Steve said. It would be a big step – but there was no other way to re-fill the vessel quickly and they had to get the core cooled down as soon as possible.

"We'll probably crack some fuel too."

"Right." *Just what I told Chambers. Fuel gas into the torus, and maybe further. We'll need to filter the building air if we can.* "You think we should get ARAFS running first, before the VEPI pumps?"

"Worth the risk. Doesn't take much juice."

"Agreed. ARAFS, then VEPI." *And, please God, let it work...* "What else?"

"Drywell's warm, but I'd worry more about the torus overheating. We'll be dumping a lot of steam in that tank to get pressure down so VEPI can inject." Keeping the torus cool was crucial, so that it could absorb more steam if that became necessary.

"You're right -- run torus cooling right away. We can wait a bit before going after drywell temperature. I don't want to push that diesel too hard."

"We'll be ready when Karl is," Cervantes said. "Maybe we'll get lucky. Not crack the fuel tips."

Steve closed his eyes. *Just maybe... God, let it work.*

****

Awkwardly holding the copper tubing and duct tape in his burly arms, Gary opened the airlock door and stepped back into the reactor building. The beam of a flashlight caught him in the face, and Gary recognized the woman as she approached. Like his wife, she was a health physics technician.

"Where you going?" the HP asked.

"STurDI-1. Fix the turbine." *No time to talk.*

"You better take one of these." The woman held out a finger-sized tube. "Accident-range dosimeter. Goes to one R."

Gary's hands were full. "Stick it in my chest pocket." He understood what the device was for: his other dosimeter couldn't record such high values. "Are rad levels up?"

"Not yet," the HP said as she clipped on the tube.

The mechanic motioned back toward the door. "My partner's right behind me."

"Give him one, then." The HP attached another to his pocket.

"Yah." Gary started towards the stairs to the STurDI-1 room.

"We'll check on you as soon as we can!" the HP added.

****

Wendell flipped a switch. All equipment but the most essential was being turned off to lessen the load on the emergency diesel generator when it was finally started.

Nearby, Fleck was briefing Phil Guthrie. The NRC site resident inspector had just arrived. "...So Leeman thinks he's getting there. We're waiting."

Guthrie nodded. "Bad rad levels yet?"

"No, torus and drywell are about normal. Looks like the fuel's holding up." Fleck ran a hand through his sweat-soaked hair. "Now, if we'd just get the diesel back."

****

In the STurDI-1 room, Gary manhandled a piece of copper tubing into place across the gap separating the startup oil pump from the rest of the system. His flashlight lay nearby, pointed at his work. Kneeling, Gary saw beads of sweat drip onto the pump casing, and he wiped an oily hand across his forehead. Until then he hadn't noticed the room was hovering around one hundred degrees. He also realized he hadn't put on a hard hat or glasses. *No time for that now.*

With a pipe wrench, Gary gave the tubing a twist, then looked at his handiwork, his heart pumping. *Bend the pipe back. Get things more in line.* He grabbed the free end of the slippery line and hammered it with the back of the wrench. Behind him, someone came through the door.

"Goddamn, oil is heavy shit," Tama said as he set two buckets down with a thud, his face flushed. "What now?"

Gary glanced up. "Give me a hand. Then get the cover off the oil tank and start filling." *And we'll get this turbine rolling.*

****

Vitaly was only a mile from home when he pulled into a darkened parking lot along the edge of South Bend. Stripping off his leather jacket, he wormed his way into a bright green windbreaker and then grabbed a thermos bottle off the floor and poured a chunk of ice into his hand. He stuck the cube beneath his nose and pulled back onto the main road. It was time for John Donner to be sick again.

At the all night grocery, Vitaly tossed the half-melted ice cube onto the asphalt. Once inside, he cruised up and down several aisles until he located a stockboy refilling some shelves. "Cold medicine?" Vitaly asked, as if he could not breathe through his reddened nose.

The boy pointed. "Two aisles over. Down at the end."

"Thanks." Vitaly coughed. A short time later he approached the checkout lanes balancing cough syrup, tissues, two cans of soup, and a half-gallon glass jar of orange juice. There was a young woman on duty at the register reading one of the tabloids as Vitaly began dumping his purchases onto the conveyor belt. The bottle of juice was slick with condensation. There was a crash, and a puddle of orange fluid began spreading across the floor. "Oh, shit." Vitaly looked over at the girl. "Sorry." He wiped his nose.

"That's okay." The young woman tried to smile. She picked up the phone. "Kevin to the front." Her voice boomed through the store. "Bring a mop."

****

Paul came to a halt at the traffic light, his foot tapping to the music. He wasn't finding it hard to stay awake -- after all, he had an appointment to identify a drug smuggler for the FBI. Would he get to watch the arrest itself, he wondered? Or point out Donner in a lineup? Whatever happened, it would be an interesting morning.

****

"One more," the electrician said to Leeman, who was hovering behind the kneeling man and shining his light into the dark interior of the cabinet. The electrician moved a wire, tightened a screw, then looked back. "That's it."

"Vessel level is minus twenty-two," the assistant operator reported.

"Final check," Fleck announced, as everyone grew silent. Alongside him, perched on the operators' table, Cervantes had the phone pressed to his ear while his free hand nervously twirled a pen. The rest of the growing staff, along with Phil Guthrie, stood a few paces back "We got the diesel bus cleared?" Fleck asked, looking at Wendell.

"Yes. Ready," Wendell said. *Jesus, let it work.*

"Control!" the radio bellowed.

Wendell stiffened. It was Leeman.

Fleck lifted the mike. "Control. Go ahead, Karl."

"We're ready to go," Leeman said.

"Roger." Fleck briefly scanned the room. "Okay. Proceed with manual start."

"Stay here," Leeman said to the electrician in the back of the panel. "Watch them master relays." He moved around to the front, alongside the turbine building operator, then peered over at the massive machine a few feet away. "Start it," Leeman ordered.

An alarm cut through the control room. From his spot at the diesel controls, Wendell looked up at the blinking rectangle: #1 DIESEL START.

"Do it, damn it, do it ...." the assistant operator said through clenched teeth. The short, chunky figure beside Wendell had his eyes fixed on the diesel's R.P.M. gage.

Wendell, too, stared at the meter, trying to will the huge engine into operation. *Come on!*

The thick black needle shuddered. *Yes!*

"Got it! R.P.M.s rising!" the assistant operator said.

Wendell watched the needle climb. There was a red line at 900. Once the diesel engine reached that speed, the generator could begin to produce electricity. Passing 400, the needle began to slow its ascent. *Too early....*

"Problem!" the assistant operator announced.

Jesus, come on! Wendell ordered. But the needle came to a stop well short of the red line.

"No good! We only got to idle speed."

Wendell closed his eyes. *It can't stay like this. It can't.*

The diesel generator rumbling behind him, Karl Leeman stared at the R.P.M. meter, then shook his head in disgust. Fingering the walkie-talkie, he headed for the door.

242

****

Steve listened on the phone as the diesel start was attempted. Encouragements could be heard ... and then curses. The plant manager grimaced.

"No good, Steve," Cervantes finally reported. "Only got to idle."

"Oh, God," Steve whispered. *Another failure! ... Why? ... Why? Never mind! Keep moving ahead.*

"Leeman wants blueprints on the electronics." Cervantes said.

"Okay. Hang on." Steve cupped his hand over the receiver and spoke to Tarelli, who was just returning to his desk with Crutch Pegariek in tow. "Lou, get Leeman all the prints for the diesel logic."

"I got it," Crutch said, stepping away. Tarelli picked up his phone to listen.

"Okay, Ted. Lou's on the line. What's our status?"

"Level's at -25," Cervantes began. His voice was steady, but to Steve it sounded like the operations supervisor was walking a tightrope, keeping his anger and trepidation in check. "Drywell temp's up around 283. Too damn hot. Torus temperature is still okay, considering we're blowing steam down there every few minutes. No high rads either, so the fuel's holding up."

"How about STurDI?" Steve asked.

"Still troubleshooting the controls on STurDI-2. No phones, and radios go dead in there. We got operators running messages. We're checking with the mechanics at STurDI-1."

"Good."

"Are we prepping to vent the drywell?" Cervantes said. "Jacking open those valves takes thirty minutes. We'll be hitting the temp limit by then."

"The team is heading out," Tarelli said.

Thirty minutes, Steve grimaced. If he could blow hot air out of the drywell this instant, he would. At least it wouldn't contain fuel gas.

But in thirty minutes, the gas would surely be there. By then, the fuel tubes would have cracked from their own heat, or perhaps from cool water returned to the vessel by STurDI. "Let me know when we're ready to vent," Steve said to Tarelli. "Unless we restore power and can cool down the drywell, we'll have to proceed." *No matter what we release. Containment must stay together.*

Steve finished with Cervantes and hung up. *If we'd gotten somebody on the drywell valves right away, we could be venting clean air right now.* He massaged his aching hand. *God, did we send folks to the wrong places? Did I miss something? ... No. We were trying to get water back in the vessel. That had to be the top priority.* But now his plant was backed into a corner, with a core that would soon start crumbling, and the release of a strong cloud of radioactivity also a possibility. He had always prided himself on finding solutions -- on leading people towards the best answer possible -- but no path seemed likely to clean up this mess in time. The thought of failure was building in the back of his mind, but Steve fought it. His father had shown him the cost of giving in to despair: living in a fog of alcohol and self-pity while his family struggled to get by. Steve would never be like that. Something had to go right. *Something.*

The phone rang. It was Chambers, the offsite emergency manager. Steve brought him up to date.

"We ought to consider upgrading the evacuation," Chambers said. "Things aren't getting any better."

"You think clearing out five miles downwind, and sheltering to ten?"

"Yep. That's the next step up the ladder."

Steve sighed. "Very well. I can't disagree." He brushed his graying hair from his forehead. *We're doing everything we can -- and it's not enough.*

Time: 3:48 am.
Time from Start of Event: 57 minutes
Reactor Water Level (above Fuel): -22 inches

Kneeling at the front of the STurDI-1 turbine, Gary wound duct tape around a short piece of copper tubing at its connection to the oil system. Soaked in sweat, his clothes were smeared with grease and his black hair was a tousled mess. Nearby, Tama was removing the cover of the oil tank.

Gary caught something bright out of the corner of his eye, and he looked back into the beam of a flashlight.

"You guys need help?" The light dropped, revealing a tall, thin operator in a hardhat labeled BAKER.

"We're gettin' there," Gary said as he worked on. "You'd just get in the way. How's the plant?"

"Level's down around the fuel."

Crap. Gary didn't look up. "Tell Control we'll be ready in five minutes." There was an edge to his voice.

"Five minutes, right!" The operator reached for his walkie-talkie, then stopped. "I forgot, it won't work down here." He hurried out the door.

On top of the oil tank, Tama continued turning the cover bolts, his wrench slapping against the metal of the container. "Five minutes?" he said. "How we gonna get that pump anchored in five minutes? It's loose as hell."

"We're gonna sit on it."

"Will that do it?"

"We'll give it a try," Gary said. *It can work.* "We only gotta hold the thing down for thirty seconds to get the steam valve open. Then the shaft-driven pump takes over."

"You think the motor can take it?" Tama said. "What if its bearings are shot?"

"We'll find out."

"Do a quick sweep for seal leakage," Wendell said into the microphone, "then check again."

"Roger. Zabowski out."

Damn! Wendell set the mike aside. The operator had reported no progress at STurDI-2. The young supervisor stared at the instruments showing the condition of the reactor. The readings were only getting worse -- but what could be done? *Christ, there must be a way out of this. Must be.* He felt a deep burn in his gut from the frustration. He wanted to lash out, to <u>demand</u> that something work. But that wouldn't help... *Calm down. Think clearly.* Wendell stepped back, and took a deep breath as he looked about the room. The staff had grown, and was working in small groups. Fleck was peering over the shoulder of those gathered around the diesel drawings, while Cervantes remained on the line with the emergency center.

"Control!" the radio blared.

Wendell responded. "Control."

"This is Baker," the breathless voice said. " I just came from STurDI-1. They're piecing together an oil set-up. They think maybe five minutes."

"Five minutes till we can try it?" Wendell said. It sounded too good to be true.

"That's what they said."

Wendell looked at Cervantes and saw the operations supervisor was listening.

"We'll be ready," Wendell said. *Let it work. Jesus, just let it work.* He turned to the personnel spread across the room. "Listen up!"

****

Five miles. They'll be moving people out for five miles downwind. Shelter to ten. Steve looked at the county map on the wall, the wind direction marked on it with a blue arrow. Northwest to southeast. Right towards Brixton. His home was eight miles from the plant, just outside of town. Marie and the kids would soon be hearing sirens and getting shelter warnings. Of course, his wife already knew something was wrong. She would be okay, Steve reassured himself. She could handle it. *Just check all the windows and hold tight.*

In the bleached glow of the fluorescent lamps, the plant manager surveyed his increasing staff. Nearly thirty people were spread among the tables: digging through procedures, arguing over drawings, updating the rad maps, all with tension and fear lining their faces. Beneath a NO SMOKING, NO EATING sign, Phil Guthrie, fresh from the control room, was on the red phone with his NRC superiors. And just down the hall, Steve knew, the staging area was being set up. In a few minutes it would begin to control the movements of the in-plant teams. Overall, the emergency plans were working well. But the plant wasn't. If things kept going at this rate, they'd have to start thinking about cutting the staff down to a minimum. Just in case.

Tarelli had been on the phone. "Steve," he said, as he stood to leave, "pick up the control room."

Steve punched the button. "Yes, Ted."

"Got a report from STurDI-1. We can try it in a couple of minutes."

"Understood. Great." *Maybe this time.*

"Your end okay?"

Cold water on hot fuel. Tarelli was now leaning in the doorway of the radio room. "Lou, how are we set for a release?"

"We've got one team at the site boundary," Tarelli said as he returned to his phone, "and Langford is dispatching someone out to the yard. We've also got folks in the reactor building, and we were sending one down to look in on the STurDI rooms."

"Any guess how much fuel we're gonna bust?" Cervantes asked.

"The tips have been in the air for ten minutes."

"Hard to say," Tarelli replied, running a hand across his bare scalp. "Basically, my guess is it won't be too bad. Torus rads will tell us." Steam from the vessel would travel through STurDI and then into the huge tank, carrying any fuel gas with it. "We'll also keep checking to see if anything seeps into the hallway."

****

Gary heard someone coming down the stairs, and the operator re-appeared just as Tama finished emptying the first bucket of oil into the low-slung STurDI-1 tank and tossed the container aside with a clunk. "Another," Gary said, handing over the second bucket.

"How long?" the operator asked. "They want it bad--"

"Hang on and I'll tell you!" Gary snapped as he watched the angle of the bucket rise.

"Done." Tama chucked the container against the wall and slid the hatch cover back in place. He smeared his hands across his blue jeans, grabbed a bolt, and began screwing it in.

Gary joined his partner, leaning across the front of the tank, the startup oil pump pressed against his leg. "Get the cover on, and we're ready," he said for the benefit of the operator. *Then we'll roll.*

The two mechanics quickly had half the bolts inserted. Gary handed his wrench to Tama, slithered off the tank and took another wrench from the tool rack on the wall. He knelt and tightened two more bolts. *Almost there. Don't need 'em all.* Gary looked at the operator. "Okay," he said, while Tama worked feverishly behind him, "tell'em to start it up in one minute. I'm countin' now. Got it?"

"Got it!" The operator disappeared.

"One thousand one! One thousand two!" Gary began.

Tama joined in. "One thousand five! One thousand six!"

248

Wendell stood beside the radio, fidgeting with his collar. *Come on. Anytime.* Nearby, Cervantes was listening to a report from the Emergency center. The pen kept twirling in his hand. At the STurDI-1 controls, the chief operator stood ready, with Fleck beside him. The assistant operator was monitoring reactor level, while further along the curving panel, another man was also on duty.

Wendell checked his wristwatch in the dim light. It had been four minutes since the last report. *Come on ...* "Level?" he said.

"Minus 32."

"Control!" A voice shot out of the speaker.

Yes. "Control," Wendell said.

"This is Baker." The operator was breathing hard. "STurDI-1 will be ready in 45 seconds! .... Repeat: 45 seconds! .... They were counting it off. You ready?"

Wendell looked to Fleck, who nodded. "We're ready," he said.

"One thousand thirty-seven! One thousand thirty-eight!" Gary chanted along with his partner. He turned a final bolt, then squirmed off the tank. Tama continued working.

"One thousand forty! One thousand forty-one!"

Peering over his shoulder, Gary lined himself up with the startup oil pump, which rested just off the floor in front of the tank. Carefully, he squatted onto the bread-loaf sized machine, letting his legs sprawl out in front as he shifted to keep from sliding off the pump's smooth, oil-splattered surface. He tried not to disturb the repaired line running up the left side of the tank with its damaged coupling patched by tape and copper tubing. Just behind him were several pipe supports, and he wiped his hands on his shirt and grabbed on.

"One thousand forty-seven! One thousand forty-eight!"

"Done!" Tama announced.

"On my lap!" Gary said. "The weight'll help." Besides being slippery, the oil pump was too small to make a good seat, and Gary gripped the supports tighter as Tama sat down on top of him. "One thousand fifty-eight!" Gary chanted, his heart pounding. *I'm not gonna let this goddamn pump fly around. This is gonna work*!

Steve's ear was pressed to the phone, as was Tarelli's at the next desk. The rest of the emergency center had also grown quiet. *This time....*

His skin sticky and moist, Gary labored to suck in the hot air as Tama's weight pressed hard against his thighs and chest. They had stopping counting.

"Let's go!" Tama said.

In the stillness, Gary heard a jingling of keys, and operator reappeared. "They're gonna start it!" he yelled, as he examined the two mechanics. "What the hell are you doing?"

"Holding the pump down!" Gary said from behind Tama's shoulder. "Grab the outlet line and try to steady it, just in case,"

"Got it!" The operator knelt to the left of the two men and gripped the thin pipe near the repairs. His hard hat began to slip forward, and he tossed it over his shoulder. "Ready!"

The control room was quiet. Wendell's eyes were fixed on his watch.

"Minus 34 inches," the assistant operator said. He yanked off his glasses and wiped a shirt sleeve across his eyes

Wendell saw the last seconds tick away. *Finally.* "Forty-five seconds is up, " he announced. He looked toward Cervantes.

"Give them a few more," the operations supervisor said, his eyes narrowed, his face set in a tense gaze. The chief operator waited at the STurDI-1 controls, with Fleck hovering nearby. The additional staff had gathered in a semi-circle a few paces back. Cervantes took a deep breath. "Do it," he ordered. "Start STurDI-1."

"Starting STurDI-1!" the chief operator said as he flipped a switch. "Startup oil pump is ... on!"

CLICK!

"Now!" Gary felt the pump beneath him whir to life. It promptly jerked up and to the left. "It's fightin' us!" he said, trying to hold the machine down by pulling at the pipe supports behind him. Tama's back pressed into his face, while Gary could just see the operator grimly hanging on to the outlet pipe. With luck, oil pressure was building, and soon the steam inlet valve would be forced open and the STurDI-1 turbine would begin to roll.

The pump bucked again, harder this time, and Gary summoned every ounce of strength in his muscled arms to pin the small motor to its concrete base. "Son of a bitch!" he forced out between clenched teeth. *Shit!*

"Hang on!" Tama yelled.

"The oil pump is running!" the chief operator said.

Come on! Wendell could just see the indication for the STurDI-1 steam inlet valve. *Green.* The valve was still closed. *Come on! Red!* An open valve would allow steam into the STurDI-1 turbine, and then it's attached pump would begin putting water back in the vessel.

Come on!

Gary continued to fight the jerking, mis-aligned pump. His shoulders ached as he pulled the supports, and he could feel the heat beneath him from the electric motor. Gary's seat tried to move yet again, and on his lap, Tama shifted to compensate. *Open up, you fucking valve!* Gary demanded.

There! Over his shoulder, at the limit of his vision, Gary saw a puff of white steam and heard a hiss.

"It's going!" Tama shouted.

First came a groan and a shudder, then a low rumble. His arms begging for relief, Gary sensed that the turbine wheel behind him was beginning to turn. *Move, you son of a bitch!*

THERE! Wendell saw it. The red light was on.

"Steam valve coming open!" the chief operator said. "... Turbine R.P.M. up! Pump pressure up! ... Inject valve opening ... WE HAVE FLOW! WE HAVE FLOW!"

"Level drop to minus 45!" the assistant operator said. The chilled water STurDI was now pouring into the vessel had quenched the boiling froth surrounding the fuel.

Wendell's hands balled into fists. *Come on!*

"Minus 48 ....slowing!..."

"Back up," Fleck ordered the water level.

Up! Wendell urged. *Up!*

"... Slowing ...minus fifty!" the assistant operator continued.

Wendell squeezed his fists even tighter. *Turn around! ... Come on, turn!*

"... Wait! ..." the assistant operator said, ".... going ... up .... Level's going up! Here it comes! ... 49! ..... 48! ..... minus 45!"

Jesus, Wendell sighed. He unclenched his fingers. *Thank you.*

Hold...Hold...Hold! His eyes squeezed shut, Gary fought the startup oil pump. A stinging sensation crept its way into his compressed buttocks, and he caught a whiff of acrid, metallic smoke.

"It's running ...!" the operator yelled over the pervasive roar now filling the room.

The pump bucked yet again, and Gary's arms spasmed in pain. *Crap!* Then, suddenly, the forceful movement beneath him stopped. It was over. Gary let his arms go slack, his muscles crying out at the release, his numbed fingers still wrapped around the pipe supports. "It stopped!" he said in Tama's ear. "It stopped! Get off!"

Tama pitched himself onto the oil-smeared floor and carefully climbed to his feet while the nearby operator released his grip on the outlet pipe. Gary tried to push himself upright, but his arms were useless. Focusing his attention, he coaxed the thick fingers on his right hand from around the steel beam. With a grimace he reached out and Tama yanked him off the pump and onto his knees. Immediately, Gary swung his aching frame around. Tama crouched down with a flashlight, and together they inspected the makeshift joint in the oil piping. It had held.

The operator had stepped behind the turbine to read some gauges on the far wall, and he came back wearing a smile of relief. "It's okay!" he yelled in Gary's ear as the mechanic rose to his feet. Gary could hardly hear the man. The operator patted the walkie-talkie on his belt. "... upstairs! ... Control!" His arms limp at his sides, Gary watched as the operator disappeared out the door.

Tama leaned closer. "Fucking great!"

Gary nodded.

****

It was quiet at the site boundary. A light breeze drifted in from the direction of the plant, a few hundred yards distant, and there was only an occasional click from the geiger counter on Carol's lap. The radio carried some brief traffic as the second offsite team got their own truck into position further downwind.

"Marty, what time did we pull up?" Carol asked.

"About five minutes ago." The driver peeled back his rubber glove to check his watch. "We left around 3:50."

"Fine. Thanks.' Carol continued to stare towards the darkness of Fairview Station, wishing she knew what was happening. Where was Gary? She tried not to worry, but with nothing to keep her occupied, it was hard. *He's doing his job*, she reminded herself, *just like me.* The thought didn't help.

"Team One, Team Two, this is Offsite Leader," the radio said.

Carol picked up the mike. "Team One."

"We are now currently in a General Emergency, two mile evacuation, shelter to five downwind, animals on stored feed."

Shoot.

"No release in progress," the report continued. "Hold position."

"Man, it doesn't sound too hot," Marty said.

"No," Carol agreed . *Lord, they're at a General.* She struggled not to let concern overwhelm her. "At least nothing's gotten out," she said. "That's good news."

"If something does happen, you think they'll have us take some of those pills?" Included with the truck's supplies were potassium iodide tablets.

"Not unless it looks really bad. They can make you sick."

"This whole thing's making me sick already," Marty said.

****

"Do you know anything more?" a deputy inquired over the radio. "People are asking."

"Nothing new," Phyllis replied from her post at the sheriff's office. "The evacuation is a precaution." The patrol car was near Fairview Station. "What's it like out there?" Phyllis asked. "Can you see anything?" *Maybe a fire? A glow?*

"It's dark at the plant. But I can hear the sirens. Traffic's been steady, and folks are scared."

As she signed off, Phyllis saw the blinking light for the line to Civil Defense headquarters. "Phyllis, we've got a big change," the sheriff said in his rough voice. "No radiation yet, but C.D. has decided to go to a ten mile evacuation zone. Sectors D, E, and F. That's downwind."

Phyllis looked at the county map. *Brixton.*

****

Vitaly pressed on the gas as the car headed up the incline towards the end of the cul-de-sac. He felt proud, and strong. In this, the most difficult challenge of his life, everything had gone according to plan. Vitaly Kruchinkin had succeeded in his mission.

Still several houses away, Vitaly turned off his headlights, and punched the button for his garage door. Guiding his car by the glow from a streetlight, he cruised inside and closed the door behind him.

Across the street, in a darkened sedan, there was movement. Taylor Winn had something to report.

****

"Level is still rising! Minus 33!" the assistant operator said.

"Torus temperature now 132," the chief operator added. Steam from the STurDI-1 turbine was heating up the water in the big tank.

Looking good. Wendell stood back, watching the three men at the panels. At 3500 gallons a minute, the reactor vessel would soon be refilled.

"We've got high rads in the torus!" the third operator reported. "700 R!"

"Well," Fleck said, "we cracked up some fuel."

"Steve, bad news," Cervantes said into the phone.

"Damn," Steve murmured as he heard the report. Gas from cracked fuel rods was now passing through the STurDI-1 turbine and down into the torus. Radiation levels in the huge tank had risen to a hundred times normal. Steve looked over at Tarelli, who was shaking his head in disappointment.

"Didn't get lucky," Tarelli said.

"As long as it stays where it is," Steve replied, "I won't complain."

Gary stood beside the rumbling STurDI-1 turbine, his buttocks still feeling the heat of the pump. He sniffed at the air, which carried a hint of singed insulation and electrical smoke. *Burnt out the pump, but we got the turbine running.* Tama tapped him on the shoulder. The thunderous noise made conversation almost impossible, and in the dim light, the mechanic held up a wrench and motioned toward the oil tank.

Finish tightening the tank cover. Gary nodded. *Can't hurt.* He knelt beside the startup oil pump and grabbed a flashlight and wrench. Gary played the beam across his taped-up handiwork, then began tracing the rest of the oil piping, which was still needed to keep

STurDI running. *Hold it!* ... He flinched as the light caught a glimmer and some movement. *Crap!* A short distance beyond the first repair there was more pipe damage. He hadn't noticed it before. The line was bent slightly, and to his horror, Gary could see it was rapidly working itself loose from a coupling. Oil was starting to spray from the joint.

STurDI-1 was in trouble again.

"Minus 10!" the assistant operator said.

"Torus temperature?" Fleck asked.

"140. Slowly rising."

"Not too bad," Fleck said. The blond, burly supervisor stood back from the panels: his arms crossed, his features more relaxed. He had resumed chewing his gum.

"Torus rad levels still going up," the third operator reported. "Starting to see it in the drywell too."

Wendell remained beside the radio, both elated and disappointed. *We didn't come through clean.* There was damaged fuel. Still, the excess radioactivity remained within primary containment. That could be dealt with later. Soon, either the diesel generator or the offsite power lines would be repaired, and the plant could be returned to a stable condition. With any luck, drywell air temperature would stay below 300 degrees until they again had power for the cooling system.

"Minus five!"

"STurDI running good," the chief operator said. "Rated flow." He looked up from the controls, a smile beneath his bushy mustache.

"Here we go!" the assistant operator said. The room grew quiet. "Minus one! .... ZERO! Level is passing the top of active fuel. Still rising!"

On one knee at the oil tank, Gary urgently nudged Tama with his flashlight. He pointed to the thin streams of oil, then swung around to grab a roll of duct tape. Turning back, he found the leak had increased, and Tama was using one hand to cover the spray of warm oil and the other to prevent the finger-sized joint from vibrating completely apart.

God damn! Gary had a sinking feeling as he slid on his knees to get closer. A hand landed on his shoulder, and, startled, Gary turned to see the operator's concerned face. "Can we bypass it?" Gary yelled, but the man couldn't hear over the rumble of the turbine, and he leaned in closer. "Bypass! Bypass!" Gary screamed. The operator nodded and hurriedly began tracing the maze of piping, trying to find a way to divert the oil flow around the leak. Without continued oil pressure, the valve directing steam into the turbine would close.

Turning back to the source of the crisis, Gary pulled a strip of tape and signaled Tama to let go of the leak. The hand came off, and Gary was sprayed with warm, fragrant oil as he attempted to wrap the joint. *Shit!* He blinked his eyes and struggled to fix the coupling. He couldn't get the tape on tight enough -- it wouldn't stick -- and oil continued to stream out. It was only getting worse. A few inches away Tama was still clamping down on the vibrating pipe. Gary tried again to wrap more tape around the leaking joint. *Don't let it split apart! Wrap it tight and let it stick to itself!* The spray increased and the oily, shaking pipe began to slip around in Tama's hands. *Hold it! Hang on!* Suddenly, the line gave a hard shudder, and the two mechanics were showered by a frantic burst of oil as the end of the pipe shook itself loose of the coupling. Above them, there was a puff of steam and the noise level began to drop. The steam inlet valve was going closed. The STurDI-1 turbine was shutting down.

"Level at plus 8."

An alarm sounded, and above the STurDI panel an annunciator began to flash. The chief operator looked up from the controls: "STurDI-1 low oil pressure!"

Oh, Christ. Wendell took a step closer.

"Oil pressure dropping!" the chief operator said as Fleck rushed up beside him. In the back of the room, all conversation ceased.

"Steam inlet valve moving," Fleck announced.

"She's dying!" the chief operator said. "R. P. M.'s dropping! Flow rate dropping!..."

Jesus. Wendell watched in horror, Cervantes now standing alongside. There was nothing that could be done.

"Come on!" the chief operator said, "hold up!"

Wendell watched the valve's indicator. A green light appeared. He winced.

"Inlet valve closed," Fleck said. "STurDI-1's gone."

"Damn!" the chief operator said. "God damn! God damn!" His face beet-red, he pushed away from the control panel. A book of procedures lay nearby and he flung it towards the bare side wall, the binder slamming against the plaster surface. "Fucking piece of shit!" There was tense silence as he stared down at the floor, his lean body trembling in anger.

"What's level?" Cervantes finally said.

The assistant operator turned back to the center panel. "We're at 10 inches."

Cervantes briefly spoke into the phone and hung up. "All right." He voiced the words as a command. "We bought ourselves some time to get power back. That's a start." He looked to the chief operator, whose gaze was still fixed on the floor. "Larry, you're relieved. Take ten minutes."

The man smacked his palm against a leg and moved toward the door.

"Arnie, take over," Cervantes said to the third operator.

Wendell turned to watch the chief operator stalk out of the control room. The belief that the crisis was ending had drained away. But something had been done. *Ten inches over the fuel. We've got a little time now. Not much, but a little.*

In the emergency center, Steve and Tarelli listened over the phone to STurDI's demise. Cervantes had set the receiver down and stepped away.

"They're losing it," Tarelli said.

Not now. God, not now! Steve heard Darrel Fleck report the steam inlet valve was shut. The plant manager's head sagged. *Not now.* There was cursing in the background.

Cervantes came on the line. "We lost STurDI-1. I'll get back." He hung up.

"Bad deal," Tarelli said. He turned to Steve. "What was the last level you heard?"

"Plus ten, I think."

"Strange, him cutting us off. Not like Ted."

"I think he wanted to take care of his people," Steve said softly, as he struggled to absorb the latest blow. He looked up to find all eyes in the emergency center fixed on him. *Straighten up. Command.*

Time: 3:58 a.m.
Time From Start of Event: 67 minutes
Reactor Level (above Fuel): +10 inches
Torus Radiation: 100X normal   (Damaged Fuel)
Radiation Release to Environment: None
Evacuation Orders: Ten Miles Downwind

As the shock of losing STurDI-1 began to wear off, Wendell moved alongside the assistant operator at the center panel. Temperature and pressure in the reactor vessel had fallen, and water level was holding at ten inches above the top of the fuel. *It'll go up a bit more, then turn.* As heat from the fuel seeped into the new, cool water, the liquid would expand. But soon enough it would begin to boil, and level would start to drop once again.

"Control!" the radio speaker said.

Wendell picked up the mike. "Control."

"This is Baker!" The operator was gasping for breath: " We lost STurDI-1! ... A main oil line ripped off. ... It's a mess!"

Wendell glanced at Cervantes and Fleck to ensure they were listening. "Can we bypass it? Or do a quick fix??"

"I don't think so. But I'll go back down."

****

Joel Wermager sat in his patrol car beside Brixton's main intersection, re-reading the emergency instructions. It had been three-quarters of an hour since the first order to take shelter had come out of Fairview Station and twenty minutes since the first evacuations around the plant had been announced. Traffic, which had been non-existent, was beginning to appear. Families now passed by, the driver hunched over, the other parent speaking to the sleepy children in the back seat. There were also older couples -- the husband at the wheel, the wife seated stiffly beside him -- and other combinations of frightened men, women and children. Many showed their anxiety by racing through the light, but Joel allowed them the extra speed. It was understandable. He fingered the thin tube clipped to his pocket, then held it up again to the light. The needle still rested on zero.

Suddenly there was a new sound, a whine that crescendoed to a bellowing pitch. The siren from the fire department. Joel listened. The alarm was not rising and falling, as it would for a fire. It stayed high and piercing. *Oh no....*

"All units," the radio broke in. "10-33. 10-33 IN BRIXTON! Civil Defense has called for evacuation of town. Everything is being cleared out for ten miles downwind of Fairview Station. 10-45, acknowledge with location. Out."

Joel picked up the microphone. *God help us.*

****

Maybe it's another Chernobyl, Liz thought when she heard a police dispatcher announce the larger evacuation. She thought of the pictures of the smoldering Russian complex. Many workers had died there. Was that happening at Fairview? Was she safe, speeding by a few miles to the east? On the radio, the police were firing back questions, wanting to know more. But there seemed to be precious little to tell.

South Bend was not far, and Liz was on schedule to meet Kreveski on the southern edge of town. Where was Donner now? Paul Hendricks had said the operator was ill at the end of his shift, but that could have been a ploy. Assuming he was finished with the sabotage, what came next? There was no precedent for this type of Soviet operation in the U.S. Was it a suicide mission? Was he supposed to run? Or was Donner just to lie low, playing the innocent?

A Soviet operation. The implications were enormous. They would need to keep this quiet. Washington would want time to deal with the event. But Liz had her own part of the puzzle to deal with. John Donner must be brought in. *There was still time to find him.* Unless it really was a suicide mission, Donner was either on the move or playing dumb. In either case, he wouldn't be expecting anyone to look for him so soon. *We've got surprise on our side.* Liz hoped that would be enough.

****

The emergency center was alive with activity as the staff searched for new solutions in the wake of STurDI-1's failure. The damaged fuel was one concern. Meanwhile, drywell air temperature was continuing its rise toward the 300 degree limit. The enclosed atmosphere was now much more radioactive as well.

Langford came out of the radio room and caught Steve's and Tarelli's attention. "Readings are increasing in the reactor building first floor hallway. 200 m.r. They believe it may be going airborne." The supervisor ducked out of site once more.

"Sounds like we're getting gas out of torus," Tarelli said as he stepped away.

Steve grimaced. It wasn't entirely unexpected, but if radioactive air was indeed leaking out of the huge tank into the hallways of the reactor building, it would complicate every repair the plant tried to make. And it meant the only thing left between the gas and the outside world were the walls of the reactor building itself.

The phone rang. It was Cervantes. His tone was sour. "We got to plus ten, then STurDI's oil system gave way. No quick fix."

"Understood." Steve had already assumed the worst. "We've just gone airborne on the first floor," he said.

"Shit. Didn't get away with it."

263

"We bought ourselves some time, at least. Anything from STurDI-2 or the diesel?"

"Nothing new."

Finished, Steve hung up. He squeezed the stub of his thumb as he tried to think differently, to find a new way of approaching the crisis, a solution that would get his plant back on the road to recovery. But there was nothing. Just failure after failure. A weight growing heavier. *How much longer? How much more before things turn around?* He curled his aching hand into a fist. *There must be a way.*

****

In the ominous quiet of the STurDI-1 room, Gary and his partner wiped themselves down with a drop cloth. The coarse material did little more than skim off the thickest layers of the oily fluid that had drenched both men and filled the air with its scent.

"Shit!" Tama said. "We had it running."

"Yah," Gary sighed. "It was pumping." He kicked at the greasy floor. "But god damn, if I'd just seen that other bend! We could've fixed it, too!"

"It's a fucking maze of piping, Gary. It's dark -- all we had was flashlights. We tried."

"I should have seen it!" Gary repeated. *Shit!* He cleared more oil from his eyes.

A light appeared in the doorway, and a short, chunky man with a clicking meter stepped inside. Gary recognized the health physics technician. "This thing been running?" the HP asked as he moved closer, using his flashlight to observe the meter.

"Yeah, it rolled for a minute."

"Well, something's screwed up. You're over 4 R. background in here."

Gary was caught off guard. *Four Rems an hour? STurDI never gets that bad.*

The HP looked up from his meter. "Unless you got something to do quick, we're out of here. Too high."

****

Steve stared at the plant maps tracking the flow of radioactive gas through the hallways of the reactor building. Workers now needed to wear anti-c's and masks, and he knew getting them dressed would take up precious time.

Tarelli returned from the radio room, "HP in the yard just picked up something. Airborne."

Steve's heart sank. *God, no. A release.* The last barrier, the reactor building, had been breached.

"Five milli-rem so far," Tarelli continued. He pointed over his shoulder. "Southeast corner. We'll have more in a sec." He stepped back out of sight.

Just let the plume be small. Please, just let it be small. But no matter what the size of the release, Steve knew, it was a disaster. An uncontrolled cloud of radioactive gas was now outside. His plant had failed. Somehow. Some way. Despite all the good people and all the expensive equipment.

Tarelli returned, along with Langford. "We've got a 40 milli-rem plume in the yard. Still increasing."

"Let's hope it levels off quick," Steve said.

"Hard to say. We're at a thousand Rem per hour in the torus. Now there's some oozing out. First floor's around 400 milli-rem. Obviously, there's a further pathway out of the building."

"Where's our people?" Steve asked. *Limit their dose.*

"We have an HP in a mask performing a brief survey," Langford said, "and we're removing the crews from STurDI-1 and 2. There's a team on the third floor setting up the drywell vent, and we'll be

monitoring that. The diesel and control room should not be affected."
He looked around the room. "Levels here should also stay low."

Steve nodded. "How about off site?"

"The truck at the site boundary is reporting background levels.
The second truck is traveling to a mile downwind. We're ready."
Langford and Tarelli returned to the radio room.

We must track that cloud. No questions on that when we're done.
Steve stared down at his desk. *God, how did we get this far?* It was
T.M.I. all over again. And right after Chernobyl.....

The phone buzzed. Bill Chambers was calling from South Bend.
"Steve, you should know we recommended evacuation to five miles,
but the county C.D. director upped it. He's clearing things out for ten
miles downwind."

Ten miles! "That's a hell of an accident, Bill." Steve glanced at
the county map and its arrow for wind direction. "Understand, you're
talking about clearing out Brixton."

"Yeah, the director wasn't happy, but he said things seemed out of
control at your place. He didn't figure he had much choice."

Steve soon placed the phone back on its cradle, and looked again
at the map of Potowatomie County. There was now an orange star,
labeled "40 m.r.," at the plant's location. The outdoor dose number
was small -- at least for the moment -- but it was a release. And the
radioactive plume was going to keep moving with the wind. Toward
Brixton.

****

The bad news was relayed to the site boundary. There had been a
release. Forty milli-rems.

"Oh, Christ," Marty said. "Something's getting out."

"Yes," Carol said softly, her thin lips barely parting. The worst
had finally come. *I wish Gary ... Concentrate!* On her lap, the geiger

counter continued to show background. She checked the window to make sure the probe was facing toward the plant.

"Team One, Offsite Leader," the radio said.

Carol picked up the mike. "Team One."

"Release is ground level, northwest side of plant. It's now at 100 m.r."

"We're still reading background."

"I can't believe this," Marty blurted out, his face creased with shock. "It's actually happening."

Carol didn't reply. She focused on the counter. Click . . . . . Click . . . . Click ... The meter was still showing a low value, the audible counts coming at random, seconds apart. Click . . . . Click . . . . Click . . . . Click Click . . . Click Click.. Click Click Click Click. *Shoot!* The meter gave off another series of rapid counts, like static.

"It's coming," Carol said. She grabbed the mike. "Team One beginning to pick up the plume. Out." She worked quickly, retrieving the probe from the window. The audible monitor was a sensitive device that could tell when a cloud of radioactive gas was approaching, but the other meter at her feet would take more accurate readings once the plume had arrived. Carol swapped the two instruments and stuck the new probe outside. Unlike the other device, this meter made no sound. There was only a dial with a thin, red needle. The reading was at zero.

Carol felt a light breeze drifting over the flat, round sensor and her gloved hand as she stared at the dial on her lap. The red needle soon shuddered. "It's starting," she said. "Marty, get the time." The needle began to creep up the dial. "Two m.r." Carol read off. "Now five." Within half a minute, the reading had reached 20 milli-rems per hour, and it was still increasing.

"I'll check plume elevation," Carol said, as she reached outside and covered the probe face with her free hand. The reading on the meter instantly dropped by half. Carol uncovered the probe and the needle jumped back up. "Ground level confirmed," she said. The truck was immersed in a cloud of invisible, radioactive gas.

"We're at a minute," Marty said, checking his watch.

"Fine." Carol grabbed the mike. "Offsite Leader, This is Team One. We are one minute into the plume. Ground level confirmed. We're reading 35 m.r. -- and rising."

****

Steve studied the in-plant maps. As he had feared, some of the fuel gas in the torus had drifted up through ventilation ducts into the drywell, and that cavernous structure now contained an atmosphere a hundred times more radioactive than before. Of even greater concern, the air inside the concrete and steel shell was approaching the 300 degree stability limit. He bit down on his lip. *If we don't get power back and drywell cooling in service, we'll have to vent. And we'll dump a hell of a hot cloud out to the atmosphere. But there won't be any choice.*

Tarelli returned from the radio room. "Okay, Steve, here's the scoop on our release. We've got 120 milli-rems out in the yard now and 35 at the site boundary." He motioned with his hand. "So far it's not much. And the plume's definitely on the ground."

"We're still releasing?" Steve asked

"As far as we can tell. The yard says levels keep inching up. In-plant we've basically got-"

"I've been looking at the maps."

Tarelli glanced at the information. "Okay, well, beyond that .... the STurDI-1 team is on their way out. The rad levels in the room shot up when the turbine ran."

"Busted fuel makes crappy steam," Steve said.

"Right." Tarelli continued. "STurDI-2's not looking too bad, and the team down there told the HP they're staying. He wasn't gonna argue. We'll get them masks and an air monitor." Tarelli shrugged his thick shoulders. "If it gets worse, we can always club them and drag them out."

"Just keep them under the limit," Steve said.

****

At the site boundary, Carol continued measuring the vaporous plume, her eyes fixed on the thin red needle as it inched upward: 50 . . . 60. . . . 70 milli-rems per hour.

"Two minutes in," Marty said. "Damn."

Carol clicked on the radio mike and reported the numbers, while in the back of her mind she struggled to accept what was happening. At this early hour, with little sleep and darkness surrounding the truck, the whole thing was like a dream. But she knew the truth. It was very real. A cloud of radioactive gas was flowing past, though except for her meter there was nothing to warn of its existence. There was no smoke, no oddly-colored curtain of mist. The window was cracked open for her to hold the probe, but Carol could smell nothing unusual, nor feel anything but the breeze against her small hand. But, still . . . the plume was there.

The red needle passed a milestone. "100 m.r." Carol said aloud. *Shoot.* The thin line continued to glide up, but she soon detected a change. "110 and slowing," she said.

"Three minutes," Marty reported.

Carol tried to will the needle into stopping. *Stick!* she ordered. *Stick!* The red line inched up past 115, then a little further ... a little further ... "120 m.r." Carol announced. The needle began to waver. 120 . . . 120 . . . 120 . . . Carol picked up the mike. "Offsite Leader, this is Team One. We are holding at 120 m.r. We are over three minutes in. "

The reading remained steady as the plume drifted over and around the truck. *What are we seeing?* Carol wondered. *Just a puff? A steady stream?* The needle was wavering a little more now. To

Carol, it seemed to want to go down. Or was that wishful thinking?
120 . . . 120 . . .

The needle hesitated, and then the thin line start to fall. "It's dropping."

"Good deal," Marty said as Carol radioed the news.

"Roger, Team One. Can you traverse?"

Carol nodded and turned to her driver. "Okay, let's see how wide this thing is. Cut across it." Marty put the idling truck into gear and nudged it forward on the dirt road. After fifty yards, the radiation levels fell off sharply. "Stop, Marty, we're at the edge," Carol said. "Turn around and we'll find the other side." The driver complied with a sharp U-turn, and as they crossed back within the cloud, Carol noticed the radiation values throughout were now much lower. *It must have been a puff. Just a little burp of gas. It's passing.* Her meter soon hit zero again. "How far did we come?" she asked. "Maybe eighty yards?"

"I'd say a hundred."

"Fine. Take us back to the middle." Carol radioed in the new data as Marty lurched the truck around once more and soon brought it to a halt."

"Team One, what is your current reading?" the radio asked.

Carol checked her meter. "We're near the centerline. I've got 5 m.r. and falling. Looks like we're on the back end of it."

****

His tape deck pounding out a steady beat, Paul pulled into the empty Donut World lot at the South Bend city limit. He was early. Settling back, he gazed at the deserted counter and tables inside, and let loose a tired grin. So far, the night had been unreal. And it would only get better.

The music faded out and Paul ejected the cassette. Sparse traffic

on the highway behind him was the only sound. At the approach of
each car he expected his wait to be over, but none turned in, and he
soon grew restless and switched on the radio. Immediately, Paul
sensed something was wrong. It was in the man's voice. The report
came at him in bursts -- short, ugly sentences that hit hard:

> "Problems at Fairview . . . no release of radiation . . .
> recommended shelter . . ."

Oh, God. A knot formed in Paul's gut. *The plant.*

> "3:55 am . . . now evacuation . . . . precautionary . . ."

The announcer repeated the message and Paul listened closely,
hoping it was all a mistake. "Additional details as we get them," the
deep voice concluded.

Urgently, Paul began scanning the other stations. He caught most
of another report, but it was identical to the first. Fairview. Accident.
Evacuation.

Paul's head fell back as a sinking feeling washed over him. He
stared at the dark, featureless roof. *How could it happen? . . . Maybe
I should get out there. Maybe I could . . . No.* He dismissed the idea.
No. I'd just be in the way. I'm not on the team. There was nothing to
do but wait -- wait for the FBI, and wait for news about Fairview.
Paul closed his eyes. *How?*

****

With the others behind him, Gary reached the power block
entryway. The scene had changed from the darkened passage he had
navigated thirty minutes before. Portable lights had been set up, and
HPs were now on station. Gary was brought to a halt.

"Arms and legs out!" the man holding the geiger counter ordered, as he began running probe along Gary's leg. "Check your dose while I frisk you!"

Gary reached into his shirt pocket and found three dosimeters. *Damn, I was supposed to give a high-range to Doug.* He held his normal-range tube up to a light. As the scale inside came into view, Gary had trouble finding the needle. *There.* It was at the far end, beyond the highest mark of 200 m.r. *Off scale high. Crap!* Next, he tried one of the high-range dosimeters the HP in the plant had given him -- and sighed with relief when he saw the needle at 900 m.r. He had been exposed to nine hundred milli-rems of radiation during his short stay in the STurDI-1 room. *Not so bad.* In emergencies, personnel were allowed several times that amount.

There was a sharp thud on his leg, and Gary looked down. The HP had hit him with the probe to get his attention. "I said these are crapped up! Pants off! Now!"

****

"So half an hour," Wendell repeated back to the load dispatcher. "What happened? How'd we lose two different lines?"

"Don't know for sure. They saw foil near the west line. Could've been a metal balloon."

"All right. Just get us power. We're hurting bad."

"I know. You've got evacuations going on out there. Our trucks have had trouble getting through the road blocks. We're working as fast as we can."

Wendell put the phone down. *Evacuations.* Cervantes had already informed the crew that Brixton was being cleared out. Wendell could only hope Karen had gotten on the road early with the dog and headed for her sister's in Fort Wayne. She'd be worried about him, but there was nothing he could do. He stepped back into the control room. The water in the reactor had swollen a few more inches, but now it was boiling again and level was going back down – though the drop was slower this time. The lessening heat in the core could not produce as much steam as it had an hour before. "Tom," Wendell asked the STA, "how fast we dropping?"

"Inch a minute. Maybe less. We just hit eighteen."

So eighteen minutes and we uncover. Jesus. Too soon to get offsite back. If only they had offsite power, they could use a feedwater pump and slowly raise level at high pressure without cracking more fuel. *Slowly up. Inch a minute drop. Diesel...* Wendell's thoughts came together. *Maybe...* "How many gallons for each inch?" he asked, though he already knew the answer.

"A hundred, I think."

Wendell nodded. "Right." *Maybe it would work...*

****

At the site boundary, the geiger counter continued to read zero. The cloud of radioactive gas had drifted on by. Carol pulled the probe back inside and covered it with a plastic bag. "That's it, Marty," she said as she peeled off the rubber glove she had extended through the window. "We're out of it."

"Good," her driver said, "and thank God."

"We'll know for sure in a second." Carol slipped on a new glove and swapped rad monitors, returning to the more sensitive audible meter at her feet. She thrust its probe out the window and the device registered only the widely-spaced clicks of background radiation. "Looks fine," Carol said. "Let's cruise back and forth."

The vehicle slowly covered the route, but the readings did not change. Carol called in her findings, then scribbled some notes in her log. The second offsite team reported they were a mile downwind from the plant, and had yet to detect anything abnormal. The breeze was still light, and the plume seemed to be taking its time.

Carol put her book aside. *One hundred and twenty,* she repeated to herself, echoing the plume's biggest punch. She wished it had been lower, but many times she had worked in radiation fields greater than 120 milli-rems per hour. At that level, the release would pose little threat to the public, and as the cloud fanned out the dose would get progressively lower. Iodine might still create some problems, but as far as nuclear accidents went, things could be much worse. *Just think of Chernobyl....*

****

To Steve's relief, readings in the yard had tapered off to virtually nothing. Now it was a matter of tracking the cloud that had escaped. *But how did it get out?* Tarelli was at the wall maps. "Lou," Steve said, "do we know the source of the release?"

"Not yet. Basically, it seems to have been a puff of bad air." Tarelli shrugged. "Some kind of ventilation leak, maybe? I don't know. We've sent Crutch and an HP out to look."

"In-plant status?"

Tarelli pointed. "They're setting up to vent the drywell. Not too long on that. Leeman's still troubleshooting the diesel, and it's the same at STurDI-2." He paused. "Nothing on the immediate horizon, Steve."

Time: 4:08 am.
Time from Start of Event: 77 minutes
Reactor Water Level (above Fuel): 16 inches
Drywell Radiation: 20X normal (Damaged Fuel)
Radiation Release to Environment: Limited (Puff) Plume of
120 milli-rems per hour.

"So here an' here?" Leeman asked the two men kneeling beside him.

"Right. The rest of the points check out."

"Mmmmm, let's see..." The grizzled supervisor massaged his back as he peered down at the blueprint through his bifocals. Emergency diesel generator #1 sat silently nearby. "Yeah, that'd do it all right," he finally said. "You'd slip back ta idle."

"Gonna be hard to pin it down further," a technician said.

Leeman pointed. "Don't have to. Resistors here ... tap in at 6 ..."

"Yeah ..." the tech nodded, as he began to understand. "You're right, we could go around! There and there. I got those in my box. Quick fix."

"Do it, boys" Leeman said as he painfully climbed to his feet. "I'll holler at Control."

****

The assistant operator set the radio mike back on the table. "God, I hope Karl's right."

"He'll get it this time," the chief operator said. He had returned from his enforced break.

"Get another man down there," Cervantes ordered. He was perched again on the operator's table.

Wendell stood nearby, trying to keep his hopes in check. *Come on.* With the diesel running, the drywell cooling system could be started, and ARAFS could filter the air leaving the reactor building. The torus could be cooled down. And there was the opportunity to refill the reactor vessel by blowing down and then using the low pressure VEPI pumps. But there was a second option Wendell had been thinking through. He turned to Fleck and Cervantes. "We could go with the control rod pump for inject. Run it off the diesel. We can hold level stable and wait for offsite power. No blowdown." *Cleaner, less risk.*

Arms crossed, Fleck peered at the center panel. 'How fast we losing? Inch a minute?"

"Right," Wendell said. "A hundred gallons."

"And the CR Pump is 120 g.p.m.," Fleck said.

"So we gain a little, get offsite back and then use feedwater," Cervantes nodded. "No more fuel damage."

"Twenty-five minutes to offsite?" Fleck said.

Wendell checked the clock. "About that."

Fleck looked to Cervantes. "Could be the way to go." He paused. "Yeah, I think so."

In Cervantes hand, the pen twirled back and forth. His eyes narrowed. "Okay," he said. "Get set for it." He picked up the phone. "But be ready for blowdown, too."

"Great." The news of the diesel fix was the break Steve had been waiting for. *Karl, be right this time.* "Where we at?" he asked Cervantes.

"Level's at plus 16. Boiling now. Drywell's at 290."

Too close to 300. "If we get the diesel, drywell cooling is first."

"Agreed. How about ARAFS?"

"Understood. That'd be next."

"Then we deal with level," Cervantes said.

"So we blowdown."

"That's one way. Or we can use the control rod pump. Hold up level until feedwater is back.

Oh. "How long on feedwater?" Steve asked. "A half-hour?"

"They tell us twenty-five minutes for offsite power."

"Procedures say blowdown."

"Yeah, but you and I know they weren't written for this situation. They're for pipe breaks, not an intact system. The regs allow us to deviate with good cause."

"Understood. "

"Steve, we can do this," Cervantes said. "Come out with a little core damage. Nothing more. We can save this reactor. Keep the plant alive."

"That can't enter into it." *Public safety, not jobs.*

"Of course. No bullshit. If a blowdown were best, you know I'd say it."

Steve nodded. Cervantes surely would.

"But this is our way out," the operations supervisor continued. "We sit tight and hold level with the CR Pump. Then feedwater comes back and it's all over."

"You're assuming the diesel will keep running," Steve said.

"The problem is starting it. Leeman gets it rolling, it'll be fine."

"Okay, I understand. Give me a minute, Ted." Steve covered the phone with his palm. He stared down through his desktop, thinking. Using the control rod pump made sense. But so did blowing down. On the one hand, they could prevent more fuel damage, while on the other, after a blowdown the reactor would remain cool and stable for hours. So what was the downside? Cervantes' idea called for the plant to hang tight on the cliff edge until offsite power came back – in twenty minutes, or thirty, or an hour. They could pull out of this with a halfway decent core and no more releases. But the ARAFS filters were built to stop releases. And they'd be running. Then there was the power supply. The blowdown and fill would only take a minute. But there was no turning back. It was like popping the lid off a pressure cooker. Once it was up and running, the diesel should keep going for at least sixty seconds, even if it started to tear itself apart.

But could they count on it for an hour? And the procedures… was this the time to look past them?

So what was the answer? Steve understood the issues, but the call would be driven by instinct as well as facts. What was his gut telling him?

He lifted the phone. "Ted?"

"Here."

"I want you to blow down."

There was a pause. "CR Pump's a better way to go, Steve."

"Understood. But I don't want to be left with nothing if the diesel fades away, and I don't want to ignore the procedure. Either way we go, we'll end up in the same place. Let's get there as quick as we can. Blowdown and fill up with VEPI."

"Okay." Cervantes issued a few orders, then came back on the line. "We're on it. It'll work."

"Right."

"ARAFS first. Shouldn't take long to pull a vacuum on the building." Given a little time, the suction of the ARAFS fans would allow no air to leave the reactor building without first being filtered. That would include anything that escaped from the torus when the blowdown sent a huge amount of steam hurtling into the tank.

"How does torus temperature look?" Steve said. If the pool of water within the tank began to boil due to the additional steam from the blowdown, the huge container could burst open.

"It can take it. But anything else goes wrong, we better find another place to put the heat."

"Understood. So you can wait on torus cooling."

"Right. We do ARAFS, start the VEPI pumps, then take a good look at the diesel. Then we blow down." Cervantes sounded confident.

"All right, Ted. That's the plan. Make it work. And good luck."

Steve hung up. He looked around at the frenetic activity in the emergency center. "Lou!" he said to his second-in-command, who was conferring with Langford. Both hurried back. "Leeman may have the diesel going in a few minutes," Steve said. "Then we blow down."

"And maybe get another release," Tarelli added.

"Where we at on offsite teams?"

"The first two are pursuing the plume," Langford said. "They're still nearby. We're attempting to dispatch a third one. There seems to be a shortage of HPs."

"You think Leeman's got it this time?" Tarelli asked.

"I know Karl doesn't like to be wrong twice," Steve said. *And I've got to believe he won't be.*

****

Carol steadied the probe outside the window as the truck accelerated down the country lane. She and Marty had not encountered the plume in their zig-zag path towards a spot two miles downwind of the plant. The radio reported no further releases, but people were now being evacuated out to ten miles. "God," Marty said, "what's going on?"

"I wish I knew." Instinctively, Carol looked over her shoulder. Gary was back there somewhere.

The truck slowed as the headlights caught the white glint of a road sign. "Rose Road," Marty said. The driver turned and soon coasted to a halt. "How long before it gets here?" he asked.

"Awhile, I suppose," Carol said. "It hasn't reached the team at the mile mark yet." She noticed Marty looked pale, his skin drawn tight across his face. "Are you all right?"

He stared out through the windshield. "I'm worried. Scared maybe. This is too much."

"It'll be fine." Carol put her hand on Marty's shoulder. "They'll get things under control. And the plume isn't big, really."

"Right now, maybe not," he said. "But you saw what it was like at the plant. Something's fucked up really bad." Marty turned toward Carol. "It's not me so much. I got three little kids. And my wife. They must be scared to death."

Carol nodded. "Don't worry," she said, trying to sound reassuring, "they'll be taken care of. People have a way of getting through these things."

"Yeah, I suppose so." Marty sighed. He shifted his gaze to the floor. "But, man, I can't just sit here." His gloved hands squeezed the steering wheel in frustration. Suddenly, he looked back at Carol, the spark of an idea in his eyes. "We got some time, right?"

Carol considered the question. The truck was at least a mile beyond the plume. "We probably have a few minutes."

"I want to make a phone call," Marty said, strength creeping back into his voice. He pointed. "There's a campground over there. I've brought the kids out a few times. I know they got a pay phone." The driver fell silent, then jerked the truck into gear. "Fuck it, I'm doing it. We'll get back in time."

"Fine," Carol said. She thought of her own fears. *I understand.*

****

The radio reports hadn't changed since Paul had first tuned in. Waiting now for the FBI, he recalled his first visit to Fairview, then Hoosier Electric making him an offer. *A nuke plant? Well . . . the people seem nice ... it's a job ... give it a try...* He jumped back to the present. *What happened tonight?* A pipe break? A valving error? He could picture the bedlam in the emergency center: his coworkers sweating it out, searching for solutions. Paul tried to reassure himself. It might not be so bad. Even the radio kept stressing everything was being done as a precaution.

Paul rubbed his eyes. Whatever it was, there was nothing he could do -- for now. It was the future he would have to deal with. What would he find when he returned to work? He'd have a role piecing together what had happened -- a task that would surely go on and on. *They're still cleaning up at TMI... That isn't what I want! Not for a career.* He stared through the windshield. There would be a lot to do in the next few months. Dealing with work, sorting through his options, looking around. *So much ...* His spirits sinking, Paul grasped for the one thing that could him afloat. *Vickie.* There was Vickie. That was good. *I'll need to call her. Let her know I'm okay. And maybe I'll be able to tell her about this FBI thing.* But crime-busting didn't seem like such a big deal now.

There. Liz spied the Donut World and pulled her car off the highway. There was one other vehicle at the front of the closed store as she guided the black FBI sedan to a halt nearby. Liz gave Paul a nod. He started to get out of his car, but she waved him back. *Better talk to Walt first.* She hailed Kreveski several times, but South Bend's senior FBI agent did not respond. Then another voice cut in:

"Agent Rezhnitsky, this is Agent Winn. Where you at?"

Liz recognized Taylor Winn's voice. "Taylor, this is Liz. I'm at the rendezvous. Walt isn't here yet. Are you at the target?"

"Affirmative. The target is available. Over. Out."

"I understand," Liz replied. "Out." *So Donner is home.* Winn had played it smart, revealing little. It was always possible Donner was monitoring the radio. Now it was time to talk to Hendricks. On the drive up, Liz had decided to stick with the cover story of the drug runner. It was better if knowledge of the Soviet spy and his connection with the problems at Fairview were kept under wraps. But perhaps Paul could tell her something about what was going on at the power plant. Whatever it was, the reports indicated it was getting worse. Rolling down a window to keep the radio within earshot, Liz climbed out of her car, as did her contact.

"Good morning." Liz managed a smile. "Thanks for coming.

Have you heard about Fairview?"

"Yeah, on the radio."

"Any idea what's going on out there?"

"Not really. But something's gone bad. They've got an evacuation out by the plant."

"The State Police just said Brixton's being cleared out too. Everything up to ten miles downwind."

"Oh." Paul's shoulders slumped. "Did they say what happened?"

"It sounds like radiation got out."

The young engineer grimaced. "How much? Anybody give a number?"

"No, nothing like that."

"Things really have to be screwed up to go for ten miles," Paul said. "That's the limit for the emergency plan."

"Should you be helping?" Liz asked.

Paul shook his head. "I'm not on the team. If Brixton is getting cleared out, I'd be evacuated like everyone else." He sighed. "It's just as well I'm here. I guess I can't go home. What do you want me to do?"

Liz glanced around the empty lot. "I'll be able to tell you in a few minutes. We should have some company soon."

****

Amidst the hectic activity of the staging area, Gary climbed into a yellow jumpsuit. His arms still ached from holding back the STurDI pump, and a stinging sensation in his rear told him he might have a burn. He wasn't sure if they would let him go back in the power block. The higher rad levels meant repair crews had to work quickly, and due to his recent experience his own time would be even more limited. But he wanted to help. Then there was Doug Tama.

282

Lacking a higher range dosimeter, his exposure would remain unknown for a day at least, until his film badge was developed.

Gary pulled on rubber gloves. A respirator sat nearby, ready for use. He might have sucked something into his lungs already, but now was not the time to dwell on that. The plant was in deep trouble – and somewhere, out beyond the gates, his wife was chasing down a plume. *Crap.*

****

Carol fidgeted in the truck as Marty, at the payphone in the deserted campground, reached through the front of his jumpsuit to dig out change. For the first time, Carol noticed a low, droning sound in the distance. *The sirens.* The second team reported the plume had reached the one mile mark, and the radiation level was only a third of what Carol had recorded beside the site fence. In the cool spring wind, the invisible cloud was spreading out and its heavier particles were beginning to settle on the ground. An air sample had revealed more good news -- the iodine content of the plume was low.

Marty paced with the phone, waiting for someone to answer. Carol saw him hang up and try another number. At least she and Gary didn't have kids to worry about and their families were back in Michigan. But what of her husband? She could picture Gary struggling over a valve, cursing as he tried to piece the broken device back together. Dead heroes were not part of the Emergency Plan... but this was real life, not a drill. Things had been going so well. They might have found a house. And now this...

Marty ran back to the truck, his chubby body looking even more ungainly in the loose anti-c's. "No one home," he said, slamming the door. "Not at our place or her parents."

"They've gotten out then. It's all fine."

"I hope so," the driver sighed. "You sure you don't have anybody to call?"

"I'm sure."

They soon reached the point two miles downwind of the plant, near a darkened farmhouse. The plume had not yet arrived when Carol climbed back in the truck after seeing if anything had stuck to it during the first encounter. The radiator grill showed minor contamination. Waiting now, probe in hand, she stared out at the blackness, the thick grass edging the roadside bursting in and out of view in time with the truck's flashers. Ahead, she knew, was a flat, open plain, broken here and there by stands of trees, that reached on into Brixton.

Lights briefly came up from behind and then sped into the distance as a car hurtled past.

"Damn!" Marty said. "How fast do you think he was going?"

"Eighty, maybe ninety. He's a scared boy."

"Hard not to be …. Cop." Flashing blue lights appeared up ahead.

Shoot. "I'll talk, if we have to," Carol said, her mouth pulling tight in a frown as the county police car pulled up alongside.

"I guess we have to." The deputy rolled down his window and Marty did the same.

"You're from the nuke plant, right?" the officer asked, examining the occupants of the Hoosier Electric truck in their yellow suits, orange gloves, and skull caps. "What the hell is going on?"

Carol leaned across Marty's lap toward the window. "There's been a small release of radiation, and we're keeping track of it."

"Oh, God," the deputy responded. "That's what the dispatcher said. How bad is it?"

"It's not much," Carol said, trying to sound reassuring. "Not enough to hurt anything." *That's the best I can do.*

"Is the place gonna blow up or something?"

Carol studied the man's face. He had a look of concern, rather than fear. "We don't know much about what's going on inside," she said, tilting closer to the window, "but from our radio reports, it sounds like things are getting better."

"Where's the radiation that got out? Here?"

"It's closer to the plant. A little cloud drifting along the ground. With the wind."

"God." The deputy's voice was heavy with disgust. "Well, keep an eye on it." Throwing his car into gear, he sped away.

Vitaly bit into a cookie and listened to the radios atop the steamer trunk that served as his coffee table. The police scanner was tuned to the county sheriff, while the local FM station beside it alternated between music and tense updates. From a third radio, tuned to Hoosier Electric's frequency, he was learning more details. *It's all there. A release. An evacuation. Panic.* When he returned home to his wife and child, Vitaly Kruchinkin would have done his duty to the fullest.

And his co-workers at Fairview? Vitaly was sure they would do their best as well. Did the ten mile evacuation mean more damage than he had planned? A higher dose to those doing the repairs? Were people taking big risks, beyond those that normally went with the job? He hoped that wasn't the case, but from the start he had known it could happen. Better a worse night at Fairview than for his mission to fail. There was too much at stake.

The phone startled him, but Vitaly quickly regained his composure. *Call out,* he guessed. He looked at the clock. *About right.* He turned off the radios. "Hello?"

"John Donner, please."

"This is John." Vitaly spoke as if suffering from a cold.

The caller was Cervantes' secretary. "We have a real mess at the plant," she said.

"What's going on?"

"I'm not really sure, but they're calling in everyone they can."

"Oh, shit." Vitaly cleared his throat and coughed. "I'm sick as a dog. How bad are you hurting for operators?"

"We've got some people coming but we'll need relief crews in a few hours."

"Maybe I can do that, if I sleep this off," Vitaly said. "I can hardly breathe right now, and I've got a fever going."

"All right. We'll contact you later. Stay by your phone."

John Donner would be well enough in a few hours to work, Vitaly knew. The Hoosier Electric employee would be tired and coughing, but also very determined to make a contribution. Donner was a good operator. He would do what needed to be done.

****

Joel cruised the residential street, briefly adding his own siren to the fire station's. He made the announcement again:

> "Attention! There is a problem at the Fairview Nuclear
> Plant. Brixton is being evacuated. Tune to your radio
> for details."

It had been only fifteen minutes, and much of Brixton was still waking up to the news, lights flicking on as the squad car passed by. With a phone call, Joel had made sure his wife had a head start. The young policeman was about to accelerate when a figure in sweat pants and a torn T-shirt flagged him down.

"Has the nuke plant blown up? We gettin' fallout?" The man was unshaven, his hair a tangled mess.

"Sir, I can't tell you much. There's a problem at the nuclear plant and civil defense wants the town evacuated."

"Those fuckers out there finally did it! What happened?"

"I don't know," Joel said. *Keep it calm. Keep it simple.* "We've just been told to evacuate. If you need somewhere to go, they're

286

opening up Norsay High School, so head up there."

"The hell with that! I'm driving east 'til I hit Ohio."

"Fine, sir. Be careful." Joel tapped on the gas before the man had a chance to reply. *It's just gonna get worse.*

****

Steve waited. It was up to Leeman now. If anyone could jury-rig a solution, it was him. *Soon Karl, soon.*

Tarelli appeared. "Steve, the guys working the drywell vent think they can crank the valve in another five minutes."

Steve frowned. "Understood." It was an option -- but not the one he wanted. "If we get the diesel back, we'll start the cooling system. Otherwise, we vent. We can't wait for offsite power. Too close to 300, and I won't risk the drywell." *It must stay intact.* "If we do vent," Steve sighed, "what will the rads be like?"

Tarelli frowned. "Ballpark, we think the gas would be around 75 Rem an hour."

God. 75 Rems. Steve knew the situation was bad, but to hear the numbers... It would be a huge release, thousands of times larger than the cloud the trucks were chasing. It could pose a genuine hazard.

"At least we can blow it through ARAFS," Tarelli said, "and keep the iodine out of the food chain."

"I suppose that's some consolation. It's better than having the drywell split open."

Tarelli's expression brightened. "But if Karl's right about the diesel..."

In the cabinet behind diesel generator #1, the instrument technician made the connections, with Leeman guiding the work. The room was quiet, save for the sound of shallow breathing.

"One more, right?" the tech said, not taking his eyes off the maze of wires. Sweat dripped across his jaw.

"Yessir." Leeman checked the blueprint. "F-9. That'll do it."

...then cycle the chiller valve... At the dimly-lit control panel, Wendell went over the steps needed to start the drywell cooling system. From there, he would slide over a few feet, and when the order came to blow down the reactor vessel, he would open the pressure relief valves. He didn't understand fully why they weren't using the control rod pump instead to buy precious minutes, but he could guess some of the reasons – and there wasn't time to worry about it.

"Control! Leeman!"

Wendell looked back at the radio. *Make it run, Karl.*

Fleck picked up the mike. "Control. Go ahead."

"We're fixin' to start this son-of-a-bitch. You set?"

"Hang on." The shift supervisor surveyed the room. Wendell and three operators stood at the control panels, while Cervantes remained perched nearby, the phone on his shoulder. More staff members were in the back of the room. Fleck looked hard at the assistant operator in front of the diesel controls. "You ready?"

"Ready."

"Drywell cooling?" Fleck looked toward Wendell.

Wendell met his partner's gaze. "Ready."

Once the diesel was running, the reactor building's air filters would be the first equipment put in operation. "ARAFS?" Fleck asked the extra operator.

"Yep."

A few feet closer, the chief operator stood at the VEPI controls. If all went well, the pumps would soon be re-filling the vessel. "VEPI?" he asked.

"Let's do it."

Fleck turned to Cervantes, and the operations supervisor nodded grimly. "It's up to Karl."

Cervantes' voice came through loud and clear over the phone. "Here we go, Steve."

Steve looked at Tarelli, who was listening in, and his second-in-command held up crossed fingers. "Attention!" the plant manager announced to the busy room. "We're about to try the diesel!" The staff fell silent.

Steve waited. On the other end of the line, the control room was quiet.

God, it's got to work. It's got to.

Karl Leeman took his spot at the control panel of the diesel generator, an operator beside him. The three other men in the room surrounded the massive engine, training their flashlights on dials and meters.

"Y'all set?" Leeman yelled. The replies were immediate. Leeman turned to the operator at the panel. "Local start. Go."

The tense quiet of the control room was broken by an alarm and a flashing light.

"Diesel start!" the assistant operator said. "R.P.M.s coming up!"

Come on! This time! Wendell demanded. The engine should only need a few seconds to reach full speed.

"R.P.M.s at rated!" the assistant operator said.   A second alarm began to blink. "On the bus! Diesel is on the bus!"   The emergency generator was now ready to provide power to the plant. The operator gave a control handle a firm turn. "Diesel cooling pump on! ... No problems!" He punched a button and the alarm horns stopped. A sharp silence returned; all eyes still fixed on the diesel controls.

Jesus, it's working. We're gonna do it! Wendell's hands poised above the controls for drywell cooling.

"Still looks good!" the assistant operator said. " R.P.M.s normal. Voltage normal." He glanced back at Fleck. "It's running fine."

Fleck nodded. He looked at Wendell. "Drywell cooling on."

NOW! "Drywell cooling on!" Wendell repeated, as he turned the switches and watched the lights above change color. "Inlet valve .... going open. Cooling pump on! ...." He saw a meter swerve. "We've got flow!   System running .... flow normal."   He flipped more controls. "Fan number 1... on. ... Fan number 2 ... on." *And that's it.* Wendell looked over his shoulder at Fleck. "Drywell cooling in service."

Wendell's partner crossed his arms, and then let out a deep breath. "Okay, let's hold steady till we hear back from Leeman."

More nervous quiet.   Cervantes, still on the phone with the emergency center, paced the two steps the cord would allow.

Wendell checked drywell cooling. *No problems.* Cold water was now racing through pipes within the huge shell, while fans circulated its hot air over and around them.

"Control! Leeman."

Fleck grabbed the microphone.

"So fer, looks normal," Leeman drawled. "T'ain't much of a load, though."

"Roger. Hang on a second." Fleck turned to Cervantes. "We'll get ARAFS going, then have him check again."

Cervantes nodded.

Fleck's eye fell on the panels at the far right. "Okay, start ARAFS."

"Starting ARAFS!" the operator said. "Got the fan! .... Got the heaters .... Air flow increasing ... More .... More .... Normal flow!"

Fleck lifted the mike. "Karl, we're running ARAFS now. Check everything again."

The tense atmosphere in the control room continued. "How we doing on drawing a vacuum?" Fleck asked.

"No negative pressure yet," the operator reported. With the ARAFS fans sucking air from its rooms and hallways, the reactor building atmosphere would soon drop to a lower pressure than the world outside, which meant any gap in the outer walls would be filled by harmless outside air rushing in. The ARAFS filters would then be the sole path for any escaped fuel gas to leave the building.

"Okay so far," Cervantes murmured into the phone.

Wendell moved over to the center panel. *The next step...blowdown. It's got to work. Got to.* Two VEPI pumps would be started, and then Wendell would open all the pressure relief valves, allowing the remaining steam and water in the reactor vessel to roar down into the torus. Vessel pressure would plummet from the current 950 pounds per square inch. At 500 p.s.i. a valve would open, connecting the VEPI pumps to the reactor. Pressure would continue to fall until, at 250 p.s.i., the two pumps could finally force water into the huge steel capsule. By then, there would be nothing but a little steam surrounding the core. If water wasn't quickly pumped in, the fuel would begin to melt. *Jesus, it's got to work.*

"Control! Leeman! Second time, all readin's good. Do what'cha gotta do, boys."

"Hang tight right there," Fleck said. He turned to Cervantes: "We'll wait a couple of minutes and let ARAFS get a good negative pressure. Then start VEPI and do a final check."

"Right."

Wendell stared at the controls for the P.R.V.s. *Almost there.*

Time: 4:20 am
Time from Start of Event: 89 minutes
Reactor Water Level (above Fuel): + 13 inches

In the emergency center, the staff worked in whispers. Steve pressed the phone hard against his ear, trying to make out every word said in the control room. He fought any elation when the diesel first came on line. *Good news, but still a ways to go.* Yet, no matter what lay ahead, cooling the drywell air was removing a heavy burden from him. The thought of venting a horrifying cloud into the atmosphere was receding with each moment. He would have made the decision if he'd had to, but ...*Thank God.*

And now came the blowdown. It was an all-or-nothing call. If something went wrong, they would have a crumbling core, and very soon, a pool of deadly, molten slop at the bottom of the vessel. How could they pump water through such a mess to cool it down? How could they be sure there was no ongoing nuclear reaction, no debris so hot with atomic fire that it would eat its way right through the vessel? But the alternative to a blowdown was to wait for offsite power. Soon, the fuel would be uncovered again, and the tips of the damaged bundles would grow white hot a second time. When it was finally dowsed again with cold water, the core might then shatter like glass. Would the transmission lines be fixed in time to prevent such a catastrophe? And how stable would the connection be? Too many questions. It was time to refill the vessel. Now.

"ARAFS is on," Cervantes reported. "Should have a solid vacuum soon. Then we go."

Steve's grip on the phone tightened. "Understood. Good luck."

"Drywell temperature is creeping down," Wendell said, checking the meter. The hush in the darkened control room had only been broken for such updates, the crew and the onlookers behind waiting while the ARAFS fans drew more air out of the reactor building.

The room grew brighter. Wendell blinked.

"That's better," Fleck said. A bank of lights had been plugged into the diesel generator circuit.

After his eyes had adjusted, Wendell stole a look at Darrel Fleck. The tall, heavy-set shift supervisor, his sweaty blond hair plastered against his forehead, appeared in control, but exhausted. Wendell could feel his own damp shirt clinging to his back and he reached around and pulled it free. *How long have we been at this?* By his watch he saw it was 4:20. *Eighty minutes, maybe ninety.* An eternity ago, Karen had helped him make his lunch and then he had left for a quiet shift at Fairview Station. When he had arrived, the plant was running, with no major problems. Then a power line had gone down a few miles away. And then another ... Now Brixton, and Karen, were being evacuated. *Jesus...*

"Pressure in the building is still falling," the operator at the ARAFS panel reported. "We're starting to pull a vacuum."

"One more test for the diesel," Fleck said. He looked toward Cervantes, then gave the order: "VEPI in idle."

The chief operator turned a black handle. "Starting VEPI pump #1! .... Start is successful... idle flow confirmed." He repeated the sequence for the second pump.

Over the radio, Fleck asked the operator stationed outside the diesel room to check with Leeman on how the machine was handling the increased burden. He then trained his eyes on the assistant operator. "How's it look from here?"

"Fine. It took the load okay. No problems."

"Good." Fleck motioned to the center panel. "Give Wendell a hand."

Wendell stood by as the assistant operator shifted over. The short, chunky man, his brown mane more unkempt than usual, had been a quiet and solid presence.

"I'll pop the P.R.V.s, then cover pressure," Wendell said.

The operator nodded. "I'll take level. Watch VEPI do its thing."

Behind his glasses, his eyes were lit with expectation.

Wendell turned to the four buttons, a green light above each. When given the order, he would open the pressure relief valves, and the steam and water remaining in the reactor vessel would escape into the torus. After that, it was up to VEPI. Many times in the simulator he had performed the same task, never believing it would become a real necessity. No NEB reactor had ever been forced to do it.

"Vacuum improving. Nearing required."

Soon now. Soon. Action was always better than waiting, but the feeling in Wendell's gut was not anticipation. There was no reason to think anything else would go wrong -- but so many things had broken. Why not one more?

"Control!" the radio beckoned. "Leeman says the diesel still looks fine! Running smooth."

"Roger," Fleck said. "We're going for blowdown and VEPI injection. Anything happens, do what you can."

"Diesel's okay, Steve," Cervantes relayed over the phone. He continued to pace, his wide features drawn, his dark eyes squeezed to a thin, intense line.

Fleck lay the radio mike aside. "Gentleman, we're gonna be at required vacuum real quick. Then we go."

Wendell's hands flexed. *Just tell me, and I'll start the blowdown.*

"Larry, take VEPI out of idle," Fleck ordered. "Put the system in auto."

"VEPI to auto." The valve separating the VEPI pumps from the reactor was now set to open once pressure in the vessel had dropped by half. Soon afterwards, the VEPI pumps would force fresh water into the huge tank.

"Required vacuum!" the operator at the ARAFS panel announced. "We're there."

"Reactor status," Fleck asked.

"Vessel level is plus 12 inches," the assistant operator said. "Reactor pressure is 960, torus temp 140."

Cervantes spoke into the phone, then laid the receiver on the table.

He turned to Fleck. "Do it."

"This is it!" the shift supervisor announced to the room. He looked to the center panel and the P.R.V. controls.

Wendell tensed as he caught his partner's eye. They had been through a nightmare together, standing by helplessly as the water in the reactor had slowly boiled away. Now it was time to turn things around.

Fleck called out the order: "Blow down the vessel! NOW!"

"Blowdown!" Wendell stabbed at the four buttons, alarms sounding as the light above each changed from green to red. "All P.R.V.s open!" As the pressure relief valves lifted, the thirty thousand gallons of scalding water still surrounding the reactor core instantly flashed to steam and escaped in a screeching torrent.

"Level's gone!" the assistant operator shouted. "Downscale!"

Wendell could feel a dull rumbling in the floor as steam raced down into the torus. The pressure indicator for the vessel, a thick red pointer, was plummeting. "Pressure 800!" he said. More alarms began to drone, but all were quickly stopped, and except for the muffled, distant roar of the blowdown, the control room was silent. Pressure continued to fall.

"700!"

"Torus at 160 degrees, rising!" the assistant operator reported. The water in the massive tank was being heated by the new steam.

"Pressure 600!" *The valve will open at five.*

Fleck stepped up beside the chief operator, and both stared at the light for the VEPI valve. It was green -- valve closed.

"550!" Wendell reported. *Come on, open ...* "500!"

The green light held steady ... steady... and then became red. An alarm sounded. "Inject valve coming open!" the chief operator said.

Good! Now for the pumps ... "Pressure 400!" Nothing stood between the vessel and the VEPI pumps, and at 250 p.s.i., they would be able to force water into the huge steel capsule. Wendell stared at the red pointer. The pressure loss was beginning to slow, but the value kept drifting down ... down... "300!" He began calling out the numbers: "290!....... 270!....260!...." *Come on! Come on!* "... 250!"

"Go!" the chief operator said.

".. 240! .. "

"GOT IT!" the chief operator screamed, as yet another alarm came in. "I got flow! I got flow! ....One and two ramping up!... Both past 7000!"

Yes! It was happening! *Jesus, thank you!* The VEPI pumps were pouring water into the reactor at 14,000 gallons a minute.

"Level still downscale!" the assistant operator said. The swirling water within the vessel was not yet high enough for the instruments to record.

"Get there," Fleck said. He moved behind Wendell.

"Pressure 175!" Wendell read off. He glanced at the nearby level indicator. The black pointer still hugged the bottom of the scale. *Come on! Up!*

"Level is still down-" the assistant operator began. The pointer jerked.

Now! NOW! Wendell's heart skipped a beat as the indicator began shooting towards the ceiling.

"Level up! Level up!" the operator yelled over the alarms. "Minus 90! Moving fast!"

"Yes!" the chief operator said. "YES!"

"That's it, that's it." Fleck added. Behind him, Cervantes punched at the air.

Wendell stood transfixed, watching the pointer move up the scale. A button was pushed and the alarm horns stopped. The rumble of the blowdown had also ceased. There were now only voices, and the control room staff promptly quieted as the new countdown for level began.

"Minus 40! ... Minus 30! ..."

Wendell felt a massive weight being lifted away. He kept his eyes fixed on the pointer. *Come on ...*

"Minus 20! ...."

The center panel was the sole focus of attention.

"Minus 10! ...." the assistant operator read off. "... Minus 7 ... 4 ... 1 ... ZERO AND RISING!"

There were cheers. Claps. Broad grins. Wendell felt the remaining burden disappear as a wave of relief swept over him.

Cervantes picked up the phone. "Core's covered, Steve."

"We've re-covered the core!" Steve said to his waiting staff. "VEPI is running." The stuffy, darkened room erupted, and the plant manager felt his own tension start to drain away. There was still much to do, but the decisions they had made were beginning to pay off. He leaned back and closed his eyes. *Thank you. Oh God, thank you.*

Emergency diesel generator #1 was rumbling steadily as Karl Leeman inched around it, the beam of his flashlight playing across the machine's surface. His face, flecked with white stubble and lined by age and tension, now bore a new expression -- a slight, satisfied smile.

****

"200 inches!" the assistant operator said.

Wendell, too, was now watching the level indicator. One of the VEPI pumps had already been turned off, and it was time to stop the other before water began to slosh over into the steam lines. He looked toward Fleck.

"Larry, shut down VEPI," Fleck said, and the operator flipped a handle.

"Level is 210 -- and holding." The assistant operator let out a deep breath and leaned wearily against the panel. Seventeen feet of water now covered the core.

There was silence. Fairview Station had just pulled back from the brink of disaster. The chief operator broke the spell. "YES!" The room burst out in excited chatter.

Wendell, too, finally let go. *Jesus, we made it.* He was almost laughing. *We made it!* He caught Fleck's glance, and the two shift supervisors exchanged a look of relief, and triumph.

****

The emergency center brightened as half the overhead lights came on. Ventilation also returned, and Steve allowed himself a moment to enjoy the cooling breeze. He looked to the door of the radio room, where Tarelli was standing. "Lou, anything more on the release after the blowdown?"

Tarelli stepped closer. "Langford says ten milli-rems was the max in the yard. Site boundary got up to two and then dropped off.. Basically, the only plume out there now is the first one."

Another break.

"ARAFS helped us out," Tarelli said. "Crutch hasn't found the first leak path yet."

Steve looked at the county map, and the orange star inching toward Brixton. "How about the plume?"

"They're picking it up at two miles." Tarelli pointed at the map. "It probably won't hit twenty milli-rem."

It's dropping off quick. "Levels in the plant?"

"About the same. We got all the teams out of the reactor building before the blowdown, just in case." Tarelli looked around. "We've hardly seen a blip on the meter in here. Same for the control room."

"What about inside the reactor? Any idea what we've got?"

"Basically, we figure core damage is around five percent. Most of the cracked tubes are probably still in one piece. We'll have a better idea once we get a water sample."

A frown crossed Steve's tired face. *Any fuel damage is too much. Way too much. But -- after all this, five percent I'll take.*

Langford came up behind Tarelli. "The load dispatcher estimates five to ten minutes now on the west line."

Steve heard the good news. *Offsite power. Then we'll really start recovering.*

****

Sprawled across his couch, Vitaly listened to the radios. The police were struggling to cover the evacuation, while the local stations had little new to say. On Hoosier Electric's frequency, the teams were still tracking the release, and it sounded as if the radiation leak at the plant was under control. The pathway Vitaly had created out of the building was closing itself off.

What will it be like when I go back there? Did the core get screwed up? How much contamination? And how would his fellow employees deal with the disaster? So many things had gone wrong. Would there be suspicions, or just self-recrimination about bad maintenance and poor design? Vitaly told himself not to worry. His plan had been excellent.

Then there was John Donner. The operator must remain at Fairview Station for a time, working hard on the plant's recovery. Of course, there would be an exodus from the Fairview staff, and eventually John Donner would move on. He would talk of somewhere exotic -- South America or Australia perhaps. And finally... it would be over. Home. To be with Yelena, and not face the certain pain of saying goodbye. To be with his child. To know for the rest of his days that he had done his duty. It was a future he longed to embrace. *Soon.*

Besides the peaceful music from the FM station, there was a lull in the radio noise, and Vitaly punched the search button on the police scanner. It flipped back and forth, discharging snippets of conversation:

> "...two, but they were okay..."
> "... 25 to station...."
> "...Out."

Vitaly leaned forward to adjust the other radios while the scanner continued:

> "...the Donut World on the corner. Check in with detective and special agents. They will direct. Out."

Special agent, Vitaly repeated as he fiddled with the FM dial. *That could be ... what? FBI? ... Maybe... Yes, that's right.* The thought made him pause, and for an instant his worst fears came into view, but he dismissed any concern. If he'd been under suspicion, they would never have allowed him to complete the job. And it was much too soon after the event for him to be a suspect. The scanner moved on:

> "...en route. 2-2-3-1 Elm. Out."
> "...from Brixton, but we'll let you know...."

Time: 4:28 am.
Time from Start of Event: 97 minutes
Reactor Water Level (above Fuel): 211 inches

"How far are we from Fairview?" Liz asked, as she and Paul waited in the deserted lot. *Too close?*

"Maybe fifteen miles." There was a catch in Paul's voice. "Far enough. And the wind isn't right."

A standard issue FBI sedan turned in, followed by two patrol cars. "Wait here." Liz walked over to the agency car and climbed inside. "Hi, Walt."

"I'm getting too old for this stuff, you know," Kreveski said, shoving up his black-framed glasses. "And what did your suspect do to Fairview, anyway?

"All I know is what I've heard on the radio. I've got to assume he's involved. That's my contact from the plant over there. He says the evacuation means it's pretty bad."

"Sounds like it. Damn shame too." Kreveski's tone grew serious. "So how much did Taylor tell you?"

"We kept it short," Liz replied. "He just said Donner's at home."

"Somebody is anyway. Is that all?"

"I don't think he wanted to say much more over the air."

"Yeah," Kreveski nodded, "we were careful too. Taylor said the house seemed dead when he got there. He just figured Donner was asleep, but then about four o'clock a car pulled into the driveway."

He was out! Liz was not surprised, but the news still hit hard -- it was a final confirmation.

"It looked like a man driving," Kreveski went on. "Car pulled in the garage. Had to be Donner. You wouldn't figure him to have any roommates."

"Right," Liz agreed. *It was him. It was HIM!* "When did Fairview start having problems?"

"The police here first heard about it around 3:15. It'd been going on for a while by then. So with the distances, and the time, Donner could have been there."

Liz threw her head back against the seat. *Damn!* She turned to Kreveski in the darkened car. "How we set for picking him up?"

"About ready. I got the judge up and got a warrant. He's a friend of mine. And I let your boss know."

"Thanks." *Keep this quiet.* "So how many people know about Donner, anyway?

"The warrant doesn't mention Fairview. The judge and chief of police know he's an illegal, but it's still narcotics to everyone else."

"Good. Same with my contact. How soon can we move?"

"I just came back from the place," Kreveski said. "Got as good a look as I could in the dark." He flipped on the dome light and displayed a hand-drawn map. "Donner lives at the end of a cul-de-sac on the edge of town, a few miles from here. The street goes up a little rise. Juts out into a cornfield."

Liz studied the drawing. "It's the spot an illegal would choose."

"Well, this one did. Taylor was worried about him sneaking out the back way, so we've got a car cruising each of the nearest roads."

Liz kept her eyes on the map. "How should we go in?"

"What are the chances he'll resist?"

"I don't know. This is a whole new ballgame as far as illegals go."

"He came home," Kreveski noted. "There's a light on now. I'd say he's not expecting anyone."

"So you think try for a standard pickup?"

"Yeah. But go in unmarked. Ring the doorbell and then put the cuffs on him."

****

"Car Four, what are the conditions?" The sheriff's deputy was only a mile from Fairview Station, and Phyllis feared for his safety.

"It's still dark over by the plant."

"Any radiation?"

"I just checked the little tube they gave us. Still reads zero."

"Remember, the sheriff says to stay inside the car if you can. Keep your windows up." Phyllis clicked off the mike. The news of a radioactive cloud had sent a shudder through her. Hoosier Electric said it wasn't dangerous, but that was not very reassuring. Somewhere out there was a black fog, ready to bring pain and death. What would it feel like if she ended up in the cloud? Would there be tingling? Burning? Would she go blind? At Fairview Station, Phyllis could picture men and women in lab coats, desperately turning switches, while others in bulky spacesuits battled their way into rooms filled with a misty, greenish glow. All were doing their best to hold back the tide of disaster. But it wasn't enough.

She looked at the picture of her grandson taped to the wall. At least he was safe. But what of her neighbors, her friends? And what would be left in the morning, once the toxic mist had gone by? Would homesteads have to be abandoned -- the animals killed, the crops plowed under? Would a big chunk of Potowatomie County be a dead zone? And what kind of gruesome scene would be found at the plant itself? Peering at the county map, Phyllis traced the path of the deadly cloud over the country fields and on into Brixton. She said a prayer.

****

There was another round of smiles in the emergency center as the remaining lights came on. Offsite power was back. Tarelli returned from the radio room, and Steve saw the red golf shirt on his second-in-command was soaked with sweat.

"Plume's breaking up well," Tarelli reported.

"Is there any chance of another release?" Steve said. "Any way we could burp out more gas?"

"I don't think so. Basically, ARAFS is running fine, and we're not moving steam around any more."

"So what's the in-plant situation?"

"Well, it could be a lot worse. Still airborne in most of the reactor building, but rad levels are dropping."

"Good." Steve knew it might be hours, or days, or weeks before the staff could re-enter some areas without masks or anti-c's. But things were headed in the right direction. "Let's get a plan together to clean up. Then we'll figure out what happened." *And where did we go wrong? Why didn't the diesel start? A loose connection from the last overhaul? Dripping coolant causing a short? And the STurDI systems: Poor maintenance? Did we push a work crew too hard? -- did they make mistakes? Did we train them right?* So many questions.

****

Rounding a Brixton residential corner in his squad car, Joel saw a vehicle blocking most of the street. The car was dented, and two men were arguing beside it, with a cluster of people nearby. Even before he had climbed out, the police officer could hear the men screaming:

"... stupid fucking thing to do! Watch the road!"

"Fuck you! If you'd kept going-"

"Phil, stop it!" a woman said. "Let's take the other car and get out of here!" A young girl beside her was crying.

Joel approached the two adversaries. One had a pronounced height advantage. "You'll be paying!" the taller man said.

"Hell if I will! I show you what-" The shorter man lunged and took a clumsy swing that caught his opponent in the chest.

304

"Stop! Now!" Joel ordered, as the men reached out to grab one another. The policeman shoved himself between the two combatants. "NO ... MORE!"

"He wrecked my car!" the shorter man said, pointing to a second dented vehicle in a driveway.

"Looks like you did each other's," Joel said. *Get them calmed down.* "Now just relax." Cautiously, he put his arms down. "You've had an accident here. I can see that."

"He backed into me!" the taller man said.

"Daddy, I'm afraid!" the little girl cried. "Let's go!"

Joel looked hard at the taller man, and spoke with authority. "Right now, at this moment, I don't care who did what. We can sort that out later. I'll take your names, and then you go. Understand?"

The man's fierce glare softened a little. He nodded. "Okay."

Joel looked at the other adversary.

"Yeah," he said, waving his hands. "Fine by me."

****

"Thanks." Wendell stepped aside for his replacement, then weaved his way through clumps of personnel. Weariness flooded over him. For a while at least, he could give in to the fatigue. Wash up. Get a drink. In the bathroom, he splashed cold water on his face. The chill felt good. Looking up, he saw his reflection in the mirror, his copper hair darkened with sweat, his blue eyes dulled by shock and exhaustion. Wendell stared back at the taut face, following a drop of water as it streamed past the freckles on his cheek. In a little while, when things had really calmed down, he would try calling around to find Karen.

At his desk, Wendell checked the log book. The last entry was his own:

> "2:42. Lost backup offsite power (east line). LD says down a few miles from plant. Dispatched operator to check onsite readings. W.A."

He thought back to the moment. He had just finished writing when the lights had gone out. The night's events then became a jumbled collection of images enveloped in tension, anger, and fear. Darkness. Alarms. A scram. An isolation. No diesels, STurDI-1, STurDI-2. Wendell grimaced. The water over the fuel had kept boiling away…

Wendell closed his eyes and thought of what lay ahead. Questions. Endless reviews. Hearings. And when that was finished? He was twenty-eight years old. He had been at Fairview six years. What of his reputation? What kind of a career could he have now?

****

The truck came to a halt at the outskirts of Brixton, six miles from Fairview Station. On one side of the street, framed by the brightening eastern sky, were new suburban homes, while across the road a plowed field stretched back toward a distant line of trees. Not far beyond those woods, Carol knew, a plume of radioactive gas was drifting invisibly towards them. It was more than a mile wide now, its radiation level creeping down towards five milli-rem per hour.

Carol studied the well-kept houses, each with a wide driveway of asphalt and a yard of fresh sod. The neighborhood looked as peaceful as one would expect for an early Sunday morning. But the sound of blaring sirens that seeped through the windows told a different story.

Minutes passed, and there was only the occasional background click from the geiger counter. Carol wished the cloud would arrive so she could quiet her mind with work. She had asked over the radio if Gary was all right, but all they could tell her was that no injuries had been reported. With time now to reflect, she was beginning to glimpse a very different future for them, and the idea frightened her in a way radiation never would. They were in the middle of the next T.M.I., and she couldn't imagine raising a family in such an atmosphere. Their new home was only a few blocks away, and they'd be lucky to sell it at all, at a hefty loss. But where would they go? Another plant, or an industrial job? Or would they head back to Michigan, to somehow chase Gary's dream of a boat? And what of her friends here -- at work, at church -- what would they do?

The radio came to life, announcing the state of Indiana had also dispatched a chase vehicle to track the plume.

"Fine," Carol murmured. Searching for a distraction, she peered over at the nearest house, and was surprised to see a woman, gray hair draped across the shoulders of her bathrobe, staring out from a window. Her face spoke of terror. Carol looked back into the frightened eyes. *It's all right. It's going to be all right.*

Time: 5:15 a.m.
Time From Start of Event: 144 minutes
Reactor Level (above Fuel): 211 inches (stable)

The impending sunrise colored the sky as Paul waited beside the patrol car, hands thrust into his jacket. Up ahead there was a huddle around another of the vehicles. All were parked along a plowed field, beyond which lay a well-lit intersection where a street branched off and turned up a hill. Homes lined both sides of the inclined road. There was nothing unusual about the place, Paul thought. A typical small subdivision. Except John Donner lived there.

The map was spread out on the hood, and Liz studied it along with Kreveski and Taylor Winn, now relieved of his stakeout duties. Behind them, two uniformed policemen and a plain-clothes detective also peered at the sketch. Liz had studied the officers closely when she was introduced. Steadiness and calm were needed now, not some gung-ho types. The men seemed to fit the bill.

Kreveski pointed with a weathered finger. "Donner's home is here -- eight houses up, almost to the top, on our side of the road. It's a small one-story with an attached garage. The neighbors on either side are blocked off by a wooden fence about my height. The suspect's yard is open to the back. There's a strip of field and then these woods." The senior agent moved his finger from mark to mark. "We've got two officers in place: one in the woods behind, and the other in our car across the street." He turned back to the three policemen. "Two more of you go up the hill."

"Me and Frank go," the detective said. He looked at the third man. "Bobby, you stay. Keep an eye on us."

"Now here's what you do," Kreveski said. "One goes up the far side of the street, behind the houses." The agent pointed across the intersection.

"Frank, you got that," the detective said.

Liz turned to the officer. "Understand, you and the guy sitting in our car up there are the first backups. Anything goes wrong and you move in. Quick."

"Detective," Kreveski said, "you and I will go up to the house just below Donner's." He gestured at the nearest line of homes climbing the hill. "Then I'll move on into his backyard if I can."

"Walt, I figured I'd do that," Winn said. "You and Liz can make the arrest out front."

"That's how I had it figured, too" Liz said. *Senior agent gets it.*

"No, let the old hunter do the sneaking around," Kreveski said with a grin. "You two bring him in. It'll look good on your records. Doesn't matter to me -- I'm about done with all this stuff anyway."

Liz looked over at Winn. The tall, black agent shrugged. "It's what the man wants."

Liz folded up the map. "That's it then. Let's go."

Paul remained at a discrete distance, hearing enough to know that Donner's home was out of view, near the top of the incline. *This will really be something.* An officer headed toward the intersection, stopping to peer around the house on the corner. After a moment, he darted behind a large tree near the street, then sprinted across the pavement until he was again screened from the hilltop. The policeman gave a quick wave and disappeared. Two more figures now moved away. In the lead was an older man wearing a dark blue windbreaker with FBI in bold yellow letters on the back. The two came to the corner home's back yard, turned, and started up the hill. Nearby, a dog began barking.

Liz stood with Winn and the remaining officer, watching Kreveski and the detective fade into the twilight. "Won't take him long," Winn said, as he adjusted the wire running from his earphone to the walkie-talkie in his overcoat. "Walt can move pretty quick when he wants to."

"Good." Liz cradled her own radio, drumming her fingers against the case.

"Quite a feat, you finding this guy," Winn said. "It was hard to keep from going after the bastard right when he drove up."

"I can imagine." Liz looked at the darkened hillside. "The evidence just came together. I had a lot of help." She took a few slow, deep breaths. But her concerns remained. Was Donner suspicious? Would he come to the door? His house lights were on, and Liz assumed he was following the news about Fairview Station. Maybe he'd just give up quietly. Act confused and play dumb. ...Yes ... that's probably how it would go. She grabbed her purse off the car hood and slung it across her right shoulder. Opening the bag, she felt for her revolver.

Kreveski picked his way along the edge of the back yards, the detective close behind. The dog near the bottom of the hill continued to bark. "One more house after this, and then Donner's," the agent whispered. "It's a little white place. You peel off as we pass by the next yard. Cover the side fence."

The detective nodded, and the two moved ahead in a crouch. A dozen more steps and Kreveski signaled the officer to take his position. The senior agent then crept forward to the rear of Donner's lot, behind the metal garden shed of a neighbor. The small outbuilding was pressed up against the tall wooden fence that separated the two yards. From the corner of the shed a few loose strands of barbed wire stretched up the incline across the back of Donner's property. Another high, wooden fence marked the uphill

310

edge of the lot. Kreveski peered into Donner's back yard. The twilight revealed a deck attached to the rear of the house, with bushes surrounding it, and a tree nearby. No lights were visible in the rear rooms, and the curtains were drawn, but there was a faint glow. He ducked back and keyed his radio. "Kreveski. In position. Looks quiet. Over."

"This is Rezhnitsky," came the response in the earphone. "Understood. All posts in position. We're coming up. Repeat, final team is coming up."

Liz opened her purse and crammed her walkie-talkie in next to the revolver. Resting her hand atop the bag's loose flap, she looked at Winn. "Let's do it."

The remaining patrolman followed the two agents until all had reached the corner house, then he peeled off as Liz and Winn headed up the sidewalk. "You think Donner had something to do with Fairview?" Winn said, once they were out of earshot. "It looks that way to me."

Liz peered up the incline at the homes lining both sides of the street. "It had to be him. Too many coincidences."

"Crazy thing to do."

"Risky, yes. But hard to say crazy. We just got the right information at the right time." Liz thought back over the case, and shook her head. "I don't know. They must have believed he could get away with it."

Halfway up the hill, a terrier that had been asleep under a porch suddenly rushed out, barking. His chain yanked him back.

"Shhhh," Winn said. "We're the good guys."

Waiting by the cars parked around the corner, Paul soon lost sight of the two agents. At the intersection, the lone police officer dashed out and took cover behind a large tree close to the street. He could probably see Donner's house from there. What would the arrest be like? Would they kick the door down? Would Donner fight back? After all, he was a dangerous fugitive. He'd smuggled drugs and killed an FBI agent. Paul debated whether he should move in closer but thought better of it. He'd stay out of the way. Both the FBI's -- and John Donner's.

The lights of an approaching vehicle glared in Paul's eyes. The patrol car cruised by the entrance to the cul-de-sac, where the officer behind the tree gave it a signal, then continued beyond Paul before pulling over. A patrolman and a man in street clothes got out. "Where's the FBI?" the man asked Paul.

"They just headed up the street to make an arrest."

"I'm the chief of police," the man said. "Who are you?"

"Paul Hendricks. I came with the FBI. I can identify the guy they're after."

"Just stay here," the chief said. The two men headed towards the intersection, but stopped before they passed the corner house when the officer behind the tree motioned for them to go no further.

The radio traffic had slackened and a dog was barking in the distance as Vitaly got up from the couch. His knee was stiff, and he did some stretching, then turned toward the bathroom just as a second dog began to sound off closer to home. *Probably the paper boy.* Vitaly peaked through the front curtains, expecting to see a boy or girl in the twilight, but instead there was a man and woman coming up the incline. And something seemed odd. The couple didn't look right together. The black man was wearing a tan, dress overcoat while the woman beside him was in jeans and a sweatshirt. Both seemed uncomfortable, almost rigid, and they were not strolling, but

312

moving with a sense of purpose.

At the base of the hill, a vehicle approaching the street entrance caught Vitaly's attention. It was a patrol car, and he saw it slow and debate whether to turn before passing on out of sight. *Police?* Deep in his gut, Vitaly felt a twinge. *You're just tired, that's all.* Still, he kept his eyes on the bottom of the incline, well illuminated by streetlights. *Just tired.*

Near the intersection, behind a tree, he saw movement. *Imagining things ... No, there!* A man leaned out and stared up the hill. Vitaly peered at the image. *Who is that? A cop?* The police car had slowed, then just driven by ... The figure now ducked back out of sight. *No, couldn't be a cop,* Vitaly tried to convince himself. *That wouldn't make sense.* But then the scanner message replayed in his mind. "Check with the special agent..." Special agent meant FBI. For the first time, Vitaly sensed real danger. He looked again at the couple coming purposefully up the hill. It all came together. *SHIT!*

Vitaly hurriedly flipped the scanner to the South Bend police band, then returned to the window. The couple was drawing closer. They hadn't gone into another house. *Damn!* Still, sensing a danger did not make it real. What proof was there? *So just calm down. It's nothing. It can't be. Not now.*

"This is 145," the scanner broke in. Vitaly looked back at the radio.

"145, Dispatch. Go ahead."

"We've arrived at the location. It looks like the agents are moving in now."

The agents. Moving in... Vitaly felt as if the floor were giving way. *They know. Somehow, they know!* His disbelief mixed with panic. *How could they? How?* He peered back out the window. The couple was now little more than a house distant. Vitaly's strength began to drain away. *After all this ...*

No. Hands clenched into fists. *... NO! NO! NO!* Vitaly pushed the hopeless feelings aside. It was time for action, not for weeping. *Think clearly. Don't do anything stupid. And move!*

He had an escape plan. It wasn't elaborate, but such a scheme was not supposed to be. And if he was wrong, he could come back and laugh. But if he was right ... He must not allow himself to be taken. If that happened, there would be no hope of seeing Yelena again. He would never know his unborn child. And, eventually, they would make him talk. *Never a prisoner. Never!* Like a good soldier, he would fight. *Now MOVE!*

"So you think he'll come peacefully?" Winn asked.

"I hope he does," Liz said, her eyes glued on the small home up ahead. "He's got to be wary, but he also came back, so he must feel safe for the moment." She saw there was a light on in the house, filtering out through the curtains beside the front steps. "If we're lucky, we'll catch him off guard." *Please, make it that easy.*

From his position at the corner of Donner's back yard, Kreveski peered over the roof of the metal shed at the thin slice of street and sidewalk visible along the fence line. Rezhnitsky and Winn passed by, and the senior agent dropped back down, peeked into Donner's yard, and then moved forward. He stepped over the barbed wire and took cover behind the only tree, ten yards from the bushes that ringed the home's rear deck.

Her heart pounding, Liz shoved her hand into her purse and gripped the stock of her revolver. She and Winn turned off the main sidewalk and headed toward Donner's front door. She tried to peer through the curtains but only a pale glow was visible. *Just come to the door. Give up!*

314

Move! Vitaly raced into the kitchen. He reached under a shelf, pulled out an envelope, and stuffed it into his pants. *Move!* He was on the cellar steps when the thought struck. *Weapon!* He had no gun -- that was one thing his superiors would not allow -- but he needed something. Vitaly burst back into the kitchen and grabbed a small knife, then locked the basement door behind him as he flung himself into the cellar. *Move!*

Her senses on edge, Liz crowded alongside Winn on the small porch. She pushed the doorbell once, then again. There were dampened chimes. *Come on, answer!* She listened, hoping to detect some movement inside. Voices drifted out, muffled and indistinct. It sounded like TV. No one came to the door. Liz raised her fist and knocked.

No response.

"One more try." *Answer, damn it! Answer!* She pounded on the door this time. "FBI! Open up!"

Vitaly heard the doorbell just as he hit the cellar floor, and it shredded the last bit of doubt in his mind. He was the target! He vaulted onto an old desk beneath a ground-level window. On the other side of the dirty glass lay the crawl space under the back yard deck. Clutching his knife, Vitaly flipped up the window frame and hooked it to the ceiling. A musty smell drifted in.

Move! Vitaly jumped back to the floor. Someone was knocking now. He hit the light switch at the base of the stairs and in the darkness took two strides and climbed again to the open window.

There was a louder pounding at the door. *Move!* The bottom of the window sill was chest high, and letting the cool breeze guide him, Vitaly felt for the edges of the opening. He laid the knife outside along the wall, then grasped both sides of the frame and crouched.

Do it! He exploded upward into the clear space. His chest thudded against the moist ground, and he clawed at the rocky soil, struggling to pull the rest of his body out into the night air. Reaching up, he grabbed a crossbeam and heaved himself forward, squirming until his feet were clear. Then he jack-knifed around and gently closed the window. He felt for the knife. *There.* Vitaly clutched the thin handle, squatting in the darkness beneath the deck. His breathing heavy, his jeans and sweatshirt smeared with dirt, he stared out at the faint, early morning glow of the outside world. *I've got a chance now. A chance.*

At his post in the backyard, Kreveski waited. There was a breeze, and the birds in the tree overhead were presenting their morning songs. Dogs barked in the distance, and an insistent pounding now came from the front of the house.

"No go," Liz grumbled to Winn. She leaned around to peer through the hazy curtains, but there were no shadows, and no sounds of footfalls. *Damn!* She pulled out her gun and set her purse aside. "I guess we do it the hard way."

"I'll take the honors," Winn said. He held his revolver barrel up and kicked at the center of the wooden door. There was only a resounding thud. He tried again and this time the door showed signs of giving way. "One more."

Winn drew back and kicked. The door flew open and smashed against the wall. "FBI! Freeze!" he yelled as he burst inside in a shooting crouch.

Liz followed. "FBI!" She surveyed the room down the barrel of her gun. The small living area was lit by a single lamp, and John Donner was nowhere to be seen. But he had been there recently. Three radios sat atop a steamer trunk; one playing a steady rock beat, the other two belching out messages as Liz crept forward. *Scanners. Did he hear us coming? We were careful, but...*

A few steps away, Winn braced against the wall at the entrance to a darkened hallway. He turned the corner and froze in firing position. "FBI!" There was only silence in response. His eyes trained ahead, he reached over and flipped on the hall light. "Come on!" he said. "John Donner, show yourself!"

Vitaly heard the door being kicked in as he crouched beneath the deck. The crawl space was three feet high and empty. There were bushes and latticework on all sides, blocking both his view and that of anyone watching, but here and there were gaps he could squeeze through. He wiped the sweat from his eyes with a dirt-smeared hand.

They'll have someone covering the rear. How do I get by? Vitaly knew surprise was his one advantage, but heading straight for the rear of the lot would still be foolish. Covering open ground in the twilight, he'd easily be seen. He shuffled over to one edge and peered through the bushes at the fence that separated his yard from his neighbor's further up the hill. *There.* Once over the wall, he could work his way to the nearby woods.

They'll still see me. When I hit the wall, at least. A decoy was needed. Vitaly pictured the layout of the yard, and found an answer. The handle of the knife wedged between his teeth, he scurried across the crawl space, sifting dirt through his fingers. By the time he reached the other side his hands had closed around several small stones. They would have to do. Overhead, he could hear the dull thumping of footsteps inside his house.

Near the edge of the yard, Kreveski waited behind the tree, peering at the rear exit that lead to the deck. He had brought out his revolver. The front door could be heard giving way and someone shouted. Then it was quiet again.

Clutching the stones, Vitaly gently squeezed out from under the downhill edge of the deck into a hidden space behind the bushes. In the murky light he peered along the fence line towards the back corner and his neighbor's metal tool shed. He peered over his shoulder, trying to visualize his return path, then chose two rocks. Careful not to raise his arm too high, he lobbed the stones toward the roof of the shed. The small objects seemed to fall short. There was no sound.

Harder this time. Vitaly took aim. It felt right, and even before the rocks had arced back down he was in motion.

DANK!-TANK!

Kreveski turned toward the sharp sounds.

His knife in hand, Vitaly frantically crawled to the far end of the deck and forced himself between two bushes. Branches scraped at his face.

There was another noise, a softer sound, and Kreveski swerved back to face the house.

With one strong push Vitaly was out in the open, his sights set on the tall wooden fence. *Three steps and over.* With enough speed, the former gymnast could dig his foot into the side and vault the barrier.

"Halt, FBI!" Kreveski yelled at the figure that had burst from beneath the deck.

Vitaly's second stride hit the ground. *One more ...* His bad knee pushing down hard, he hurtled toward the wall. *Grab it!*

Kreveski steadied his gun as the figure reached out for the top of the fence.

Vitaly swung his foot up to make contact with the wood barrier. His hands stretched toward the rim. *Get over!* . . .

ICE-STAB! PAIN!

The Russian shuddered as something drove hard into his thigh just

318

as that foot touched the fence. His leg collapsed beneath him and he slammed into the wood, then crumpled to the ground.

Inside Donner's house, Liz was cautiously entering a darkened bedroom when she heard the shout from outside and then the crack of a gunshot. She ran back down the hallway, burst through the front door and jumped off the porch. *Did he make a run for it?* She headed for the back yard, with Winn not far behind.

Kreveski edged through the puff of smoke from his revolver toward the prone, limp figure sprawled face down in the grass.

Vitaly lay on the moist ground, stunned for a moment before his mind began to clear. His leg was throbbing. *No!... NO! ... Yelena! ... Baby! ... Never a prisoner! ...* He sensed someone approaching and remained motionless, resting on his right side and twisted at the waist so that his chest was pressed against the lawn. His arms were tucked underneath. There were footsteps. He listened. *Only one person... Knife?* Vitaly squeezed his right hand. He had the weapon.

Kreveski kept his gun barrel pointed at the sky as he knelt down beside the motionless suspect.

Liz's shoulders bobbed with her heavy breathing as she jumped around the house and into firing position, then peered along the fence line. In the dawn glow she could see Kreveski bent over an inert figure.

Vitaly felt someone kneeling beside him. He tensed, his fists pressing harder into the dirt. *Only one ...*

With his free hand, Kreveski reached out to roll the body over.

Vitaly felt a grip on his shoulder. *Wait ...* He was being turned. *Wait ... NOW!* With desperate strength, he thrust off the ground.

Liz saw the motionless body suddenly jerk and twist sharply, and then a hand, clutching something, rose into the air. "WALT!" she screamed, as the senior agent threw up his arm as a shield.

Die! Vitaly brought the knife down hard on his enemy. But just as the blade hit home, there was a POP! and, in an instant, he felt very weak. *Too weak ... to ... move.*

Liz' hands snapped back from the recoil as Donner went limp with the bullet's impact and flopped over on his stomach. She prepared to fire again, but Donner remained still.

"I'm covering!" Winn said from behind. "Get Walt!"

Liz hurried ahead. *Damn it!* Kreveski had been pushed backwards by the assault, and he sat on the ground at the suspect's feet, his revolver now firmly pointed in Donner's direction. Liz saw the nylon of Kreveski's windbreaker had been torn at the left shoulder, and a wet blotch was spreading across the fabric.

"Walt, you all right?" she said as she knelt beside him.

"Top of my arm. Probably a lotta stitches." He waved his gun at the body. "Check him."

Liz moved to the motionless torso. *Damn you, be alive. Talk!* Face down in the grass, Donner had not made a sound since he'd been hit the second time. Liz saw the stain on his upper thigh, and then, between his shoulder blades, the dark, sticky hole she had created. *Bad.* Hesitating, she reached down and felt along the side of Donner's neck. It was sweaty and cold -- and she could find no pulse. Hoping she was somehow wrong, she grabbed an arm at the wrist and squeezed it between thumb and forefinger, trying to discern the beat of Donner's heart over the pounding of her own. There was nothing. Liz scooted back from the body, clamped her hand onto the shoulder and yanked. The lifeless figure flopped over, and Donner's eyes stared upward, unseeing. *Be absolutely sure.* Turning her head away from the waxy face, Liz put her ear to Donner's chest. Silence.

"Dead?" she heard a voice ask. It was Taylor Winn.

"I'm afraid so."

"Shouldn't have happened," Kreveski said. "Sneaky son-of-a-bitch, wasn't he?"

Winn squatted down beside the senior agent, and with his help, began to peel off the blood-stained jacket. "Nothing like easing into retirement," Kreveski grimaced.

Liz stared at Donner's face. It had a look of surprise: the mouth slightly open, the matted brown hair laying disheveled across the dead man's forehead. *"Pochti proskachil,"* she whispered as she climbed back to her feet. *You almost got away with it.*

****

A steady murmur from the four hundred refugees drifted out the entrance to the gym. Inside, there were small children asleep on exercise mats, while others were wide awake, giggling and shrieking as they chased each other around the families that sat in tight groups on the floor. Older, school-age youth were wandering in small packs around the tops of the bleachers, while teenagers gathered below in the farthest corners. Some adults stood talking alongside the basketball court, where a coffee machine had been set up, while in the first row of the stands older men sat quietly, their wives grouped behind them, exchanging concerns. Other evacuees clustered in the bleachers around portable radios, listening to the latest news: the women fighting back tears, the men slumped over, staring down at nothing. Throughout the gym was the sound of whispers and loud voices as refugees spread and squelched rumors, cursed Hoosier Electric and Fairview Station, and worried aloud what would become of their homes and their lives.

****

"Mommy, there's a noise."

The woman lay tucked into one corner of the double-bed, saving space for her absent husband.

"Mommy!"

The woman came awake. She opened her eyes and saw the crib against the wall, then looked down the bed at the outline of her daughter.

"Mommy, listen!"

"It's too early." The woman rolled over and closed her eyes, but before she faded back into sleep she heard it. The odd, distant howl. High pitched ..... a siren. It might be the one in Brixton whose sound occasionally drifted south. But it seemed louder this time. *A tornado?* It was that time of year. *That's got to be it.* "All right," the woman sighed as she climbed out of bed. She followed her daughter into the kitchen, turned on the radio, heard music, then peered through the curtains. Blue sky.

The music stopped.

> "Again, the big story this morning -- there has been an accident at the Fairview Nuclear Plant, and Brixton is being evacuated. Police urge calm and ask motorists to drive safely. A Hoosier Electric spokesman says there is no immediate danger."

Oh God. Fear rushed through the woman. It wasn't a tornado. It was something far, far worse. *Oh God, oh God.* She had seen this in movies. It would be horrible. An atomic bomb! "Susie, get your shoes on right now, and put on a coat!" the woman yelled as she ran down the short hallway. She leaned into a room and flicked on the light. "Little Sammy! Wake up! Get up and put your shoes on! We have to go right now!"

Hurry! Oh, please God, let us get away! Back in her bedroom, the woman shoved her feet into slippers and scooped the baby out of the crib, then checked on her son. The boy had not yet stirred. "Sammy, get up this instant! You heard your mother!"

The boy opened his eyes. "Noooo! I don't wanna!"

"Don't make me smack you!" The woman yanked her son up by one arm. "We're leaving. Now!"

****

Paul stood by the patrol car outside John Donner's house, watching the police deal with the neighbors clustering around the edges of the yard. He stared at the small home. Where was Donner now? What were the shots he had heard? Had anyone been hurt? Apparently so -- an ambulance pulled into the driveway, and the EMTs were directed to the back.

Liz appeared around the corner of the house and spoke with one of the policemen. The officer pointed, and Paul saw the agent coming toward him.

"Well, Paul," she said in a flat voice, "I've got an unpleasant task for you."

Paul wasn't sure how to respond. "What happened? Have you got him?"

"Donner tried to run. He stabbed one of the other agents." Paul was unnerved. This wasn't TV now, it was the real thing. "How bad?"

"He should be okay."

"What about Donner?"

"He's dead."

"Oh." *Dead.*

"So," she said, "now I've got to ask you to do a tough job. Identify John Donner for us. That would help."

Paul swallowed hard. "I can do that."

"Follow me."

Paul trailed Liz around the corner of the house. He saw the EMTs kneeling, and caught a glimpse of the older FBI agent between them. Then, nearer the fence, he spied a pair of legs stretched out on the ground. Two policemen blocked the rest of his view. Paul shuddered.

"FBI. Step back, please."

The rest of the body came into view, the torso covered by an faded green blanket. Paul halted, but then edged nearer as Liz knelt at the corpse's shoulder. He kept an eye on his shoes, not wanting them to touch the body or the blanket.

Liz looked up. "Okay, Paul," she said softly. "Remember, it's just a face." She pulled back the covering.

Paul forced himself to keep looking. It took a moment to register the image, to come to terms with the vacant eyes, the tousled hair, the stubble covering the chin. Paul tried to make the connection to the human being he had known. When he had talked to John Donner, the operator's expression had always been rather impassive, but it had still shown the life within the man. The eyes had moved about; the jaw muscles had shifted as he spoke. The cold, gray visage before him now bore none of those traits. But it was the same face.

"Can you identify the body?" Liz asked.

"It's John Donner," Paul said. "John Donner," he repeated, nodding. "For sure."

"Thanks," Liz replaced the blanket. "I'm sorry you had to see that," she said, standing back up.

"Yeah," Paul murmured. He felt a numbness now. He wanted both to move away and to look again.

"I'll need you to sign some forms. Then you can get some rest."

"Sure," Paul said. He was certainly tired -- but it would be a long time before he would feel like sleeping.

****

The road was a thin strip of pavement leading the woman's car east, away from the danger. Her baby lay on the seat beside her, and the other two children sat sleepily in the back, the little girl crying. *Got to get away.* The woman pressed her foot down harder. *Got to get away!*

Early morning sunshine was warming the cropland beyond Brixton as Carol held the probe out into the breeze. The plume had split when it went through town, and she and Marty had turned to the south, while the other truck stayed with the northern half. But the cloud's radioactivity had also continued to fade away, and now both teams were reading only background. Carol's thoughts turned again to her husband and the future. Running a boat in Michigan didn't sound so bad. They'd work it out somehow.

The baby fidgeted, and the woman reached over to adjust its blanket, as trees flew by on either side.

"I guess we'll be collecting samples, huh?" Marty said, as the fields gave way to a patch of woods.
"Yeah, that'd be next." Carol sagged into the seat.
Marty slowed as they approached an intersection, letting the truck drift toward the stop sign.
The woman released the accelerator of the speeding car when it was well into the curve, and she struggled to bring the vehicle back from the shoulder of the road. A warning sign for an intersection flashed by.

Marty checked the crossroad arcing back into the woods, then let the truck creep into the intersection.
The car careened into view, still fighting the curve. There was no time for either driver to react, and the passenger side of the truck received the full force of the blow. The two vehicles, each now a mass of crumpled metal, briefly twisted and rolled together before following separate, flaming paths into the trees.

Time: 6:08 a.m.
Time from Start of Event: 197 Minutes

The initial shock of identifying the corpse had worn off as Paul waited in Donner's front yard. *Vickie just won't believe this.* He would call her as soon as he could. She was probably still asleep, but if she had somehow heard about Fairview, she would be worried. From what the police were saying, the evacuation was still going on, and there had been a release. Was it really that bad?

The future. Paul didn't want to think about it at the end of a long and strange night, but there was no way to avoid it. His whole life had changed. Would it be worth staying at the plant? What would his job be like? *Later,* he sighed, trying to clear his thoughts. *Later.*

Liz was in the back yard looking over Donner's escape route when the chief of police appeared.

"Anything from the house?" he asked.

"Not much so far," Liz said. Only she and Winn had been conducting the search. The police commander, she knew, had been informed of the real reason for the FBI's involvement, and as long as nothing too obvious was said, she was willing to discuss it. "We found a good short-wave radio," she added. "You'd expect that, but it's not exactly incriminating."

"Chief," an approaching policeman said, "we've got Indy on the line now. The FBI special agent in charge. He'd like to talk to the agent on the scene."

"Yes, he would," Liz said. She and the chief headed around the house. "The S.A.C. would have come himself, if he'd known it would turn out like this." They reached the front yard, and Liz saw Paul Hendricks standing off to one side as she moved towards the street.

"Hard to believe he actually caused all that," the chief said.

"Yes," Liz replied. Having spotted Paul, she was now

uncomfortable talking about the case.

"Lot of people got moved out," the chief sighed. "Bad news."

Liz cringed. *That's enough.....*

Paul had been within earshot, and he ran over the remarks again as Liz and the chief moved away. *He caused all that ... lot of people moved out...* It took him only a moment to tie the pieces together. *Fairview?* He thought it through again. *Fairview ... Donner ... operator .... accident .... FBI had to find him now. NOW.* It all fit. *Oh, man!* But why would he do it? Just who was John Donner?

When she reached the chief's car, Liz peered back at Paul. She saw his expression change.

****

"Yes, 8:30, that's correct," Steve said into the phone. Out of habit he glanced at his wrist, but he had neglected to wear his watch. "Yes, our corporate headquarters in South Bend. .... All right. Yes, I understand. .... Thank you, sir. Bye." *Well, that's over.* Talking to the chairman of the NRC had been no easy task.

Tarelli approached. "Done with the admiral?"

"He's one angry man," Steve said. "But professional. I'll give him credit for that. His biggest concern right now is how we're handling the public."

"You mean at the press conference?"

"That, and how we're releasing information. And he wants his team on site before we go digging into equipment to figure out what happened. They'll start arriving around ten."

"I'll see they're taken care of," Tarelli said.

"Thanks. I might not be around. Depends on what happens in South Bend."

"You going to the press conference like that?" Tarelli said, casting a critical eye on the plant manager's polo shirt and blue jeans.

Steve shrugged. "I can't go home. Brixton is still off-limits." He thought a moment. "Chamber's people can find me a suit. Somebody must be about my size."

Tarelli cracked a smile as he walked away, "Well, if nothing else, at least put your shirt on right side out."

Steve looked down. He laughed at himself, but only for an instant. *"The next T.M.I."* That was the way the chairman had put it. Steve studied the county map, with its arrow leading from Fairview to Brixton. *It was a small release. But that won't matter.* He closed his eyes and flexed his aching hand. *We're done.* He had carried the thought like a weight from the moment the fuel was first uncovered. And he had fought it, not giving in to the idea even after the release drove the point home. But now, with the plant stable and slowly recovering, he could no longer avoid the obvious. *Even if we can clean out the vessel... even if we can fix all the problems .... We're done .*

Steve opened his eyes and peered again at his bare wrist, the gold watch still at home on the dresser. His father had arrived at work one morning to find his business in ruins, his partner on the run. And now, Steve reflected, it was his turn. He, too, had missed the signs of an impending disaster. He hadn't done his job. Fairview Station had fallen apart.

Steve let his frustration burn for a time, then began to wrest his emotions back under control. Self-pity would not be his way out. He would accept the consequences, as he had the honors. He wouldn't turn his back on his family. Marie and the kids must be provided for. *And my staff...* He looked out at the activity around him.. *What about their jobs?* He thought of the possibilities. *There'll be lots of cleanup work ... Most of them can stay on.*

The plant manager sighed. *Most.*

****

The aide stood ill at ease before the massive desk, watching the piercing eyes fix on him in anger and disbelief.

"You have confirmed this?" Party Secretary Gorbachev asked.

"Yes," the aide said, fighting the impulse to look away. *He doesn't shoot messengers.* "It has been confirmed by Comrade Chebrikov. He will be phoning with more details in a few minutes." *Leaving me to do the dirty work now.*

"How did this happen?" Gorbachev pounded his fist on the table. "What the hell were they thinking?"

The aide retained his stiff posture. "It appears, sir, that the plan was advocated by a mid-level official in the First Directorate, a Colonel Bykov. His superior, Major General Sveshnikov, agreed. The criteria for plan activation stated that, in emergencies, the operation need only be approved by two Central Committee members. Sveshnikov apparently gained such approval."

"From whom?"

"This is not known. Comrade Chebrikov is attempting to find out."

"It's some of those old bastards!" Gorbachev rose to his feet. "Those sons of bitches, they will never learn!" The leader of the Soviet Union turned away from the aide and stepped to a window. "We've got to deal with our own problems! Screwing with the Americans doesn't solve anything! Think of the risks!" He fell silent, his hands clasped tightly behind his back.

The aide did not move. The party boss's bitter anger was like a physical force, trying to push him toward the door.

Gorbachev turned. "Who else knows?"

"Besides those I've mentioned, and the unknown Committee members -- maybe one or two others."

"The trail must be stopped," Gorbachev said icily.

"Yes," the aide responded in a voice devoid of emotion, "Comrade

Chebrikov echoed those sentiments."

Gorbachev turned back to the window. "If the Americans ever find out..." he said quietly, his voice trailing off into silence.

****

Sergei took slow, gentle steps as he made his way down the corridor of Moscow Clinical Hospital Number Six. He was weak from the infections and his feet were tender. But, he knew, he was among the lucky ones. While the reappearance of his own radiation sickness had been relatively mild, a number of firemen and operators had already died, their bodies shriveled, blistered and blackened.

Sergei had witnessed much before he was finally evacuated. Hundreds of men and women at the plant had toiled to bring the situation under control. Dosimeters and other radiation monitoring devices remained in short supply, and often the workers went without. Soldiers were brought in to remove the graphite and fuel strewn across the ground, and they had gathered it up by hand, all the while exposed to its fierce, invisible energy. Within a few days of the accident the reactor fire had reached a low ebb, but the rubble in the core continued to shift like logs in a fireplace, sending new plumes of ash streaming into the sky. Tons of sand were dumped on the atomic pile as a protective measure, but soon there was concern that the added weight might push the hot mass of the core right through its bottom casing and into a water tank underneath, resulting in an enormous cloud of steam and dust. Divers, braving intense radioactivity, had finally managed to open some underwater valves and drain the tank. Now preparations were underway to pump liquid nitrogen into the ground around the reactor for better cooling, and there was already talk of encasing the whole structure in concrete. Pripyat, the city built for Chernobyl's workers, remained a ghost town. All land within eighteen miles of the plant had been cleared out. In Kiev, eighty miles away, streets were still being washed to remove the contamination. Sergei had heard that radiation levels in the Ukrainian capital reached 100 milli-rems per hour in the days following the accident. The city's population had left in large numbers, and vodka became even more popular due to the mistaken belief that alcohol would cleanse the body of radioactivity.

The hallway of Clinic Number Six suddenly seemed very long, and Sergei's slow walk came to a halt. He leaned against a wall to gather his strength. What did the future hold? In America, too, a plant had recently experienced an accident, and the outcry there against nuclear energy was intense. But in his own nation, Sergei knew, too much was invested in the power of the atom to turn back. The remaining reactors at Chernobyl had been shut down within a day or so of the explosion, but others of similar design were still in operation throughout the country. The electricity they produced was too vital to be taken away. His room was just ahead, and Sergei shuffled forward. There was much work to be done in the Soviet nuclear industry. And, Sergei told himself as he finally lay down, he would do his part.

****

Merzhinsky never asked why. He knew better. And he never turned down an assignment. That too would be a mistake. Now, as they headed down in the service elevator, he stole a glance at the man beside him. The officer was short, with the stocky build common among ethnic Russians. What little hair he had lay along his temples. His name was Dmitri Bykov: KGB Colonel Bykov, Division S, Subsection One, of the First Chief Directorate.

He knows. Merzhinsky had recognized The Look -- the slow nod and sad-eyed stare an officer would give when presented with his papers. The colonel stood ramrod straight as the elevator dropped towards the sub-basement. Arrangements had been made to clear the area. The van would arrive in twenty minutes.

The quiet was broken by Bykov's voice. He spoke calmly, staring straight ahead. "You know, if I were twenty years younger, I would try to stop you."

"Yes, comrade, I know," Merzhinsky answered. *And it never works*. His self-defense skills were one reason he had been chosen for the job. He knew there were others.

The elevator glided to a stop. The doors opened.

"After you, Colonel," Merzhinsky said.

"Yes, of course." Bykov strode out of the elevator in the purposeful style of an important KGB official. Behind him, Merzhinsky pushed the HOLD button and reached inside his tunic. The colonel had not gone far when the weapon was raised. There was a soft pop, and the officer fell forward. His legs twitched for a time, and then he lay still, a pool of blood forming beside his head. Merzhinsky knelt by the body and felt for a pulse. Nothing. He jumped back on the elevator, and the doors closed.

****

Wendell turned off the mower and pushed it back toward the garage. It was more humid than hot, and he ducked inside the house for a beer. He let the dog out as he came back onto the porch and sat down. He sipped slowly, smelling the freshly cut grass, watching the dog sniff around the bushes.

Three more days and he was back on shift again. It would be good to return to the control room, after all the time spent rehashing the event and his role in it. Of course, things would never be the same. He would be helping to manage the cooling of a damaged core, rather than the production of electricity. But it would do for now.

He looked at his watch. Karen would be home soon. With such a high profile case shoved in the lap of the company's lawyers, Karen had gotten the opportunity to do the kind of challenging legal work she had always wanted, and she was thriving at it. She had also shown him a side he had never seen before: a strong belief in her husband, and an inner strength he had leaned upon during those first weeks, when he had been wracked with self-doubt.

In time, they would move on -- together. He could picture them back in Philadelphia, Karen working for a high-powered firm while he slowly crawled up the ladder in a corporate engineering job. It would be a challenge, but a good one.

****

Gary opened the hatch and stepped out onto the slippery deck. On the greenish-gray horizon, the sun was setting into a haze of thin clouds. The huge ore carrier was halfway down the western side of Lake Michigan, its engines running smoothly enough for him to take a break and get some fresh air. The job paid well, and its long hours gave him little time to think of anything beyond wrenches and grease. His fingers wrapped around the guardrail, Gary stood watching the three foot swells, the endless stretch of restless, churning water seeming to echo what he felt inside.

A gull skimmed low across the water, heading back toward the invisible shore. Carol was gone. The woman who had loved him, their life together, was gone. Gary felt the twisting in his gut grow worse, and he turned back to the hatch, and his work. Someday, he would take the insurance money, buy a boat, and start over. But not yet.

****

Steve listened, tugging at the stump of his thumb as one of the senators gave his opinion on the state of nuclear power in the United States. It was the final hour of the final day of hearings regarding the Fairview event. A lot had happened in the three months since the crisis. Many nuclear units were now shut down, and the strain on the nation's power grid had been felt most acutely in the eastern half of the country, where utilities were making constant pleas for power conservation as their customers suffered through periodic blackouts.

John Donner's part in the Fairview event quickly became a source of discussion in the press, and it wasn't long before the FBI acknowledged he had played some role, though they chose only to speculate on his motives. The idea that the Soviet Union had been involved had been offered up by the press, but officially it remained a closely guarded secret. Steve himself had been privy only to hints and knowing glances from the upper echelon government personnel he had spoken with, but these were enough for him to know the truth. Fairview had been sucked into an international power struggle. It was some consolation -- but only some.

His own life had been a grinding succession of investigations, interviews and press conferences. The citizens of Brixton had been allowed to return within forty-eight hours, and after that it soon became clear that the home of the Fairview plant manager was a target for every angry citizen and demonstration. He and his family lived in South Bend now, in a house already owned by Hoosier Electric. The company had been good to him, particularly after the truth about the cause of the event was understood, and arrangements were being made that would allow him to continue his career outside of the nuclear arena. A new office was opening up in Australia as part of an effort to entice businesses to come to Indiana, and he would be put in charge.

Steve glanced over his notes as the senator began to wind down

Rad Decision

his monologue, cramming in a few more sound bites and statements of indignation for public consumption. An aide to one of the more senior senators on the panel had told him a few days ago what the final question of the hearing would be. He was ready with his answer.

"One last question, Mr. Borden. Upon reflection, what would you say was the biggest mistake here?"

Steve straightened in his chair, then leaned forward towards the mike. He looked to the table and his pad of notes for a moment, and then at the panel of distinguished legislators. "Senator, I've thought a lot about that. We've all heard the expert testimony regarding the decisions made that night at the plant, for which I have always taken full responsibility. We've also heard about possible design flaws, and problems with the evacuation.

"But I think we need to look beyond that. We live in a nation that depends on electricity. It is essential in every home, and as the recent outages have shown, without it our economy comes to a standstill. Steps clearly will need to be taken if the events of this summer are not to be repeated.

"It is viewed as a fundamental right in our country that we have access to electricity that is both cheap and has a minimal impact on the environment. But I am afraid that to most of our citizens, the creation of electric power remains a process little removed from magic. And in the case of nuclear energy, perhaps black magic. Now the event at Fairview has touched off a national energy crisis. A single incident -- which was not, and could never have been, another Chernobyl -- has the public clamoring to shut down the entire nuclear industry. If that is done, it will eliminate a fifth of our nation's power production. At the same time, there is also increasing outrage over the high cost and shortages of electricity."

"Our biggest mistake, Senator? I believe it was allowing ourselves, our nation, to reach this point." Steve held up a lone finger. "One plant, one event. And now the power grid we all depend on is hanging by a thread."

Steve sighed. He placed his hands on the table. "I can only speak from my limited experience, but I think the burden now falls heavily on those responsible for informing and guiding our nation regarding its energy decisions. By this I mean industry, the government, educators, the press. Every day that we fail to correct the public's perception that electricity can be limitless, cheap, safe and clean, we serve only to make the situation worse. All must understand that there is no free lunch when it comes to energy."

Steve glanced at his notes. He was making his point with far more eloquence than he could have hoped. "Senator, I've often heard the statement that 'Somebody will figure out a solution' to our energy problems. I must tell, sir, that we are that 'somebody.' We must help our fellow citizens understand the situation: how much power is used, the methods available to produce it, and the cost to both pocketbooks and the environment. Someday, perhaps, there will come a time when the average citizen can balance the pros and cons of energy sources and make educated decisions, just as they now weigh their options when buying a car or a house." Steve shook his head. "But, right now, I don't see us headed in that direction. I fear the event at my plant is serving more as a way to make political points and sell newspapers than as a catalyst for any thoughtful change."

Steve straightened. He'd said enough. "Senator, I've spent my professional life at Fairview. My career there is over. I can accept that. My life will go on. And like many in this room, I have children. Someday, maybe grandchildren. I would hope they could look back at these days and say it was a turning point toward a brighter future. But unless we really learn from what has happened, I fear their judgment will be harsh."

****

The late summer sun beckoned through the window as Paul finished signing the documents and slid them across the table.

"Thanks," Liz said, filing away the papers. *He looks tired.*

"Sure. If there's anything else, let me know." Paul hesitated. "By the way, I didn't say anything until it came out in the papers."

"Good. I didn't think so."

"I thought about it that morning -"

"Well, it wasn't hard to put the pieces together."

"You know, we still haven't figured out some of what he did," Paul said. "Your folks have been around too, but if they've found more, I haven't heard."

"I'm not up to speed on the results." *Just that Donner was very good.* "And even if I did know -"

"You couldn't tell me." Paul nodded. "Can you say why he did it? First they mentioned drugs, then Mafia, then something like Iran or Russia."

Liz cracked a knowing smile. "Don't believe everything you read in the papers, Paul. Especially if it's a good story."

"That's all, huh?"

"That's it. I can't say anything more." Liz herself knew only a few additional details. Apparently, the Soviets had claimed it was a renegade KGB operation, and Gorbachev was cutting deals. Nobody wanted another Cuban missile crisis. Thus far, the leaks from the state department hadn't been too bad. But it was only a matter of time.

Liz changed the subject. "Sorry we had to bring you in again."

Paul sighed. "Actually, I appreciate the break It's been long days and not much time off."

"What exactly are you doing?"

"I've been interviewing the folks who were in the emergency center. Now we're finishing up a blow-by-blow account."

"Then what? Will you stay at Fairview?"

"I doubt it. It's a long-term cleanup, and that's not for me. I've been looking around when I get the chance. Maybe solar, or a fossil plant. I don't know." Paul shrugged. "Compared to some of the staff, I'm lucky, I guess. I've got a few years experience, but I'm still young. And I don't have a family. My girlfriend's a teacher, and she can move."

Liz smiled. "At least you'll have company."

"Yeah. She's put up with a lot. Everybody has."

"I heard they fired some people."

"A few. Once the word on sabotage got out, the security supervisor was let go. Donner's paperwork was in order, but that didn't matter, I guess. They also got rid of some guys who ran away instead of reporting that night."

Liz recalled a picture in the newspaper. "I saw the protesters have shown up too."

"Some, but mostly at the corporate office, or tromping through Brixton. Only the really brave ones come out to the site."

"Is it bad out there?"

"Nah. The grounds are all cleaned up, and they barely had to touch the office areas. The only rough spots are deep inside the plant. Nothing much got out, really. Despite all the talk, the plume was a real dud."

"They moved a lot of people for a dud."

Paul frowned. "Yeah, and now we've got lawsuits because of the radiation <u>and</u> the evacuation. And our own truck got smashed up."

"That sounded terrible."

"Six killed. A mess."

"So will Fairview ever run again?"

Paul shook his head. "No. No way. Even if we didn't have the fuel damage to deal with. I think there'd be a riot."

"But some plants are running, right?"

"Less than half. The grid's hurting."

"So what do you think will happen?"

"I don't know," Paul said. "We can conserve more, but that won't do it. Fossil gives you acid rain and the greenhouse effect. Dams are nice, but they kill a lot of fish. And despite what some of the protestors say, we can't replace a hundred nuke plants with a few windmills and solar cells. They don't seem to understand the difference between kilowatts and megawatts. The numbers just don't add up. Not even close."

"You don't sound very optimistic."

Paul sighed. "A few years ago, I would've said we'll just have to get the top minds together and work out a solution. Then we'd all make the best of it." He reached up and brushed a stray lock off his forehead. "But it's not that simple, is it?"

<u>The End</u>

Afterword and Acknowledgements

The Richmond, Indiana explosion that begins this story was a tragic event that got little press coverage, as it came on the heels of Martin Luther King's assassination and the riots that followed.

Fatality estimates from Chernobyl run from less than one hundred to half a million, depending on the source. Almost all agree there was a dramatic increase in thyroid cancer among children (which was not entirely unexpected.)

For those of us on the inside, the minute details of the U.S. nuclear industry have changed quite a bit since 1986, but in the broader sense – and compared to the overview provided in *Rad Decision* – it has remained essentially the same. Federal personnel radiation limits are unchanged, though there is increased emphasis on lowering worker exposure. No permanent spent fuel storage facility has yet been established. There has been increased attention paid to offsite power access and grid stability. Staffing levels continued to increase into the mid-nineties, then for most sites they leveled off. (A single reactor plant such as Fairview would now likely have from five to seven hundred people on site.) Many nuclear sites are applying to extend their approved operating licenses from forty to sixty years. One innovation is that most, if not all, sites have switched to using medical scrubs or similar clothing as "modesty" garments, so the days of trotting about in one's underwear are no more. (U.S. nuclear plants also have an aging work force, so perhaps this is best.)

The U.S. has had no further events on the scale of TMI. The number of near misses range from zero to hundreds, depending on the source and their definition (and often their agenda). Perhaps the most significant "event" was the discovery in 2002 of a near breach through the top of the Davis Besse reactor vessel caused by acidic corrosion. The water in PWRs like Davis Besse contains some boric acid for reactivity control in addition to the boron-filled control rods. In PWRs, the control rods drop down through the top of the vessel as well, and in this case the acid worked its way up through cracks in the control rod housings. The area was not being examined frequently enough to catch the problem in its early stages.

The public's current attitude in the U.S. toward nuclear energy is hard to measure. There does seem to be growing acknowledgement of climate change as an environmental problem, coupled with the realization that nuclear is the only large scale electric power producer available for immediate expansion that does not also contribute a sizeable amount of greenhouse gases to the atmosphere. (Some are generated in mining, construction, etc.)   The true test will be when new nuclear plants actually begin to be constructed and brought on line – a process that may be underway in the near future.

In discussing radiation, I like to use the phrase "a drop is not a gallon." Radiation is not nerve gas, where a minute amounts can kill you in short order. It takes a lot of radiation to do damage to the human organism (with somewhat less required for children). Contamination – particularly internal contamination with radioactive particles – can do the job quicker, but this again depends on the amount of radioactivity present.

One issue that has yet to be resolved in the public mind is the disposal of high level (very radioactive) waste from civilian nuclear power plants – mostly used fuel bundles. My expertise in this area is quite limited so I have chosen not to address it in any detail in the text.   Used fuel is really nasty stuff, no doubt, as are many other industrial byproducts. My background does lead me to believe that high level nuclear waste concerns have been somewhat overblown. Addressing the waste issue involves working through classic engineering problems of ongoing heat transport, corrosion prevention and structural permanency – complex, for sure, but not necessarily cutting edge.

Transportation of the high level waste is a similar problem – a shipping container must be used that can withstand a train crash or a significant fall.   (Based on the testing films I've seen, these are available.) If a radiation "leak" in a shipping container were to occur,

I suspect the actual health effects would be similar to that of the train accidents each year involving tanker cars that release toxic gas. Of course, the effect on the public mood would undoubtedly be much greater because radiation is involved.

Currently, many containers of high level radioactive waste sit at nuclear sites in temporary "above ground" dry storage. Radiation levels are very low, the area is secure, the containers are thick and sturdy, and shielding and fission control are not dependent upon a spent fuel storage pool. (This pool will likely always have some of most recently removed fuel to allow for a decrease in its radiation levels before further movement). The onsite, dry storage method is not ideal, but it does seem like a reasonable temporary solution.

Terrorism is a topic of public concern when nuclear power is discussed. The *Rad Decision* story should help provide some perspective regarding the complexity and extent of the systems and structures in place to ensure reactor safety. I do not claim any security expertise, and it would be inappropriate to comment upon this aspect in any case. One terrorism concern that can be addressed to some extent is the nuclear plant as a target from the air. The target profile of the key safety areas at a nuclear plant site is small and low to the ground compared to skyscrapers, making a successful impact by an aircraft of any size and speed much more difficult to achieve. I will leave it to the civil engineers to debate the effects of such a strike. I suspect the public fear caused would likely outweigh the actual adverse results.

Regarding terrorism and nuclear waste – high level waste cannot be used as a nuclear explosive without extensive reprocessing. This requires a sizeable infrastructure that likely only a national government can provide. High level nuclear plant waste could also be used within a simpler, conventional "dirty bomb" to spread contamination, but there is already a great deal of nasty radioactive garbage on the planet that is not as well secured – particularly in the old Soviet Union. (Small comfort.) In the U.S., at least, it is also difficult to see how reactor-based nuclear waste could be successfully stolen from a site and transported. Security issues aside, the waste's shielding requirements to avoid detection (or health symptoms within hours) are so massive that even suicidal terrorists would have a tough time moving it around.

Another terrorist fear involving waste is an attack upon a high level waste container during transportation. If such a container can survive a train crash it is hard to imagine it being quickly broken open except by powerful weaponry. (And a truck driver can't be forced at gunpoint to open it with a key. There are large bolts and welded seals involved.) One could postulate a shipment being hijacked and the proper explosives then being installed while on the way to a high profile detonation site, but this requires the successful completion of multiple, complex steps while in the public eye, which makes final "success" much harder to achieve. Again, I believe it's likely the public terror from a waste shipment attack would be out of proportion to its actual danger.

When discussing our nation's overall energy picture, I again fall back on the saying "A drop is not a gallon." In this context: if you are going to replace one energy source with another, the new source should provide just as much energy and be just as reliable as the old source. This concept is often missed or glossed over, and I encourage the reader to always seek these details.

The developed nations use a huge amount of energy that (unfortunately) is not easy to replace by "cleaner" alternative means. For this and other practical reasons, it is clear to me that the first, second and third priorities of any energy policy should be *conservation* (or call it *efficiency improvement* if you wish). The cheapest, safest, and most environmentally-friendly energy of all is that which is not used.

Rad Decision has a website, *RadDecision.blogspot.com*, at which reader reviews are available, along with a great deal of additional commentary by myself and others on various issues raised by the book.

I owe a great deal of thanks to many people for the development and production of *Rad Decision*. Long Drive Bill sat down with me one evening and helped develop the accident scenario, and individuals such as Storyteller Ron and Coach Jeff helped me flesh out sections – particularly with respect to Operations activities. Also lending a hand in some form or another were LS, Cannon John, Risky Terry, Dick B, VP, TV, GC, Deb R, Dave M, Brian S, Bill D, WL, MB, CS, Vitaly R, John C, James W, Chris C and others who I'm sure answered some curious questions from me. Miss L was a fearless typist in the early stages. Jane Rafal provided much useful editorial direction through the years. My parents offered me a place of sanctuary where I could concentrate (and eat well). Nancy! offered not only editorial support, but a near-limitless patience and occasional chocolate fudge. Steve S provided early technical assistence, and Henry S some emergency support, as did Dick W. Mark C, Dr. db, and Cousin Jeff also provided editorial and logistical aid. Al Zwitty was there from the beginning.

As I moved on from the writing to the publication of *Rad Decision* I was fortunate to have the help of a number of popular authors – fiction and non-fiction alike – who provided some great advice and encouragement (and sometimes more) as I worked through issues unfamiliar to me. Among these are included a non-fiction Pulitzer Prize winner and a National Medal of Science recipient. So I extend my great thanks to Joe B, Roger P, Richard R, Dr. Richard G, Samuel F, Dr. John C, David C, Sara A, Rich W, Sara M, Richard P, Douglas P and a host of others kind enough to lend a hand. As I moved into the blogosphere, Dr. Jennifer R of LabLit.com [check it out], Maxine from Petrona, Tom Ev at dotHill, Carla N, WW Lynne S, Judith L, Dr. Ian H, Cobol H, Grumpy OB, Frank R, Daniel R, David B., Gavin L, McQ, Jason B, Scooter, Bill L, Pliable, Wn'W, Nethawk,

Darnell C, Ben W, Brad M, Marshal Z and Dr. B D were among those on the net who were of great help, and many others also kindly passed the word. Thanks to the Ambivalent Engr, Phillep H, Beev and Kaptian for finding errors in the online text. The Hoosker Dude put in many, many hours of effort and struggle on the internet project, for which I cannot adequately express my thanks. Finally, I also owe a special debt of gratitude to Stewart Brand, who came along as I was struggling and offered some keen advice and support.

The opinions expressed in *Rad Decision* are sometimes my own (and often not even that) and do not represent any official perceptions or conclusions of any companies involved in the U.S. nuclear energy industry or advocacy groups (pro or con) on the topic, or any government agencies. The symbol on the front and back covers is an upside-down and altered international radiation symbol. Actual radiation symbols should only be used when appropriate.

James Aach
November, 2006

About the Author

James Aach has been employed in the American nuclear power industry as a staff engineer for over twenty years. During this time his duties have included the investigation of numerous equipment malfunctions and emergency reactor shutdowns. Mr. Aach has also investigated several incidents involving excessive radiation exposure, as well as a number of cases where federal regulations were violated. During his career, Mr. Aach has had the opportunity to discuss the challenges facing the nuclear industry with atomic workers from across the nation and he has developed many contacts with expertise in areas as diverse as reactor physics, public evacuation planning and the Chernobyl and Three Mile Island accidents. James Aach has a degree in Engineering, with his primary area of study having been electric power production, including the use of fossil fuels and alternative sources such as solar energy.

Mr. Aach can be reached via his website *RadDecision.blogspot.com* or at jimaach@comcast.net

Impressive Imprint
3073 S. 337 E.
Kokomo, Indiana, 46902